THE COMPETITION

Also by Marcia Clark

Fiction

Killer Ambition

Guilt by Degrees

Guilt by Association

Nonfiction

Without a Doubt (with Teresa Carpenter)

MARCIA CLARK

THE COMPETITION

A NOVEL

MULHOLLAND BOOKS
LITTLE, BROWN AND COMPANY
NEW YORK BOSTON LONDON

The characters and events in this book are fictitious. Any similarity to real persons, living or dead, is coincidental and not intended by the author.

Mulholland Books / Little, Brown and Company
Hachette Book Group
237 Park Avenue, New York, NY 10017
mulhollandbooks.com

First Edition: July 2014

Mulholland Books is an imprint of Little, Brown and Company, a division of Hachette Book Group, Inc. The Mulholland Books name and logo are trademarks of Hachette Book Group, Inc.

ISBN 978-0-316-22097-2 (hc) / 978-0-316-40473-0 (large print)
Library of Congress Control Number 2014937384

10 9 8 7 6 5 4 3 2 1

RRD-C

Printed in the United States of America

We pass through this world but once. Few tragedies can be more extensive than the stunting of life, few injustices deeper than the denial of an opportunity to strive or even to hope.

—Stephen Jay Gould

THE COMPETITION

PROLOGUE

MONDAY, OCTOBER 7
6:51 A.M.

Christy Shilling rolled over and squinted at her nightstand for the fifth time. Why hadn't her alarm clock gone off? She pushed the Kleenex and can of Icy Hot spray out of the way. *Still* too early, but at least she could get up now. She hadn't slept more than two hours total, and it wasn't a good sleep. She'd had constant nightmares of waking up, going to her closet, and finding it wasn't there. The pain was still so real Christy was afraid to look at her closet door.

But there it was. The plastic dry cleaner's bag, hanging in front of the mirror, right where her mother had left it. Christy's heart soared. The Marion J. Fairmont High School cheerleading uniform in that bag was the realization of a dream she'd had since third grade, when the Newport Junior High cheerleading squad came to her school. She'd never forget the moment those girls ran out onto the auditorium floor. Christy had watched in openmouthed awe. Always the smallest in her class, she'd kneeled on her chair to take it all in. And from the very first shout, Christy had known she'd do anything to be one of them.

She'd made the junior high squad, and those tryouts had been tough. But they were nothing compared to varsity. Weeks of practice in the school gym, the rec center gym, her backyard. The sore hamstrings, the bruises, the falls, the constant anxiety. She'd been so nervous the first day of tryouts she'd had to run to the locker room to throw up. And after

Christy made the first cut, the pressure only got worse. At that point just the cutthroats were left. She'd been proud—and a little amazed—to find herself among them.

Throughout the next two weeks of practice, rumors flew about what the judges were looking for. Hair in ponytails, hair in pigtails; no makeup at all, light makeup, glam makeup; rail thin, muscular thin, "healthy"—whatever that meant; short, medium, tall; blonde but not bottle blonde, brunette, auburn. Christy threw up so often her clothes got baggy. Her mom had threatened to make her quit if she got any thinner. Christy tried using safety pins to make her clothes look tighter, but her mom had seen right through it and instituted morning weigh-ins. Desperate, afraid to ask anyone for help—if the coach found out she'd be cut for sure—Christy had searched the Web. She'd found her salvation in protein shakes and Ensure. Finally, the needle on the bathroom scale held steady at 103 pounds. Christy's eyes had filled with tears of relief. But nothing worked when it came to sleeping. She'd tried melatonin; warm milk; long, hot baths; even counting sheep. All useless. The last four days of tryouts, she was running on fumes.

But she'd made it. The varsity cheerleading squad.

Today would be her first pep rally. In just a few hours, she'd run out onto the gym floor to do her first routine in front of the whole school. Christy's breath caught as she pictured the packed bleachers, heard the roar, the stomping of feet, the whistles. She saw herself yelling to the crowd, taking her first run for her handspring-roundoff combination—and her final move, a climb to the top of the pyramid, then a somersault through the air into the basketed hands of the bigger base girls. Christy thrilled to the imagined cheers and fist pumps, hugged herself as she savored the moment. Her cell phone rattled on her nightstand. A text from Harley Jenson. They'd been besties since they pulled their nap-time rugs together on the first day of preschool. *"The big day! Break a leg—KIDDING. You'll be awesome! Xo, Harley."* Christy hugged the phone, jumped out of bed, and headed for the shower.

THE COMPETITION

7:42 A.M.

"Honey, don't stress. You'll do great—"

Harley Jenson looked up, forced a smile, and sprinkled more brown sugar on his oatmeal, then dropped back into his world history notes.

"Harley, listen to me." His mother pulled out a chair and sat across from him. "I don't want you to pressure yourself. If you don't get the scholarship, we'll find a way to make it happen, I promise." She squeezed his arm. "Okay?"

Harley covered his mother's hand with his own. "Sure, Mom." He tried to give her a genuine smile. "I just want to give it my best shot, that's all."

His mother sighed. "Of course, sweetheart." She squeezed his hand, then got up and moved to the sink to hide the tears that burned in her eyes. The truth was, she didn't know that they'd find a way to make it happen. With Andrew laid off, nothing was certain anymore. At least, nothing good. They'd planned a family trip to Greece that summer, knowing it might be their last chance to travel together before Harley went off to college at MIT in the fall. Now those plans were a taunting, bitter memory. Family vacations? A pricey, prestigious school for Harley? That was for rich people with steady incomes. *This* family would be lucky to keep the house. But she didn't mourn for herself or her husband. They'd had their chances to shoot for the moon. It was Harley she mourned for. The unfairness of it all made her heart ache. He'd done everything right. Made the grades, done the extracurricular résumé builders—and he'd been duly rewarded with early admission to MIT. But that was back when they'd been paying customers. Now, the only way he'd get in was on a scholarship. And the competition for the few slots that afforded a full ride was breathtaking. Harley never complained, but she knew he was working night and day, seven days a week, to make it happen.

Harley closed his notebook, forced down one last bite of oatmeal—it was hard to get food past the knot in his stomach—and took his bowl to the sink. He rinsed it quickly before his mother could see how little he'd eaten. He'd studied hard, but he still didn't feel ready for his exam. And he had to ace it. If he didn't, he'd ruin his perfect 4.2—and probably his one shot at the scholarship for MIT. He needed more time. Even one more hour would help. His cell phone buzzed. It was a text from Christy. *"Thx, Scooter! See you there! Xoxo."* Scooter—as in the opposite of Harley Davidson—had been his nickname in elementary school. Only Christy still called him that. He didn't love it, but it was better than Vespa. Harley frowned at the phone. He hated to miss her pep rally, but it was his only chance to sneak in more study time. Besides, she'd never know if he didn't tell her.

Harley leaned down to kiss his mother's cheek. "Bye, Ma. Don't work too hard."

As was her habit, she walked Harley to the door.

He slid into his backpack. "Love ya!"

"Love you back!" His mother swallowed hard as she watched him head out, his heavy backpack swinging behind him. He still moved like the little boy who'd given her a nervous-brave smile as he left for his first day of school—a side-to-side roll that reminded her of a skater. She smiled with wistful eyes as he headed down the front walk and out into the world.

1

10:45 A.M.

Principal Campbell's voice blared through the classroom loudspeakers. "As you know, it's Homecoming, and I'm sure you're all as excited about it as I am. Pep rally starts at eleven a.m. sharp. Show your school spirit and greet our new cheerleaders. See you there! Go, Falcons!"

Groans went up in nearly every classroom as the students rolled their eyes and traded disgusted looks. The truth was, they didn't mind the break. Any excuse to get out of class.

10:59 A.M.

The gymnasium buzzed with heat and raucous energy; the bleachers, designed to hold three thousand, were nearly packed to capacity. Girls' high-pitched notes and boys' hornlike, cracking bleats mingled and snowballed into a roar. Wincing at the din, geometry teacher Adam Levy leaned toward Hector Lopez, the Spanish teacher. "Bet you wouldn't mind having library duty today."

Hector sighed. "Yeah, no kidding. Sara totally lucked out."

Finally, Principal Dale Campbell walked out to the center of the floor, the wireless microphone invisible in his large mitt of a hand. He still carried himself like the linebacker he'd been when he was in high school. The principal loved these rare opportunities to see all the kids together like this. To him it was a family gathering. He tapped the mic, waited for everyone to settle down, then thanked the crowd for coming—as if they'd had a choice—and read off the announcements: a bake sale for the Woodland Hills Home for the Elderly, the job fair next month, and the upcoming performances of the junior and senior orchestras and jazz bands.

"And since our fantastic jazz singer Sheila Wagner has graduated, it's my pleasure to announce that her replacement will be Dimitri Rabinow—"

Girls shouted out in singsong tones, "We love you, Dimitri!" and "Dimitri's so hot!"—sparking a wave of laughter.

Principal Campbell chuckled along with them. "Seems we've made a popular choice." Then he pushed his hands down, gesturing for them to be quiet. "And now, the moment we've all been waiting for: Fairmont High's new, world-class varsity cheerleaders—I give you...the Falconettes!"

The locker room door at the far end of the gym opened, and a single line of girls in blue-and-gold pleated skirts and blue sweaters bearing the gold outlined image of a falcon in midflight came bursting out, cheeks shining.

They went into their V formation. Christy Shilling tilted her head and smiled at the crowd. Cheerleading 101. Captain Tammy Knopler, in position at the apex of the V, shouted the cue for their windup chant, "Hey! Go! Hey! Fight!" They clapped out the rhythm for four beats, then started to yell the words. The students joined in, stomping and pounding the wooden bleachers as they shouted, "Go!" and "Fight!"

After a few rounds, the squad threw their arms straight up in the air and called out, "Go, Falcons!" The crowd obediently roared back, "Go, Falcons!" The V stretched out into a line, and Christy took the brief run to start her first tumbling pass. Just as she launched into her handspring, the double doors behind the top row of bleachers flew open. At first, no one noticed the two figures who stood there, rifles in hand. The crowd continued to clap and shout; Christy went into her roundoff. As she turned in the air, the shorter of the two figures raised an assault rifle and fired off four rapid shots. The blasts ripped through the noisy gym. A hush fell, and for an instant, wide-eyed students turned to stare at one another. Christy landed heavily and stuttered backward on her heels.

Heads craned, searching for the source of the foreign sound. They found it at the top of the bleachers. Two figures clothed in camouflage coats and black balaclavas, assault rifles held high. Shrieks rang out.

"Time to die, motherfuckers!" The shout came from the shorter figure on the right. The taller figure yelled, "Run, assholes! Run!"

One of them gave a weird, high-pitched laugh. Then they both aimed their weapons down at the crowd. Staccato gunfire pierced the air. Screams of terror filled the gym as students hurtled down the bleachers, pushing, falling, trampling over one another as they desperately searched for cover. The acrid smell of fear mingled with panicked shouts as the black-hooded gunmen fired into the sea of bodies. Bullets tore through arms, legs, torsos, sending bright-red sprays of blood through the air.

Tammy ran toward the locker rooms. Christy knew she should run too, tried to make her feet move. But her body and brain felt disconnected. *Run! Run!* Christy sobbed to herself, even as she thought, *This can't be real, it has to be a nightmare.* Finally, feeling as though she were moving underwater, she began to follow Tammy. As she reached the locker room door, Christy stretched out a hand. She started to push the door open. She was nearly inside, nearly safe, when the shorter of the two gunmen turned to his left and fired. Christy's head exploded in a red mist as she dropped to the gym floor.

Somewhere, someone had pulled a fire alarm, and the shrill clanging underscored the frenzied screams of the crowd.

The killers moved down the bleacher steps in tandem at an almost leisurely pace, shooting into the crowd below as they went. They yelled at the students with a vicious glee, "Fuck the jocks!"

When the gunmen reached the gym floor, a bloodied hand groped the air blindly. "Help me, please...," the boy whimpered.

One of the killers laughed. "Sure, no problem." He put his gun to the boy's temple and pulled the trigger.

The bleachers had turned into a battlefield. Bodies everywhere—flung over benches, splayed out on the steps, curled under the seats, crumpled in heaps on the gym floor. Blood, bone, brain matter, splashed the walls, the bleachers, the floor.

The shorter killer gave a sign to his partner, and now they began to move more quickly, heading for the gym entrance, which was clogged with teenagers clawing and scrambling over one another to reach the doors.

Angela Montrose, the girls' soccer coach, threw her arms around as many students as she could, shielding them with her wide, sturdy body. Then came another barrage of shots. Just ten feet to her right, three boys and a girl spun and fell to the floor. Angela stretched her arms to the breaking point and pushed the students forward with all her might. If she could get them past the bottleneck, out to the open hallway, they'd have a chance.

She'd just crossed the threshold when another wave of shots rang out. Searing fire spread through Angela's right side. Suddenly, her knees buckled. She stumbled as black spots swam in her eyes. Mustering her last ounce of strength, she shoved the students out from under her wing and yelled, "Run!" Then, clutching her side, she crumpled to the ground. One of the gunmen walked over and looked down at her. They locked eyes. He raised his gun and pointed it at her face. Angela closed her eyes and silently said good-bye to her sister, her partner, their dogs. Bracing for the shot, she startled at the sound of an empty metallic click. The gunman cursed. Something heavy clattered to the floor next to her. Angela opened her eyes and looked up. He was gone. Her eyes fluttered closed.

Students screamed as they poured out through the double doors of the gym. The gunmen moved behind them like deadly sheepherders and took in the chaotic scene. Another high-pitched laugh, then the shorter one calmly took aim at a group of girls running for the main entrance, fired a few shots. Without looking to see if anyone was hit, he gave another signal to his partner.

The taller figure nodded and fell in behind him, pulling a handgun out of his jacket as they headed for the wide staircase that led to the second floor and the library. At the foot of the stairs, they stopped and fired at the students fleeing up the steps. Hector Lopez, who had just cleared the landing, cried out, "No!" He'd led a group of students to the stairway, hoping the gunmen wouldn't come this way. He dropped back and pushed the two girls nearest to him up the stairs. "Go! Go!" Hector deliberately slowed, praying that the gunmen would take him, the easiest target, giving the girls more time to escape. More shots. Hector's back muscles went rigid, anticipating the sting of bullets, but he kept moving forward.

Up ahead, he saw that the girls had made it to the top of the stairs and were sprinting down the hallway to the right. As he reached the last step, he heard another set of shots. Closer, much closer. Hector grabbed the handrail to pull himself up, but his fingers slipped off and he nearly tumbled backward down the stairs. He teetered, arms windmilling to regain balance. At the last second, Hector managed to seize the handrail and climb the last step. Only then did he notice the blood running down his side. He glanced over his shoulder, saw the gunmen had reached the landing. He took the hallway to the left, hoping to draw them away from where the girls had fled. Hector's stomach lurched, and he felt bile rise in his throat. Stumbling past the library, headfirst, body almost parallel to the ground, he held the wall for support. Had they followed him? Where were they?

As he neared the boys' restroom, he risked another glance over his shoulder. Saw them behind him, heading toward the library. Hector leaned into the lavatory door and fell to the floor inside. Using his left hand, he slid his cell phone out of his pocket and pushed 9-1-1. He managed the words "Fairmont...shooting." The last thing he saw before blacking out was the time on his cell phone: 11:08.

Harley had been in the library for the past hour, head down, desperately cramming factoids on the War of the Roses, when the fire alarm began to ring. He'd ignored it. Probably just a prank or an accident. But the shrill clanging persisted. Harley looked around, sniffed the air. No smoke. He got up and headed toward the windows that looked down on the front of the school to see if they were being evacuated. He'd gotten only halfway across the library when he heard screams, pounding footsteps—and then a voice bellowing from somewhere out in the hallway. "Hey, assholes, have a nice day!"

A series of loud pops—they sounded like firecrackers, but...were they *shots?* Then laughter, ugly and brutal. Another shot. Then another. Closer this time. Just outside the library door. Harley frantically turned to Ms. Sara Beason, the teacher on duty. She stood at the front counter, staring wide-eyed at the doorway. He started to move toward her, when she suddenly screamed, "Hide!"

Harley quickly scrambled behind a bookcase and ducked down. A blonde girl was standing near the storage cubbies at the front of the library, frozen, mouth hanging open.

"Get down!" Harley whispered to her. "Down!" He gestured to her wildly.

She stared at him, uncomprehending at first. Harley crawled over to her and yanked at her hand, pulling her to her knees. She dropped woodenly to all fours and curled up under a nearby desk. Harley scurried back to his hiding place.

Seconds later a mocking voice came from the doorway. "Where're all the good little kiddies? Helloooo?" Footsteps, then the same voice, closer now. "Hey, who's got library duty? Guess what? It's your lucky day!" Harley heard Sara Beason scream. Then, the boom of gunfire. It rattled the windows, shook the desks.

Harley thought only a bomb could be that loud. More footsteps, Harley couldn't tell exactly where, and more shots. How many? It was impossible to know. It all blended together in one continuous deafening roar. From the other side of the library he heard moaning, then a low swishing sound. What was that? Harley heard a weird, high-pitched laugh. Someone—one of the killers?—snickered and said, "Losers." Again footsteps, this time moving his way.

Harley swallowed hard, pressing his lips together to keep from screaming. He peeked through a gap in the books and saw someone—*A killer? It had to be*—walk over to the desk where the blonde girl had hidden. Shaking with terror, Harley tried not to breathe. He couldn't think beyond the words *Go away, go away, go away* that ran through his brain on a continuous loop. The killer moved past the desk. Harley briefly closed his eyes in gratitude and dared to take a shallow breath.

Then, without warning, the killer doubled back and rapped sharply on the desk.

"Knock, knock, anybody home?" He laughed, leaned down, and looked at the girl cowering on the floor.

The girl sobbed, "No! Please! Please don't—"

"Please don't," the killer mocked in a high falsetto. "Well, since you said *please.*" He took two steps away, then abruptly turned back. "Then again, that's a stupid, bullshit word." He swung the barrel of the gun under the desk. Fired point-blank into her face. Blood and brains splashed the wall behind the girl.

Harley jammed a fist into his mouth and clutched his chest with the other hand to muffle the pounding of his heart. Ears ringing from the deafening sound, he squeezed himself into a ball and took shallow little breaths. He knew he was next. A warm, wet trickle made its way down his right leg.

He heard footsteps, the brush of pant legs. It sounded like they were near the windows, but he couldn't be sure. Could they see him from there? Harley didn't dare turn his head to look. He thought of his mom, his dad, pictured them during one of their last happy dinners together, and squeezed his eyes shut to hold on to the memory. One of the killers was speaking. The voice seemed very close. Just feet away. Harley willed the ringing in his ears to stop as he strained to make out the words.

One of the killers spoke again. "Ready?"

An affirmation. "Yeah."

Then both voices. "Three... two... one."

A beat of silence.

This is it, Harley thought. He curled up knees to chin, wrapped his arms over his head, and sobbed silently into his chest.

2

I glanced at the clock on the courtroom wall for the fiftieth time. It was seventeen minutes past eleven, which meant I'd been waiting exactly twenty-seven minutes for my case to be called. I hate waiting. Especially in a noisy courtroom where I can't get anything else done. Usually I could stay in my office until the prosecutor assigned to the courtroom called me with a five-minute warning—it was all I needed, since my office was just upstairs—but this particular home-court deputy district attorney wasn't exactly a fan of mine. We'd locked horns a couple of years ago when he screwed up the murder of a homeless man. Deputy DA Brandon Averill was just too big a hotshot to be bothered with low-rent, pedestrian crimes like that. I'd grabbed the case away from him in front of a packed courtroom and wound up proving he'd had the wrong guy in custody. My bestie, fellow Special Trials prosecutor Toni LaCollier, says Brandon's a dangerous enemy. I say Brandon's a tool. We're probably both right.

I could've asked the court clerk to give me the five-minute heads-up, but that's a risky proposition. Even if they're willing to help, clerks are busy people. And some might even "forget" to call just for the pleasure of seeing a judge ream you. But I knew Sophie wasn't like that. And besides, I'd run out of patience. I headed for her desk, but at that moment Judge J. D. Morgan glared down at the packed courtroom and made an announcement. "Since I can't seem to find a single case where both sides are up to speed, we'll be in recess." He banged his gavel. "Get it together, people. I expect a better showing when we reconvene at one thirty."

Damn. Now I'd have to come back for the afternoon session. I refused to get stuck down here for another hour. Better to take my chances with the clerk. I moved toward the line of attorneys queuing up at Sophie's desk, but the judge gestured for me to approach. He leaned over the bench and covered his mic. "Rachel, where's your worthy adversary?"

"My worthy...you're kidding, right?" I nodded toward the back of the courtroom, where defense counsel Sweeny was schmoozing the defendant's family. He'd put the case on calendar so he could postpone the trial for another month. Said he needed more time "to prepare"—i.e., squeeze the family for more cash. I'd told the clerk I wanted a full hearing on Sweeny's reasons for delaying the trial. Again.

The judge sighed. "Look, I'm giving him the continuance this one last time. So agree on a drop-dead date for trial and stop busting my chops."

I gave him a sour look, but I nodded. He was right. The endless delays pissed me off, but another month wouldn't matter. The case was basically all physical evidence, and my experts were local. My cell phone vibrated in my purse. I reached in and sneaked a look. The screen said "Bailey Keller." My other bestie, who also happened to be a top-notch detective in the elite Robbery-Homicide Division of LAPD. Her call might mean she was free for lunch—a welcome distraction from the irritating morning I'd had so far. I turned back to the judge. "Okay if I have someone stand in for me if I get His Nibs to agree on a date?"

"Sure." The judge started to head off the bench, then turned back. "Hey, by the way, you and Graden still on for dinner Saturday?"

Graden and I—Graden, the lieutenant of Robbery-Homicide—had been dating for over a year now. And Judge J. D. Morgan had been dating Toni for the past two years. It's a cozy, some would say quasi-incestuous, group. But we work seventy-hour weeks—at least. Where else are we going to meet someone? The parking lot?

"Absolutely."

"Good. Now go make nice to Sweeny and pick a date."

J.D. trotted down off the bench and headed for his chambers. I did my lawyerly duty with Sweeny, then called Bailey back.

"Hey, Rachel," Bailey answered, her voice tense. "You get pulled in on that school shooting yet?"

I had just pushed my way into a packed elevator. "What school sh—?" I managed to close my mouth before saying "school shooting" out loud.

"Just happened."

"Oh my God. How bad?"

"We still don't have a body count. I'm putting a team together."

Body count. We used the term all the time, but about children? Never.

"Rachel? You still there?"

"Yeah, I just...give me a sec." I had to push away from the horror of it all and make myself think. If the case was already big enough to justify bringing in the Robbery-Homicide Division, then District Attorney William Vanderhorn, affectionately known by me as the Dipshit, would insist that we have a presence in the investigation. It gave him a chance to show up at the scene and get free publicity. And if Bailey had anything to say about it, that presence would be Yours Truly. "You on your way out there now?" I asked.

"Yeah. You may as well let me pick you up. Odds are you'll wind up getting sent out anyway."

Bailey was right. Vanderhorn's obnoxious press grab aside, it is SOP for the Special Trials Unit to show up at the crime scene, because we usually get our cases the day the body is found. That means we're involved in the investigation. And that makes for a lot more work—normally prosecutors don't even get the file until they start picking a jury—but it lets us put together a much tighter case. It's an honor to be chosen for Special Trials, but it's not a job for anyone who wants normal working hours. Free evenings? Free weekends? Fuggetaboutit.

The elevator bounced to a stop at the eighteenth floor of the Criminal Courts Building, one of the two floors occupied by the district attorney's office. It's a long-standing, not-so-funny joke that the contract for the elevators went to the lowest bidder. They operate like one of those cheapo traveling carnival rides. "Okay." My voice was as leaden as my heart. I didn't even want to imagine what I was about to see.

"We think we've already identified the shooters."

I punched in the security code on the door that led to my wing and headed for my office. "Then why...?" If they already had the shooters, there wouldn't be much for me to do. I unlocked the door to my office and dropped the case file on my desk.

Bailey sighed. "Yeah, now that I think about it, Rache, maybe you don't need to come. This one's gonna be... really bad."

I couldn't remember ever wanting to take a pass on a crime scene before, but I did now. Though homicides are always grim, nothing compares to the tragedy of a child victim. Let alone a mass murder involving children. I *didn't* want to see it. I *didn't* want to know about it. I *didn't* want it to be true. But it was. And I had to do something about it. Even if it was too late.

3

"What do we know?" I asked, as Bailey pulled away from the Criminal Courts Building.

"Precious little. Everyone's got cell phones, so between the kids and the teachers, we have about a thousand reports. And they're all over the place. 'There were two gunmen. There were four gunmen. They had AKs. They had handguns. They had grenades, they had Molotovs.' The only thing we know for sure is that they yelled at the jocks. But when they fired they didn't seem to be targeting anyone specific. A soccer coach, maybe. And she might've just been in their way."

"Any idea how many casualties?"

"Not yet."

"But the building is cleared already?"

Bailey nodded. "SWAT went in through the library window. Word is that's where the last shots were fired."

"And that's where they found the suspects?"

"Yes."

I looked out the passenger window as we made our way down the 101 freeway. It was an incongruously glorious fall day, the kind I imagine L.A. used to have in abundance before we fouled the air with modern conveniences. Piercingly blue skies; brilliant yellow sunlight; and a clean, mild breeze that carried the burnt orange and ochre smells of autumn. The palm trees swayed gracefully in that breeze. At this moment I hated the sight. It felt like proof that the world didn't care.

Our destination was Woodland Hills, a suburb in the San Fernando Valley that lies north and west of Los Angeles proper. Bailey got off at Tampa Avenue, and I distracted myself by counting the number of storefronts advertising Asian "foot massage" for twenty dollars. When I reached six, Bailey turned south and headed us into the maelstrom that surrounded Fairmont High School.

Fire engines, police cars, and ambulances—more than I'd ever seen in one place—packed the front entrance. Overhead, police helicopters competed for airspace with news copters. Their deafening *whump-whump,* the flashing blue and red lights, the piercing scream of ambulances, created a dark swirl that made the whole scene feel apocalyptic.

More than two hundred stunned civilians crowded the grass quad in front of the school. I guessed that most were the families and friends of the students who hadn't been accounted for. Many were hunched over, holding cell phones to their ears, or staring at them as if willing them to ring. The air was thick with anguish. Circling like vultures were the inevitable news crews. I watched in disgust as reporters held out microphones to catch every drop of misery from the anxious crowd.

Bailey double-parked next to a squad car on the corner, and we headed to the police barricade at the side of the building, where things were quieter. The school was big—two stories high—and relatively new-looking, with a facade of light-colored stucco. The stairs leading to the main entrance were filled with local police officers.

A sobbing couple hovered over a gurney that was being loaded into one of the ambulances. The woman called out in a quavering voice, "Don't worry, baby, you're going to be okay! We'll be right behind you!" The paramedic slammed the rear door shut and jumped in, then the ambulance flew down the street, siren screaming.

Bailey and I stopped just outside the tape that had been placed around the perimeter of the school and she flashed her badge at the nearest officer, a wiry guy who seemed almost young enough to have been a student himself.

"I'll have to check with the sergeant before I let you in," he told Bailey. He glanced over at me. "But she'll have to wait. I've got strict orders: no civilians allowed."

"I'm not a civilian," I said, irritated. I pulled out my badge and held it up. "I'm a deputy district attorney—"

The officer studied my badge, then shook his head. "I'm sorry, ma'am, orders are not to let—"

"She's on the case," Bailey interjected.

He gave me a skeptical look. "I'll get the sergeant." The officer started to go, then turned back and pointed at me. "But wait here till I get back."

I watched him walk away. "What, did he think I was going to rush the line?"

"It's the glint of madness in your eyes, Knight. Screws you every time."

"You're not funny, Keller."

"I wasn't kidding."

We waited in silence as we watched the scene in front of the school. A line of police officers held back the surging crowd that was getting louder and more desperate by the minute. Keening cries mixed with voices grown hoarse from pain and frustration. A man shouted, "I just want some goddamn information!" That sparked a wave of cries from the others. "Please, we just need to know!" and "Can't you tell us something?" and "It's our kids, for Christ's sake!" I could see by the expressions on the officers' faces that they felt the parents' pain but there was nothing they could do. In this chaos, it would take time to get accurate information. And the truth was, nothing short of seeing their children alive and unharmed was going to reassure these parents.

Finally, the kid—I mean officer—we'd spoken to came back. Without a word, he lifted the tape. As we ducked under, he said, "Sergeant said for you both to get on some booties and gloves before you go in."

We nodded and started toward the main entrance. Behind us, voices shouted out, "Rachel! Rachel Knight! Bailey Keller!" Stunned, I turned and found myself staring into the black lens of a video camera. Behind the camera, reporters were leaning over the tape, holding out microphones. A female reporter in a red suit asked, "What can you tell us?" A heavyset male behind her called out, "Do you have a body count?"

Nice thing to say in front of all those families. Assholes. Luckily for them, I'd left my gun in Bailey's car. Bailey saw the look in my eye and grabbed me by the arm. "Zip it, Knight—you don't need to star in tonight's headlines."

I forced myself to turn back and move up the front steps. As Bailey and I went over to the boxes that held the booties and gloves, I heard shouts of recognition bounce through the crowd of reporters.

"Hey, aren't those the two that did the Ian Powers case?" Another called out, "Yeah, that's the prosecutor!"

Bailey and I had been in the center of the spotlight last year when I handled a high-profile trial involving the murders of Hayley Antonovich, daughter of world-famous director Russell Antonovich, and her boyfriend, Brian Maher. But that'd been almost a year ago. I'd thought—hoped—everyone would forget what Bailey and I looked like. So much for that.

We pulled on gloves and booties and made our way inside. I've been to a lot of crime scenes. Never have I seen the kind of grim, bruised expressions I saw on the faces of the cops, techs, and paramedics in that school. Even before we reached the area where students had fallen, I could smell the sweat, the panic, the blood. We walked down the main hallway and got as far as the principal's office before we hit more yellow crime scene tape. I looked past it and saw jackets, shoes, backpacks, and purses strewn up and down the hallway; garbage cans lay on their sides, spilling out wrappers, torn notebook pages, and empty soda cans. Farther down, I saw paramedics working urgently over a body. I started to move forward to get a closer look, but a steely grip circled my arm and pulled me back.

Annoyed, I yanked my arm away. "I'm authorized—"

"I know. By me."

The familiar voice made me stop. I looked up and, for a brief moment, even smiled. "Hey." I shouldn't have been surprised. After all, Graden Hales was the lieutenant of Robbery-Homicide. I started to lean into him, then caught myself and stepped back.

Graden gave my arm a quick squeeze, then turned to the area inside the crime scene tape. "I just finished walking through the school," he said. "I've seen bad, but nothing comes close to this."

That was saying something. Graden hadn't scored an early promotion to management by cozying up to the brass. He'd worked his way up through the ranks, serving in some of the most violent divisions in the city.

"How many?" I asked.

"We've counted twenty-seven dead so far, and those are just the ones who were pronounced at the scene. We don't have an accurate count of the wounded yet, and may not for a few days. The local hospitals filled up fast. They've had to reach farther and farther out to find beds."

Twenty-seven dead and counting. That made this one of the worst school shootings since…the thirty-three killed at Virginia Tech—but that was a university. As far as public school shootings went, it was worse than Columbine or Sandy Hook. Graden looked at me intently. "You sure you want to see this?"

No. I really wasn't. "I have to."

Graden signaled to Bailey, who'd been talking to one of the officers at the door.

"Lieutenant," she said, when she'd joined us. Graden nodded. "I just got another update." The tension in her voice told me it wasn't a good one. "Hospital just pronounced two more."

"Twenty-nine confirmed," Graden said. "So far."

4

Bailey's cell phone buzzed on her hip. I didn't want her to answer it. I didn't want to hear about yet another dead child.

"Dorian's on her way," Bailey said. "Says nobody better be touching anything."

Dorian Struck, aka "she who must be obeyed," was the best criminalist and crime scene analyst in the business—and she knew it. She ruled her roost with an iron fist and woe to the fool who didn't follow her orders.

"Then we'd better get moving," Graden said. "I'll walk you through in chronological order. They hit the gym first, so we'll start there."

Bailey and I followed as he skirted the crime scene tape and led us through the wide hallway that ran from the main entrance to the back of the school, where the gym was located. "How many shooters?" I asked. "Do you know yet?"

"We're pretty sure there were just two."

The fluorescent lighting penetrated every inch of the scene with cruel, sharp clarity. A body covered with a sheet lay in the hallway just outside the open door to the gym. As we drew near, the thick, metallic smell of blood grew overwhelming. I slowed to look around the stretch of hallway that led into the gym—and to push down the nausea that threatened to bubble up into my mouth. Blood was everywhere. There was a pool near the sheet-covered body, a fine spray on the walls and the doors just outside the gym. When we reached the entryway to the gym I saw numbered evidence cards that marked the killers' path through the bleachers and across the floor to our left.

Graden stopped and pointed at them. "Keep to the far right and stay close."

We fell in behind Graden, moving slowly, careful to stay away from the evidence markers and the cops, crime scene techs, and coroner investigators. As bad as the hallway had been, the scene in the gym was worse—much worse. Bodies—eleven by my count—were strewn like rag dolls across the bleachers, the aisle stairs, and the floor. The sight and the smell of the carnage made me swallow to keep from heaving. I forced myself to take it all in. The air still felt thick with panic, tears, and terror. What kind of monsters could have done this?

"The killers were students?" Bailey asked.

"That's the theory at this point," Graden replied.

We left the gym, and Graden stopped at the foot of the stairway that led to the second floor, where crime scene techs were taking measurements and dusting for prints.

"We had another four victims on the stairs and three more in the hallway leading to the library. We'll take the elevator."

When we got to the second floor, I was able to look down on the stairway. The bodies had been removed, but the clothing that had been ripped and cut away by paramedics draped the steps. And once again, blood was everywhere. I closed my eyes for a moment, overloaded by the gore and the terrifying violence that had ripped through the school like a demonic cyclone.

"This is the last of it," Graden said, as he led us toward the library.

He pointed to a desk on our left and I saw a pink sneaker on the floor in front of it. "We found another two victims there. A teacher and a young girl. The girl had a close-range shot straight to the forehead."

I didn't even try to make myself look under that desk. Graden moved farther into the library, and I trailed behind, knowing I couldn't take much more.

"And here is what passes for good news," Graden said. He stopped outside a taped-off section of the room where photographers and coroner investigators were congregated. At the center of the activity were two dead bodies. It took me a few moments, but from what I could see, they looked like two teenage boys. It wasn't that obvious at first. To call the sight gruesome wouldn't do it justice. The faces were masses of red pulp and exposed bone, the features completely obliterated—no doubt by shots fired at point-blank range—and their bodies were just a couple of feet apart. Black balaclavas lay next to each of them and there was a handgun at each of their right sides.

"So the suspects shot each other?" I asked. "Or themselves?"

"We think they shot each other," Graden said. "But we'll have to wait for the coroner to give us a definite on that." Graden stared for a long minute, then continued, his voice brittle. "At least you won't have to sit in trial and listen to a bunch of shrinkers talk about how it was all mommy's fault for giving them an Atari instead of an Xbox."

"Yeah," I said. But it was cold comfort. Their deaths wouldn't bring all those children back.

Bailey pointed to the small handguns near the bodies. "I thought they used AKs."

"They did," Graden replied. "We found one on the floor just outside the gym. Looks like it might have jammed—"

"So he dumped it—" I said.

Graden nodded. "And we found the second one at the top of the stairs with an empty magazine."

"So the other one kept firing the AK—" Bailey said.

"Until it emptied. But the one who'd dumped his AK downstairs had at least one, possibly two, handguns on him. We found shell casings from a forty-four caliber and a three-fifty-seven on the stairs."

Bailey pointed to the guns that lay near the bodies in front of us. "But those aren't forty-fours or three-fifty-sevens."

"No. They're both cheap twenty-five-caliber Saturday night specials."

"Man, they were carrying an arsenal," Bailey said.

I stared at the guns. "Doesn't it seem weird that they'd use low-caliber, trashy stuff like that for their finale?" I asked. "I mean, why settle for dicey junk that might only wind up maiming them?"

"My guess is they wanted to use the reliable hardware on their moving targets," Bailey said, her voice cold with anger. "They could afford to use the cheap stuff on each other. They weren't going to miss at point-blank range."

"And the dicey junk did do the job," Graden added.

"Got ID on them?" Bailey asked.

"Not yet," he said. "Haven't had the chance to get their prints. Hopefully they have driver's licenses—"

"Or rap sheets," I said. If they didn't, their prints wouldn't be in the system.

"Any of the survivors get a good enough look to make an ID?" Bailey asked.

"Not yet. But we've got a few kids who had the presence of mind to take videos with their phones, and we're checking into the school's surveillance footage."

"Anybody give a description?" I asked.

"All kinds." Graden's tone was glum. "The only consistent one—and it's not totally consistent—is that they were wearing camouflage jackets."

I pointed to the bodies on the floor. "I don't see any on these guys."

"I know. But like I said, even that description wasn't consistent. Some kids didn't notice any camouflage jackets. The video footage should resolve that question. And even if the suspects were wearing camouflage jackets, they could've taken them off and dumped them somewhere before they got to the library."

The library, the talk of two bullied, disenfranchised losers going ballistic—it all seemed too familiar. "Doesn't it kind of sound like a rip-off of Columbine?" I said. "With a different 'uniform'?" The Columbine killers had worn trench coats and hadn't covered their faces.

Graden nodded. "Yeah, it does. Like a deliberate copy, in fact."

"Seems pretty obvious the suspects knew the layout of the school, and knew there'd be a pep rally in the gym today—" I said.

"Had to be students," Bailey said.

I dredged up what I could remember about Columbine. "But no propane tank bombs?" Eric Harris and Dylan Klebold had set up propane tank bombs in the cafeteria of Columbine High, but they'd malfunctioned and never went off. If they had, the death toll would have topped three hundred—more than the Oklahoma City bombing. Their goal, according to Harris's journals.

"No," Graden said. "And we haven't found any pipe bombs or Molotovs like the ones they used at Columbine either—"

"But they still managed to top the Columbine body count," Bailey said.

Graden nodded. We stood in silence for a few moments. Finally, Graden spoke. "Seen enough?"

"For a lifetime," I said.

We headed out of the Hellmouth.

5

Graden took us to an ambulance that was parked behind the school where a surrounding wall and steep hillside provided a measure of privacy and quiet. He gestured to a figure wrapped in a blanket sitting on the gurney inside. "This is Harley Jenson. He's still a little shock-y, obviously, but he's pretty coherent, all things considered."

We walked over and introduced ourselves. Pale, baby-faced, and slender, his dark hair cut conservatively short, Harley was the quintessential studious high school nerd. But right now, huddled inside that blanket, he looked more like a frightened sixth-grader.

In halting sentences, he told us what he'd seen. As he described how one of the killers put the gun to the girl's head, he began to shake and his teeth chattered so hard he had to stop. We waited in silence until he found his voice. Finally, speaking in a monotone, his eyes staring, vacant, he told us how he'd been momentarily deafened by the shots that killed the girl under the nearby desk, how he'd heard the killers do the countdown, and how he'd been sure he was going to die.

"Did you see their faces?" I asked.

"No, I—I was afraid to look."

"Did you see what kind of shoes they were wearing?" I asked. "Or their pants?"

Harley shook his head and began to shake again. "I must have, right?" Harley said. "But every time I try to remember things, I just keep hearing that girl saying 'Please, please don't'..." Tears filled his eyes and he swallowed hard.

I knew the sights and sounds would haunt him for the rest of his life, so I didn't offer any platitudes about the healing effects of time. I don't lie to victims. They deserve the respect of honesty. I gave Harley a few moments to recover, then asked whether he remembered what the suspects said.

"They really didn't say anything, except 'Knock, knock' and the things I already told you. And then the countdown."

"Did either of the voices sound familiar?" I asked. Harley shook his head. "They didn't say anything about jocks?" I continued. The "why" of this atrocity was going to be the focal point of the investigation. The more I could gather from the survivors about the suspects' words and behavior, the more we'd learn about their possible motives.

"No. But I heard that they called out the jocks when they were in the gym. Everyone's saying they probably got bullied by them."

" 'Everyone's saying'?" I asked.

Harley held out his cell phone, the bane of most investigations. We always try to keep witnesses from talking to each other and influencing each other's memories. But it was obviously a hopeless cause in this case.

Harley leaned forward. "Can I ask you a question?"

I nodded.

"Have you seen Christy Shilling? I've been calling and calling, but I keep getting her voice mail. She's a cheerleader. She was in the gym when..." Harley licked dry lips that barely moved. "Is she okay?" His voice cracked.

"I don't know, Harley," I said. "It's going to take a little while to find everyone. I'm sorry."

Harley's mouth trembled as he nodded. He'd been holding it together pretty well, but I could see that wasn't going to last much longer. I fought the urge to put my arms around him. The paramedic gave me a warning look. I nodded. I wasn't going to ask him any more questions. At least, not right now. Whatever else he'd seen—and I didn't think it was much—he was too traumatized to remember it. We'd come back to Harley when he was in better shape. I looked at Bailey, who shook her head. We thanked him and headed for Bailey's car.

"You said some kids got video?" I asked.

"Yeah, we've been collecting their phones," Graden said. "Which really made them happy."

"Who's got them?"

"I'll check."

"No, I'll do it," Bailey said. "You've got bigger fish to fry. Thanks for the walk-through."

Graden nodded to Bailey, gave me a warm smile, and walked off to do lieutenant business.

Bailey started to scroll on her cell phone but stopped abruptly as she stared over my left shoulder. "Well, what do you know."

I turned to see the head coroner, Dr. Shoenmacher—affectionately known as Dr. Shoe—and my buddy, coroner's investigator Scott Ferrier, walking briskly behind him. The head honcho showing up at a crime scene was a first for me. And it was even more surprising given the fact that the perpetrators were dead. But I was all for it. In a tragedy of this magnitude, we had to pull out all the stops to answer the how, the why, and—the most impossible question of them all—the what to do to make sure it never happens again. But I was sure it was also a political move, a grand CYA to head off the lawsuits that were probably already being cooked up in law firms around the county.

"Want to go watch him do his thing while I chase down the cell phones?" Bailey asked.

"You mind?"

"No. I'll meet you up there when I'm done. I'd like to watch the master in action myself."

I started to head back into the school, then remembered a question I'd meant to ask Graden. "Hey, Bailey!" She stopped and turned. "Who's getting the footage from the school surveillance cameras?" Most schools had them nowadays. And I had a feeling that would soon beg the question as to why they didn't also all have metal detectors.

"There's some unis on it," she said. "We should have it pretty soon."

I hurried back into the school. When I got to the library, I found Dr. Shoe standing to the right side of the suspects' bodies, hands on his hips, wearing a frown that made him look like a bald eagle. He moved down to their feet, backed a few steps away, and tilted his head to the left, still frowning. "Scottie, get me the—no, wait." Dr. Shoe scanned the surrounding crowd of officers, crime scene techs, and paramedics with narrowed eyes. "No one moved these bodies, did they?" In near unison, the group shook their heads and said, "No." Dr. Shoe looked skeptical. "Where's the first officer?"

A blonde man with a runner's physique raised his hand. "I was the first EMT, but a SWAT officer was already here. He told me to forget about these guys and sent me over there"—he pointed to the area where Harley and the girl had been hiding.

"So you're telling me you never touched these bodies?"

"Yeah. I mean, it was obvious there was nothing to be done for them."

"You have the name of this SWAT officer?" Dr. Shoe asked.

Another officer spoke up before the paramedic could answer. "It'll be in the log, Doctor. I can get it for you."

"Don't get me the *name*. Get me the *officer*. I want him here. Right now."

A low murmur rolled through the room as the logbook was located and examined. I'd heard that Dr. Shoe was a charmer in the courtroom, but I'd never heard about this side of him—the crime scene martinet. I wondered if he was married. He and Dorian would be a perfect match.

When Bailey joined me, she scanned the hushed room. "What's going on?"

I filled her in and asked her about the cell phones. "Still checking," she whispered.

A burly SWAT officer dressed all in black clomped into the room. He faced the coroner with a clenched jaw. "I was the first officer on scene in the library. What can I do for you?"

Dr. Shoe, who'd been directing Scott's photography, peered closely at the officer. "You can answer a question. I need that answer to be completely and perfectly accurate. Did you touch these bodies?"

"Yes. I put two fingers to each of their wrists to check for a pulse. I didn't want to touch the neck because..."

"Yes, I know, I know, too much blood and it was obvious they were dead." He waved an impatient hand. "Last question: did you move any part of them in any way, no matter how slight?"

"Absolutely not. As soon as I confirmed they were dead, I taped off the perimeter." The SWAT officer looked around the room. "After that I believe an officer was posted here to make sure nothing got disturbed. But that was out of my purview."

The police officer who'd offered to help earlier now spoke up. "I'm pretty sure someone was continually posted because I relieved the officer who'd been standing guard before me."

"I'll need a list of all the officers who got posted here," Dr. Shoe said. "Who's the investigating officer in charge?"

Bailey stepped forward and introduced herself, but they didn't shake hands.

"I'd like to talk to you privately," the doctor said. He led Bailey out of the room, and I fell in behind them. When we got to the elevator, he frowned at me. "This is a private discussion."

Again? Now *he* was going to throw me out? "I'm the prosecutor on the case. Whatever you have to say, I need to hear it."

Dr. Shoe looked at Bailey for confirmation, and she nodded. "Yeah, she's okay."

We exited the school and headed for the area at the back. It was the only spot that was safe from prying microphones and cameras. Dr. Shoe motioned for us to sit down on a stone bench.

"I suppose you're here to prepare this case for trial?" he asked me.

"Usually I would be," I said. "But in this case... well, obviously, there isn't going to be a trial."

"You're the lawyer so I won't presume to tell you your job. But I am the pathologist, and I *will* presume to tell you this: the position of the bodies in that library does not fit with the scenario everyone seems to have accepted."

Bailey and I shared a look. "You're saying they didn't shoot each other?" I asked. "So, what? They shot themselves?"

"I'm saying neither. The angles are way off—for everything. The bodies wouldn't have fallen in those positions. The handguns wouldn't have landed where they did. And I thought I saw a faint blood trail on the carpet leading up to the bodies. You'll need a good tech to test that carpet to make sure—"

"We've got one," I said. "But what—"

Dr. Shoe raised his hand, cutting me off. "Even the balaclavas seem...oddly placed. Too close to the bodies. If you pull off an item like that—especially if your intent is to shuffle off this mortal coil—you toss it away. Those balaclavas were right next to their heads. One body might coincidentally land with the head near the balaclava, but two? No. Everything about this is wrong."

"Then...what's your theory?" I asked.

"Just between us, understood?" We nodded. "I need to check lividity, get a better look at the wounds, get the gunshot residue test results, and obviously the luminal results on the carpet. But if that all pans out as I expect, my conclusion will be that a person or persons shot these kids, dragged their bodies into position, and staged it to look like a mutual suicide."

"Then if you're right, those bodies in the library—" Bailey said.

"Are not the killers," I finished.

Dr. Shoe looked up in the direction of the library. "They most certainly are not," he said.

6

His words hit me like a sucker punch to the gut. The killers were still at large. I could feel my breath getting shorter as the implications sank in.

"Thank you, Dr. Shoe," I said. "And you're right. We need to keep this theory quiet until we're absolutely sure. So watch out for those parabolic mics..." I shifted my eyes to the throng of reporters in front of the school. Backup in the form of a flotilla of satellite trucks had now arrived to clog the street. "The sooner we can get final confirmation from you, the better."

"Obviously. But I won't be able to do that until I get the bodies on the table, and I'd like to let the crime scene tech do his work before I move them—"

"*Her* work," Bailey said, reading her cell phone. "It's Dorian Struck."

For the first time, I saw Dr. Shoe smile. "Excellent."

What'd I say about the perfect match? The doctor strode off to finish his work in the library.

"The killers wore masks—" Bailey said.

"Why bother to hide your face if you're planning to off yourself?"

Bailey nodded and stood up. "It all fits with Shoe's theory. The principal is cuing up the surveillance footage for us. He's got to have it ready by now."

"Did he say what areas it covered?"

"Front entrance, back doors, cafeteria, the door to the gym, and one upstairs. He wasn't sure what that one covered."

"There were no surveillance cameras inside the gym?"

"No."

It figured. We headed back to the main entrance and found Principal Campbell downstairs standing just inside the doors. His hands were clasped together so tightly I could see the whites of his knuckles from twenty paces. When Bailey asked if he was able to answer some questions, he nodded eagerly, but his ashen color worried me. He looked like a heart attack waiting to happen. Bailey started by asking how many shooters he saw. Now that the murder-suicide theory was effectively nixed, we couldn't assume anything we'd heard was accurate; every detail had to be reexamined. Principal Campbell believed there were two shooters, but he couldn't swear to it.

"I was sitting near the door of the gym when the shooting started, so I couldn't see that much," he said. "But as soon as I realized what was happening, I led as many students as I could out through the side door next to the cafeteria. It's the closest exit to the street."

His breathing quickened; I could practically see his blood pressure rise as he relived the horror of it. He was stuck in the memory and couldn't get out. Eyes wet, he stammered, "I-I should've gone back in sooner. And Angela...my God, if it hadn't been for her...covering them with her body...she was so brave—" He broke off and blinked back tears. "I-I don't think she made it. Do you know?"

"I can check," I said. "But Angela who?"

"The girls' soccer coach. I heard she was pushing a bunch of kids out of the gym, but I haven't seen her..."

I shook my head. "It'll be a while before we know the status of everyone who was wounded, Mr. Campbell—"

"Dale. It's Dale—"

"Dale. It's over now. You did all you could. It's time to take care of yourself. Have you been checked out by the EMTs yet?"

"I...uh—" His gaze dulled. "D-don't worry about me, I'm fine. I'm okay."

Obviously, appealing to his sense of self-preservation wasn't going to cut it. "Look, the only thing we need from you right now is to show us how to view the surveillance footage. We'll come back to you soon. And when we do, we'll need you to be in shape because it's going to be a detailed interview. If you land in the hospital, you'll slow down the investigation. You wouldn't want to do that, right?"

He nodded slowly.

"So you need to stay healthy for everyone's sake. Let the paramedics give you a once-over, okay?"

He didn't like the idea, but he finally capitulated. He took us to the room where the video monitor for the surveillance footage was kept, showed us how to scan the footage, and left.

"Let's start with the cameras closest to the gym doors," Bailey said.

Black-and-white images of the hallway just outside the gym doors jerked across the monitor. A woman holding a clipboard to her chest came into view. Her heels snicked loudly on the linoleum floor as she passed under the camera, then faded as she moved away. For another few seconds the screen showed an empty hallway, and I heard faint echoes of a voice speaking into a microphone—Principal Campbell, probably—then cheering, like waves breaking on a distant shore. It was another few seconds before I heard the screaming. At first, it sounded like any ordinary crowd watching a basketball game. Then I heard the flat *crack* of gunshots—faint at first, but growing louder as the killers moved down the bleachers. A few moments later, the screen filled with the images of bodies desperately clawing their way out through the gym doors, climbing over each other as they struggled to make it through the clogged exit. In the background, the sounds of gunfire, continuous, relentless, grew louder. Finally, the gunmen came into view.

The balaclavas and camouflage jackets covered them so completely I could only get a general idea of height and weight. One was taller than the other and looked to be around six feet. They both carried assault rifles and wore gloves. I saw the shorter one take aim at a person who, with outstretched arms, was trying to shield a group of students. Most likely Angela, the coach we'd just heard about from Principal Campbell. The killer fired. He threw back his head. Was he laughing? Jesus.

The taller one took aim at someone on the ground, then held his weapon up in front of his face and shook it. He smacked it with his palm once, twice, then dropped it to the ground. As he moved away, I saw him reach inside his jacket and pull out a handgun. By that time the shorter gunman had already moved out of camera range, but I could hear the *crack-crack-crack* that told me he was firing continuously.

Eventually, the sounds of gunshots and screaming faded into the background, leaving only the shrill clanging of the fire alarm. The screen showed an empty doorway and three inert forms sprawled on the floor.

Bailey started the next tape. "This is the one upstairs. I'm not sure it has anything for us."

It didn't. The shriek of the fire alarm echoed down empty hallways, though I could hear screams and gunshots in the distance that had to be coming from the stairway or the library.

"And this will be the cafeteria exit," Bailey said.

The monitor showed Principal Campbell holding the door as panicked students tumbled and staggered out. He faced the inside of the school as they ran, looking over their heads. "He's acting as the lookout. But what was he going to do if the killers showed up? Throw a lunch tray at them?"

"My guess? Take the bullet."

Angela, the principal...and probably many more had shown such bravery and selflessness in the face of such vicious, gratuitous violence. It struck me that the alpha and omega of human existence had crashed into each other here in this suburban high school.

I refocused on the video. Between the screaming and the constant ringing of the fire alarm, I couldn't hear whether the killers were saying anything, and the picture quality was so poor, there was no way to distinguish one student from another.

"I was hoping for better clarity than this," I said.

"Yeah, this is pretty fuzzy. Let's try the front and back doors."

But that was a bust too. The back door had been locked, so the students who'd run that way were forced to turn around and head for the main entrance. The path to the front door was so jammed with kids scrambling to escape, it was hard to make out anything of use.

"Okay," I said. "We'll have to do it the old-fashioned way and talk to witnesses. Maybe someone noticed a couple of guys carrying rolled-up camo jackets—"

"Sure, and a couple of guns. And holding a signed confession. Why not? If you're gonna dream, may as well dream big."

"So unfair that people call you a smartass." But I had another idea. "Has anyone started the outside search?" I was betting no, since the working theory had been that the killers were lying dead in the library upstairs.

Bailey saw where I was going. "Good point."

We found Dorian in the library.

"We need you to work on the outside of the school," Bailey said. "Keep this to yourself, but Dr. Shoe says—"

"Stop," Dorian said, holding up a hand as she glanced around the room. "I know what Dr. Shoe says. And I was just about to move outside."

Bailey and I looked at each other.

"Please," she said, with a disgusted look. "You think he'd tell you anything he wouldn't tell me first?" Dorian shook her head and stomped off to pack up her kit. When she finished, we headed out through the rear exit. "You got a priority in mind?"

I pointed to the side of the school where Principal Campbell had ushered the students out. "The cafeteria door. I'm guessing the killers chose the exit that was least visible," I said. Which, if I was right, meant they'd waltzed out right under the principal's nose.

"Why wouldn't that be the back door?" Dorian said.

"Because it's locked during school hours," Bailey said. "So the kids who ran that way had to redirect to either the front or the side door. The front door is more exposed."

"And from the killers' perspective this exit has another benefit." I pointed to the Dumpster ten feet away.

Dorian looked up at me and nodded. "Pretty impressive."

"Thanks." A compliment from Dorian. That never happens. I admit it: it felt good.

"Impressive how you think like a deranged teenage boy." She gloved up and opened her kit. Bailey smirked openly.

I ignored her. As Dorian climbed into the Dumpster, I pictured the scene in the library again. "Did you get a look at those balaclavas near the bodies?" I asked.

"Yeah," Dorian said. "If you're going to ask whether I'll rush the analysis, don't."

"I wasn't." Because I knew better than to do it in person. I'd take the coward's way out and do it on the phone. "I was actually thinking they looked pretty new."

Dorian gave me an incredulous look. "You're thinking these kids were smart enough to bring extras to throw down so they wouldn't leave me anything?"

"Maybe." With all the crime shows on television that featured so much trick shit—some real, some fictional—it wouldn't take a genius to figure out that a mask worn over the face and head could have hairs, fibers, or DNA.

"We'll find out soon enough."

Ten minutes later, my hunch about the Dumpster paid off. Dorian pulled out two camouflage jackets. "Hand me a couple of those paper bags."

I gave her the bags and whispered to Bailey, "I'd say this clinches it. They took off their coats and blended in with the crowd."

"Yeah, but I'd still wait for Shoe's final answer before we go public with it. He won't take long. Besides, they're just kids. We'll catch up with them pretty quick."

I looked at my watch. "Except those 'kids' have already cost us two hours. They could be almost anywhere by now—especially if they have fake IDs."

Dorian's low, rasping voice came out of the Dumpster. "Vegetable matter, all kinds of junk in here," she groused. "Probably ate up any DNA."

Bailey sighed and whispered, "I'll go in and check on Dr. Shoe. You stay here with Mary Sunshine."

I gave her a look that would've made her weep. That is, if she hadn't turned and walked off.

I answered Dorian. "But the coats haven't been in there long," I said. "And if you get hair, it'll probably still be testable, right?"

"Probably. And then I guess we can just assume the hair we find is the killer's...not the salesclerk's...or the packer's...or the sewing machine operator's...or the—"

"Yeah, I get it, Dorian. Can you tell if there's anything in the pockets?"

"Like a driver's license? Maybe a student ID?" Dorian asked. "Maybe while I'm at it I can look for a signed confession."

I wondered what my horoscope for today said. Probably "Stay away from women in law enforcement." Dorian humored me and carefully parted the pockets.

"Nada," she said. "But if I was you, I'd take the information off the labels and see who sells 'em."

"That's what I was planning to do."

Dorian gave me a "yeah, sure" look. She was never a walk in the park, but she was unusually caustic today. She'd be the last to admit it, but I had a strong feeling this case had gotten to her in a big way.

She had lots of company.

7

Dorian continued to root around in the Dumpster for a while longer before determining there was nothing else of value. She stayed outside to work on the area between the cafeteria door and the parking lot, and I headed back to the library. Dr. Shoe was stripping off his gloves as the bodies were being loaded into bags and readied for the two nearby gurneys.

Bailey motioned me over. "He found entry wounds just under the jawline on one and behind the ear on the other."

"So they were already dead when the suspects shot their faces off."

"Right. It's another page out of the Columbine playbook."

Eric Harris and Dylan Klebold had committed suicide in the school library. Our shooters had played on that scenario so we'd jump to the conclusion that they'd done the same, which would buy them some precious time. It killed me to admit that it had worked. Any doubt I'd had that our shooters had studied the Columbine case was gone. There were too many similarities to be coincidental: the full-on style of the attack, the way they stormed through the halls, the final act in the library. And I had a feeling Graden was right: the body count was no accident either. They'd set out to "beat" the Columbine killers in every way: top their death toll *and* escape.

"But in the meantime, we need to figure out who those kids in the library are," Bailey said. "Hopefully their prints are on file somewhere. But if not..."

I took stock of where we stood. Surveillance cameras hadn't panned out, the bodies on the floor weren't the killers, the camouflage jackets might—or might not—tell us who the killers were, but it would take days before we knew one way or the other. And even if we did manage to get usable DNA from the coats or the balaclavas, since the killers were high school students, we probably wouldn't find them in the criminal DNA database. That meant we'd have to get parents' DNA and do a paternity match—a crazy amount of work. We'd need to narrow down the suspect list considerably before the crime lab could even start.

"Time to talk to the kids," I said. "We've got to get to them while it's all fresh."

Bailey gave me a grim nod. Talking to victims of a violent crime is always hard. But this would be worse by a factor of about a hundred. These kids had been through a massacre that would've made battle-hardened soldiers weep.

"Best to do it in their homes, where they feel safer," Bailey said. "I'll get some unis to help. We've got a lot of ground to cover."

And we had to cover it fast.

"I'll call Graden," Bailey said. "Guess you better hurry up and call Vanderhorn."

William Vanderhorn, known on the inside as Vanderputz and by the outside world as the district attorney of Los Angeles County, was everything I detested in a manager or politician—which was like saying he epitomized the worst of the slimiest ooze that inhabits the blackest of lagoons. Politicians and managers—to me they're cut from the same useless, unproductive, endlessly self-promoting, ass-covering, you-scratch-my-back-I'll-scratch-yours cloth. Vanderputz's sole talent lies in currying favor with the people who can get him elected. He couldn't handle a trial if his life depended on it. The only thing he could do was look good standing at the podium with the flag behind him. I'd call him an empty vessel, but it would be an insult to empty vessels. And he's just as fond of me as I am of him. Ours is a relationship in perfect balance, steeped in a deep, abiding mutual loathing.

It satisfied Bailey's sadistic streak to watch me squirm whenever I had to meet with him. But this time she wouldn't get her wish. For now, I figured I could dodge that bullet and report to my immediate boss, Eric Northrup, head deputy of the Special Trials Unit. Eric was everything

Vanderputz was not. Smart, experienced, savvy, and unflappable, he was a lawyer's lawyer, and that unique person who could try lawsuits *and* be a good manager. As a result, he was beloved by all—no easy feat in an office full of big egos and power players.

I called Eric and got Melia, his secretary. Though generally unmotivated, Melia had shown a whole other—downright efficient—side when I picked up the Antonovich case. Prosecuting a Hollywood big shot had made me a weird kind of celebrity, and Melia, an unrepentant celebrity junkie, instantly became my devoted fan. Suddenly, I got my messages on time, I got through to Eric faster than anyone else, and she personally escorted witnesses to my office. I knew my shine wouldn't last forever, so I intended to enjoy the ride for as long as I could.

"Hey, Melia. Is Eric around? It's pretty urgent. Oh, and it's Rachel."

"Rachel, come on, I know your voice." There was a warm smile in hers. Ah, the perks of fame. "I'll get him right away. Hold on." Toni would turn green if she could see the Melia-love I was getting.

Eric got on the line and I brought him up to speed.

"Just a bit of advice," he said. "Get the students' cell phones and watch any footage they got before you do the interviews. The kids will probably still be a mess, so you'll need to know what makes sense and what doesn't."

"Right. And I'll tell the crime lab to put a rush on everything."

"You won't have any problem with that," he said. "The press is already all over it. When they find out the killers are at large—"

"It'll be completely batshit. So what are they saying about the shooting so far?"

"That the shooters were a couple of fringe-type losers who'd been victims of bullying by the jocks—"

"But they fired at random—"

"But they targeted a pep rally, and specifically called out the jocks," Eric said. "I'm not saying you rule anyone out based on that. As far as we're concerned, everyone who isn't accounted for has to be considered a possible suspect. All I'm saying is, it wouldn't hurt to start there. Get a list of kids who fit the profile."

I ended the call and went to find Bailey. I had to get the cell phones and start the interviews ASAP. With traumatized kids running all over the place and being treated at who knew how many hospitals, just figuring out who hadn't been accounted for was going to be a daunting task.

And that was only the beginning.

8

Bailey had the cell phones brought to us in Principal Campbell's office. The paramedics had ordered him to go home, and he'd generously offered us the space so we could work in private. I braced myself for what we were about to see. We'd only viewed the footage from a camera positioned outside the gym doors. These phones would show us the scene inside the gym.

Though the images were shaky and out of focus, and the sound was tinny, this footage gave us our first real glimpse of the kind of monsters we were dealing with. The killers, looking like evil personified in their camouflage jackets, boots, and black balaclavas, stalked down through the bleachers and strafed the students with a bloodlust that was palpable even on these small screens. One of them laughed as he fired into the face of a young girl cowering on the floor, a high-pitched, almost manic-sounding giggle. I was sick with fury.

"Which one is Chuckles?" I asked. "The short shithead or the taller one?"

Bailey pointed to the shorter of the two. "Him, I think." She held up the phone that had the most close-range footage. "See how his head tilts up when you hear the laugh?"

I wanted to tilt his head up myself. Up and off. I picked up another cell. This one seemed to have been held by someone who was on the floor just inside the doors to the gym, behind the shooters. A brave soul who might already be dead. At first, the images were jumbled, a bouncy montage of students running, stumbling, and screaming. Then, the taller of the two shooters came into view. I recognized the motion he was making from the surveillance video. He was shaking the assault rifle. I now knew it was because the gun had jammed. He extended his arm and the skin of his wrist was exposed. I saw something on it—a dark spot. I hit "pause" and tried to enlarge the image. Something was definitely there. A bruise? A birthmark? A tattoo? It was too blurry to make out. I showed Bailey.

"We'll get the lab to work on this," she said.

"Is the kid who took this...?"

"Alive?" I nodded. "Is there a name on the evidence bag?" she asked.

"Yeah," I said. "Hugh Filoma."

"I'll check right now."

"Did you get any footage with a better shot of the shorter guy?" I asked.

"No. But I think I know why. It looks to me like he was doing most of the shooting. The kids closest to him are either hiding, on the run, or already down. The only reason this Hugh kid could get a shot that close is because the shorter one was gone and the taller one was right in front of him. This is the best lead we've got so far."

It was also the only one. We packed up the cell phones and headed out to start our interviews. We'd just reached the main entrance when a small, slender man in a black parka waved us down from the front steps of the school.

Bailey smiled. "Hey, Ed. Since when do they let you out in public?"

"Since they lost the key to my cage." He glanced at me. "That your partner?"

"Sort of. Rachel Knight, Special Trials, DA's office, meet Ed Berry, senior firearms examiner."

We shook hands. His was leathery. "You here to check out the weapons?" I asked.

"And all the casings. Got more brass here than a shooting range." He shook his head.

"Can you tell us anything?" Bailey asked.

"I can tell you that one of these assault rifles was fired a hell of a lot more than the other. They both had fifty-round magazines, but one rifle about emptied the clip in that gym. Only had a few left by the time he got out to the hallway. The other one only fired a few in the gym before it jammed."

That would've been the taller shooter's gun. "And outside the gym, on the stairs and second floor?" I asked.

"So far, it looks like a mix of forty-four- and three-fifty-seven-caliber casings. Mostly forty-fours. Those guns haven't shown up—"

"I think they hung on to them," Bailey said.

"Well, maybe we'll find some prints on the guns they left behind," he said.

"Hate to tell you this, but we looked at the footage," Bailey said. "They wore gloves. But hey, feel free to check the casings for prints."

Bailey was being sarcastic. They always try, but I have yet to see anyone get prints off casings.

"And you feel free to lift some prints off your victims," Ed said. Finding decent prints on skin is another near impossibility. Cop humor. "Sorry I can't do much more for you right now, but if you get hold of that forty-four and three-fifty-seven..."

Bailey clapped him on the back. "I'll bring them to you myself."

Bailey had arranged for us to interview the first batch of witnesses from the gym at the home of one of the students, Charlotte Kerrigan, who lived just a couple blocks away. I wouldn't ordinarily be all that thrilled to have witnesses hanging out together until I'd gotten each of their statements recorded, but there was no way to keep them apart. The ones who hadn't been injured had banded together from the moment they'd escaped. And it probably didn't matter anyway. According to the first responding officers, no one had seen the shooters' faces or had any idea who they were.

The house was a sprawling ranch style, and Charlotte's mother ushered us into the den. "I feel so fortunate that my Charlotte wasn't hurt...but those poor parents who..." She stopped and swallowed hard. "Anything I can do to help, just let me know, okay?"

I took in her pale face and shaky voice, knowing that from this day forward, every time Charlotte left the house, her mother would choke on the fear that it might be the last time she saw her.

We ushered in groups of three and four at a time, mainly to let them have one another for support. Any more than that and we wouldn't be able to keep the statements straight. When we'd arrived, I'd estimated there were about fifty students lined up outside for interviews, but I was wrong. It was more like a hundred. And we saw what we were in for after the first six: disjointed glimpses of figures in camouflage jackets and ski masks, seemingly endless gunfire, students flying or falling down the bleacher stairs…or dropping to the ground like broken puppets. Some thought there were four gunmen; most remembered hearing them yell something, but weren't able to make out the words. A few said they were sure the gunmen shouted something about jocks. But they couldn't add much to the general descriptions of height and weight we'd already gotten from the cell phone and surveillance footage.

They'd all heard the reporters speculating that the killers were bully victims, but getting the kids to give up names of students who might fit that description wasn't easy. They didn't like the idea of putting someone on the suspect list just because they'd been targeted by asshole jocks. I didn't blame them, but we spent precious minutes explaining over and over that we wouldn't take anyone into custody based solely on that criteria and that we had to start somewhere. It took longer than I would've liked, but they eventually gave us some names. By seven o'clock, we'd done more than twenty group interviews and amassed eighteen names of "possibles."

We still had about forty students waiting, but the kids looked exhausted. It had been a long, draining day. I wouldn't have minded working all night, but I had to admit that the statements were starting to run together. The fact that they were all so similar didn't help.

"What do you say we pull the plug?" I said to Bailey as the group left the room.

Bailey yawned. "Yeah." She rubbed her neck. "They look like they've had it. But I hate to make them all come back tomorrow. Think we can squeeze out one more hour?"

I did. We forged ahead. And finally, we hit something that felt like pay dirt.

It was in the group that included Charlotte and her two besties, Marnie and Letha. All three girls wore jeans tucked into UGGs and had long, straight hair streaked with various colors. Like so many of the other girls, they held hands and sat close to one another on the sofa. Letha chewed the fingernails of her free hand, and Marnie, who sat in the middle, squeezed her friends' hands so tightly I saw them wince. Charlotte seemed the calmest of the trio, but even she nervously pulled at the whiskered threads on the knees of her jeans.

"We were on the far left side, in the middle," said Charlotte. "I think they just didn't shoot at the kids sitting at the top of the bleachers where we were—"

"And it was just luck that we wound up there," said Letha. "It was the only place left where we could all sit together. But Christy..." Slow tears rolled down her face.

"Christy wasn't sitting with you?" I asked.

"Christy just made the varsity cheerleading squad," Marnie said. "It was her first pep rally." Marnie stopped to wipe her tears, and Charlotte bit a trembling lip. "I didn't see it, b-but we heard she got shot in the back. We still haven't heard...anything." Marnie looked at me with fearful eyes. "Do you know...?"

"We'll find out for you," Bailey said.

I remembered Harley had asked about her too. Bailey wrote down her last name. I gave them a moment to recover. "Can you describe the suspects?"

"One was definitely shorter, smaller—" Charlotte began.

"And wasn't he the one with that creepy laugh?" said Marnie.

"Yeah!" said Letha. "It was freaking twisted."

"Do you know anyone who laughs like that?" Bailey asked.

The girls all shook their heads.

"And the other shooter, what did he look like?" I asked.

"Real tall," Marnie said. "I'd say over six feet, like six feet five or something."

"And he seemed skinny to me," Letha said.

"Yeah," said Charlotte. "I couldn't see their bodies or anything.

But the way they moved...it's like, they weren't fat or anything, you know?"

"Could you see their feet?" Bailey asked. "What kind of shoes they were wearing?"

A smart question. When the shooters put their outfits together, they would've thought about coats, gloves, and masks, but it was unlikely they'd worry about their feet. So, whatever boots or shoes they wore might be distinct enough to be identifiable. The only problem was, who'd be looking at feet when gunmen were leveling rifles at their heads?

The girls exchanged glances, then gave us an apologetic look. "We got down on the ground and hid when we saw the guns," Charlotte said.

"Do either of you know someone as tall as six feet five who has a birthmark or a tattoo on his wrist?"

The girls stared off into the distance. "No," Charlotte said. "Not that I can think of." The others shook their heads in agreement.

"Could he maybe have been a little shorter than that?" I asked. It was natural for witnesses to exaggerate unusual characteristics—especially height—and especially when the suspect has a gun. An assault rifle can make even a skinny guy look like the Hulk.

"I don't know," Marnie said. "He just seemed really tall to me."

"Do you know any guys who've been bullied by jocks in the past year or so?" I asked.

Another long pause. They all shook their heads. "But we don't hang with the jocks," Letha said. "You'd have to ask them."

"I heard on the news that they're thinking the shooters might have hung around with the Goths," Charlotte said.

"You think Goths were involved in this?" Bailey said.

"No way," Charlotte said. "They're just emo wimps with eyeliner."

"Do you know any Goths?" I asked.

"Not really," Letha said.

"And besides, I don't know any who're that tall," Marnie said.

But since they didn't know any Goths, and their estimation of height was a bit suspect, the Goth possibility would have to remain in play for now.

"You said you remember one of the shooters had a weird laugh," I said. "I know you said you didn't recognize that laugh, but you were under a lot of stress. Can you listen to it and tell me if you recognize it?" They moved closer together. I pulled out a cell phone and played the short snippet.

The girls stared at each other with wide eyes. At last, Marnie answered. "Yeah, but it couldn't be him. I've known him since third grade—"

"What's his name?" I asked.

"Otis Barney."

"Are you close?" I asked.

"No, but we've been in the same schools practically forever." Marnie's expression was tortured. "Otis couldn't have been involved in something like this. He couldn't have."

"Have you ever known him to be bullied?" Bailey asked.

"N-no," Marnie answered.

"But he's the type, isn't he?" I asked.

Marnie looked down. "I don't know. He's kind of...geeky, but he's always trying to be cool."

"Who does he hang with?" I asked.

Marnie shrugged, but she kept her gaze focused on the floor. "I don't know. I've never seen him with anyone in particular. I guess he keeps to himself." When Marnie looked up at me her eyes were wet with tears. "Ms. Knight, I really don't want to get Otis in trouble. I just don't believe he could have..."

"You know him?" Bailey asked the other two.

They did. "But not well," Charlotte said. "We just know who he is because Marnie told us she knew him back when we all started at Fairmont High."

"Can you give us a description, Marnie?" I asked.

"He's medium height, about medium weight—maybe a little on the skinny side."

In other words, the same build as the smaller of the two shooters.

And he had that laugh.

9

Finally we had something to work with. But I wanted at least one more student to confirm Marnie's statement before we moved on Otis Barney. We didn't have time to waste on dead ends. Energized, we knocked out ten more interviews. I asked about Otis Barney, but I was careful to toss his name into the mix with no particular emphasis, along with several others on our list of possibles. A wiry-looking kid in glasses said Otis had been in his freshman Spanish class. And he remembered that weird, high-pitched giggle.

"Is Otis into guns?" I asked.

"No, not that I ever knew."

It wasn't a DNA match, but it was enough to make it worth our time to find out whether Otis Barney had been accounted for. We rescheduled the rest of the interviews for the following day and hurried out to Bailey's car.

"I don't want to red-flag this guy before we're sure he hasn't shown up anywhere," I said.

"We can check EMT lists, hospital lists, and police reports without getting noticed."

I took the hospital and EMT lists; Bailey took the police reports and the school liaison who'd access the attendance records for us. An hour and a half later, I had my answer: eighty-four wounded, thirty-three dead, and none of those who had been positively identified were named Otis Barney. The numbers were so staggering, just hearing them was beyond comprehension. I felt numb as I waited for Bailey to finish her calls.

"And?" I asked.

"He doesn't show up on any police log and he wasn't checked in at homeroom. He might've just gotten to school late."

"He might have. There's one way to find out for sure." I looked at my watch. "Almost ten o'clock. If his folks haven't heard from him they're not sleeping. Assuming they're even home."

"And if they are, and he's there, we apologize for waking them up and say we're checking in on everyone and have to talk to him," Bailey said. "I just don't want any reporters to run with this. We've already mentioned his name to some of the kids. If the press sees us at Otis's house and asks the kids..."

It was a problem. We'd warned all the students that it could seriously undermine the investigation if they talked to reporters, and we'd asked them to warn all their friends about it. But it was a big school—more than three thousand enrolled—and reporters knew how to make people feel important. Odds were, someone would cave to the siren song of momentary fame. And even if the kids stayed strong, reporters were bound to have their own sources in the hospitals or in LAPD. Hell, I was sure they had sources in my own office.

"All the more reason to move on it now," I said. "The press probably has interns comparing lists of wounded and dead to school records even as we speak. I—wait, do we?"

"Have people working on the lists? Yeah. But the attendance records aren't entirely accurate. Like I said about our buddy Otis, if a kid skipped homeroom, played hooky, or a teacher just made a mistake taking roll, that'll take a while to sort out."

Bailey got the number for Tom and Sonny Barney fairly quickly. She paused before punching it in. "For our sake, I hope this is our guy. But for their sake..."

I nodded. I could hear the phone ring. No one picked up. Not even an answering machine.

Bailey ended the call. "Could mean they're on the phone or—"

"At the rec center, looking for their son." The community recreation center had been designated as the gathering place where family and friends of missing students could wait for reports. "Let's hit the house first." It'd be easier to talk to them there. "You have an address?"

Otis lived five miles away, in a small Spanish-style house adorned with colorful tiles just under the roofline. Bailey and I approached the house quietly, listening for any sounds coming from inside. When we reached the front door I heard a woman's voice, shrill with tension, then the deeper tones of a male voice. Bailey and I exchanged a look.

With one hand on the holster of her gun, she knocked. The voices abruptly stopped. After a few seconds the male voice responded, "Who's there?"

Bailey identified us. "We're here to ask you about your son, Otis."

The door opened, and a man in socks and corduroys stared at us for a moment before asking to see our IDs. As I held out my badge, I saw a petite woman with short, dark hair peeking out from behind him. She was holding a Kleenex to her nose, and her eyes were wet and red. Tom and Sonny Barney.

The man stood back to let us in and gestured to the couch against the wall. Before we even sat down, the woman asked, "Have you found our boy? Do you know where he is?"

"No, ma'am," Bailey said. "We were hoping you'd heard from him."

At this, the woman squeezed her eyes shut and shook her head as tears leaked out and ran down her cheeks. There was a framed photograph on the side table next to the couch that showed Otis standing between his parents. He could definitely be described as medium height and build—for what it was worth.

"We're so sorry we don't have better news," I said. "You've heard nothing all day?"

Tom Barney shook his head. "We've been at the rec center—just came home to change clothes. And we've called all over the place, but no one seems to know anything."

Bailey and I exchanged a look.

"We can tell you that his name has not shown up on the list of injured or...deceased," Bailey said. "But he doesn't seem to have been in school today either. Do you have any idea where he might have gone?"

"Not in school?" Sonny asked, her tone incredulous. "That's impossible. I dropped him off myself this morning."

"Did you see him go inside?" I asked.

"N-no. There was a line of cars behind me. I had to move. But he doesn't ditch. He might play sick, try to stay home, but..."

"Do you remember what he was wearing?"

"His usual: hoodie and jeans," Sonny said.

"Have you checked with his friends?" Bailey asked. "Asked whether they've seen him?"

Sonny dropped her head slightly. "He really doesn't have many."

Tom frowned. "I've been trying to remember the name of that kid he did that science project with. Jason...something. He came over here a couple of times, didn't he?"

"That was last year, Tom. He hasn't come around since." Sonny looked at us, her eyes filled with pain. "Otis is a very sweet boy, but not much of a socializer. I-I'm afraid I don't know of any friends he'd skip school with."

"Do you mind if we take a look at his room?" Bailey asked.

Sonny stopped, looked at Bailey, then at me for a long moment. "Wait a minute...what's going on?"

"Now, Sonny." Tom put a hand on her shoulder. "They're probably just checking on all the students who're still missing." Tom Barney looked from me to Bailey. "Right?"

Bailey and I were silent.

Sonny's breathing quickened. "No. They're not." Her eyes flashed, her voice was low and raw. "You think he's one of them! Don't you? Well, I'm telling you right now, that's impossible! I know my son! He had *nothing* to do with this! Do you hear me? Nothing!"

"Mrs. Barney, we're not accusing your son of anything," I said. "But we have to follow up on all leads. We have reason to believe someone involved in the shooting may still be at large," I said. We hadn't released the fact that the killers had escaped, so I had to keep it vague. "If you won't cooperate, we'll just have to get a search warrant. It'll cost us precious time, but..."

I was bluffing. I didn't have enough to get a warrant. We *might* be able to justify a quick search right now as hot pursuit of a fleeing felon. But getting consent would be a lot safer. I waited and tried to act confident.

Sonny's gaze dropped to the floor. Her body began to shake, whether from rage or fear or grief—or all three—I couldn't tell. Tom put his arms around her, his expression tortured. After a few moments, he spoke. His voice was raw, angry. "Sonny's right. Whatever kind of 'leads' you got that pointed to Otis are wrong. But we have nothing to hide. Look all you want." Tom led us down a short hallway, to a room with navy-blue walls covered with posters of bands I didn't recognize. Bloodstained Boots, Crew XXX, and Der Fuehrer. They all showed white guys with shaved heads, most sporting swastika tattoos.

"Mind if we look around?" Bailey asked.

Tom made a sweeping gesture. "Have at it."

We went through everything—his chest of drawers, the bedding, the closet—searching for guns, ammunition, any mention of a weapons supplier, any notes or photos that might relate to the school shooting. Nothing. I glanced up at the posters on Otis's wall again.

Sonny saw me. "I know how it looks. We hate them too, but Otis isn't...he's not that guy. It's just a...phase he's been going through. We think it probably makes him feel powerful, tough. But he's a good kid. Really."

I didn't answer. Tom saw my expression, and his features hardened.

Bailey scanned the room. "It'd help if we could have a crime scene tech in to test for gunshot residue or—"

Tom cut her off. "We've already helped enough. Now how about *you* help *us* and find our son, goddamnit! Otis had nothing to do with this! So if you want to waste more time searching here, you'd better get a warrant."

He turned and left the room and we followed him out. There was no point arguing. If we got anything more to tie Otis to the shooting, we'd get that warrant. Short of that, we had no choice but to leave.

From what we'd seen, Otis did look like the typical angry, alienated loner who hated the world enough to lash out, but that didn't mean he was one of the shooters. At least, not yet.

10

By the time we left Otis Barney's house it was almost eleven p.m. The autumn air had a bite that made me pull my peacoat closer and wish I'd brought my cashmere scarf. When we got back to Bailey's car I reached for the heater.

"It's not that cold," she said.

"It is for me."

Bailey closed the vents on her side. "Maybe you should transfer to the DA's office in Dubai." We rode in silence as she steered us toward the Tampa Avenue freeway on-ramp.

"Those posters were pretty strange," I said. "But we didn't find anything else. Maybe his parents are right. Maybe he isn't one of the shooters."

"And maybe his parents are in denial about who their son is. They wouldn't be the first. But I don't blame them for being pissed off at us. It's a hell of a thing to hear your kid accused of mass murder."

"Yeah." I sighed. It was hard to even imagine how that must feel. I pictured Otis's room again. Those posters. And something I hadn't seen. "I didn't notice a computer," I said. "He must have one."

"Yeah, probably a laptop. But I didn't want to bring it up and give them any ideas. If Otis does have one, I'm hoping they won't think to wipe it before we can get a warrant." Which meant we had to dig up some probable cause for a search warrant, and fast. "Home?" she asked.

"May as well. Can't get anything more done tonight." I put my hands next to the vents to warm them. "We need to have the unis ask around about Otis. Talk to students, teachers, and counselors and find out if he was into guns or made any threats, that kind of thing. But they can't make it sound like—"

"He's our guy. One of 'em, anyway. I know."

Traffic was light, and before I knew it, we were heading into downtown Los Angeles. Bailey cleared her throat. "Feel like a drink?"

I was tired and depressed and in no mood to hang out, but Bailey's voice was uncharacteristically strained. I looked at her closely. She had a death grip on the steering wheel, and her jaw was clenched so hard the cords in her neck stood out. She needed company—and a stiff drink...or seven. Come to think of it, so did I. "Sure. And why don't you crash with me?"

Bailey gave me a tight smile. "Sounds good."

Twenty minutes later, Bailey pulled up in front of the Biltmore and parked next to a fire hydrant. Bailey believes illegal parking is one of the few perks of being a cop. But it's not just a matter of convenience. She'll pick the red zone over a closer space every time. It's a religion with her. "You know, eventually, someone's going to bust you for this shit."

"Good thing I know a lawyer then, huh?"

"Please. I'll be the first to testify against you. You want to know who'll be second?" I pointed to Rafi, the Biltmore valet, who was shooting daggers at Bailey.

Bailey threw him a smile as we walked past the valet stand. "Catch ya next time, partner."

Rafi nodded sullenly.

"That's what you always say," I said, as we reached the front entrance.

Angel, the doorman, opened the door and chuckled. "I believe she's right about that, Detective," he said.

"Good idea, Angel, side with her," Bailey said. "You don't care about getting that Christmas bottle of scotch anyway, right?"

Angel put on an earnest expression. "On second thought, I believe you *have* let him park your car on many prior occasions," he said.

"Shameless," I said.

"Nicely played," Bailey said.

Angel smiled. "Marriage has taught me many things." We stepped inside. "Have a nice evening, ladies."

The familiar faces of home. It was the best I'd felt all day. And I knew it was comforting to Bailey too. Even so, as we crossed the lobby and headed for the bar I noticed her steps were heavy. We had to lighten up. There was no way of knowing how long it would take us to wrap up this case. If we didn't find some emotional balance we'd wind up wearing jumpsuits with very long arms. I grabbed the large brass handle of the bar door, pulled it open, and gestured for her to enter. "Your Highness."

"Your Highness?"

"There're plenty of other things I could call you."

Bailey and I took our usual spots at the end of the bar nearest the wall. It was a classic, well-appointed bar, mahogany with plush swivel stools and a mirror that was lit softly enough to prevent depressing news if I accidentally caught a glimpse of myself. Our spot at the end offered the most privacy. But that wasn't a problem tonight. The bar was relatively empty. Just a few businessmen whose loosened ties and red faces told me they'd finished their business for the day at least three drinks ago.

"I don't see Drew," I said. Drew Rayford is the head bartender and, more important, Bailey's boyfriend.

"No, he's off tonight. We were supposed to have dinner, but..."

"But a mass murder got in the way."

We exchanged a look and sank back in our chairs. I'd hoped Drew would be here tonight. It would've been good for both of us to see him. Cliché though it is, he became my confidant and buddy from the day I first moved into the hotel. And he's plenty easy on the eyes, which is also helpful. Tall, with a muscled V-shaped torso and skin the color of mahogany, Drew had women falling into his lap when he wasn't even trying. When he and Bailey got serious, I could practically hear the weeping from all corners of L.A. County. I probably would've been one of them myself if I hadn't been such an emotional wreck when we first met. I had been staying with my mother, nursing her through her battle with breast cancer. But after she died, I couldn't bear to be there anymore. I had a high-profile murder trial that was about to start, so I'd temporarily moved into the hotel because it was within walking distance of the courthouse. The murder victim was the Biltmore CEO's wife, and she'd been killed in the parking garage during a robbery. Between the stress of that trial, my mother's recent death, and the breakup with my long-term boyfriend, Daniel Rose, I wasn't looking for love. Drew poured my drinks while I poured out my heart, and a deep, long-lasting friendship was born. As a side perk, after I'd won the trial, the CEO had made me an offer I couldn't afford to refuse: a permanent residency at the hotel. I hadn't planned to stay longer than a year—two at the most. But it's been three years now and it still hasn't gotten old. The truth is, it's hard to give up a life with no laundry, no dishes, and room service.

A young bartender who'd started a few months ago took our orders: Ketel One martinis straight up, very dry, very cold, olives on the side. Bailey asked for an extra tray of Crunchies, the only food we could get at that hour.

"We need to nail down a list of who's accounted for and who isn't," I said. "Have all the bodies in the hospital and the morgue been identified?"

"Not quite. Not all the kids carried ID with them when they went to the pep rally. We've got officers on loan from the burglary desk working on it. A lot of kids ran home, but not all. The parents have been blowing up the phone lines at the Valley Division."

"It would help if we could round up all the students and take roll call—"

"Like they'd be doing if they had a school to go to?"

I sighed. "Yeah." Fairmont High School would be out of commission for the next few weeks while every inch was combed for evidence. In the meantime the students had to be relocated, but finding the space for them in the overcrowded L.A. Unified School District was going to be a nightmare.

"I hate to tell you this, but it's even worse than you might've thought," Bailey said. "The unis said there were a ton of kids who were ambulatory whose parents took them to hospitals and clinics all over the place. If they weren't brought in by paramedics, they might not show up on any of our lists."

"But I heard the parents who haven't found their kids are all waiting at the local rec center. That should give us a pretty accurate missing list."

"Not necessarily. Not all of the parents are there, and even those that are keep coming and going. Like Sonny and Tom. Plus, some kids got taken to the hospital by other kids' parents. Some kids went on their own. And I've heard some just ran to friends' and relatives' houses. It's pretty crazy."

So even if students were reported missing, that didn't mean they really were. "The fastest way to find out who's really unaccounted for is to go public with the fact that the shooters are still at large and ask all students to check in at the local police station. But that'll tip off the killers—"

"Not to mention cause a riot," Bailey said. "But we've got to do something or it'll take us days to figure out who's missing—"

"And we don't have days." I rubbed my forehead. "We're going to have to let it out pretty soon no matter what."

"If it doesn't get leaked first."

"I just wish we could get the killers ID'd before we go public with it," I said. "At least we'd be able to tell everyone who to look out for."

Bailey leaned back and sighed. "Yeah, that'd be nice."

The waiter brought our drinks, and I raised my glass. We clinked and drank, but two more miserable toasters would have been hard to find.

11

TUESDAY MORNING, OCTOBER 8

Bailey left early to go home and change. Though she had a drawer of clothing in my dresser, she didn't have anything that was warm enough for this weather. The clothes Bailey still had at my place were left over from the time she'd moved in to help me deal with a psychopath who'd nearly succeeded in killing us both.

That psychopath, Lilah Bayer, was responsible for at least three murders and she was still at large. Though not a serial killer, Lilah was an "ends justify the means" kind of person, and if those means happened to include murder, so be it. But generally speaking, other than the ax murder of her husband—a crime for which she, incredibly, had been acquitted—she'd left the messy work for her employees. And if it was messy *important* work, she gave it to her main guy, Chase Erling.

Bailey and I had managed to nail Erling, but when Lilah found out that he was in custody, she hired an inmate to kill him. He'd always been loyal to her, but she couldn't be sure that loyalty would last when he was facing a sentence of life without parole. A Nazi Low Rider serving a lifetime sentence shanked Erling.

Certain that Erling would soon be sleeping with the fishes, Lilah hopped a private jet to parts unknown. But right before takeoff, she'd texted me with information about my sister. Reports that might prove Romy, who'd been abducted more than twenty-five years ago, was still alive. The text was Lilah's way of saying that if I left her alone, she might get me more information on Romy's whereabouts. But if I kept after her...well, whatever form her retribution took, it was almost guaranteed to be lethal for Bailey and me.

But I one-upped Lilah: Erling had survived the attack, barely. He was in a coma. I answered her text with a photo of him in the hospital. I left out the part about him being in a coma, the better to make her sweat.

Graden had checked out the reports she'd sent me about Romy and found they were legit. But they were more than twenty-five years old and so far there's been no further trace of my sister. Nor has there been any trace of Lilah, though both Graden and the district attorney investigators have been actively hunting for her.

If it were anyone else, I wouldn't have had any concerns about my personal safety, though I certainly would've been pissed off that a criminal had escaped justice. But Lilah was a whole different story. Bailey says she's got a bizarre obsession with me. I can't argue. At one point, Lilah followed Graden to a downtown bar and hit on him—and said just enough to make sure he'd tell me about it. To make matters worse, Lilah had the resources to disappear—or reappear—almost anywhere, at will. I try not to dwell on the fact that she's still out there, but since she's unlikely to get therapy for her obsession, let alone her sociopathy, I keep one eye on the rearview—and a loaded gun in my purse.

I lingered over coffee, thinking about our next move. We needed to push forward harder and faster on Otis Barney. I'd hoped we could track him through his cell phone, but his parents told us he'd lost it recently. It seemed to be true. There had been no activity on his number for the past five days. The unis had checked out his calls and texts for the past month and found nothing of interest. The calls were mainly to and from his mom and dad, with a few to video game companies and electronics stores. So he really did seem to be the loner Marnie and his parents had described.

That was bad news for us, because it made it that much harder to get information on where he might be. Worse, it meant that identifying his buddy, the second shooter, would be like looking for the proverbial needle in a haystack. We'd have to talk to everyone in his classes—and maybe the whole school—and hope someone could give us a lead. It would be a major time suck, and it might not even pay off. The only other option—and one that would give us much faster results—was to get into Otis's computer, if he had one. But for that, we'd need a search warrant. I looked at my clock radio. It was a little after seven. J.D. would be in his chambers soon. If I headed for the office right now, I could bang out the warrant in time to catch him before he got swamped with his daily calendar.

But there was one thing Bailey could do in the meantime. I called her on the way to the courthouse. And caught her in one foul mood.

"I said I'd meet you at the station," Bailey said. "What couldn't wait another half hour?"

"We've got to get that photo of the shooter's wrist enhanced so we can show it to—"

"Already done, Knight. It should be on my desk by the time I get to the station. I'd ask if there's anything else, but I don't want to know."

"Actually, you might." I told her I was going to put together a warrant for Otis's computer.

"Shouldn't take you long," she said. "We've got diddly-squat. Who're you going to take it to?"

"J.D."

Bailey snorted. "Way to work the friend angle, girl. Guess it's worth a try. You need me there?"

"Nah, I can sign this one. I'll meet you at the station." I like to do my begging in private.

Bailey was right, it didn't take me long to write the warrant. I pumped up the probable cause as best I could, even waxed a little poetic about the shooter's crazy laugh, and got down to J.D.'s courtroom by eight o'clock. I was in luck. The hoards hadn't descended yet. The clerk let me straight into chambers. I kept my pitch short and handed J.D. the warrant with a silent prayer.

I watched his face as he scanned the probable cause affidavit; I squeezed the arms of my chair to keep from fidgeting. I guess it was true that I was banking on his friendship to make him a little more sympathetic to the cause, but I was also counting on J.D.'s experience as a former detective in Robbery-Homicide to know how badly we needed to speed up the investigation. He finished reading and dropped the pages on his desk.

"I've seen a lot of search warrants in my time," he said. "This one's a hands-down winner for the most well-written—"

"Thanks, I—"

"And skinniest excuse for probable cause I've ever seen. I'd ask if you were kidding me with this, but I know why you took a shot at it and I don't blame you. The problem is, this warrant's so thin, it'll be my ass if those parents decide to file a beef. And anything you find will get tossed out so fast it'll put a hole in the wall. I'm sorry, Rachel."

No sorrier than I was. I trudged back upstairs to my office to drop off the case file and noticed that Toni's door was open. I missed her. Since picking up the school shooting, I hadn't even had the chance to call. Toni was glued to her computer screen. I knocked on the door frame. "Hey, Twan. What's new?"

"Huh. You tell me." She peered at me. "The way you look, it ain't good. Come sit, catch me up."

I did.

When I finished, Toni drummed her fingers on the desk, then asked, "Have you considered bringing a shrink in on this?" I looked at her. She held up a hand. "I know, you're not a fan. Me either. But strange times call for strange measures. You need to make sure Otis is your guy, and you need to identify your second shooter. And you're in a bad time crunch—"

"The worst—"

"You can't be talking to all three thousand kids in that school with your killers flying around out there. You've got to narrow down your search. Only way I can think of is to get some idea of who you're looking for, what type of kid. You need someone who can help you figure out the teenage brain—"

"The twisted teenage brain," I said.

Toni nodded. "Even harder."

She had a point. We'd never tracked killers like these before. And we definitely needed to pull out all the stops. Having a shrink on board couldn't hurt. Toni helped me put together a list of psychologists we liked—or at least didn't hate. "Thanks, Tone. Gotta run. Bailey's waiting for me at the station and I've got to check these names out—"

Toni waved her hand. "Go, go. I'm here if you need me. Call when you come up for air."

I went back to my office, did some research, and winnowed our list down to three names, then headed to Eric's office. I told him I was considering bringing in a psychologist. "What do you think?"

"It won't hurt. And it'd be good PR. Shows the public we're doing everything we can." He sighed. "Jeez, I sound like Vanderhorn."

"If it makes you feel any better, I thought the same thing." I handed over the list of names. "Anybody you like?"

Eric read the list. "They're all good. I've got one more you might want to check out. Ran into her when I was in juvy."

I took down the name and headed for the station at a fast trot.

When I got there, Bailey was standing at her desk, tapping her watch. "You're half an hour late and we've got a boatload of—"

I put up a hand. "Hold your fire. I haven't exactly been lying around in my fat pants with a spoon and a can of frosting." I told her about J.D.'s no-go on the search warrant and my plan to bring a shrink on board.

Bailey gave me an incredulous look. "A *shrink?*"

"Actually, two shrinks. Eric liked my idea of Dr. Malloy, and he suggested Dr. Shelby."

"Dr. Malloy sounds familiar. Didn't he testify in that pedophile case last year?"

"Yep," I said. It was a case involving seven victims who'd been molested by a summer camp counselor. Not one of them had reported the crime, and when police first questioned them, five denied it. The jury was falling for the defense claim that the police coerced the kids into saying they'd been molested—until Dr. Malloy showed up.

"But does he have experience with teen freaks?"

"That I don't know." But how many shrinks could there be who had firsthand experiences with psychos like these?

"What did Eric say about Dr. Shelby?"

"She's a child psychologist too, but she's got more hands-on experience with juvenile offenders. And she's done studies on Columbine and some of the other school shootings."

Bailey nodded. "Sounds like a good team. How fast can you get them on board?"

"I'll call them right now. How fast they'll come is another matter." In my experience, forensic psychologists—at least the good ones—were usually overbooked. I dialed Dr. Malloy's number, expecting to hear that at best he might be able to fit us in sometime next week.

But I'd underestimated the powerful pull of this case. Not the media-whore factor—in fact, both doctors demanded that their names not be released to the press. I mean the desire-to-help factor. They agreed to drop everything for this case simply because they wanted to help us find the shooters. In this job it's easy to forget that there are people like that in the world.

I asked them to meet us at the station as soon as they could. They said they were on their way.

12

"Got coffee?" I asked. I'd been up since five thirty, and my engine was starting to sputter.

"I'll see if I can snag some of Graden's. The shit we've got probably had dinosaurs stuck in it. In the meantime, check this out." She handed me a large manila envelope. Inside, I found the blowup of the taller gunman's wrist. When Bailey came back with two steaming mugs, I held it up. "What the hell is that? A dagger through a rose? A spider? A screwed-up iron cross? I can't believe this is the best they can do." I'd hoped this picture would give us a solid lead on the second shooter.

"It's not great. I've got the lab working on getting us a better enhancement, but don't expect much. It'll probably never be super clear."

"We need to show it to Charlotte and her buddies."

"We will."

I held the photo at arm's length to see if it helped. It didn't.

"Rache, don't obsess. It'll be good enough if we find someone who knows him. At least you can tell it's not just a birthmark."

That much was true. It was better than nothing.

A patrol officer with two civilians in tow headed toward us. Our doctors had arrived. Bailey and I thanked them for showing up on such short notice and for agreeing to help us. "I know you had to push a lot out of the way to get here," I said.

"Please," Dr. Malloy said. "I'm just glad to be able to help out. And you'll have to call me Michael if we're going to work together.

He looked like a Michael. And he looked like someone kids would have an easy time opening up to. Of average height and sporting a hint of a belly, he had warm brown eyes and thick, wavy brown hair that in spite of his best efforts kept falling into his eyes. To top it off, he wore a sweater vest. Nothing says "cuddly" like a sweater vest.

Dr. Shelby, who likewise insisted on her first name—Jenny—was slender and attractive. Not the frilly type, she wore a brown turtleneck sweater and black slacks. Her shoulder-length dark blonde hair hung straight and simple in a side part, and she wore minimal makeup that enhanced her gray eyes and high cheekbones. She too had an easy, approachable vibe. Even without a sweater vest.

They declined my offer of Graden's coffee—it really was pretty good—and Bailey led the way to one of the smaller conference rooms. We got right down to business. I told them what we knew so far and what we needed from them. Then I played the video footage from inside the gym. When it ended, Michael rubbed the side of his head as though he were trying to wake up from a nightmare. Jenny looked pale.

"How many dead?" Jenny asked.

"Thirty-three as of now," Bailey replied. "We're hoping it stops there."

"Jesus," Michael said. "That's worse than Sandy Hook."

"And much worse than Columbine," Jenny said. "But from what you've told me, I'd agree that may be exactly what they intended. They wanted to prove they were better, so they exceeded the body count *and* managed to escape."

"Yes, that much seems obvious," Michael said.

"As for what type of person you're looking for, that's less obvious," Jenny said. "The angry loner, bully victim—which seems to be Otis Barney—is a stereotype, but it doesn't always hold. Columbine is instructive. Eric Harris was very socially adept—"

"And popular with the girls, if my memory serves," Michael said.

"He was," Jenny said. "Even Dylan Klebold was fairly social. So there are no hard-and-fast rules. Studies show these mass shooters are a heterogeneous group. They come in all stripes. But there are certain markers that show up with some consistency."

"The sense of feeling persecuted or victimized is very common," Michael said. "They frequently feel mistreated or undervalued by the school, their teachers, their parents—"

"Great," Bailey said. "How're we going to spot that?"

"By asking other students to tell you if they've heard anyone talk about feelings of persecution and plans for revenge," Jenny said. "Individuals with this type of pathology often vent to others, may even demand an audience."

"You should also ask students if anyone has seemed overly invested in guns or military paraphernalia, or romanticizes guns and weaponry in general," Michael said.

"What about the video gamer theory?" I said. "Some shrinks—uh, sorry, psychologists—say the first-person-shooter battle games desensitize kids, get them addicted to violent fantasies, and make them forget people are real. I heard there's even a game called School Shooter." Which sickened me on every level: both the fact that someone dreamed it up and the fact that people bought it.

"First of all, we call each other shrinks, so no apologies necessary," Michael said. "Second of all, no normal kid turns into a mass murderer because he played too many video games—"

"But if a kid has pathological homicidal tendencies, an addiction to violent video games can tip him over," Jenny said. "So the games may exacerbate the tendency, but they don't create it. In fact, someone who's already planning to commit this type of crime might use the video game as a form of practice and perhaps to further desensitize himself—"

"Just to play devil's advocate, isn't it possible the games act as a form of release?" I said. "You know, like porn?"

Jenny smiled. "They may. If you're normal. In that case, certainly, porn or video games can be beneficial. But for a sexual predator, or someone with a homicidal pathology, the opposite is true. The porn might offer the predator temporary release, but in the long run it'll just cause the pathology to escalate until he explodes and acts out. Same thing with the homicidal types. The games might provide transitory relief, but ultimately the games aggravate the unbridled rage and lack of focus that's intrinsic to their pathology."

"Lack of focus?" I asked. "Seems to me the games require a lot of focus."

"Only in a superficial sense," Michael said. "You have to pay attention to what you're doing, but the focus is constantly shifting from one obstacle to the next, with only fractions of a second per target. So the focus is extremely fragmented."

"In general, though, the games may encourage what's already there. But they don't create it," Jenny said.

"You said they like to talk to people about their pisstivity with the world and their plans to get revenge," Bailey said. "Isn't that what you guys always say people should do? Talk things out? How come it doesn't do anything for them?"

"Because they're not talking constructively, with the purpose of understanding their feelings," Michael said. "They're just venting, spewing. When you talk to a friend or lover about your feelings, you're trying to understand, to gain some awareness of your situation. Not these people. They're just looking for an audience. So talking only feeds their rage."

"I assume Otis Barney is a gamer?" Jenny asked.

"Yes," I said. "So I guess that doesn't necessarily prove anything."

"Not in and of itself," Michael said. "But what is significant is that, based on what you describe, Otis is a follower. That means your second shooter is certainly the leader. I can't think of a case in which there were two leaders."

"Okay," Bailey said. "We've got a leader and a follower, and we shouldn't bother canvassing video game sites. We should ask around about kids who did a lot of venting about being persecuted or waxed on about gun stuff. What else?"

"Have someone who's good with computers check the Internet," Jenny said. "This type of criminal almost invariably writes about his desire to kill. I'd be very surprised if you didn't find writings, blueprints, or drawings showing how they planned the attack. Check out Tumblr, Instagram; I hear Pheed is getting hot these days. I'd also check with English teachers for any poetry, short stories, or essays that depict homicidal fantasies."

"What about someone who's been diagnosed as mentally ill at some point?" I asked.

"Typically, no," Jenny said.

"No?" Bailey said. "You've got to be kidding. You're saying these sick fucks are normal?"

"No," Michael said. "We're certainly not saying that. We're just saying they're not necessarily mentally ill—"

"They have personality disorders," Jenny said. "Usually borderline personality disorder or antisocial personality disorder. But those are not mental illnesses. In fact, people with those disorders are usually highly intact, organized, and articulate. Frequently, very intelligent."

"What about Adam Lanza, though?" Bailey asked. "Didn't he have Asperger's?"

"So I've heard. But again, that's not a mental illness," Michael said.

"Regardless, our shooters are different, aren't they?" I asked. "Don't these guys usually kill themselves? Like Harris and Klebold?"

"Yes," Michael said. "And your shooters probably will too...ultimately. I doubt they plan to be taken alive."

I mentally replayed the images on the video footage taken from inside the gym, our walk-through at the school. "Fine by me."

13

TUESDAY AFTERNOON, OCTOBER 8

We promised to keep the doctors up to speed on the investigation, and they promised to review any "interesting" writings we found on the Internet or at school. After they left, Bailey glanced at the clock on the wall, which was slightly crooked. It had bugged the hell out of me through the whole interview. Maybe I lacked focus too.

"It's lunchtime," Bailey said. "You feel like eating?"

"Not really."

She picked up the manila envelope with the photo of the shooter's tattoo. "Then we may as well go see Charlotte and company."

The traffic wasn't bad. We made it to Woodland Hills in just under forty minutes. This time I had the chance to take in the neighborhood. It was pretty uniformly middle- to upper-middle class. Mature pepper and weeping willow trees and '50s-style ranch homes showed that it wasn't a new development. But it had always been a fairly nice one. Nothing flashy, but nice. Families had moved here, at least in part, to get away from the crime and violence of the inner city. The bitter irony was that at least two of those families had spawned the most vicious predators of all.

We found Charlotte, her mother, and Charlotte's friends Letha and Marnie sitting over steaming cups of tea in a bright-yellow breakfast nook. The flowered curtains were parted to let in the pale sunlight. Bailey and I joined them at the table. I declined their offer of coffee. I'd had three cups in my room and a fourth at the station. Any more than that and I wouldn't sleep till next year.

I took a moment to look at the girls. It had only been one day, but their haggard faces and haunted eyes showed the enormity of the trauma they'd suffered. I wished we could leave them alone to grieve privately and regain their balance. The whole world probably felt like a precarious high-wire act for them. On the other hand, maybe talking to us would give them a sense of control over the situation. In any case, we had no choice.

Bailey pulled out the photograph of the taller shooter's wrist.

"Do any of you recognize this?" I asked.

Each girl examined the photograph, shook her head, and passed it on.

"What is it?" Charlotte said.

"I was hoping you'd tell me," I said. Charlotte shrugged. "I heard Otis had a friend named Jason. They did a science project together a year or so ago. Does that ring a bell?"

They frowned in unison. "Jason...the only Jason I know graduated last year," Letha said.

But that didn't mean he wasn't our tall shooter. "What did he look like?"

Marnie made a face. "An Ewok. Real short and really hairy."

So much for Jason. Or at least *that* Jason. Maybe there were others. "Do you happen to remember the names of the science teachers for last year—which would've been what, your junior year?"

"Yeah," Charlotte said. "I had Mr. Forster."

"Who'd you guys have?" I asked Marnie and Letha.

Letha pulled her long hair forward over her right shoulder and began to stroke it. "Marnie and I had Ms. Sherman." Her mouth turned downward. "We got sent to the principal's office because we wouldn't dissect a frog—"

"How can they kill animals just so high school kids can cut them up?" Marnie said. "It was so...brutal." She hadn't meant it to be ironic, but it landed hard anyway. On all of them.

We wrapped it up shortly after that and walked out to Bailey's car. I stopped at the passenger door and spoke to her over the hood. "Is Principal Campbell back in act—"

"Dale, and yes, he's reachable."

We got into the car and Bailey called Dale, who got us the numbers for the evil Ms. Sherman and Mr. Forster. Both answered on the first ring and offered to meet us anytime, anywhere. It was a grim upside to a case of this magnitude: no one thought they had anything more important to do. We told them for now, we only needed a few minutes on the phone.

Ms. Sherman, who sounded more like Betty Crocker than Cruella De Vil, was a model of efficiency. She kept records for the past four years on her computer.

"I didn't have any student named Otis Barney," she said. "I did have a Jason a couple of years ago, but I think he would have graduated by now."

Jason the Ewok, I guessed. We thanked her and moved on to Mr. Forster.

"Otis Barney? That name sounds familiar," he said. "Hang on, let me go get my laptop." A few minutes later, he was back. "Let's see, this was last year, you say?" I confirmed it. "Okay, yes, I did have Otis Barney. No Jason though."

Damn. "Who was Otis teamed up with, then?" I asked.

"Carson. Carson James. Why?"

Bailey and I exchanged a look. Carson…Jason. Close enough. A parent could easily misremember. "Mr. Forster, would you mind if we stopped by for a few minutes?"

The science teacher lived on the outer edges of the neighborhood that fed Fairmont High, where the homes and the lots they sat on were a good deal smaller. A teacher's pay doesn't go far. But no worries, the universe provides balance. Britney Spears has mansions in at least three states.

When Mr. Forster opened the door I was momentarily speechless. Why do I expect teachers to be old? I guess because way back when I was a student, they all looked old to me. The fact that Mr. Forster not only looked young, but hot—in a science nerd kind of way—was upsetting for so many reasons.

He wore a gray waffle shirt and jeans. His black, curly hair was charmingly messy and complemented by heavy-framed black glasses. His welcoming smile seemed to stretch a little farther than he'd planned when he saw us. That helped assuage my "I'm so old" blues a little.

"Thank you for seeing us on such short notice, Mr. Forster," I said.

"Uh, it's Liam, okay? I get enough 'Mr. Forster' at school." Liam ushered us into a small living room that was furnished in Early Bachelor. Ikea couch, coffee table, two chairs, a television. No flowers, no paintings, no knickknacks. There were a few framed photographs of people who looked like family on the mantel over the fireplace. "Would you like coffee or tea? It's the extent of my culinary skills, but I do those pretty reliably."

We declined, and Liam sat down in one of the chairs across from the couch. I started by asking him whether he'd been in the gym at the time.

He shook his head. "I stayed in the classroom so I could set up for our weather experiment." He'd eventually heard the gunfire, but his classroom was on the second floor, at the opposite end of the hall from the library. He hadn't seen anything.

"Can you tell us what you remember about Otis Barney?" I asked after Bailey and I had settled into the couch.

"I figured you'd ask that so I've been thinking about him. He was pretty quiet, intense, you know? He seemed like a sensitive kid who was trying not to be, if that makes any sense."

It did. But it was probably true of half the school. "Was he a problem in class?"

"Not really. He was never disruptive. But there was something...anxious about him. It felt like he was trying very hard to fit in, be one of the guys. I kind of got the impression he was getting picked on." Liam sighed. "He never told me, and I never saw anyone attack him in any way, so I couldn't do anything about it. And maybe I'm wrong about that. It was just a feeling. But no, he never caused me any problems. Why? Are you thinking...?"

I didn't want to answer that question, not until we had solid evidence of Otis's involvement. "We're just following up on all leads. Otis is one of the many we're looking into." Not true, but the safest answer for now. "Any information you can give us will be helpful."

Liam nodded. "I remember being surprised that Otis volunteered for the extra-credit team project. He didn't really seem all that interested in science."

But it didn't surprise me. If Otis was looking for a friend, signing up for a team project gave him a safe way to make one. "And he teamed up with Carson James," I said. "What can you tell us about him?"

"Carson was kind of a loner, and a rebellious type—sat in the back and never talked in class—but he loved science. And he was good at it. He didn't want a partner, didn't want to have to collaborate with anyone, but I told him that was the deal. Otis was happy to let Carson call all the shots, so it was a good fit. And I'm sure Otis also liked the fact that no one messed with Carson."

"Why?" I asked.

"For one thing, he was over six feet, and he seemed to be in pretty good shape."

The pieces were starting to fall into place. I didn't have to look at Bailey to know that her ears had perked up too. "Mind if I show you a photograph?" I pulled out the enhanced cell phone photo of the taller shooter's wrist. "Do you remember seeing any student with a marking like this on his right arm?"

Liam studied the photograph carefully. "No. Several of my students have tatts, but I don't recognize this one."

"Did you ever see any kind of tattoo on Carson's wrist?" I asked.

Liam paused. "Not that I can recall. Sorry."

It was a letdown, but not a game ender. He might've just missed it. "Do you happen to know any of Carson's friends?" I didn't want to go to his parents yet. If he did have the tattoo, they'd jump to the right conclusion. And possibly help him run.

"I don't. But I can give you the names of the other students in the class. Maybe one of them can help you."

Someone had to. And soon.

14

TUESDAY, LATE AFTERNOON, OCTOBER 8

Bailey started the car but let it idle. "I think this Carson dude is exactly what the doctor ordered."

"Agreed." I snapped my seat belt into place. "Just because Liam didn't see the tattoo doesn't mean it wasn't there—"

"Or it might be very recent. The kid could've even done it the night before the shooting."

"Yep. I say we put the unis on Carson, find out if he's shown up anywhere. In the meantime, we can ask around about him while we keep running on Otis Barney. Are Tom and Sonny still hammering Graden?"

"Every five minutes," Bailey said. "Graden keeps telling them Otis isn't the only one who's still MIA, that they're working twenty-four/seven to account for everyone, but—"

"They know he didn't have any friends to run to, and he hasn't turned up in the hospital or the morgue. And they don't like what that means. But they haven't gone public yet, right?"

"Not yet."

"We need to whittle down that list. Is anyone going through juvy cases? Maybe one of our shooters has a record."

"That would be refreshing," Bailey said. "And of course we're checking juvy cases. So far, all they found were some curfew violations and minor drug busts. All those kids are accounted for. The only thing we can do is move fast on the interviews. We've already got Liam's student list, so we may as well start there. I'll call Dale and get student lists for the rest of Otis's classes. Start with this year and work our way backward."

"Shit." That might mean hundreds of interviews. While two murderers ran the countryside.

"You got a better idea, Sherlock?"

I folded my arms and tried to come up with one while Bailey made the calls.

We managed to line up immediate interviews with four of Liam's students. One of the moms, Meredith Charnosh, volunteered to let us use her house. "I just think it'd be nice not to traumatize them any further by making them go to a police station," she said.

I considered telling her it might actually be reassuring for them to see law enforcement at work, but I had the feeling she just didn't want to let her son out of her sight. I didn't blame her.

We gathered in the living room, which was overfurnished but oddly comforting. The three boys, Mark, Vincent, and Harrison, took the sofa. The only girl, Paula, perched on the matching ottoman. All of them had that hundred-yard stare usually reserved for battle-scarred soldiers.

"Were you all in the gym when it happened?" I asked. They were. I asked what they'd been able to see of the gunmen.

"Just that they were wearing camo jackets and masks with eyeholes," Paula said.

The boys agreed. They'd all noticed that one was taller than the other. Estimates of the taller one's height varied between six feet two and six feet six.

"One of them yelled something about jocks," Mark said. Vincent and Paula heard that too.

In short, nothing new. Time to move on to Otis and Carson.

I had to be careful not to get too heavy with specific questions about them. If I did, it'd hit the grapevine in seconds and some kids might suddenly "remember" things that were more a product of imagination than reality. Not necessarily to get attention, but just because some people are susceptible to suggestion. Plant the idea and they'll fill in the blanks. So I started by asking the open-ended questions suggested by our shrinks: did they know anyone who vented frequently about feeling persecuted and hating the world or talked about taking revenge—

"On who?" Mark asked. "Lots of kids feel screwed over and talk about payback against their teachers or"—he craned his neck to see if Mrs. Charnosh was within earshot—"their parents."

"Or other kids," Vincent Charnosh said.

A fair question. "I mean someone who was always venting about everyone screwing him over, and wanting to kill them. Not just someone who spouted off once about wanting to kill the math teacher because he got an F. Someone who's angry at the world and talks about payback—a lot."

"I can't remember anyone talking like *that,*" Paula said.

"I'm pretty sure I would've turned in someone who went off like that," said Harrison, the most conservative-looking of the group. "After Sandy Hook and that freak in Colorado, we all know what's going on."

"Yeah," Mark said. "Ever since Sandy Hook, they've been talking about putting in metal detectors."

I'd been thinking about that when our shrinks gave us the checklist. Given how many shootings there'd been, and recently, I had a feeling most kids thought they were on top of it, could spot the dangerous types. But knowing that homicidal nutbags could walk among them didn't mean they knew whom to take seriously. It was the typical hubris of youth to think they had it all figured out. If the shooters turned out to be Otis and Carson—or anyone else they'd actually known—what few shreds of false security they had left would dissolve like spun sugar in the rain. But they didn't need to hear that right now, so I sat back and let Bailey take over.

"Do you know anyone who's heavily into guns?" she asked. "Anyone who talks about going to the range a lot or about having a lot of military paraphernalia?" They didn't.

She asked a few more gun questions, got more nos, and then asked whether they knew anyone who'd written about homicidal fantasies. When she again got a chorus of nos, I decided it was time to bring up Otis Barney and Carson James. I started by asking if any of them did the extracurricular team science project. I was betting Vincent, yes, the others, no. I was right. Sometimes, you just know.

"Did you get friendly with any of the other teams?" I asked.

"Some," Vincent said. "Not a ton."

"Did you ever hang with Otis and Carson?" I asked.

"No. They pretty much just did their own thing."

"So they were tight?" I asked.

"I guess. I didn't hear them argue or anything."

I pressed on with a few more questions about Otis and Carson—and threw in a few about the other teams just for cover—but got nothing, so I had to let it go and move on. I played the recording of the weird laugh that Marnie had identified as Otis's. "Do any of you recognize that laugh?"

"Uh, I don't know," Vincent said.

Mark gave him a surprised look. "Dude, that totally sounds like Otis," he said. He nudged Harrison. "Don't you think?"

"Yeah," Harrison said. "It does."

"Vincent?" I asked. "You don't think so?"

Vincent stretched his neck. "I guess, maybe. Yeah, probably."

I guessed Vincent was nervous about tagging his classmate. The wonders of teen loyalty. I kept at it a little while longer, but just kept hitting dead ends, so I wrapped up by showing them the blowup of the tattoo on the shooter's wrist. "Do any of you recognize this?"

They passed the photo around. Nada.

Four down, twenty nine hundred ninety-six students to go. We were cooking.

Dale Campbell had volunteered to set up the next batch of interviews. Based on our shrinks' advice, Bailey asked him to make English class the top priority. He started with Otis's current class. The teacher couldn't make it. He had to fly back to Arizona to help his father, who'd suffered a heart attack. But Dale had managed to round up several students and even let us meet at his house.

As we pulled into his driveway, Bailey got a call from the unis working on Carson James. It was a brief call, and when she ended it she stared out the front window.

"And?" I said, impatient.

"No one answers the door or the phone at his house. When they called his cell it went straight to voice mail. None of the bodies at the morgue fit his description, and they haven't found him at any of the hospitals so far."

We exchanged a look. "I would say Carson James is looking good," I said. "But I'm not going to because—"

"Yeah, don't jinx us."

Our hopes cautiously lifted, we got out and headed for Dale's house. Nine students, four male, five female, had crowded into Dale's family room. The parents had been relegated to the kitchen. They'd wanted to sit in with their kids, but there wasn't room. These students didn't look quite as shell-shocked. Did they feel more secure because it was a larger crowd? Or did they just not want to show how terrified they really were in front of the others? Even so, by no means did they look calm. The girls twirled their hair and hunched forward, some with arms wrapped around their bodies. The boys bounced their knees and cracked their knuckles.

They'd all been in the gym at the time of the shooting, but none had been able to see the shooters well enough to add to what we already knew. I moved on to the questions suggested by our shrinks. And got the same results as before: no, no, and no. I segued into Otis Barney. All they remembered was that he was pretty quiet and got real nervous when the teacher called on him. I played the snippet of footage with the shooter's weird laugh. No one recognized it. We were getting nowhere. I tossed out one last question. "Do any of you happen to know Carson James?"

Nancy, a petite brunette in leggings and a long sweater that fetchingly exposed one shoulder, asked, "Is he kind of tall, has long, black, greasy hair?"

Bailey, who had pulled his school yearbook photo, said, "Yeah. You know him?"

"He sat behind me in my English lit class last year. He was always bitching about something. The other kids in the class, the homework, the teacher." She shook her head. "What a loser—"

Carrie, who'd been groggy from taking antihistamines for her allergies, sat up. "Oh, is he the one who told you—"

"Yeah. One time, I asked him to keep it down and he told me to go fuck myself and said the next time I gave him shit, he'd shut me up forever."

"Did you report that to anyone?" I asked.

"No. I didn't take him that seriously. I thought he was just being an asshole."

He was at least that. "Did he ever talk about guns? Or about shooting people?" I asked.

"He never said anything about guns," Nancy said. "But he was always talking about how much he hated the school and how the kids were all loser assholes."

"Who did he hang out with?" I asked.

"I don't know. I didn't exactly go looking for him."

Interesting that no one reported seeing Carson act like that in science class. I wondered what his project had been. If it was how to make a Molotov, that might explain his good behavior. All kidding aside, his project might've had some subtle connection to explosives. I made a mental note to check with Liam.

We kept at it for a while longer, but there was nothing more—from Nancy or any of the others.

I passed the tattoo photo around. Nobody recognized it.

Still, Bailey and I left Dale's house feeling better than we had since we'd picked up the case.

When we got into the car, I looked at Bailey. "Okay, now I can say it: Carson James is looking good."

"He is," Bailey said. She pulled out her cell. "Let's get ahold of Carson's English teacher. See if we can get a few writing samples."

We shared a grim smile.

15

A few phone calls later, Bailey had a meeting set for five thirty at the teacher's house in Tarzana, which would give us just enough time to drive through a fast-food joint and pick up a very late lunch.

"Feel like Taco Bell?" Bailey asked.

"Always."

"She had no trouble remembering Carson," Bailey said.

"She say why?"

"No, but the way she said, 'Oh, yes,' I'll bet it wasn't because he volunteered to clap erasers," Bailey said.

"No one does that anymore."

"Whatever."

"They use whiteboards now," I said. Bailey shot me a look. "Just saying."

We found a Taco Bell on Ventura Boulevard, and Bailey pulled into the parking lot so she could eat without getting it all over herself.

I savored a big, crunchy bite. "Taco Supreme—the best fast food has to offer."

"There's also In-N-Out—" Bailey's cell phone buzzed. She answered it with a mouthful of taco. "Keller." Her chewing slowed, then stopped as she listened. When she ended the call, she wadded up her taco wrapper and threw it against the dash. "Son of a bitch!"

"What?"

"They found Carson. He's in a hospital out in Santa Clarita—"

"Why the hell is he all the way out there?" That was at least an hour away from the school.

"His uncle's a resident. His parents had him transferred straight out of the ER. They've been at his bedside this whole time."

Which is why no one answered the phone or the door. But maybe he was just hiding in plain sight. Maybe he was just acting like a victim to fool us. "What're his injuries?"

"Two shots to the gut. He's stable, but they're still worried about possible peritonitis. They couldn't get all the shrapnel out of his intestines."

That seemed a bridge too far. I could see shooting himself in the hand or the foot, but not in the gut. It was too dangerous. But if he was one of the shooters and his buddy did that to him, he might just be pissed off enough to talk to us. "Can we see him?"

"The uni said yes, but we need to get going. She said visiting hours for nonfamily end soon, and traffic's going to be a bitch."

Bailey canceled the meeting with Carson's English teacher, and we headed for the Henry Mayo Newhall Memorial Hospital in Valencia. The place was a labyrinth. It took less time to get there than it did to find Carson's bed. He had just been moved out of ICU and into a private room. The natural light flowing in through his window softened the harsh glare of the standard fluorescent bulbs, but even candlelight couldn't have masked the gray pallor of Carson's face. His doctor (uncle) warned us not to push him, said he was not out of the woods yet—can no one think of a new cliché?—and told us we had fifteen minutes, max.

His parents insisted on staying for the interview, his mom hovering on one side of his bed while his father glowered at us from the other and pointedly looked at his watch. There was no time for open-ended questions, so I went straight at it.

"Where were you when you got shot?"

"In the gym." His voice was thin and strained.

I asked him to be more specific. At the top of the bleachers? The bottom? I had him describe who sat next to him, what class he'd been in that morning—questions designed to tell me whether he could've been a shooter. The answers would be easy to verify. If he was lying, I'd know soon enough. But seeing him now, I had a strong feeling they'd check out. "Can you describe the shooters at all?" I asked.

"One looked tall."

"Taller than you?"

He nodded.

"I'm going to play a part of a video taken by one of the students in the gym. Tell me if you recognize this voice." I played the snippet of the crazy laugh.

Carson shook his head, a barely perceptible move. "Is it...one of the shooters?"

"Yes," I said.

He mouthed, "Motherfucker."

"Does it sound like anyone you know?"

"Kinda sounds like Otis. But it's not."

"Why not?"

Carson snorted. "Fucking wuss. Couldn't even cut up a frog."

The frog lesson plan didn't seem to have a lot of fans. But it didn't mean Otis wasn't one of the shooters. Animal lovers can be psychopaths too. Hitler had scientists working on a more humane way to cook lobsters. Couldn't bear the fact that they were boiled alive. "But you agree, it does sound like Otis's laugh?"

"Sort of."

"Did Otis ever talk about guns?"

"No...wait. He told me about someone...this dude who said he could get stuff online." Carson's voice was starting to sound like it was being squeezed through a narrow tube.

"What kind of stuff?"

"AKs and shit."

"Do you remember who that was?" I crossed my fingers behind my back.

Carson closed his eyes. Suddenly, he gave a sharp inhale and curled into a fetal position. One of the monitors started to shriek. Papa James stepped forward and pressed the call button for the nurse. "Okay, that's all. You're finished."

Just as abruptly, Carson's body relaxed. He lay on his back, panting. "S'okay, Dad." He took a few deep breaths and I found myself doing the same. When he spoke again, his voice had dropped to a whisper.

I leaned toward him, winding my body around the father, who'd stepped in even closer. "I didn't catch that. One more time?"

"Logan Jarvis."

"Do you know him?" I asked.

Carson shook his head.

I stepped back, and his father held up a thick hand. "That's it. I mean it. You have to stop."

I was about to tell him we *had* stopped when a nurse trotted in and shooed us all away. "Officers, whatever it is you need, it'll have to wait."

As she began to check his monitors, Carson whispered, "That school...bunch of fucking assholes."

"Angry young man," I said.

The nurse raised an eyebrow. "You blame him?"

Not now I didn't.

16

TUESDAY EVENING, OCTOBER 8

The sun had dropped low on the horizon, taking the day's warmth with it. I shivered and pulled my thin wool coat closer. It really was time to break out the winter wardrobe. Bailey and I trotted back to her car in silence. We talked as little as possible when we were in public because you never knew who was listening. Especially in a case like this.

As soon as we got into the car, Bailey handed me her cell phone. "Call the unis at the rec center. It's rush hour. I want to get on the road."

The phone rang six times before someone picked up. "Sharven here. What can I do for you, Detective Keller?" The din of frantic parents swelled over the young officer's voice. And mine. I had to yell my question four times before he could make out the name.

"Logan Jarvis?" he asked. "Is that *J* as in *John*, *V* as in *Victor?*"

"I think so."

"Hang on."

I started to bite my cuticles—my go-to stress coping strategy when there was no room to pace. Bailey slapped my hand. "Knock it off, Knight. What are you, twelve?"

I turned my back to her and attacked my right hand. I'd just gone to work on my thumb when the officer came back on the line.

"Detective Keller? Looks like your guy was reported missing—assuming the spelling's correct."

My heart began to pound. I told him to have the parents meet us at their house and got the address, then punched it into the navigation system. When I hung up, neither of us said anything about Logan looking good. No more jinxes.

We hit the 101 freeway in the middle of rush hour. We'd roll a few inches, stop, roll a few more, stop. I couldn't stand it. I had to *do* something. "What else can we check?"

"You could get the unis to check the juvy records, see if he's got anything."

"Didn't they already check the kids who had records? I thought they were all accounted for."

"Doesn't hurt to double-check."

It kind of did. I needed progress, forward motion. I stared at the line of cars ahead of us. "Wait...if the killers left the scene, at least one of them had to have had a car, right?"

"I'd guess."

I called DMV, got Logan Jarvis's license and registration, then called the unis and had them check it against the cars in the school parking lot.

"And?" Bailey asked.

I kept my eyes forward. "Not there."

Having one idea pay off gave me another.

I put in a call to my buddy in the coroner's office, investigator Scott Ferrier. "Hey, Scott, how you doin'?"

"What do you want?" His voice was wary. Not that I blamed him. Generally speaking, a phone call from me meant two things: (1) I wanted him to get me something I wasn't supposed to have and (2) I'd bribe him with lunch at Engine Co. No. 28, his favorite restaurant, to get it. So Scott was always conflicted about taking my calls.

"Just one bit of information. Has Dr. Shoe finished the autopsy on those two kids in the library?"

"Yeah, took him a while. They were a mess. He just finished a couple of hours ago."

"Can you check out his report—"

"It's not typed yet."

"You only need his notes to see what I'm looking for—"

"Rachel, I'm not supposed to—"

"Come on, Scott. This one's easy." I heard him sigh. "And I'll still buy you lunch at Engine Company Number Twenty-eight."

"No, that's okay. What do you need?"

"Did either of the two boys in the library have a tattoo or any kind of marking on his right wrist?" We already knew one of them was close to six feet tall.

"That *is* easy." He sounded relieved. "No, neither of them has any kind of marking on the right wrist. At least, nothing that's in the notes. Anything else?" His voice had that wary note again. He couldn't believe he'd gotten off that lightly.

"Just one thing. Do we have results on the gunshot residue?"

"Yeah. No GSR on either of them. Is that it?"

"Then the report confirms they're not the shooters?"

"Well, the official report isn't done yet—"

"But the answer's yes."

Scott sighed again. "Yes. They are not the shooters. But I can't get the report for you. Not this time, Rachel. The case is too hot, I might really get fired—"

"Scott, what are you thinking? I would never ask you to jeopardize your job."

"Would and have, Knight."

True and true. "Well, I'm not doing it now. Just one more thing." I waited a beat to build suspense. "How about lunch in a couple of weeks?"

I could practically hear him exhale. "You got it."

I ended the call and told Bailey what Scott had said. We continued to inch along, and I leaned forward in my seat, straining against the seat belt. I sat on my hands to keep from biting my cuticles. I looked at my watch, then the car clock, then back at my watch. I must have done it fifteen times before we finally got off the freeway and headed into Logan's neighborhood.

17

Bailey turned onto a quiet street lined with trees that had grown so large their roots had buckled the sidewalks. The houses were a mix of ranch, Tudor, and Cape Cod styles, but all were in the four-thousand-square-foot range and well maintained. Bailey pulled over and pointed across the street to a beige two-story house with off-white trim situated on a large lot at the end of the block. Red and white roses lined the walk leading up to the front door, and still-leafy jacaranda trees shaded the front yard—the very epitome of upper-middle-class suburbia. I wondered if it housed one of the nation's most heinous mass murderers.

We headed across the street and when we reached the door Bailey used the brass knocker to give two sharp raps. I felt footsteps approaching from somewhere in the house. Seconds later, a tall, stoop-shouldered man answered the door. His eyes were red rimmed behind wire-framed glasses, his short brown hair was matted on one side, and his clothes—a long-sleeved T-shirt and jeans—looked slept-in.

Bailey produced her badge, and I did the same. "Mr. Jarvis? I'm Detective Keller and this is Deputy District Attorney Rachel Knight. Thank you for meeting us here."

I saw alarm and misery in his face. He opened his mouth, but just stared at us silently for a moment before gesturing for us to come in. We followed him down a short hall and turned right, into a tastefully furnished living room. We settled on the sofa and he sat down in the wingback chair across from us, his hands on his knees. He cleared his throat with a harsh cough, took a deep breath, and made himself ask the question. "Have you found him? Have you found my son?" He looked from me to Bailey.

I could see how much that question had cost him. We shook our heads. "I'm sorry, Mr. Jarvis," I said.

He blinked slowly, nodded.

"Does he usually drive his car to school?" Bailey asked.

"Yes. But it's not there. We've been calling everywhere trying to find him. No one seems to know anything—"

A woman's voice called out from the hallway. "Brad? Are they..." A small, slender woman in jeans, whose face and body sagged as though attached to lead weights, entered with quick, nervous steps.

"Yes, it's the police, Bonnie—"

Her swollen eyes asked the question she was too afraid to voice.

"We have not found your son yet, Mrs. Jarvis," Bailey said.

The mother sank onto the other end of the sofa and twisted a Kleenex in her hands. The anguish in that room was heartbreaking. They had no idea why we were really here. Their only fear was that he was a victim. What we would tell them in the next few moments would make them long for that relatively simple form of agony.

"Can I ask you if Logan has a tattoo anywhere on his body?" I asked.

Bonnie lifted her head. "Yes, he has a tattoo of an iron cross on his right wrist."

I pulled out the photograph of the taller shooter's forearm. "This is a little fuzzy, but could this be it?"

The mother leaned forward to look but didn't take the photograph from my hand. She pressed her lips together and nodded. I showed the photograph to the father. His face turned white.

"Where... when was this taken?" he asked.

I glanced at Bailey. We wanted to hold off on telling them for as long as possible.

"Would you mind if we had a look around Logan's room?" Bailey asked. "We might pick up on some clue as to where he might be."

Brad Jarvis's face lifted with surprised relief. "So you're saying he's still alive?"

"He might be," Bailey said. "We don't know yet."

He looked from Bailey to me. I saw his expression harden as relief turned to suspicion. "You didn't answer my question, Detective," he said. "Where and when was that picture taken?"

There was no avoiding it now. Bailey looked him steadily in the eye. "It was taken during the shooting in the gym." She waited a moment for that to sink in, then continued. "This is a blowup. The original photograph shows the entire hand. It's holding an assault rifle. It's the hand of one of the shooters."

It felt for a moment as though we were suspended in space, with no gravity, no oxygen. For several long moments, there was dead silence. Then suddenly a shriek broke through the vacuum.

"No!" Bonnie Jarvis jumped to her feet. She stared at us, wide-eyed, then slowly shook her head. "No! It can't be! You're wrong! Not my Logan! Not my son!" Tears began to stream down her face. She clutched her husband's arm. "Tell them, Brad! Tell them!" She dropped her head and sobbed, the hoarse, choked sob of someone who'd already cried herself raw.

Brad Jarvis remained sitting but drew himself up and clutched his knees even more tightly. His face had paled, but his eyes spit fury. "I refuse to listen to this...crap! It can't be Logan." He threw a contemptuous glance at the photo. "That picture's so grainy, you can't possibly say it's his tattoo. Hell, you can't tell *who* that is! My son could never, *never* do a thing like this! You're out of your minds!"

Bailey let the air clear. When she spoke, her voice was low and calm. "Mr. Jarvis, I do not for one moment believe we have enough evidence to charge your son with anything right now. We're following leads. That's our job, and that's all we're doing."

Bonnie Jarvis slowly sat up and dried her tears on her sleeve. I hoped she might be able to listen to reason. I leaned toward her. "Mrs. Jarvis, it's just as important that we clear the innocent as convict the guilty. We need to search Logan's room because given what we know so far, it's the next logical step in this investigation. It may yield evidence that clears him. If he isn't involved, we need to know that as soon as possible so we can move on. I'll be honest with you, I think we have enough to get a search warrant. So you can delay the search but you can't stop it. The problem is, the longer we wait, the more time the killers have to get away." I paused for a moment to let her process what I'd said. "And I'm sure you, as a parent, want us to do everything in our power to catch them."

Bonnie Jarvis drew several ragged breaths, then looked at her husband through eyes that were now nearly swollen shut. "Brad, I think we have to—"

Her husband folded his arms and shot daggers at her. "No, we don't, Bonnie. They're on a witch hunt, can't you see? They just need to put someone in jail to get the public off their back. I refuse to help them frame my son!"

"We only need one of you to consent," I said. Then clamped my mouth shut. Fighting with Brad Jarvis would only force Bonnie to defend her husband. Bonnie looked at her husband imploringly, but he stomped out of the room. She wrapped her arms around her waist and watched him go as tears rolled down her face. Finally, she spoke.

"I'll show you his room."

18

Bailey had a search team on round-the-clock standby and she called them in now as we followed Bonnie Jarvis down the hall to Logan's room. The first thing I noticed was that it had a sliding glass door to the patio and pool area. More important, a gate on the far right side led out to the street. That kind of setup meant Logan could get up to just about anything without his parents knowing. If he were so inclined.

The mother looked around the room distractedly, her eyes darting from one end to the next, as though afraid to land on any single spot.

"Mrs. Jarvis, can you give me a list of Logan's friends?" I asked.

"Bonnie. It's Bonnie," she said absently. Tears continued to leak from the edges of her eyes. She didn't seem to notice them. "There never were very many. Logan's been friends with Caleb Samuelson for years, though I haven't seen him around here lately. There was a boy...Kenny...Epstein. They were good friends back in junior high, but I don't know how close they are now." Her mouth trembled, and she bit down hard on her bottom lip. "Evan Cutter, I remember meeting him a few months back. I'm not sure how close they are, though."

"What about a boy named Otis Barney?" Bailey asked. "Did you ever see him here? Or did Logan ever mention him?"

"I-I'm not..." Bonnie closed her eyes and rubbed her temples. "Wait, yes. Now I remember. Last year. I remember because he stayed for dinner."

"And that's unusual?" I asked.

Bonnie nodded. "Brad and I own a temp agency. It doesn't leave us a lot of time for family dinners."

"Was that the only time Otis was here?" I asked.

"As far as I know, but..."

"He might've been here when you weren't around?" Bonnie nodded, her expression troubled. "You had some misgivings about him?" I asked.

"Not exactly. It was just, he had kind of a...whipped-dog look about him. As though he was expecting to get hit or caught for...something." Her gaze shifted to the desk where a laptop sat open, its screen dark. "I asked Logan whether Otis was having problems of some kind—with other kids or at home, but he didn't know."

The search team arrived, and Bailey peeled off to direct them. I suggested to Bonnie that we get out of the way, and she led me back to the living room. I noticed Brad had not returned. Bonnie and I sat on the couch. "What about Kenny or Caleb or Evan?" I asked. "What was your sense of them?"

"Nothing out of the ordinary. I haven't seen Caleb in a while. He and Logan were pretty close in junior high, so that's when I saw more of him. But unless he's changed a lot, there was nothing unusual about him. He was a nice kid. And Evan, he was sweet, charming even. Kenny...I only saw him once when I was on my way out the door, so I didn't really have an impression one way or another."

"Anyone else you can think of?" I asked. Bonnie dug around in her memory and came up with a couple more names but no details that distinguished any of them as potential suspects. I wrote them all down. "Were any of these kids here in the past few days that you know of?"

Bonnie shook her head. "But we didn't see much of Logan in the past few days either. He's been working to put together enough money to trick out his car, and this past week he took on extra shifts. I told him he had to keep his grades up or those extra shifts would have to go."

"Where does he work?"

"At Cut-Rate Kicks. It's in the mall on Topanga Canyon Boulevard."

"So what was he going to do to his car?"

"You'd have to ask his brother about that." Bonnie's face broke into the nearest thing to a smile I'd seen. "Luke's the mechanic in the family." She shook her head in disbelief.

"You're surprised by that?"

"I'm surprised any child of ours would be into cars—neither of us is mechanically inclined. But after Luke enlisted in the Army and got assigned to transpo, he discovered a real passion for mechanics. He's planning to open his own gas station and repair shop."

"Are he and Logan close?"

"As close as two brothers with eight years between them can be. When Logan was little, he worshipped Luke. And I think Luke was a pretty decent big brother, but they didn't have much in common. How could they? When Logan was in second grade, Luke was already in high school and almost never around." Tears began to roll down her cheeks again, and she swiped them away. "But they did seem to get closer after Luke finished his tour and came home. I think helping Logan with his car brought them together."

I got Luke's information and moved on. "What about girlfriends? Was Logan seeing anyone? Or did he break up with anyone recently?"

"No, there were no girlfriends. At least not that I knew of. Logan is pretty shy. But Brad might know more about that."

"Did Logan play sports of any kind?"

A sad smile lifted the corners of her mouth. "No. They pushed him hard to play basketball in junior high. He was very tall for his age even then. But he had no interest. In basketball or any other team sport. He thought they were for 'knuckle draggers.'"

"Any school activities?" Bonnie shook her head. "Did he have any problems in school recently? Any fights with other students? Teachers?"

"No. Logan never fought with anyone." She frowned. "The only person I ever saw him angry with was himself. He'd get furious about messing up the littlest thing. I remember the first time, when he was eight. Me and a couple of other moms took our sons fishing. Logan accidentally dropped all his bait into the water. He stood up in the boat and screamed at himself so long and so hard I thought he was going to faint from lack of oxygen." Bonnie bit her lower lip. "I'd never seen him act like that before. It scared me."

"Did you ever see that happen again?"

"Yes, a couple of other times. But it was always directed at himself. Never at anyone else."

"Did he continue to have those...outbursts when he started high school?"

"At first, but then it stopped. He did have sad spells, when he'd hole up in his room. But he'd always come out of it before too long. It didn't seem terribly unusual. The teenage years...it's a tough time for kids. Luke went through the same thing at that age."

"Did Logan ever show any interest in guns?"

Bonnie's eyes widened. "Never." She shifted on the sofa and looked down the hall toward Logan's room. "How much longer are they going to be in there?"

"I don't know. I can go check—"

"Yes, please."

We stood up, but at that moment Bailey walked in with a uniformed officer. She was carrying an evidence bag.

"Mrs. Jarvis, I'm afraid we're going to have to search the rest of the house," Bailey said. The uni moved in, one hand hovering near the butt of his gun. Bonnie stared at him, white-faced, then turned to Bailey. "Why?" she asked.

Bailey held up the bag. "Loose ammunition in one of Logan's dresser drawers. It's the same caliber and make as some of the ammunition used in the shooting."

19

Bonnie swayed, and I reached out and grabbed her arm to keep her from falling. She put a hand to her chest and struggled to catch her breath as I settled her on the sofa. After a few moments, she recovered enough to argue that a friend had to have left the ammunition. It couldn't be Logan's.

There was no honest answer I could give that she'd want to hear. I asked the uni to get her a glass of water, then excused myself and went out to the front porch, where Bailey was waiting.

Bailey held up her cell. "I'm waiting for a callback from the duty judge."

A judge who could approve a telephonic search warrant. Even if Bonnie gave us consent to search the rest of the house, there was no way Brad would and there was no point in taking even a minimal legal risk. We had plenty of probable cause for a search warrant, and getting a telephonic warrant would save time.

"Just loose ammo?" I asked. "Or did you find a magazine?"

"Just the ammo. But it's the same make and caliber as the ammo for the AK that jammed."

The gun wielded by the taller shooter, who was looking more and more like Logan Jarvis. "Anything else in the bedroom?"

"A notebook. I left it in the room for now."

I nodded. We'd gotten consent to do the search, and the ammunition was a no-brainer. But the notebook or the laptop, which might have the most incriminating information, could get thrown out by a softheaded judge.

Bailey's cell rang. She gestured to me that it was the duty judge and told him she was going to conference me in. I joined the call and we made our spiel. Five minutes later, we had our search warrant. Before we ended the call, the judge asked, "When are you going to go public about the gunmen being at large? Because I can promise you, the press is not going to miss all those cops piling up at the Jarvis residence."

"Yeah," I said. "We've got no choice. We'll have to do the release now."

We ended the call, and Bailey punched another number on her cell. "I'll tell Graden so he can get the chief ready to call a press conference. You'd better call your people."

I hoped I could avoid Vanderhorn and get away with just talking to Eric. If I had to go in and brief Mr. Potato Head, I probably wouldn't get back to the Jarvis house before midnight. I punched in the number and crossed my fingers. "Hey, Melia, it's Rachel. Is Eric in? It's urgent."

"Sure, Rache! What's going on?"

So I'm "Rache" now. Me and Melia, we're totes BFFs. "Uh, I can't really talk—"

"Oh, sure, right. Hang on. He's on a call, but I'll see if I can get him."

A few seconds later, Eric came on the line. I brought him up to speed. "I'm guessing the chief will say the killers are still out there, but he'll play it safe with Logan for now and just say he's a 'person of interest.'"

"Holy shit, Rachel. This is huge. But no release on your possible second shooter, Barney...something—"

"Otis Barney. No. We don't have enough yet. But we're closing in on it." An unmarked car pulled up, and three detectives I recognized from Robbery-Homicide got out and headed for the house. We exchanged nods as I pushed open the door for them.

"Vanderhorn's going to want to put out his own statement, so he'll want to see you."

"I can't, Eric. We're serving the warrant right now and I've got to be around in case they find something that needs follow-up. We've got two killers out there; I don't have time to spoon-feed the—"

"Stop. From now on watch what you say on your cell. You know these things aren't secure. I'll try to take care of him myself, but stand by."

I thanked him profusely. "I owe you big-time."

"Yeah, you really do."

Another unmarked car and a couple of patrol cars had arrived by the time I ended the call.

I found Bailey in Logan's bedroom, where she was talking to the search team. The room hadn't felt small when it'd just been Bailey, Bonnie Jarvis, and me. But with two detectives and three unis, it felt like a closet. Bailey gave them the list of what they could seize. It allowed just about everything—including the kitchen sink if it showed signs of recent use by Logan. "And remember to take a couple of his coats. Check the hall closet as well as this one."

We could use Logan's coats to see if the size matched the larger of the two camouflage jackets found in the Dumpster outside the school cafeteria. The officers got to work.

"We've got three more detectives on the way to handle the upstairs," Bailey said.

"We're not waiting for Dorian?" I asked.

"We really can't—"

"I get it. I just want it on record that I was the one who said we should wait."

Dorian would hit the roof when she saw the cops pawing through the house before she could process it. It wouldn't matter to her that they were all gloved and bootied up. She trusted no one but herself. Bailey made a face. "Heartwarming the way you always have my back, Knight."

"And how many times have you thrown me under the Dorian bus to save yourself?" I asked. Bailey answered by turning a stony face toward the sliding glass door. "Exactly."

I noticed that the buff detective in the tweed jacket had a spiral notebook opened on the desk. "Is that the one you saw?" I asked Bailey. She nodded. I clasped my hands behind my back to make sure I didn't touch anything and moved in next to him to see what was written in it. Drawings of sunsets and hearts with a name interwoven through them—I looked more closely and made out the name. "Amanda?" The detective nodded. "See anything related to the shooting yet?"

"Nope," he said. "I was hoping we'd at least see some names we could track down. But so far, nada."

The detective had opened the notebook to the last page in order to start with the most recent writings. I read as he moved backward through the journal. *"I'm the lowest most useless worm on the planet. I'm a blight on humanity. Why am I even here?"* Page after page of self-hatred. Then, suddenly, the sun would break through the clouds: *"Everywhere I look I see the miracle that is life, and I want to tell everyone that they're beautiful."* A few pages later, Logan's sky would darken again and he'd reflect on his *"worthlessness and the pain of drawing breath and having to exist on this miserable sphere."* But there was nothing about any real plans to even commit suicide, let alone a mass murder. Finally, I gave up and joined Bailey in the hallway.

"Ready to go?" she asked. "We've got another warrant to get to."

Otis Barney's house. I didn't think we had enough yet, but I didn't want to get into it with Bailey here, in front of everyone. I followed her down the hall and into the living room. The Jarvises sat side by side on the sofa, looking shell-shocked. The uni we'd left there had relaxed enough to move his hand away from the butt of his gun.

"I probably don't need to tell you that if you hear from Logan, you should tell him to turn himself in," Bailey said. "And call us immediately."

Bonnie Jarvis nodded vacantly. Brad stared at the floor.

"Did either of you know a girl named Amanda?" I asked.

It took a few moments for my words to break through. Bonnie Jarvis shook her head. Brad said nothing.

"Brad?" I said. I repeated the question.

He didn't look up, but he finally answered. "No. I-I don't recall hearing Logan mention that name."

We told them we'd be in touch and said good-bye. We'd have to talk to them again, probably many more times. But there was nothing to be gained by it now. They clearly knew nothing about his involvement in the shooting. The only information they might have for us would be coincidental, and only useful at trial: a stray remark, an unusual behavior—something fairly subtle that wouldn't have meant much to them at the time. But their minds were too frozen to be able to access those memories.

Bailey and I headed for her car. Just as we reached the sidewalk, a young woman in heels came clattering toward us. "Detective Keller! Ms. Knight! What can you tell me about this latest development? Did Logan Jarvis have something to do with the shootings?" A cameraman behind her pointed his black lens at us as the woman pushed a microphone into our faces.

"No comment," I said. Bailey and I kept walking. I barely restrained the impulse to swat the microphone out of the woman's hand.

Another news van roared up the street and disgorged yet another reporter, who tried to head us off before we reached the car, but we jumped in before he could get to us. He was still running behind our car as we pulled away.

"And that'll be our lives until we put this one to bed," I said. I pulled down the visor so I could use the mirror to check out the street behind us. We hadn't even reached the corner before another news van arrived.

Bailey looked grim. "I'm going to ask for a detail on Logan's house. Once the chief pegs him as a person of interest, those parents won't be able to burp without someone getting it on tape."

"Someone better warn them. This might be a good time for them to get out of Dodge."

"I'll call the search team," Bailey said. She turned right on Ventura, heading toward the Barney house. "So, you ready to work up a warrant for Otis's place?"

"It's still a pretty close call." We had a connection between Otis and Logan now, thanks to Carson James's statement, and we had more confirmation that the shorter suspect's weird laugh sounded like his. But the fact that he was of the same general height and weight as the smaller shooter was a wash. There were probably a thousand boys in the school who fit that description. The neo-Nazi-looking posters on his bedroom wall were ugly, but there was no indication the shootings were racially motivated. Bottom line: getting a judge to approve a warrant was far from a slam dunk. "Did any of the unis get statements about him being into guns? Or making threats of any kind in the past couple of years?"

Bailey shook her head.

"Can we get someone to dig into Logan's computer right now? If Otis is our guy, he should be in there somewhere."

Bailey nodded but didn't look happy about the prospect. "I wanted Dorian to get a shot at lifting prints before we did anything."

"Why not ask her to take a look and see if there's even anything liftable?" If not, then there was no reason we couldn't get into the laptop right away.

"Yeah, good idea." Bailey gave me a small grin. "And since it was your idea..."

Dorian hated to be rushed. But I couldn't back down now. "Fine." I pulled out my phone and made the call.

"Struck here," she answered. From the sounds in the background, Dorian was out in the field. Probably still at the school.

I told her what we wanted her to do.

"So you want me to rush my work."

"I...ah, well." There was no getting around it. "Just a little."

"Is Herrera at the Jarvis house?"

"Let me find out." I asked Bailey whether criminalist Marco Herrera was there. She nodded. I got back on the phone. "Yeah, he's there."

"Then he can do it. But have him call me first."

"Thanks, Dor—" But I was talking to air. She'd already hung up.

We headed back to the Jarvis residence.

20

The uniformed officers had already set up a barricade to keep the press away from the property. Bailey parked in the driveway this time, so we wouldn't have to outrun the media when we left.

We found Herrera setting up at a folding table in the garage, where he'd examine the laptop for prints, hair, and DNA. Bailey called the Computer Crimes Unit and asked them to send someone out to look at Logan's laptop when Herrera had finished with it. We'd worked with Herrera on our last case, so I knew the CCU guy would have plenty of time to get here. Herrera was, impossibly, even more painstaking than Dorian. I watched him work for fifteen minutes, then had to walk away to keep from pulling my own hair out. Bailey couldn't stand it either. She went back into the house to check on the search team.

I went out to the backyard and scrolled through my email. Nothing of any urgency there, which was a relief. Bailey brought our computer expert out to meet me. I'd never have guessed he worked the Computer Crimes Unit. In a beige cowboy hat, jeans, and Western boots, Nick Parsons looked more like an undercover cop—if LAPD was surveilling rodeos. He said howdy—yes, he really did—and when I told him we had to wait for Herrera to finish with the laptop, he said he'd take a stroll around the neighborhood. I was about to warn him that he'd get hounded by the press, but there was something in his eyes that said it was the press that needed the warning.

Twenty minutes later, Herrera sent a uni to tell me he'd finished and I called out to Nick, who was leaning against Bailey's car and talking on the phone. Bailey was already in the garage when we got there. Herrera was stripping off his gloves.

"Find anything?" I asked.

"Nothing," Herrera said. "In fact, it looks to me as though it's been wiped clean very recently. And thoroughly."

Bailey and I exchanged a look. Nick's expression said he was thinking the same thing. If Logan cleaned the keyboard, he probably…

Nick sat down and began to punch keys. It didn't take him long. "He wiped it," Nick said. "There's nothing here. If you want, I can get into the hard drive, but I'll need to take it downtown for that. And it'll take some time."

"What are your chances of finding anything?" I asked.

"To be perfectly honest, ma'am, I wouldn't bet on it," Nick said.

Ordinarily, "ma'am" sets my teeth on edge, but it was stylistically consistent for Nick, so I let it go. I wondered if Graden could bring back our master hacker M. Parkova. She'd come to the rescue when I'd had a computer issue on my last case. But how many times could I get away with hiring a convicted felon? I might already have exceeded my quota.

The problem was, I'd hoped to find something on Logan's computer to pump up our probable cause for the search warrant for Otis's house. "We can still try to get a warrant, but…"

"But you don't think we've got enough," Bailey said.

"It's pretty dicey." Some think the more heinous the case, the more likely judges are to hand out search warrants. In fact, it can be just the opposite. A heinous case usually means a high-profile case, and a high-profile case means lots of scrutiny. No one wants to screw up with the whole world watching.

"Then I guess we're stuck with guilt."

As in, we try to guilt Otis's parents into letting us search his room. Banking on getting consent for a search is always my least favorite option, but it was our best—well, really, our only—shot this time.

"Hey, do we have an ID on either of those boys found in the library?" I asked.

"One. Lionel Franks. We got him through the DMV database. We're confirming with DNA."

"Any known connection between him and our shooters?"

Bailey shook her head. "Right now it just looks like a poor kid in the wrong place at the wrong time."

The thought twisted my gut. I had to take a minute to refocus. "I was thinking, since we've got Herrera here, we probably ought to get the Jarvises' DNA," I said. "I know Logan's ruled out as one of the bodies in the library, but you never know when we might need it."

"Good idea." Bailey headed back to the garage to tell Herrera to swab the parents.

By the time we left the house, the entire block was packed with news vans, making the street barely wide enough for one-way traffic. Bailey navigated carefully as I sank down in my seat to stay out of camera range. It was eight o'clock, and the night air was cold and damp. I looked up at the sky and saw clouds scudding across the moon. I'd worried that the parents might still be at the rec center, but when we got to the house I saw a car in the driveway and a light on in the living room window. There was a heavy knot in my stomach. I didn't want to face another set of devastated parents. "You lead off on this one."

Bailey parked at the curb in a legal spot—and there was a spot next to a fire hydrant just one house up. That's how upset she was. "Why me?"

"Because you're the investigating officer."

"Since when has that mattered?"

"It has always mattered, Detective Keller."

"Then you'll have to live with the way I handle it. No interference."

"Fine."

Bailey raised an eyebrow. The truth? I have been known to jump in on interviews on occasion. Okay, on most occasions.

As we headed toward the front door, I admired the red and white begonias that were planted in a circle in the middle of the lawn. It was a nice, unexpected touch of color. I wanted to study them for a while. Then maybe check out the backyard, see what fun surprises they'd planted there. Basically, I would have washed their windows to avoid the meeting we were about to have.

21

Sonny Barney answered the door this time. She looked even worse than before, hollow-cheeked, deathly pale, her hair like straw—she'd aged ten years in just one day. And her eyes were filled with so much pain it sent a stab of guilt through my heart. Bailey asked if we could take a few minutes of her time. Given the way our last meeting had ended I wasn't sure how Sonny would react, but she wordlessly stepped back from the door to let us in. We gathered in the living room again. I was glad to see that Tom didn't appear to be home.

"Tom's at the rec center," Sonny said. "I just came home to get us a change of clothes. She drew in a long breath through her nose and let it out. Then, looking from Bailey to me, she asked, "Do you have any... information about Otis?" Her eyes filled with tears as his name left her lips.

"We haven't found him," Bailey said. "But we have come across some information about a friend of his, Logan Jarvis."

Sonny pulled a tissue from a box on the side table, swiped at her eyes, and frowned. "Logan Jarvis?"

"Yes. You don't know the name?" Bailey asked.

"No."

Bailey looked Sonny in the eye, and I saw the effort it took to maintain that eye contact as she spoke the next words. "We have reason to believe they may have been fairly close. It's very important that you try to remember any contact your son may have had with Logan, anything he might have said about him."

Sonny's mouth worked silently for a few seconds, like a television that had been left on mute. "Wh-why would that be import—?" Her eyes widened. "You think Logan is one of the…and that he and Otis…" Sonny grabbed her throat. "No! Please, you've got to believe me! Otis is a good boy, he's never been in trouble! We'd have known if he was… having…problems like that!"

I pitied Sonny. I knew what she was in for, this seemingly decent, loving mother. The world would judge her and Tom, and the Jarvises as well. Maybe, eventually, I would too. But right now, all I felt was profound sympathy. Sonny put a hand over her mouth. "Oh my God. Listen to me. That's what those parents said, isn't it? The ones at Columbine." She looked from my face to Bailey's. Our silence was answer enough. She bent forward, her arms wrapped around her torso.

Bailey stepped in gently. "We may be wrong, Sonny. Otis may not be involved. But we can't rule him out unless we get more information." Bailey waited. When Sonny looked up, Bailey continued. "If he was close to Logan, there should be some communication between them—and it would probably show up on his computer."

Sonny slowly straightened up, a defiant look on her swollen face. "Yes, that's right. There should be. Go ahead, check his computer. That'll prove you're wrong! Check his whole room again if you want. We've got nothing to hide." She led us to Otis's room, opened the bottom drawer of his desk, and pulled out a laptop with a red skull sticker on the back. "I can give you the password for his email."

That was significant. And surprising. But if Otis was sure she'd never snoop on him, he might not worry about what was on his computer. There was no time to call in Dorian or even Herrera to check for prints. If there was information that might lead us to Otis and Logan, we had to get it now. I pulled a pair of latex gloves out of my purse and went over to the laptop. Touching only the edges, I opened it and waited while it booted up. Sonny directed me to Otis's account and dictated the password. The most recent emails were from commercial websites selling computer gadgets, jeans, and logo T-shirts. About halfway down the list I found a message from a sender named LJ314. I opened it. There was no text, but there was an attachment.

It was a photo. And it had been sent the night before the shooting. A smiling Logan Jarvis posed with an assault rifle. One that looked a lot like the gun he'd dropped just outside the gym.

22

Behind me, Sonny screamed. "No! How...? It can't be!"

"I'm sorry, Sonny," I said.

She sat down on Otis's bed and hung her head. "I don't believe it. No...it's not right. It can't be right. I know it."

I put my hand on her shoulder and spoke to her softly. "We're going to get a search warrant, Sonny. I'm sorry."

Sonny grabbed my arm. "You don't understand. I know my son! I know Otis! That isn't him! Please, you've got to believe me!" She dissolved into tears.

I didn't have any honest words of comfort. "We're going to finish checking out Otis's computer before we bring in a search team. You can stay and watch..."

Sonny struggled to her feet and shook her head. "No, I-I need to go lie down."

I put my arm around her and led her down the hall to her bedroom. I gave her a glass of water, covered her with a blanket, and asked her for her husband's cell phone number.

"No, don't call him. Please don't. Let him not know for a little while longer."

I nodded and went to Otis's room. I sat down in front of the laptop and typed "LJ314" in the search bar. There were six other emails from that address, but none with photos. And none mentioned any murderous plans. They were all just routine boy stuff about school, girls, and video games. But Otis might have deleted the incriminating messages up until that last night. By then he was probably too busy putting the final touches on their big plans to remember to get rid of the photo of Logan and his AK. I'd have our cowboy Nick look into it. In any case, the photo, and the timing of its receipt, was damning.

Bailey had been looking around the room and now she held up a binder.

"Don't tell me we've got more musings about Amanda."

"No, it's poetry," she said. "Or song lyrics. They all look like they're about world peace and racial harmony."

"You've gotta be kidding me," I said.

"Nope."

"Is it dated?" If he wrote it back in junior high it wouldn't mean much.

"No. We'll be able to take it with the warrant, see if there are any references that can show us when he wrote this. But I'd bet we'll find more of the ugly stuff like that photo of Logan on the laptop once Nick gets into it." Bailey sighed. "Let's do another telephonic. You get the judge. I'll get the search team."

I should have felt some sense of satisfaction, of accomplishment. After all, we were pretty sure we'd finally identified both shooters. But all I felt was hollow. None of these parents were monsters. Hard as it was to believe, none of them seemed to have had a clue what was coming. They were shattered by what their children had done. When Tom finally showed up, I could barely bring myself to tell him what we'd found—or that a search team was on its way.

"I'm so sorry," I said.

Tom stood white-lipped and silent for several moments. "No." He shook his head slowly. "I know my son. Drinking? Smoking dope? Probably. Maybe even vandalism. But this? No way. I know he had some issues, but he could never hurt anyone." He glared into my eyes. "You're wrong." And he walked out of the room.

I turned back to the task at hand. The sooner we got the work done, the sooner we could get out of their hair and let them grieve. "We got a criminalist coming?" I asked Bailey. She nodded. "Make sure to have him get DNA swabs from the parents."

After an hour or so with no new discoveries, we bagged up Otis's laptop and binder and headed back to the station. On the way, Bailey called Nick and told him to meet us at her desk in thirty minutes.

Even at this hour, traffic was fairly heavy. We moved slowly down the southbound 101 freeway and I stared at the river of red taillights that stretched out before us. "Remember how everyone hammered the parents after Columbine?"

"Yeah," Bailey said. "About how they didn't know what their kids were up to, making pipe bombs and buying guns?"

"That part never surprised me. A kid can hide things like that even if the parents routinely toss his room—which most don't."

"Wait, I thought Harris and Klebold left all their weapons out in plain sight—"

"Only on the day of the shooting," I said. "When they left that morning they knew they weren't coming back, so what did they care? The thing that I always wondered before was how could they not know how crazy their kids were? There had to be about a million signs. But now I think I get it. It's one thing to know your kid has issues, but it's a whole different world to think those issues might add up to mass murder."

Bailey nodded. "Yeah. I see what you mean. So Sonny and Tom think, okay, maybe our kid got bullied and he vented by listening to hate music. There're probably millions of kids like that who'd never do anything more than talk shit on a Facebook page."

"Keyboard thugs. Exactly."

When we got back to the station, Nick was lounging in Bailey's chair, cowboy hat covering his face and boots crossed at the ankles on her desk. She swatted his legs off, and he jerked up in the chair, startled. "Hey!" Then he saw it was Bailey and took in the bag she was holding. "That it?"

"Yep, it's been bagged and tagged. Just remember to write up that I handed it to you."

"You get it looked at for prints and such yet?" he asked.

"No time for that," Bailey said. "Just glove up and do your best."

It was after Nick's normal hours, so I'd expected him to take it back to his office and let us know what he found tomorrow. But he asked Bailey for a set of gloves and opened the laptop immediately. "You're looking for mentions of Logan and any gun-related plans. That sort of thing, right?"

Bailey nodded. "I'm going to get some coffee. Want some?"

"Yeah, thanks," Nick said.

"Want anything in it?" she asked.

Nick looked up and gave her a lazy smile. "Why don't you just dip your little ol' finger in it? That oughta sweeten it up for me, darlin'."

It was a cheesy line, but Nick sold it. Maybe it was the accent, which sounded for real, but I had a feeling it was just Nick's gift. And the proof was right there on Bailey's face. She smiled and rolled her eyes. If any other guy had said that, she would've drilled him with a stare so cold his eyebrows would freeze.

For the next forty-five minutes, Bailey and I hovered as Nick worked on Otis's laptop. Finally, he looked up and rubbed his face. "Other than that nasty photo of Logan, I'm not seeing anything suspicious. And I doubt he wiped anything. The kid didn't even clear his search history. That'd be the least he'd do if he had anything to hide. I'll take it deeper to make sure, but from what I've seen, if he wrote down any of his plans for the shooting he didn't do it here."

"Isn't that kind of strange? I mean, wouldn't you expect him to have *something* on his computer?" I asked.

"Back when not many folks knew how easy it was to find old emails and search trails I'd have agreed with you. But nowadays, everyone's a lot smarter about that. Kids especially know there's a good chance that anything they type can be found. Deleting don't mean squat. So the long answer to your short question, ma'am, is no, I don't think it's strange. Not necessarily."

I winced. "Nick, do you have to call me 'ma'am'?"

"No, ma'—uh, no." He smiled. "But why does that worry a pretty young thing like yourself?"

I tried not to smile back, I really did. But I could feel the grin spread across my face. And, of course, Graden chose that moment to walk out of his office, which was just ten feet from Bailey's desk. There was no way he could've missed Nick's flirty look, and I didn't want to imagine what he could see in mine. "Hi!" I said, as I dialed up the wattage on my smile. "Nick's checking out Otis's laptop."

Graden's raised eyebrow said that wasn't all Nick was checking out. "Anything?" he asked Nick.

Nick, smooth as glass, answered, "Not yet. Which means if there's anything here, it's buried pretty good." He shook his head. "I'll take this back to my office and keep working on it."

Graden moved toward me and leaned in close. "How've you been?"

I shook my head. "Probably the same as you. And everybody else. Stressed. Angry. Frustrated. Sick."

"You and Bailey going back to the Biltmore?" I nodded. "How about if I meet you there?"

"Sure," I said.

Nick threw a glance at Graden and me as he finished packing up the laptop. It occurred to me that this was the first time Graden had acted like my boyfriend when we were at the station. I wondered if he was sending Nick a message. But Graden wouldn't do that.

Would he?

23

It was close to midnight by the time we got to the Biltmore. Way too late for dinner, even at the bar. We'd have to fill up on appetizers and snacks. On the way there, I got a text from Toni saying she was on her way home from a date with J.D. and was wondering if we were still alive. When I told her we were—just barely—and that we were headed for the bar, she said she'd meet us there; we probably needed a little *sane* company.

"What's up with that crack about 'sane' company?"

"Can't imagine," Bailey said. "She must not know I'm here."

Toni had the bar to herself, and she'd already ordered our drinks—Ketel One martinis for herself, Bailey, and me, and a Dalwhinnie scotch on the rocks for Graden—and a double order of the standard assorted nuts and crunchy bar snacks.

We hugged and I slid into the booth across from her. "Hey, how'd you beat us here?"

"J.D. and I had dinner in the neighborhood. I had a feeling you guys would wind up here tonight." Toni looked at us, sympathy in her eyes. "How're y'all doing?"

She kept her voice low, though there was no one else around. I shook my head. "It can't even be described, Tone. To say it's the worst I've ever seen doesn't begin to get there."

Toni nodded. "I can't—well, frankly I don't even want to—imagine."

Graden appeared. He gave Toni a hug and sat next to me.

I leaned in. "Has Vanderputz grabbed his face time with the press yet?"

Toni rolled her eyes. "Of course—"

"But he doesn't know anything," Graden said. He looked at me. "Unless you've been filling him in."

"Yeah, 'cause I run to him every chance I get."

"As if he needs to know something to justify a presser," Toni said. "What's wrong with you two? He didn't say anything. Just said how his heart ached for the victims and their families and that he'd see to it the case was brought to a 'swift and just conclusion.'"

That sounded about right. I dipped an olive into my drink. "Did the chief do a press conference?"

Graden nodded. "Just said the killers were at large and named Logan Jarvis as a 'person of interest.'" Graden raised an eyebrow. "But it's very reassuring to hear that Vanderhorn's promising a 'swift and just conclusion.' With him hot on the trail it'll be wrapped up in no time."

Toni and I sighed. The deputy DAs in Special Trials work closely with the detectives, but the detectives lead the investigation—not us. Vanderputz, however, never let accuracy get in the way of a good sound bite. "He couldn't be a bigger jackass if he put on the back end of a donkey costume," I said.

Graden chuckled. "Anyway, as predicted, the tip line blew up. We've got sightings of Logan Jarvis from Indio to Cape Town."

I put down my drink. "Cape Town? As in South Africa?"

"I blame the interweb," Bailey said. "It lets the crazies go global. So nothing for real yet?"

Graden shook his head. "Not yet."

"That's the problem in a city this big," Toni said. "It's easy to hide. And if he has the brains to cut or dye his hair or wear a wig, he'll slide right by."

"The only thing that'll make it a little harder for him is his height," I said. "But even that..."

Bailey nodded. "And we've checked cell phone records for Otis and Logan, Logan's license plate, his gas card, everything we can think of. Nothing. No sightings on Logan's car and there's been no activity—not on their cell phones, not on the gas card. They're off the grid."

"What about their bank accounts?" Graden said.

"We've got someone checking on that," I said. "And tomorrow we'll be talking to everyone who had classes with them in the past year."

"After that we'll hit Logan's brother," Bailey said.

"That might lead you somewhere," Toni said. "I assume you've checked his alibi?"

"Immediately," Graden said. "He was nowhere near Fairmont. Not that he fit the profile anyway."

"And I'm not that optimistic about what he can tell us," I said. "According to Mom, they had gotten closer in the past couple of years, but they weren't that tight."

Graden took a sip of his drink. "Take it from me, he'll know something."

Graden and his younger brother, Devon, were different as night and day, and they hadn't been that close as kids. But when they reached their twenties, they discovered each other. Now they were not only the best of friends but also partners in the video game they'd developed that had become the hottest thing since Grand Theft Auto.

Before Graden knew what he wanted to be when he grew up, he loved to design video games. It was a hobby, nothing serious. When he got hired by LAPD, he decided it was time to quit. Just before he graduated from the Police Academy, he created one last game, Code Three. Devon wrote the program for it. Graden had walked away from the project—it was time to put away such childish things—but Devon refused to let it go. Graden gave Devon his blessing to try to sell it, never dreaming it would amount to anything. It took a few years, but Devon found a buyer, and the game took off like a rocket. By the time Graden made detective, both he and Devon were millionaires many times over.

"Give me a 'for instance,'" I said. "What do you think the brother would know? Assuming he wasn't actually in on it, which I seriously doubt."

"I do too, though I never like to rule anything out," Graden said. "It's possible he got unhinged during his tour of duty." I raised an eyebrow. "But even if the brother's not in on it, Logan might've been less guarded around him. Maybe he let something slip. You've got his info, right?"

"Yeah," Bailey said. "He's got a place up in Oxnard. Works at a garage there."

The waiter came by to tell us it was last call, and we all decided we were ready to pack it in.

Toni looked from me to Bailey. "Listen, I know things are going to get crazy, so both of you, remember to eat and sleep, okay?" She looked at Graden. "You too. You're no better than they are."

Drew, who'd just finished for the night, came out to join us, then seconded the vote. "Yeah, you're all looking pretty raggedy."

Graden smiled, but Bailey gave Drew a sour look. "You really think that's what I need to hear right now?" she asked.

"Yes." He kissed Bailey and helped her with her coat.

Bailey rolled her eyes. "I'll deal with you later—"

"Looking forward to it," Drew said. For the first time that day, I saw an actual smile—well, half-smile—on Bailey's face.

She buttoned her coat. "Okay, Knight. Get some sleep. I'm picking you up at seven thirty."

"Why not eight?" Morning and I are not the best of friends.

"Because we're meeting with kids at Taft High School at eight fifteen."

"Taft. That's where they're housing the Fairmont students?" Bailey nodded. It made sense. Taft was closest to Fairmont High. But that meant we'd have at least a forty-minute drive. "Next time, *I* set up the interviews."

Toni laughed. "You've got my sympathy." She, Bailey, and Drew left.

Graden walked me up to my room "just to say good night." When we got inside, I dropped my coat and purse on the wing chair and turned on *Kind of Blue* by Miles Davis. We sat down on the couch and snuggled in. Neither of us felt the need to talk. As I listened to the steady beat of his heart and inhaled his scent, my chest unwound and I think I even dozed for a few minutes. Then he leaned down, tilted up my chin, and kissed me. "I should probably hit the road," he said. But then he kissed me again. A warm, lingering kiss that left me a little out of breath.

I suggested the road could wait until tomorrow.

He thought I might be right.

24

WEDNESDAY MORNING, OCTOBER 9

Morning, as usual, came too early for me. I had to fly through my shower and jump into the first thing I saw in my closet. Not Graden. Graden woke up at the crack of dawn as a matter of habit as well as choice. Probably his only obnoxious trait. When I went out to the living room, I found him reading the paper and drinking coffee.

He looked up and smiled. "Morning, sunshine. I don't think you have time to order breakfast."

"No." I sighed, poured myself a large mug of coffee, and tried to slug down as much of it as possible.

He looked me over, noticing my outfit. "I take it you won't need to be in court today."

I was wearing black jeans and an ivory turtleneck sweater. "Nope. We'll be out doing interviews, and I don't want to freeze."

Graden smirked. "Yeah, it could get down to sixty degrees. Better wear your snow boots."

I threw my napkin at him, then walked over to the hall closet and pulled out my down puffer coat. Graden walked over and put his hands on my shoulders. "Listen, I need you to be very careful. Those kids are crazy—"

"No, not crazy. Personality disordered—"

"Whatever. Which makes them unpredictable. No one knows where or when they'll surface. And remember, they still have guns."

I opened my purse and pulled out my .38 Smith and Wesson. "But I'm a better shot, and I'm a little crazy myself."

"A little." Graden smiled and kissed me.

When I got downstairs, Bailey was parked at the front entrance and chatting with Angel. "Mind if we stop and get some coffee?" I said. I hadn't had my two-cup daily dose.

Bailey pointed to a bag in the front passenger seat. "Got ya covered. Even brought bagels."

I grabbed my coffee from the cup holder and took a sip, then rummaged through the bag. Coffee, bagels…even cream cheese? This kind of service I never got. Not from Bailey. "Okay, where's the catch? What do you want?"

"Nothing. Friends buy friends breakfast, don't they?"

"No."

"But now that you mention it, we really should check in with Dorian. Let her know we didn't preserve Otis's laptop for her."

See? "So let me get this straight. I'm supposed to incur the wrath of Dorian for a measly coffee and bagel?"

"And cream cheese. And there's some jam in there too."

I put in the call and got lucky: Dorian's voice mail. I pumped a fist and gave Bailey a triumphant smile. Then I checked my own voice mail. There were fifty-seven messages. I listened to the first one. The producer of channel nine news was asking for comment on the search at the Jarvis residence. The next four were the same. I didn't bother to listen to the rest, or wonder how the press got my cell phone number. They'd gotten it during the Antonovich case too. I made a mental note to change my number. Again. Northbound traffic wasn't bad. By ten to eight, Bailey was pulling into the faculty parking lot at Robert S. Taft High School. Located on Ventura Boulevard—the busiest thoroughfare in the Valley—Taft wasn't as big or as fancy as Fairmont High. It had that '60s square-box, plain-wrap look. Also unlike Fairmont, it wasn't an enclosed building. It was your typical Southern California school, with classrooms accessible from outdoor hallways.

A secretary directed us to the classroom that had been set aside for our interviews. The door had been propped open, and the room was downright frosty. Even Bailey rubbed her hands together and zipped up her jacket. The other problem was that the only furniture in the room was a few desks. The kind that are attached to chairs. If we sat at those desks, it would put a physical barrier between us and the students. We needed the kids to relax and open up.

"I guess we could sit on the floor, hippie-style," I said.

Bailey shook her head. "A little too casual. We need to maintain some authority." She pulled a couple of desk-chairs to the front of the room and sat on the desk. I followed suit.

Seconds later, a teenage boy with shoulder-length blonde hair poked his head in through the open doorway. "Are you the cop—I mean, officers we're supposed to talk to?"

Bailey put on her warm interview smile and gestured for him to come in. "Make yourself comfortable," she said.

He slid into the chair facing us and stretched out his legs. They stuck out past the edge of the desk by about a foot. His name was Kenny Epstein, and he'd known Logan since junior high. I asked if they were good friends.

Kenny shrugged. "We weren't super close or anything, but we were friendly. We'd shoot the shit—uh, sorry."

I waved him off. Yo, me and Bailey, we were the cool cops.

Kenny gave a nervous smile and continued. "Logan was always the smartest guy in the room. A real brainiac. But not a nerd or anything. Pretty much everyone liked him—"

"Would you say he was popular?" I asked.

Kenny tossed his head, flicked back his overgrown bangs. "He didn't party a lot or anything. He wasn't Joe Social. He was kind of the quiet type, you know? But he was a good guy."

"Did you ever hear of him getting bullied or pushed around by the jocks?" Bailey asked.

"Logan? Nah."

"Do you know Otis Barney?" I continued.

"Pasty little dude?"

Pasty. I pictured the face I'd seen in photographs in the Barney house. I guess he was sort of pale. "Yeah. A little bit shorter than you, medium build. Curly brown hair."

"Yeah. Not real well, but I remember seeing him around." Kenny paused and frowned. "You asked about bullying. I think that guy got knocked around by some punk on the football team. And I heard someone once threw his books in the toilet." Kenny shook his head disapprovingly. "I don't get shit like that. He never bothered anybody, so why mess with him?"

"When was the last time you saw him?" I asked.

"No clue. Like I said, I didn't really know Otis. Just saw him around school."

"What about Logan? When was the last time you saw him?"

"I don't know, maybe a week ago?" Kenny dropped his gaze to the floor.

"Not since the shooting?" I asked.

Kenny shook his head. "But there's lots of kids I haven't seen since..." His eyes slid away, and a long moment passed as Bailey and I gave him a chance to recover. Then he looked at me with worried eyes. "I heard you guys are saying Logan's one of the shooters. Is Otis the other one?"

Bailey gave him her poker face. "We're just looking into everyone who hasn't been accounted for."

Kenny sat up in his chair and folded his arms. "I don't know about that Barney guy, but Logan couldn't have done it."

"Why's that?"

"Because...Logan never got mad...at anybody. Never talked shit about anybody or anything. It just makes no sense."

I asked him the standard shrink questions: did he know anyone who did "talk shit" about wanting to kill people or feeling persecuted? Kenny didn't. Just the usual "my 'fill in the blank' sucks."

"Did you know Logan's brother, Luke?"

Kenny's eyebrows went up. "I didn't even know he had a brother."

"Do you know who hung out with Logan?"

"Darnell, Leo, I think Caleb." Kenny shrugged. "That's all I can think of."

"So not Otis?"

"Not that I ever saw."

I got the last names and descriptions of the friends he'd mentioned and then had him tell me what he remembered of the shooting.

"I, like, dived under my seat." He described the gunfire, the remark one of the shooters had made about jocks, the horror of it all, but he had nothing new.

The next few interviews got us more of the same: Logan was a great guy, never got bullied that anyone knew of, and had never had a problem with jocks—or anyone else. A couple of others confirmed the tattoo and that it was a recent acquisition—within the past month or two.

They also confirmed that Otis was a strange guy who did get bounced around by at least one of the football jocks—Bryan Scofield—but Otis had never seemed like the violent type. I probed to find some connection between Otis and Logan, but no one had any recollection of seeing them together. At least not until we got to Caleb.

If anyone still wore a pocket protector, Caleb would be that guy. He was on the short side, but even so, his pants were floods. He had wavy hair that refused to stay in its side part and constantly fell into his eyes, and black-framed glasses. He'd known Logan since third grade and they'd bonded over their mutual love of math. This I could not relate to. Math was the reason I chose law school—lots of reading, no numbers. In spite of that, Caleb was a nice kid. Shy, quiet, but not abnormally so. Predictably, he was a Logan fan. But he'd also seen some dark spots on the halo of St. Logan.

"Back in junior high we studied together and stuff. But by around our sophomore year at Fairmont he got kind of... moody. Sometimes he'd just pop off at me for no reason."

"Did he ever get violent? Hit you?" I asked.

"No, no. Nothing like that. He'd just be... upset."

"About?" I asked.

"Nothing in particular. At least not that I could tell. He'd just get withdrawn and... down."

It sounded like depression. But it also sounded like typical teen hormones and angst. "Do you know Otis Barney?" I asked.

Caleb wrinkled his nose and pushed his bangs back. "Yeah."

"And?" I asked. "What do you know about him?"

"Nothing really. Just that he's kind of weird." Caleb made a face. "And kind of pathetic. I just saw him a couple of weeks ago. Logan and I were talking in the parking lot. He walked up and just interrupted us. Started telling Logan they had to get going. He acted like I wasn't even there."

"Did Logan say anything to him?" I asked. "Get mad?"

"No. Just told him to wait a sec."

"But you never knew them to be friendly before?" I asked.

"Well, like I said, I didn't see all that much of Logan recently, so they could've gotten to be buds without me knowing about it."

"Was that your only contact with Otis?" I asked.

"Pretty much. Other than seeing him around school."

We kept at it for another ten minutes or so, but didn't get anything more. Still, we'd found another link between Otis and Logan. Progress.

Bailey glanced at her watch, then looked outside. "We've got three more kids out there. We can either tell them to come back and get lunch or power through."

"I vote we power through." After our mini-breakthrough with Caleb, I hoped we were on a roll.

25

Logan didn't have a big crew, but he was a social butterfly compared to Otis. Interestingly, whereas Logan's fans had all been male, the only two kids who claimed to know Otis were girls.

Chloe had a head full of curls and a round, rosy face. Given that look, I expected a high-pitched Kewpie doll of a voice, but I was surprised to find it was rich and mellow. I bet she could sing. We made our introductions, and Chloe sat down in the chair and put her fringed purse on the floor. The desk didn't leave much room, but she somehow managed to cross her jean-covered legs and tuck her hands between her knees.

"I've known Otis since our freshman year. He was so sweet."

"Was?" I asked. "He changed?"

Chloe nodded, making her curls bounce. "When we started at Fairmont, we were all a little scared. You know, big school, we were freshmen, and we'd all heard the stories about what they did to freshmen..." Chloe had a wistful smile. "Otis was in my homeroom, and on our first day, he admitted he was scared. We sort of bonded over that, you know? So we got to be friends. Not, you know, hangout friends or anything, just school friends. But he could make me laugh about almost anything." The wistful smile grew bigger with the memory. "The teachers, the other kids. He got me through my freshman year."

"Did he make you laugh about the jocks?" I asked.

"All the time." Chole's smile suddenly faded. It made the room seem darker. "I guess they must've found out somehow, because one of them, this asshole—" Her eyes grew wide, and she clapped her hand over her mouth.

I waved her off. "I believe in calling an asshole an asshole. What's his other name?"

A glimmer of a smile from Chloe, and then she sobered again. "Bryan...something. He threw Otis's books in the toilet. And I heard he knocked Otis down a couple of times too."

"But you never saw it?" I asked. Chloe shook her head. "Did Otis tell you about it?"

"Never. I think he was ashamed to. When I heard what had happened, I tried to get him to report it, but he wouldn't even talk about it. He'd just change the subject." Chloe's sad eyes got to me.

"Did you and Otis stay friends after your freshman year?" I asked.

"Not as much, but somewhat. Yeah."

"Did he talk to you about the jocks this year?" I asked.

"No. So maybe they weren't hassling him anymore."

"Do you know Logan Jarvis?" I asked.

"No." Chloe frowned. "I mean, I've seen him around, but I don't actually, like, know him."

"Did you ever see Otis with Logan?"

"No." She looked from me to Bailey. "But I heard you think Logan might be one of...them." I nodded. "Are you thinking Otis is the other one?" I didn't answer right away. "Because I can tell you he isn't. Otis couldn't hurt anybody. Ever."

"Did you see him the day of the shooting?"

Chloe turned her head to the side and stared at the wall for a few moments. "I think I did. I think I saw him coming up the front steps that morning because we said hey." She paused, then continued. "Yeah, I'm almost sure of it."

"Was that the last time you saw him?" I asked.

Chloe's eyes dropped down to her lap. She nodded.

"Chloe, did Otis ever talk about getting revenge against anyone?" I asked.

"No!" Chloe leaned forward, her expression earnest. "Otis was the most nonviolent person I've ever met. I know people told you he's kinda weird, and he is. But if anyone's telling you he could've done something like this, they're full of it! Believe me, I knew him for real. There's no way!"

And the next girl—Suzanne Eckman—echoed virtually all the same sentiments about Otis.

We went through our list of shrink questions with both of them. They had no recollection of anyone who fit the profile.

Our last interview was with another of the friends mentioned by Logan's mother.

Evan Cutter had a military-style buzz cut and the kind of lean frame and ropy muscling you usually see on wrestlers. But he had none of the swagger that usually goes with the type. He shuffled in with slumped shoulders and barely met our eyes. I introduced myself and put out my hand. He held it loosely for the barest of seconds, dipped his head, and plunked down in the chair.

We asked the usual preliminary questions about how long he'd known Logan and how they'd met: one year, in gym class. It was a perfect segue.

"Did the jocks ever give Logan a hard time?" I asked.

"Not that I ever saw."

"If they had, do you think he would've told you?" I asked.

Evan shrugged. "I'd hope so."

"You wrestle?" I asked.

"I used to. But I got bored after a while. Plus, I needed the time to study. I'm not a brainiac like…Logan." At the mention of his friend's name, his face tightened, and I thought he was about to cry. But he swallowed hard and cleared his throat. Crisis averted.

"Do you know Otis Barney?"

Evan's lips twisted. "Yeah, he's a loser. He tried to buddy up to Logan this year. Kept hanging around, trying to get Logan to do stuff with him."

"Did it work?" I asked.

"Kinda, yeah. Logan said they hung out a couple of times. Probably my fault. I don't have as much free time as I used to. I got a job over the summer. Pizza delivery for New York's Finest."

So he blamed Otis for pushing Logan down the wrong path. And himself for not having time for Logan anymore. "Then you and Logan were pretty tight—at least at one time?"

"Yeah. I mean, I wouldn't say 'best' friends, but we hung out."

"Did you ever know Logan to be violent?" I asked. "Or have a temper?"

"He didn't used to. But more and more he seemed kind of…I don't know, edgy? Everything seemed to bug him." He paused, his expression troubled. "And, yeah, he lost his temper a couple of times."

"What would set him off?" I asked.

Evan shook his head. "That's what was so weird. Nothing big. An A minus in calculus, a stain on his shirt. Stupid stuff."

"Did you ever hear him threaten anyone?" Bailey asked.

"Not specifically. He'd just hate on everything. Probably why I didn't take it seriously. I mean, he wasn't going to try and take out the whole world, right?" I said nothing. Evan huffed. "Come on. Seriously? He was just venting. Look, I heard the press conference, so I know what you think, but there's no way he did this."

"Did he ever talk about guns?" I asked.

"Not that I ever knew."

"What about Otis Barney?" I asked. "Did he ever mention wanting to get guns, or being able to get them?"

"Specifically, did he say he was going to buy a gun? No. But that kid, I'd put money on it. Isn't he the typical kind of loser jerk who needs to have a gun to feel tough?"

"You tell me," I said. "Is he?"

"Yeah. I wouldn't be surprised if that kid had a whole arsenal stashed somewhere."

I was getting the distinct impression Evan was not an Otis fan.

"Where were you when the shooting happened?" Bailey asked.

"In the gym."

We asked what he'd seen and heard, but like many others, he'd ducked under a bench when the first shots were fired. He couldn't tell us anything we hadn't heard at least fifty times before.

"Did you see Otis or Logan the day of the shooting?" I asked.

"No. I wish I had."

"Because you would've stopped it?"

"I would've tried." Evan's knee began to bounce. "And I'm not saying I believe Logan's involved. I don't. I'm just saying...I...whatever." He stared at the floor.

"Let me go back to something you mentioned before," I said. "You said Logan had more free time than you. That maybe that was why he got friendly with Otis." Evan nodded. "According to Logan's mother, he had a job too," I said. "And he was working lots of hours."

"But not all the time, at least not from what I remember."

"What about in the past few weeks?"

Evan shrugged. "I don't know. I've been pretty busy myself."

Logan's job at the mall was on the to-do list we'd given the unis. It'd be easy enough to check out.

We wrapped up with the usual shrink questions. And got the usual answers. We let Evan go. He shuffled out looking fairly miserable.

I was feeling the same way. "How come the only guy anyone remembers talking shit like the shrinkers described is the guy who's hooked up to an IV in the hospital?" I asked.

"To be fair, they warned us these shooter types come in all shapes and sizes."

"True."

"Our next interview's waiting for us in the main office." She pulled out her notepad. "Otis's English teacher. Arthur Windemere."

26

Mr. Windemere did not ask us to call him Arthur. As we introduced ourselves, he nervously adjusted his tortoiseshell glasses and pursed his lips. His thinning red hair contrasted sharply with his young—albeit pale and prunish—face. The principal of Taft High School, Michael Dingboom, a heavyset man who wore a janitor-sized set of keys on his belt, was sitting in on the interview. I had a feeling Mr. Windemere had asked him to. Just to mess with Windemere, I wanted to advise him of his rights and ask where he was during the shooting, but he looked like the type who'd call the teachers' union and threaten to sue.

The small office was crowded with the four of us. Bailey and I faced Mr. Windemere across the principal's desk, and the principal sat spread-legged in a chair inconveniently placed in the corner near the door.

"Thank you for taking the time to speak with us, Mr. Windemere," Bailey said.

"What can you tell us about Otis Barney?" I asked.

"Well, I don't know what his other teachers have said." He paused and peered at Bailey and me. "But I found Mr. Barney extremely... disturbing."

I waited for him to elaborate, but when the silence stretched out, I realized he was waiting for a prompt. "Did he cause problems in class?"

Mr. Windemere shook his head. "No, nothing that overt. And of course, hindsight always gives us perfect vision, but after seeing what he wrote, I should have known." He opened a file on the desk and pulled out a page. "The assignment was to write a paragraph describing the perfect city." He gave us a dark look and passed the page to me. I held it so Bailey and I could read together.

"I suppose most people would say the perfect city is one where there's no smog, no gangs, and no violence. But to me, the perfect city is one where there are no people."

After the drumroll Windemere had given us, I'd expected an essay that promised mass destruction. Still, I decided to humor him. "In hindsight it does seem ominous." I could see that my response was not what he'd expected. He fiddled with his glasses and cast a disapproving look at Bailey and me. What did he expect us to do? Jump up, put our hands to our cheeks, and shout, "Oh my! You've cracked the case!"? On second thought, that might be fun. But it was too late now. He'd never buy it. "Is there anything else you can remember? Any remarks he made in class that indicated violent fantasies? Or that indicated he was planning to take revenge against anyone?"

He shook his head primly. "If he'd said anything that obvious I would have reported it, I can assure you."

"Did you have Logan Jarvis in your class at any time?" We already knew Logan and Otis hadn't been in any of the same classes other than science.

"Yes, I believe I did. But I have no recollection of any writings or behavior out of the norm. I was surprised to hear he is now a 'person of interest.'"

"We have a great deal more digging to do." I wanted to keep it low-key just in case something crazy fell out of the sky and proved that Logan wasn't one of the shooters. "I understand he and Otis were friendly."

"I see." He pursed his lips again and sniffed. "Well, I can't speak to that."

What a fun guy. I looked at his left ring finger. No ring. Big shock. We lobbed him a few more questions, but there was nothing more to be gained from Mr. Windemere. Bailey and I thanked him and Principal Dingboom for their time and the use of the classroom.

"Anything you ladies need," the principal said. "You just let me know."

I gritted my teeth at *ladies*. It conjured up white gloves, panty hose, and tea parties. I was sorely tempted to show him my .38. But I wanted to hit the road.

It had been downright cold outside when we'd first arrived, but as we headed for the parking lot a shaft of warm sunlight pierced a hole through the heavy bank of clouds and lifted my spirits. "Mind if we hit the mall?" I said. "I'd like to pull the unis off and talk to Logan's boss myself." The mall was only a few minutes away.

"Exactly what I was thinking."

"It's uncanny the way we do that, don't you think?"

"No."

As we rolled out of the parking lot Bailey asked, "So what did you think of that paragraph Otis wrote? A city without people."

"It wouldn't have meant much to me back when he wrote it," I said. "Really, it only looks bad now, in hindsight; I guess that's what got Windemere all excited. He thought he'd just solved the whole case—"

"Nah. You ask me, he's scared his neck is going to be on the chopping block for not sounding the alarm when Otis first turned that thing in."

I hadn't thought of that. "You think that's why he had the principal there?"

"Yeah. He's worried."

Bailey was probably right. "But to tell you the truth, all I thought when I read it was, who *hasn't* felt that way? Didn't you?"

"I'm taking the Fifth."

The mall on Topanga Canyon Boulevard was one of the big omnibus types, with a merry-go-round, a huge food court, and stores that ranged from Neiman Marcus to Sears. Logan's place of employment, Cut-Rate Kicks, was a chain store on the second floor, not far from the food court. As we wove our way through the crowds—it always amazes me how many people have the free time to float around a mall in the middle of a weekday—the tantalizing aromas of barbecued beef, marinara sauce, and pizza wafted through the air. I felt my stomach grumble. As we entered the shoe store, I pointed to the food court. "We're going there after we're done. No arguments."

Bailey put her hands up. "Hey, no problem. I'm in." The store was almost empty, and the salesclerks were clustered near the window, talking and laughing. Pretty cushy job. We walked up to the girl behind the register, identified ourselves, and asked to see the manager. Seconds later, a young Latina with her hair up in a bun, wearing dark slacks, a white blouse, and low-heeled pumps, came out from the back room.

"I'm Lupe Velasquez." She put out her hand and we shook. "What can I do for you, Officers?"

Bailey produced Logan's yearbook photo. "Does this young man work here?"

Lupe glanced at the photograph. "He did."

"He got fired?" I asked.

Lupe shook her head. "No. He quit. About three months ago."

Bailey and I exchanged a brief look. "Have you seen him since then?" I asked.

"Once, when he stopped by to pick up his last paycheck. But that was a while ago. Just a week after he quit."

I waited for her to ask about Logan's involvement in the shooting, but she said nothing. Hard as it was to believe, I supposed she might not have heard about Logan being a person of interest.

Bailey held out Otis's photograph. "Did you ever see this person in the store?"

"Not that I recall. He could have come by when I was in the back, though."

"Was Logan a good worker?" I asked.

Lupe shrugged. "He was already here when I got transferred to this store, and he only stayed for a few months. But from what I saw, he did okay. Toward the end, though, around the last month, he called in sick a lot."

"So I guess you weren't surprised when he quit," I said.

"To be honest, no. Most kids are happy to have the work—well, the paycheck anyway—but some get bored and burn out. I figure they don't really need the money."

"He seem like that to you?" I asked.

"Kind of, yeah."

"Was he friendly with any of the other employees here?" Bailey asked.

"I'm not sure, but you can ask." She called the three salesclerks and the cashier over. All were young, no more than college age. We spoke to each one separately. They didn't have much to say. Logan was kind of quiet and "okay" as a coworker. No one had ever hung out with him. And only one of them—a ponytailed girl whose ears were pierced all the way around—knew he was suspected of being involved in the shooting. I thought it was odd she hadn't told the others about it.

When we'd finished with the salesclerks, I asked Lupe whether there were any employees who'd worked with Logan who weren't there today. Lupe brought us to the back room and checked her computer. "There were two others who were working here at the same time as him. I can't say whether they were friends or anything." She pointed to the screen. "Joy Pickerton and Ava Landau." Lupe printed out their contact information for us. We'd let the unis check them out. It was unlikely we'd get anything from the kids at Cut-Rate Kicks. We thanked her and headed to the food court, where I indulged in a slice of pepperoni pizza.

I took a big bite and savored the oily cheesiness. The echoing din of the crowd gave us enough cover to talk about the case. "Three friggin' months he lied about working here. Probably spent every minute of it planning the shooting."

Bailey shook her head. "You wouldn't think kids that crazy would have the patience to do that much prep work."

Bailey's cell phone rang, and I focused on my pizza while she took the call. When she put the phone down, she looked stunned. Bailey never looks stunned.

"What?"

"They got back the DNA results on the parents. The other dead kid in the library? It's Otis Barney."

27

"But that picture of Logan on his computer—"

Bailey nodded. "And the hate band posters on his wall—"

And he fit the profile: a loner who'd been bullied by jocks, a follower who'd been Logan's acolyte—someone likely to follow his leader into hell. Who'd written that a perfect city is one without people. And who had that weird laugh. Neither of us spoke for several moments. I slid down in my chair and let my gaze wander. It landed on the jewelry kiosk to my right. The fake baubles were dazzling in the lighted glass case. Dazzled, that was us. "We fell for it. We fell for the stereotype."

Bailey raised an eyebrow. "Really? Just like that you're ready to dump Otis? Clichés are clichés because they're true, Knight. Just because he's dead doesn't mean he wasn't a shooter."

"But why would Logan kill his partner?"

"Shit. Who knows why these fools do anything? Maybe Otis was a weak link, and Logan wanted to cut the deadweight—"

"In which case maybe we only have one shooter on the loose." Not that one wasn't enough.

"Or..."

I sighed. "Or, Otis was involved but he wasn't a shooter." In which case we still had two shooters out there. I bent my straw into tiny, accordion squares. "I agree, we can't rule Otis out as a possible suspect just because he's dead. But that photo on his computer. The more I think about it, the more it bothers me."

"The one of Logan with the gun," Bailey said.

"Yeah. Why would Logan send something like that just before the shooting? If Otis's parents had seen it, that could've screwed up their whole plan."

"True. So what are you thinking? That Logan sent that photo on purpose, to incriminate Otis? Or a third mystery guy—maybe the second shooter—sent it?"

"The mystery guy, more likely," I said. "And yeah, to frame Otis."

"But that still leaves your question: why take the risk?"

"Because only Logan would've been tagged. He'd still be in the clear."

"So you think our unknown guy was willing to go through with the shooting alone?"

"Probably not his first choice. And he didn't have to go through with it. If the shit hit the fan with Logan's photo, he could pull the plug and do it another day." I let go of the straw. It uncoiled and lay semi-curled on the table. I reached for it again.

"Then you're also saying this unknown guy deliberately imitated Otis's laugh during the shooting?"

I started to fold the straw again. "Why not?"

"He would have to have access to Logan's computer—"

"Logan's got friends," I said. "And laptops move around. He could've taken it anywhere—to work, to school."

Bailey grabbed the straw out of my hands. "Give it a rest, would you?" She put the straw on her plate. "Okay, let's assume that plays. Why pick Otis?"

"If our mystery guy is a friend of Logan's, he probably knew Otis. So he knew Otis fit the profile. A fringy loser who got knocked around by football jocks. He figured we'd jump on him." I grabbed the straw off her plate. "You know, like we did."

"That's pretty friggin' smart for a kid."

"Not really. Anyone can read about these school shooters. There's stuff all over the place. And we're pretty sure our shooters did study the others. Besides, who says these guys aren't smart? Just because they're fucked-up and homicidal—"

"Yeah, 'I may be crazy but I ain't stupid,'" Bailey said. "But I'm an Occam's razor kind of guy. When in doubt, go simple. Logan sent that photo to Otis the night before the shooting to celebrate their big day. And he wasn't worried about the risk because Otis told him his parents never check his computer." Bailey glared at the straw, which I'd resumed torturing, then looked me in the eye. "And as we know, he was right. They didn't."

And they probably didn't check because having his password made them feel secure. I couldn't argue that one. "I'm just saying we can't ignore the possibility that Otis was an innocent bystander."

"Who just happened to be in the library at exactly the right time to be killed and set up to look like one of the shooters?"

"Might've just been a lucky break for them." Awfully lucky, I had to admit. But stranger things have happened.

"Whatever." Bailey sighed. "We've got to notify his parents."

And we wouldn't even be able to give them the comfort of knowing their son was in the clear. "You want me to set it up?"

"Yeah. And I'll try to think of something better to say than 'I've got bad news and... bad news.'"

I left a message for the Barneys asking if we could come by in the early evening. When I ended the call, I tried to focus on what little bright side we had. "We still have Logan. And he looks solid." I mentally went through the to-do list we'd put together for the unis. "Did anyone report in on his bank account yet?"

"No, but I can goose them. And I'll get unis to go talk to those other salesclerks at the shoe store." Bailey pulled out her phone and punched a number.

"I want to go back to Logan's buddies, Caleb and Evan—"

Bailey gestured to the phone. While she spoke, I remembered the other person I wanted to see.

Bailey ended the call. "We should get the info on Logan's financial empire by the end of the day."

"I want to get out to Logan's brother too. The sooner, the better."

"He's in Oxnard. I vote we get the local police to help us set that up before we run out there."

Oxnard was an hour and a half north of us, and if we hit traffic, it could easily be double that. We couldn't afford to spend hours in travel only to find out the brother was in the wind. "Okay, then let's hit up Evan and Caleb again." I looked at my watch. It was after three. School would be out by now. "I'd like to get them somewhere quiet."

"How about their cribs? We can tell the parents we need to talk to them privately."

We went to Caleb's house first. It looked similar to Logan's. Two stories, but with a brick-and-white, wood-trimmed front. Caleb answered the door in his socks. He looked less than thrilled to see us. "Oh, hi."

We said we had a few more questions for him, and he reluctantly stood aside, then gestured for us to follow him. Lucky for us, his parents weren't home. He led us to the kitchen. "I'm just having a sandwich. My mom hates it when I eat in the living room. You, uh, want something?"

"No thanks, Caleb," I said. His ham and Swiss on rye looked pretty tempting though. We sat at the breakfast table, and Caleb took a man-sized bite. His cheeks bulged as he chewed.

"Did you see Logan at all on the day of the shooting?" Bailey asked. "Maybe on the way to school? At a gas station?"

Caleb swallowed and shook his head. "The last time I saw him was when I told you. A couple of weeks before in the parking lot. When Otis was hanging around."

He took another bite of his sandwich. I let him swallow before I jumped in. "Do you drive?"

"Yeah."

"Did you drive to school that day?" I asked.

"Yeah."

"Did you happen to notice Logan's car in the parking lot?" I asked.

Caleb picked up his sandwich, stared at it for a long moment, then shook his head. "I can't remember. It's not something I would've been looking for, you know?"

I nodded. He took another bite. "Remind me where you were during the shooting," I said.

Caleb put down his sandwich and stared at the table. "I was in one of the lower rows, close to the floor. By the time I turned to see what everyone was screaming about, they had started shooting. I dropped to the ground and hid under the seat."

"Did you hear what the shooters were saying?" I asked.

"I thought I heard them yelling things when they were up at the top of the bleachers, but I couldn't make it out. I was pretty far down and then I got under the seat. And everyone was screaming and..." He looked away.

I felt guilty about making him relive it, but I couldn't risk missing anything. "Did you hear either of the shooters laugh?"

"No. I've already told you everything. Really, it was all just a blur. I'm sorry."

We left Caleb to his sandwich. He didn't seem as interested in it anymore.

28

Evan's house was a single-story ranch. It was smaller than Caleb's, but it was nicely maintained, and there were multicolored ice poppies lining the front of the house. Evan's mother answered the door. She was petite and dressed in a spandex workout outfit that showed off a well-toned body. Her blonde hair was gathered up in a tight ponytail. Her makeup was subtle and flawless. If not for the crow's-feet and a few laugh lines I'd have thought she was in high school herself. Bailey made the introductions.

She dipped her head. "I'm Mikayla, please come in." We followed her into the living room, which was sparsely furnished in beige and cream. The room was immaculate. There was very little in the way of ornamentation. No flowers, no framed photos. One silver Nambé-style bowl sat precisely in the center of the coffee table, and two matching beige ceramic lamps on the side tables—that was it. We sat on the couch. Mikayla perched on one of the loungers, feet together, hands on her knees.

"Do you know Logan Jarvis, ma'am?" Bailey asked.

"Yes. He and Evan became friends shortly after we moved here. I heard what they're saying about him on the news, but from what I know, he's a lovely boy. Kind of on the shy side, but very sweet." She gave us a tight "I'm trying to help" smile.

I could tell from that smile alone that we wouldn't get anything useful from her, and after a few more minutes Bailey came to the same conclusion.

"We'd like to see Evan now, Mrs. Cutter," Bailey said. "And I hope you don't mind if we speak to him alone."

She'd kept her head down, made only sporadic eye contact before, but now she looked up at Bailey with alarm. "He's not in trouble, is he?"

I shook my head. "No, not at all. It's just better—less distracting—if we talk privately."

Mikayla nodded. "I understand. I'll go get him."

Evan looked surprised to see us. He gave us a nervous "Hey" and took his mother's place on the lounger.

"I'd like to go back over the morning of the shooting," I said. "I'm sorry, I know it's upsetting, but we don't want to miss anything."

He nodded and dipped his head. Just like Mikayla. "Sure. I get it."

"Did you see Logan the morning of the shooting?" I asked. "I mean, before school."

He gripped his knees. "Uh, I don't remember."

Yes, you do. "Evan, I don't want to scare you, but it's a criminal offense to withhold information."

Evan looked down at his lap and picked at the knee of his jeans. After a few moments, he spoke. "I saw him for, like, a minute. He was in the parking lot, standing by his car."

"Did you speak to him?"

"Yeah. Just for, like, a second."

"Who spoke first?" I asked.

"I did. I said, 'Hey' and 'What's going on?' and, like, that." Evan pressed his lips together.

"And what did he say?" Bailey asked.

"Said he was waiting for someone."

"Did you ask him who he was waiting for?" I asked.

"No. I saw Otis heading over so I took off. He can be kind of a blabber sometimes, and they make you pick up trash around the school if you're late."

But that wasn't the whole story. "What else happened, Evan?"

He pulled at a thread on the arm of the lounger. I saw his Adam's apple bounce. "I told Logan I had to get to class." Evan licked his lips with a dry tongue. "He told me I should cut and not come back." Evan finally made eye contact—a brief apologetic look—then dropped his gaze back to the floor. "I'm sorry. I guess I should've told you before. But I knew it would sound bad. And I didn't want to believe...any of it."

And he didn't want to be another brick in the wall of mounting evidence against his friend. "It didn't sound bad at the time?" I asked.

"No. I just took it as him saying 'Dude, fuck school.'"

"Did you leave after that?" Evan nodded. "So you didn't talk to Otis at all?"

"No."

"Where did you go?" I asked.

"Homeroom."

I'd get that verified, though I had no doubt it would check out. It was too easy for us to bust a lie like that.

"Did you notice anything in his car?" Bailey asked.

"No, but I wasn't looking. The whole thing took maybe ten seconds." He glanced up briefly and gave us another apologetic look. "I really am sorry. I sort of told myself it wasn't important. But I guess I just didn't want to be talking bad about a friend." Evan shook his head. "Stupid, I know."

Not so much stupid as typically teenage. Or maybe just typical, period. After all, who *does* want to think their friend, son, brother is a mass murderer? "Did Logan ever talk about guns?" I asked.

Evan frowned, then shook his head. "Nothing sticks out in my mind. If the subject came up, he sure didn't say anything that made me go 'whoa.'"

"Did you ever see him with guns?" I asked. "Either in person or in photos?"

"Logan? Never. That's why this whole thing with him is so... bizarre."

"Can you think of anyone besides Otis who might've been in on this with Logan?" I asked. "Anyone else Logan was hanging out with who seemed like trouble?"

Evan frowned. "No. And to tell you the truth, I don't even really believe Otis was in on it. I know I said he was a loser and all. But after I talked to you guys, I got to thinking about it. Otis was kind of annoying, and he was a weird little dude, but he wasn't *that* kind of weird." He went back to picking at the arm of the lounger.

"Did Logan ever talk to you about a girl named Amanda?" I asked.

He looked up at me. "Amanda? Where'd you get that name from?"

"So he didn't talk to you about her?"

"No."

"Did he mention any other girls?" Bailey asked.

"What, ever?" Evan looked incredulous. "Yeah. Of course. But not in a 'love' way or anything."

"Did you ever meet Logan's brother, Luke?" I asked.

"Yeah, once or twice."

"What was your impression of him?" I asked.

Evan shrugged. "I don't know. He seemed okay, I guess."

"When did you last see him?" Bailey asked.

"Not that recently. He and Logan didn't really hang out. At least not from what I saw."

"If Logan was looking for a place to hide, where do you think he'd go?" I asked.

"No clue. He's got cousins in Colorado, I think. But I don't know where."

"Was there someplace you two used to hang out when you didn't want to be in a crowd?" I asked.

"Just his house or mine."

"Did he ever talk about friends or relatives he was close to? Maybe who lived outside Los Angeles?" I asked. These were all questions for Logan's parents, and either Bailey and I or a uni would ask them. But given how little Bonnie seemed to know, and how little cooperation we could expect from Brad, I didn't hold out much hope for those interviews. Evan was my best shot.

Evan shook his head. "Not that he ever told me."

I'd had the impression he and Logan were closer than what I was hearing. "How long did you say you've known Logan?" I asked.

"Since we moved here. About a year ago."

"You move a lot?" I asked. Evan nodded. "What's your dad do?"

"Works for an oil company based in Texas."

We weren't getting anywhere. And if Evan picked at the thread on that lounger any harder, he'd unravel the whole damn thing. "Okay, thanks, Evan. That's all we've got for now."

We stood up to go, and Evan jumped to his feet, looking visibly relieved—and a little frightened. Was he just glad to be off the hot seat? Or was it something more? The tattoo was the most incriminating piece of evidence we had so far. But Logan's warning to Evan that morning was a pretty damning piece of the puzzle too. Was he afraid Logan might remember that and come after him? It was hard to believe Logan would risk coming back to shut him up. But then again, as Bailey said, who knew what these psychos would do?

"Evan, I want you to know that whatever you tell us is going to stay under wraps until we have the suspects in custody."

Evan nodded, but wouldn't meet my eyes. "Okay, thanks."

"Are you worried about...anything?" I asked.

"N-no." Evan swallowed and stuck his hands in his pockets.

"Because if you are—"

"I'm not. Really. It's just...this is pretty strange. That's all."

I didn't believe him. But I also didn't think he was in any real danger. And if I kept pressing him, I'd only make him think he had good reason to be scared. We told him we'd be in touch and to contact us if he thought of anything else about Logan or the day of the shooting, then headed for Bailey's car.

"I'm probably being paranoid, but can we try to get some extra patrol on his house?" I said as I belted up. "Just in case."

"Yeah." Bailey pulled out her cell phone. "I can't believe Logan would come back for him, but the kid did look nervous. And while I'm at it, I'll see if we've heard back from the bank about Logan's cash flow."

"What about setting up a visit with the brother...Luke?"

"I'll check on that too."

While Bailey made the calls, I revisited the possibility that Logan might come after Evan. Logan had to know that we'd figure out he wasn't one of the dead bodies in the library and land on him at some point. Evan's information was good stuff, but it was hardly a smoking gun. On the other hand, I was being rational, thinking like a lawyer. Logan was smart, but rational...not so much. And if there was a second shooter, who knew how unbalanced and paranoid *he* was? Evan didn't know yet that Otis was dead. But he'd find out soon enough. And when he did, he'd realize he didn't even know who to look out for. Now that I thought about it, Evan had more reason to be nervous than even he knew.

Bailey ended her call. "Valley Division's putting extra patrols on Evan's house starting tonight."

"Good. And the bank?"

"Logan wiped out his checking account a month and a half ago. Apparently it'd been dwindling steadily for the past year, but he still had about five hundred dollars in it until his last withdrawal."

"Did it sound like he had enough to pay for the arsenal they had?"

"No. I'm getting copies of the statements so we'll be able to see exactly what the cash flow was, but from what I heard, I'd say the other kid had to have kicked in his share too." Bailey wore a grim look.

"So they've been building up their cache for, what? A year?"

"Give or take."

I told her my theory about why Evan seemed to be so nervous.

"Hell, yeah, that makes sense," she said. "Me, I think the kid could just be feeling guilty about not warning anyone and snitching on a friend. But you're right. Evan might have good reason to be worried. And remember, he was in that gym too. It didn't look to me like those shooters were being all that picky about who they fired on. It was just dumb luck he didn't get killed. So much for his great friendship with Logan."

I nodded and checked my cell, saw I had a message. I hit play and listened. "That was Sonny Barney. They can meet with us now."

29

We were already in the neighborhood, so it took just five minutes to get there—which meant I had no time to think about what I was going to say.

Sonny and Tom Barney sat together on the couch, their hands intertwined. The fear in their faces was a painful sight. Even worse was the small flicker of hope that still burned beneath it. I looked from one to the other, then forced out the words. "Otis's body has just been identified as one of the two boys found in the library. I'm so sorry."

Sonny jerked away from her husband and began to scream. "No! No-no-no-no-no!" Then she dissolved into tears. Tom wrapped his arms around her, buried his face in her hair, and began to sob.

I felt tears prick the corners of my eyes. I willed them back and tried to swallow the lump in my throat so I could offer words of comfort, but the words wouldn't come.

Finally, Sonny lifted her head. She spoke with a tear-choked voice. "But then Otis couldn't have been involved, could he? We told you! We told you!" She lapsed into sobs again, as she wrapped her arms around her torso and rocked back and forth.

Tom, picking up on our silence, looked from me to Bailey. "You can't still believe..."

I took a deep breath. I'd almost dreaded this more than the death notification. "We don't know. It's still possible he was involved. But I promise you, Mr. Barney, if we can clear him, we will."

Tom clenched his jaw. I watched his face as anger battled with grief. Grief lost. His voice was harsh and low. "It was crazy to call Otis a suspect in the first place, but now? It's not just wrong, it's downright cruel. I'm calling the DA! And the chief! You're incompetent...you—you monsters!" He stood up and pointed to the door. "Now get out! Get the hell out of my house!"

When we reached Bailey's car, I saw that her face looked drawn. I was sure mine looked no better, but I offered anyway, "Hey, how about you let me drive for a change?" If she said yes, it'd be a first.

"I feel like shit, but I don't have a death wish, Knight."

So she wasn't completely wrecked. But I felt pretty lousy too. I knew there was only one thing that would make us feel better. "What's the story with Luke Jarvis? Is he in pocket?"

"Yep. He's at work. Gets off at six."

"If we launch from here we can make it to Oxnard in an hour."

"Let's hit it."

Work: the great healer. Well, the great distraction.

30

We pulled up just after six o'clock. Night had already squeezed all but a sliver of sunlight from the sky. I don't know why I had the idea Luke worked at an ordinary gas station. It was actually a high-end auto-repair shop. The kind of place Jay Leno would go to have his Maseratis or Model Ts fixed. At the counter in the tiny office at the end of the repair bays sat a completely bald man whose coveralls looked like they'd been handed down by his much bigger father. The name Alfred Bedigian was stitched above the pocket on his left chest. A magazine lay open on his lap. I got a glimpse of a pouty, large-breasted blonde before he slapped it closed and stuffed it under the counter.

Bailey flashed her badge. "Mr. Bedigian?"

His eyes got big when he saw the badge, and he jumped up out of his chair. "Yes?"

I could see a smile twitching at Bailey's lips. "We're here to see Luke Jarvis."

"I already gave his time card to those other cops. They told me it was just routine. Was that wrong? Is Luke in trouble?"

We'd had Luke checked out the moment Logan was identified as one of the shooters. Luke had been at work—confirmed not only by his time card but also by a couple of customers who'd come in on the day of the shooting.

"Not at all," Bailey said. "We just want to talk to him about someone he knows."

"Because if he is, I need to know about it," he said. "He's a great mechanic, but we don't run that kind of place. He's got problems, he's out of here."

"Really, Mr. Bedigian," I said, "he's done nothing wrong."

He gave me a skeptical look. "Better not," he muttered. "Come."

Bedigian trotted around the counter and gestured for us to follow, the dirty rag stuffed into his back pocket wagging like a tail with every step. He stopped abruptly at the last bay, where a midnight-blue Porsche sat three feet up on the lift. Unless Luke was hiding in the trunk, there was no one there.

"Could he have left for the day?" I asked.

"Not without telling me." Bedigian said. He took the rag out of his pocket and nervously wiped his hands.

A tallish man with short dirty-blonde hair walked into the bay, pulling on a fleece-lined denim jacket.

"Luke Jarvis?" Bailey asked.

"That's me," he said. He favored us with a smile that crinkled the corners of his eyes. He looked like a younger version of Treat Williams—handsome in a regular-guy kind of way.

Instead of badging him, Bailey put out her hand. "I'm Detective Bailey Keller and this is Deputy District Attorney Rachel Knight. We need to talk to you."

Luke's smile fell away. "Right."

"Do you have a place we can go to talk?" Bailey asked.

Luke glanced around the bay. "Uh..."

Bedigian interrupted. "Use the office. It's time to close up anyway." He cast a glance across the three of us that was still mildly suspicious and told Luke, "Lock the door when you leave." Luke nodded, and Bedigian trotted out.

Five minutes later, we sat down in the small waiting area in the office. Bailey took the lead. "I guess you've heard Logan's been named as a person of interest in the Fairmont High shooting."

Luke nodded, and looked from me to Bailey anxiously. "Have you found him?"

"No," Bailey said. "I'm sorry to have to tell you, but Logan's not just a person of interest. We're fairly certain he was involved in the shooting."

Luke sat back as though he'd been punched in the chest. He opened his mouth to speak, but for a few seconds nothing came out. "What—how do you know?"

Bailey told him what we'd learned so far. Ordinarily, she might not have been so forthcoming. Even though we knew Luke couldn't have been the second shooter, he still might've provided some outside help. But there was no indication the brothers had spent any time together in the past few months. No one in Oxnard had seen Logan around, and no one in the Valley had seen Luke hanging out with his brother. We'd had unis track down all the checks Logan had written in the past year and go through the records of all the local auto parts stores. Logan's dwindling bank account showed he'd been spending money all right, just not on his car. So Bonnie's belief that they'd been refurbishing Logan's car together had proven to be wishful thinking. The brothers hadn't been in contact on any kind of regular basis in some time.

When Bailey finished, Luke stared out the window. Tears welled up, and he angrily swiped them away with his sleeve. "I just don't get it," he said. "Why would he do that? He was never, *never* someone who'd do anything to hurt anyone."

Bailey shook her head. "We might never have the whole answer to that." The expression on Luke's face was heart-wrenching. She gave him a few more seconds to regroup, then continued. "I understand you enlisted in the Army when he was in fifth or sixth grade?"

Luke nodded. "Yeah. Had to. I was screwing up all over the place. Flunking out at Cal State Northridge, drinking, drugging. My folks finally kicked me out of the house—rightly so. The Army was my last shot to pull my head out of my ass. I can't say I loved it, but it did the trick. And that's where I found out I loved working on engines. From there, everything in my life just kind of fell into place."

"How old was Logan when you got out?" Bailey asked.

"Let's see, by the time I got back...I think Logan had just finished his freshman year."

"Did you move back home?" I asked.

"Only long enough to find a place. I had a buddy from the service who was willing to share rent. So I moved out as soon as I landed a job at a gas station. Got a two-bedroom in Tarzana."

"That's pretty close to your folks," I said. "Did you and Logan get to see a lot of each other?"

"In the beginning. Logan wasn't driving, but I was just a short bus ride away. So we'd hang out a couple of times a week, but then..." Luke sighed. "Shane—that's my buddy from the Army—turned out to be a great trench mate but a lousy roommate. He was into everything I joined the Army to escape. Booze, drugs, the wrong kind of women." Luke shook his head, a disgusted expression on his face. "I'd come home from work and find the place just totally trashed, smelling like pot, and all these sketchy losers hanging around."

"Shane didn't work?" I asked.

"He'd work. And then he'd get fired. And then I'd get on his case about kicking in his share of the rent and he'd get hired again. No job ever lasted more than a couple of months."

"How did Shane get along with Logan?" I asked.

Luke grimaced. "Total bromance. At least on Logan's part. He started coming over just to see Shane. Shane was the cool guy Logan always wanted to be. Shane had tatts, he drove hot cars, and he was a babe magnet. Going to a party with Shane was like being the Invisible Man. Women you wouldn't think would even spit on him would slide off their chairs." His face reddened. "Sorry!"

I shook my head. "I get it. Was Shane into guns?"

"Oh, yeah." Luke stopped and stared at me as the implications sank in. "And I'd bet he still is. I know he worked at a gun range for a while. I think he still helps out there now and then. But they didn't give him enough hours to pay the rent, so he had to get a real job."

"How good is he with guns?" Bailey asked. "Does he reload his own ammo? Can he repair them, alter them?"

"Yes. To all of the above. But I found out the hard way you have to watch out for his reloads. We used to go shooting together, and one time I guess he accidentally packed a double shot in one of my rounds. Thing had so much firepower it almost blew my hand off."

"I take it you guys don't see much of each other anymore?" Bailey asked.

Luke shook his head. "I had to get away from him. Too much temptation. That's why I moved up here. I told him I had a job offer I couldn't afford to turn down."

"Did you?" I asked.

"No. I wound up sleeping in my car for a couple of months. But then I got a break. I came here looking for a job on the same day one of the guys gave notice."

"Did you lose contact with Shane after you moved up here?" I asked.

"Pretty much. I let him keep the apartment in Tarzana for the rest of the month just to make sure he wouldn't try and follow me here. But we stayed in touch for a little while. I didn't want him as a full-time friend, but I didn't want to dump him. We went through a lot together, being in the service and all." Luke stopped and sighed. "At least, that's what I wanted. But Shane couldn't leave it like that. About a week after I landed this job, he said he was thinking about coming up here. Started talking about getting a place together again. That's when I realized there was no halfway with Shane, so I stopped taking his calls. He still leaves me voice mails now and then, but I know better than to reopen that door."

"Is it possible that Logan kept seeing Shane after you left?" I asked.

"I guess. He never mentioned it, but like I said, Logan had a real boy-crush on him." Luke briefly closed his eyes. When he opened them, they looked pained and bewildered. The revelation about his brother was only just starting to sink in. It would probably take a while before he could really wrap his brain around the fact that his little brother was a mass murderer. If, in fact, he ever could.

"Would Shane have come by your parents' place to see Logan?" I asked.

Luke shook his head slowly. "Doubtful. They only saw Shane a couple of times, but it was enough for them to get his drift. They didn't care for him. I have to believe that if Mom knew Logan was hanging around with Shane, she would've done her best to shut it down."

But as we'd already learned, there was a lot Mom didn't know.

"Do you know where Shane is now?" I asked.

"Last I heard from him, he was working for a tree service up in Camarillo. I think the gun range is around there too."

"Do you happen to know the names of those places?" Bailey asked.

Luke turned to stare out the window again, then looked at us apologetically. "Sorry, no. I'm sure he told me, but I don't remember. I didn't really want to know."

But he did know Shane's last name.

31

Luke was still shaken when we finished the interview, but he refused our offer of a ride home. While Bailey called the station to check in, I watched him walk to his car. He was a little wobbly on his feet, and when he reached the driver's door, he stood there with the key in his hand, staring out into the night.

Luke had driven away by the time Bailey finished her call. I pulled out my phone as we headed for her car. "I'm going to look up our soon-to-be new best friend Shane on Facebook."

"I'm putting out the alert to pick him up." Bailey called one of the detectives who was riding herd on the unis. "I need all you've got on a Shane Dolan." She relayed what Luke had told us about his workplaces, and the description he'd given us: medium height, slight to medium in weight, dark brown hair usually worn almost shoulder length, and hazel eyes. "Pick him up if you see him, but he's not a suspect. At least not yet. And he may have good intel for us, so be nice."

I showed Bailey his Facebook photo. The wavy hair that fell over one eye, the sexy smile. He was a good-looking bad boy. No mystery why he'd been a babe magnet.

Bailey smirked. "I knew a guy like that in high school."

"Didn't we all?" She was still staring at the photo. "You have a crush on him?"

"He had a crush on me. I wasn't interested."

"Oh, excuse me, Ms. Searing Hot. *You* were the one who got away?"

"Yes."

Actually, I believed her.

"They're working on the addresses of the shooting ranges and tree services in Camarillo," Bailey said. "We should have them pretty quick."

I held up my phone. "I already got the shooting range. There's only one. Want to—"

Bailey gunned the engine. "On our way."

Camarillo was just south of Oxnard. It was almost seven o'clock, late enough to miss the evening rush hour. Bailey flew down the 101, and fifteen minutes later we rolled into Camarillo.

The shooting range was located in what had been a fairly big strip mall—before the stores had gone under. Now it looked like a ghost town. All the dark, empty windows gave it a creepy feel. At the very end of the row was a faded red wooden sign that read THE TEN RING. A reference to the bull's-eye of a target. A ramp led up to the front door, which was painted a flat black. Thoughtful of them to put in a ramp for the handicapped at a shooting range. I pulled on the door, half expecting it to be locked. It wasn't.

But it was so heavy, it only budged an inch.

Bailey raised an eyebrow. "Need some help, Knight?"

I glared back at her. "Shut up." I had to regrip and put some muscle into it, but I managed to pull it far enough to slip through sideways. I wedged my foot in the door and held it open for Bailey. "What is up with this friggin' door?"

"Cheap way to soundproof."

Which would have mattered back when the place first opened and the other businesses on the row were still in operation. Not so much now. We headed down the poorly lit hallway; its walls were decorated with cheaply framed photographs of men holding and shooting firearms of all kinds. One older man with a handlebar mustache seemed to be in all of the pictures. I deduced that he was the owner. When we emerged from the hallway and entered the main room, I confirmed it. It was a fairly large room, dominated by a three-sided glass case that housed handguns and a variety of accoutrements such as speed loaders, magazines, ammunition, goggles, and gloves. The back wall was lined with the bigger firepower: long rifles and shotguns. A window occupied the opposite wall and gave a full view of the shooting range. A father was showing his son—who looked to be about nine years old—how to load a semiautomatic clip. It brought back memories of my father teaching me the same thing. And the bruised thumbs I'd had for months after.

Standing behind the glass case was the older man in the photographs. He was wiry to the point of skinny, and his upper shoulders curved inward, giving his chest a concave look. The rimless glasses that perched on the end of his nose and his white flyaway hair reminded me of a character in an old TV show, *The Wild Wild West.* Bailey introduced us, showed her badge, and asked if he was the owner.

He held out his hand. "George Lockmire. Call me Lock."

I shook his hand. "As in locked and loaded?"

He smiled. "Always glad to do business with law enforcement. You brought your own? Or do you want to rent and try something new? I've got a great compact HK forty-five you should try."

Bailey shook her head. "Thank you, Mr., er, Lock, but we're not here to shoot. We need to ask you about someone who works here. Shane Dolan."

He jerked back his head as though we'd slapped him, then peered at us over the top of his glasses. "He's not in trouble, is he?"

"No," I said. "We just need to talk to him. He may have information on a case we're investigating—"

"He's a decent sort. Not the most punctual guy. But once he gets here he's good to have around. Not many folks can do the repairs. Most can barely clean 'em right. Shane can do it all."

"Glad to hear it," I said. "When does Shane work?"

"Well, it's kind of on an 'as needed' basis right now. Business hasn't been so good around here, in case you didn't notice." He made a face and looked out in the direction of the vacant stores we'd passed on our way in.

"When was the last time he came to work?" I asked.

Lockmire squinted. "About a week ago. Yeah. Last Thursday."

That was four days before the shooting. "Have you seen him since then?"

"No. But there's no reason I would have. This is the only place I see him. And if you want to know when I expect to have him back, I couldn't tell you. I might need him this weekend or I might not."

"He live near here?" Bailey asked.

"Not too far, from what I remember." Lock flipped through a dog-eared leather day planner. "Here you go." He pointed to an entry, and Bailey copied down Shane's address on a business card.

"Did Shane ever bring friends around?" I asked.

Lock wrinkled his nose and squinted, then shook his head. "He was friendly with customers. But I don't remember him ever bringing anyone in here."

I pulled out the yearbook photograph of Logan. "Did this person ever come in?"

Lock took the photo and studied it, then handed it back. "He does look familiar. Kinda young, though. We don't let 'em shoot alone 'less they're eighteen or older."

"But if Shane took him into the range...?" I asked.

"Well, yeah. That might've happened." Lock took off his glasses and wiped them on the sleeve of his shirt. "But if it did, it wasn't recent. If he'd had that kind of free time, I'd have sent him home. Can't afford to have him on the clock if there's no business."

"So this kid might've come in here, and Shane might have taken him into the range," I said. "You just can't say exactly when?"

Lock gave me a suspicious look. "You a lawyer? You sound like a lawyer."

I sighed. "Yes, I'm a lawyer. Is that right? What I just said?" Lock squinted at me as though he were trying to figure out what my angle was.

I folded my arms. "Lock, sometimes a cigar is just a cigar. Answer the question."

He finally caved. "Yeah, I guess that's right."

We thanked Lock for his time and left him our cards. When we got back to the car, Bailey's cell rang. She looked at the number and raised an eyebrow. "It's the station." She listened for a few seconds, then quickly wrote on her notepad and ended the call. "They found the tree service. According to the boss man, Shane was scheduled to work on Monday."

Monday, the day of the shooting. "He was a no-show. And they haven't heard from him since the Friday before."

I pulled out my cell phone. "What's Shane's address? I'll call local police for backup."

Bailey peeled out of the parking lot.

Shane lived in a dive in Ventura, a few blocks west of Main Street. His complex, called the Hacienda, was one in a connected row of apartments that faced the street. Time and neglect and the salty sea air had left the wood on the front step cracked and rotted, which made it a perfect match for the frames of the windows.

The Ventura Police Department doesn't play around. It only took us fifteen minutes to get there, but when we arrived, the backup I had called for was already waiting and ready to go. Their SWAT team was on the way. We jointly decided to check the place out and see if we could spot Shane. If we did, we'd let SWAT take him down.

We'd learned the only phone registered to Shane was a cell phone, so calling him wouldn't tell us if he was inside the apartment. And given his affinity for guns, he was likely to be heavily armed, so we strategized our approach carefully. As we worked out the choreography with the local officers, I could feel my heart pound heavily in my chest. If he was the second Fairmont shooter and he spotted us, it was more than likely he'd come out with guns a-blazing.

Everyone took their positions and began to move, slowly and quietly. In spite of the chilly sea air, a trickle of sweat rolled down my back. Bailey and I hunkered down and duckwalked to stay below the windows of the apartment, our guns down at our sides. The local police, led by a hefty but solid-looking detective with red hair named (what else?) Rusty, were right alongside us. Some officers had fanned out to guard the perimeter in case Shane decided to rabbit on us.

Shane Dolan's window was second from the last. We knelt down and listened at the door. The television was on, and a commercial for some seafood restaurant offering a good deal on lobster was playing. I tried to look around the edge of the yellowed window shade, but all I could see was the corner of a sofa that was a sickly shade of green. It looked like something he'd picked up off the sidewalk. I was about to move forward to the other window when I heard a soft thump.

I turned back to Bailey and kept my voice low. "Did you hear that?"

"I think so, but the television's so loud." She looked at me. "I don't want to wait for SWAT. Think we can call this an exigent circumstance?"

Exigent circumstances, such as hot pursuit of a suspect or the possible imminent destruction of evidence, can let police get into a house without a warrant. "Well, he does fit the description of the second shooter."

Bailey looked skeptical. "Medium build. Not exactly a DNA match."

"But we've accounted for all the other students—"

Bailey nodded. "And he didn't show up for work—"

"And no one's seen him since the Friday before the shooting. Screw it. I say we go for it. I'd rather ask forgiveness than permission."

Bailey gestured for the local officers to join us. They moved quickly to surround the small complex. Rusty and another of the sturdier-looking cops took the lead at the front door. We whispered, to make sure we couldn't be heard over the television. "Police, open up." Then they mouthed a count to three and kicked in the door.

32

The flimsy door splintered and flew open on the first kick. I was behind all the other officers so I stood on tiptoe to try to see inside. No one was there from what I could tell, but I waited for the officers to give us the "all clear." They gave it in less than two minutes.

I saw that it was just a small single room. The "kitchen" was a hot plate. But as I walked in, I heard movement coming from somewhere overhead. In one swift motion, I turned and drew my gun.

And found a cat crouched on top of the refrigerator, staring down at us. I pointed to the cat. "The thump we heard."

Bailey glanced at my gun. "You planning to take it down, Knight? I think it'll probably come peaceably with a piece of chicken. But, your call."

I glared at her and put my gun away, then scanned the apartment. It was a mess. The kind of mess that said someone had left in a hurry and didn't plan on coming back. A half-eaten meatball sub—with some cat-sized bites taken out of it—was lying on its wrapper on the coffee table next to a nearly full bottle of beer. The sub was cold and the beer was room temperature. But the sandwich didn't look stale. A few cockroaches were making a dinner of it, but given the look of the place, they were probably permanent residents. I guessed we'd missed Shane by mere hours. The dresser drawers were pulled out and empty, the only remaining clothing a few stray boxer shorts and socks that had dribbled onto the floor. In the bathroom, the mirrored door of the medicine cabinet hung open, the inside shelves nearly empty except for a couple of rusty-looking razors and an old can of shaving cream. The officers found some stray ammo inside the fold-out couch, but no spent casings or bullets. Nothing we could match to the spent rounds in the school. Still, we asked the officers to bag them up so we could see if they were the same caliber and make as the evidence ammo.

I motioned for Bailey to join me outside. "Let's get these guys out of here and get the crime scene techs in," I said. "The one good thing about this ungodly mess is it doesn't look like he took the time to wipe anything down. We should come up with some usable prints and DNA in here. If Dorian gets anything out of those jackets she found in the Dumpster, we can see if there's a match."

Bailey nodded and turned to head back inside, when we heard a shout from the apartment. We ran in and found the lead cop, Rusty, pointing to the refrigerator wedged in the corner. It had been pivoted out a few inches to reveal a yellowed piece of paper taped to the side that faced the wall. "I didn't want to pull the thing all the way out till the crime scene guys got here," he said. "But I'd guess those are his email addresses—and passwords."

Damn if he wasn't right. They all looked like remarkably unoriginal variations on the name Shane Dolan, like SDol10586 and SHLAN1086. I glanced at the officers. "Ten bucks says his birth date is October fifth, nineteen eighty-six. Anyone?" No takers.

The crime scene techs showed up, so while I copied it all down on Bailey's notepad, she told them what we were looking for—what Dorian lovingly referred to as our "wish list." Okay, maybe not so lovingly. Rusty put out an alert with Shane Dolan's DMV photo, the license plate for his black Ford F250 pickup truck, and his personal description. He assured us that would do the trick in Ventura. "If your guy's still up here, we'll find him pretty quick."

Bailey and I headed back to her car. While she drove, I pulled out the list of email addresses I'd copied down and started to tap them into my phone. Bailey turned on the radio. It'd been a long day, and the freeway was practically empty at this time of night. Easy to fall asleep at the wheel. She tuned in to a classic rock station.

"I kind of prefer jazz," I said.

"Yeah? You also prefer a head-on collision with that pylon?"

"I'll get back to you on that."

The first three email addresses were defunct, but I got lucky on the fourth: SHDOG68501. "Bailey, turn that thing down."

"What?" She did—fractionally.

I turned it down the rest of the way and ignored her glare. "Shane Dolan got an email from Logan the day before the shooting."

"No shit?"

"None at all. Listen to this: 'Hey, dog, you da man. Thanks for all of it. See ya on the other side! Ha ha.'" I looked at Bailey.

She shrugged. "Well, could be he's thanking Shane for helping with the guns. But it's pretty vague."

"Come on, Bailey. The day before the shooting? Shane's into guns, Logan thanks him 'for all of it.' At the very least, Shane had to be the gun supplier. And he might very well be more."

Bailey was silent for a moment, then nodded. "Possibly. He sure beat feet out of here, no question about that."

It was one of the few things we didn't have questions about. By the time Bailey dropped me off at the Biltmore, we were both visibly sagging.

"Get some rest, Knight. It's only going to get crazier."

"We don't have any interviews scheduled for tomorrow, do we?" Bailey shook her head. "Then I'll have to check in at the office." I got out of the car and patted the roof. "But call me if anything's shaking."

Bailey nodded and drove off. Angel pulled open the door for me. "Long day, Ms. Knight? You look tired."

"Very, very long day, Angel."

He wished me good night. I wished I could've had one. I fell asleep like someone knocked me on the head with a club, but nightmares with children crying and a stalker with a high-pitched laugh kept me thrashing most of the night.

When my hotel phone rang, I groped for the clock, sure it was three a.m. It was seven thirty. And only two people ever called me on that phone. I knew who it wasn't: Graden wouldn't dare call me at that indecent hour.

I picked up the phone. "What is it, Keller?"

"Morning, Ms. Daisy."

"I know you think that's funny—"

"Want to talk to a witness?"

I sat up. "Who?"

"Just get down here."

The Police Administration Building is walking distance from the Biltmore, and the streets between them are filled with churro stands. I love churros so much it's embarrassing. Just the smell of the hot cinnamon makes my mouth water. I picked up four and ate one on the way, congratulating myself on my restraint.

Bailey was on the phone. I put two down in front of her, and she smiled her thanks. I got my coffee and sat down at an empty desk to savor my remaining churro, careful not to get the sugar and cinnamon all over me. But when Bailey ended her call, she reached out and dusted off my chin. Oh, well.

"We've got a kid coming in who says—" Bailey stopped as a woman in a long gray wool coat led a tall, rumpled-looking young guy toward us. Bailey stood up. "Mrs. Ester?"

"Hello, Detective," she said. "I thought it'd be easier for you if I brought Jeremy in instead of having you out to the house."

"That was very kind of you," Bailey said. She introduced me and we all shook hands.

"Please call me Amy."

"Amy, why don't you and Jeremy follow me," Bailey said. Every pair of eyes in the bull pen watched as we headed to the interview room.

We might not ordinarily do a witness interview in private, but we were keeping everything about this case as much under lock and key as possible. The chief had tried to appease the press by giving updates, but he couldn't say much without compromising the investigation, so the updates basically consisted of "We're following up on leads." The press wasn't fooled. They hounded him and complained—in person and in print—about the lack of progress. So the mood at the station was tense.

Jeremy was an earnest-looking kid. Tall, with tight blonde curls—like his mom—and well-spoken. My guess that he was a basketball player panned out: he was a power forward on the Fairmont varsity team. In his spare time he worked as a bagger at the local grocery store. He hadn't been in the gym at the time of the shooting. But he had seen something he thought might be important. He started by apologizing.

"I know I should've told you guys about this right away, but I was freaked-out."

His mother pursed her lips. "He didn't even tell me until this morning, or I would've dragged him in right when it happened. Gave me some cockamamie story at first about a drunk driver."

Jeremy hung his head like a puppy who'd peed on the carpet.

"So this happened when?" I asked.

"Monday," he said.

It was Thursday. Had it only been three days since the shooting? It was hard to believe. "But you're here now. That's what matters. Tell us what happened."

He spoke in a rapid, shaky voice. "I was late to school. My car battery died, and Mom had already left for work, so I had to wait for Triple-A to come and give me a jump."

"About what time did you get on the road?" Bailey asked.

"Triple-A didn't get to me until after eleven. So, maybe eleven thirty? And I was just a couple of blocks away from school when this car comes around the corner. Heads straight for me, just like, flying. I thought I was dead. I yanked the wheel to the right just in time. He sideswiped me pretty bad. But he just kept on going, seemed like ninety miles an hour." Jeremy rubbed his palms on his thighs as he relived the moment.

"Can you describe the car?" Bailey asked.

"A white Corolla. Looked kind of new. Or...maybe just in good shape."

Not so much anymore.

"Where's your car now?" Bailey asked.

"Here. I thought you'd want to see it."

Smart boy.

"By any chance were you able to see who was driving the car?" I asked.

Jeremy pressed his lips together and shook his head. "No. I think they were wearing black ski masks, the kind that go over your whole head."

"They?" I asked. "There was someone in the passenger seat?"

"Yeah. That I'm sure about. There was definitely someone in the passenger seat."

"Did you happen to see the license plate?" Bailey asked.

"I only remember the first part. I wrote it down. It was 4JHQ." He shook his head. "Sorry, that's all I could get."

"Don't be," I said. "You did great."

Jeremy had gotten only half the numbers, but it was enough. That was Logan's car.

33

Bailey got a crime scene tech to come out and take photos and scrapings from the paint transfers on Jeremy's car. Once we found Logan's car, we'd be able to confirm that it matched. "There's no way Logan can hide that kind of body damage," she said, after Jeremy and his mom had left.

"At least it'll give the chief something to tell the press. I just don't get why no one's spotted it by now." They'd put out the alert on Logan's car the moment we had confirmation that he was one of the shooters, but so far it hadn't turned up. Maybe the description of the body damage would do the trick.

"Me either," Bailey said. "Even if they've ditched it, I would've expected someone to spot it by now."

"Or spot *him*."

Bailey shook her head. Logan's photo and all identifying information had gone national, and every source—cell phone, bank account, gas card, you name it—was being tracked. Nothing.

"But thanks to Jeremy, we know one thing for sure," Bailey said. "We've got two shooters out there."

"Right. So now there are two killers we can't find. And one of them isn't even ID'd yet. Terrific." I shook my head. "How're we doing on Shane? Do we have his military records yet?"

"Yep. And they show he's been to the VA clinic in Westwood, so we got their records. But they're not fully computerized, so we've got a ream of paper to go through, and none of it's organized. I've got unis working on it." Bailey looked at her watch. "We should head out to Camarillo." The tree service where Shane worked was up next on our agenda. "I sent a couple of detectives to check the place out. They're sitting on it for us, but he hasn't shown up yet. I want to get out there and talk to the boss man, see if he can give us anything."

"Okay, but first I've got to check in at the office."

"Want me to pick you up? We really have to move."

"No, but I'll be back here in less than an hour. I promise."

I pulled on my coat and scarf and headed to the courthouse at a fast trot. I passed by Toni's office on the way to mine, but the door was closed. She was probably in court. I unlocked my door and dropped my purse on the chair in front of my desk. Home sweet home. Everything was as I'd left it on Tuesday morning—except for the thin layer of dust. A file I'd been reviewing on Monday still lay open on my side table. Even the air felt the same. I took off my coat and scarf and draped them over my chair—a majestic judge's chair that I'd found abandoned in the hallway one night. I sat down and exhaled. It was a tiny office, but it was my sanctuary. And it boasted an awesome view of Los Angeles, something I would never take for granted.

But I didn't have time to sit and enjoy the solitude, so I picked up my office phone to check for messages. There were eighty-seven. Eighty of them were from the media. You'd think they'd have gotten the hint that I wasn't talking by now. The rest were routine business. "Hi, Rachel, it's Zack—Zack Meyer on the Valenzuela case. Just a heads-up: I'm going to ask for a continuance. Hope that's okay with you." *Beep.* I made a note and deleted the message. It wouldn't matter if it was okay with me. It was Zack's first request for more time, and the judges loved him. The other six were all variations on the same theme. It surprised me how little I'd missed. I'd expected to be bombarded. I kept forgetting it had only been three days. It felt like three months.

My in-box only had a couple of new motions. One was a routine discovery motion, the other was a motion to let a defendant use the jail law library—where he'd learn just enough to drive his lawyer crazy. I'd be glad to go along with that one. I filed them and made a note of the dates on my calendar, then headed back to the station. Bailey was at her desk, doing paperwork, her least favorite thing in the world. She looked surprised when she saw me. "That was fast."

"Told ya. So, Camarillo?"

Bailey stood up. "Yep." We were about to step into the elevator when Graden called out to us. "Hang on, guys. Can you give me a minute?" We went back to his office. He closed the door and perched on the edge of his desk. "We got a hit on the Army-Navy surplus store in Van Nuys. The cashier remembers selling two camouflage jackets in about the right sizes to a couple of guys—"

"Do they have surveillance footage?" Bailey asked.

"Unfortunately, no. It's a small operation. And we got a description from the cashier, but it's pretty vague." He picked up a report and read. "One tall guy with longish hair, one shorter guy, no further description. The shorter guy paid for both coats in cash."

"We'll get out there and talk to him," Bailey said.

"Do it fast. The tabloids are everywhere now that we're giving press conferences."

"Good," I said. "Maybe they can figure out who the second shooter is while they're at it."

"Just give them a minute, they will," he said.

"You mean they'll dig up some crank who says it's all an FBI conspiracy," Bailey said.

Graden nodded. "Yeah, the tabs will have it all figured out for us. That's why we're going to start putting a little more substance in the press releases. Better to get out in front of it and at least try to give the public the truth. So lock down all the statements you can—before your witnesses get contaminated by tabloid bullshit."

Because the more a defense lawyer can show that witnesses could have been influenced by what they saw on TV or read somewhere, the less a jury will trust their testimony.

Graden handed Bailey the report, and we headed for the door. "Oh, and one more thing," Graden said. "If you two get finished in time for dinner, let me know. It's on me."

"Depends," I said. "Where?"

"So this is where we're at now? Bribery? What happened to the joy of good company?"

"Who says they're mutually exclusive?" I asked.

"I had to fall for a lawyer." Graden shook his head. "Fine. Pacific Dining Car."

Bailey nodded. "Sounds good."

"You're on."

34

We hit the Army-Navy surplus store first. The cashier—Eddie Hemmings—was a short, skinny guy with sharp features. We'd hoped to dredge up at least a little more information than we already had, but no dice. Before we left, I warned him about the media. "I can't stop you from talking to the press, but I can say that if you do, you'll damage your credibility as a witness. And believe me, whatever they promise to do for you, they'll forget it about ten seconds after they get your statement."

I could see him weighing his options even as I spoke. But when I finished, he nodded amiably. "Got ya. No problem. I'll keep it on the down-low."

We hurried out to the car, and Bailey headed for the 101 north. "A fin says he talks to the press by noon tomorrow," Bailey said.

"So little faith in your fellow man." I shook my head. "A twenty says he's on camera before we make it to Camarillo."

Bailey groaned. "Never mind. I fold."

We rolled onto the lot of Camarillo Tree Cutters just before noon. I'd heard the loud metallic growl of a chain saw as soon as we pulled onto the street, and the smell of cut lumber filled the air. It was a huge lot that had piles of cut wood at the front and hundreds of felled trees waiting to be cut behind them. The workers I could see all seemed to be Hispanic. I pointed to a small hut on the right that had a sign over the door, OFFICE. Bailey parked in front of it.

We knocked but got no answer. Bailey tried the door and found it was open, so we walked in. Calling it an office was a stretch. It was a small room with a window that afforded a view of the lot. A couple of folding chairs were in front of a table piled high with invoices. An old Mac desktop computer sat on a short metal filing cabinet to the left of the table, a green cursor blinking on a black screen. Everything was covered in a thick layer of sawdust. The air was so filled with the stuff, I coughed when we stepped inside. A toilet flushed, and a door on the right side of the room opened. And out stepped Paul Bunyan.

Well, not exactly, but close. He was well over six feet, and though he had a bit of a paunch, his arms and chest were solid muscle. And huge. When he saw us, he tugged down his T-shirt with one hand and pushed his wavy—though thinning—brown hair back with the other. "Uh, what can I help you ladies with?"

Ladies. Again. But this time I didn't mind. I was distracted by the feeling that we'd stepped into an American fairy tale. I pulled out my badge and did the introductions. "And you're the owner here?"

"Yeah. Isaiah Hamilton."

"You have an employee named Shane Dolan?" I asked.

He half snorted. "I did. But he hasn't shown up for the past four days." Isaiah sat down and motioned for us to do the same. I took a swipe at the sawdust on one of the two metal folding chairs in front of his desk and tried not to think about what was going to be stuck to my pants.

"When was the last time he came to work?" I asked.

"Friday."

"And was he supposed to be here on Monday?" I asked.

"Yeah. Didn't even bother to call." Isaiah shook his head. "Hate to lose him though. He in some kind of trouble?"

"That's what we're trying to figure out. Was he a good worker?" It'd be a surprise if he was, given what we'd heard about him.

Isaiah shrugged. "Not the most energetic guy. But he spoke English, so I could use him to fill in for me on the phone. Take orders and such. The rest of my crew"—he jerked a thumb toward the workers outside—"are good guys, but they're strictly Spanish-speaking."

"Did Shane ever have any visitors here?" I asked.

Isaiah rolled his eyes. "Yeah, I guess you could call her that. A girl used to come around a lot, but I haven't seen her lately."

"Was that girl the only one?" Isaiah nodded. "Did you get her name?" I asked.

Isaiah looked down at the cluttered desk and drummed his fingers on it. I couldn't imagine how staring at that mess could help him remember anything except that a cleaning was overdue. Finally, he squinted at me. "Nancy. Nancy Findley. She called here about a hundred times."

Isaiah's disapproving expression made me smile. "So she was a fan of Shane's," I said.

"More like a stalker. Though why she was so hooked on him I have no idea. You ask me, the guy was a real case of arrested development."

"In what way?" I asked.

"Had a hard time doing what he was told. Didn't matter what I asked him to do—even just to get here on time—he'd give me major-league attitude."

"Then you'd say he had issues with authority?"

"Big-time. But I kept him around because, well, you know..." He gestured to the office.

But Shane hadn't had those issues with Lock, the gun range owner. I suspected tree cutting didn't have the same allure as the gun range. Go figure.

"Did he ever talk to you about guns?" Bailey asked.

Isaiah gave a short bark of a laugh. "Ho, yeah. Nonstop. Kept wanting to take me out to the range where he worked. And he was always trying to sell me one."

Sell? I leaned forward. "What kind of guns was he trying to sell?"

"Handguns mostly. Thirty-eights, forty-fours. He did mention a rifle once, I think."

"What kind of rifle?" Bailey asked.

Isaiah began drumming his fingers on the arm of his chair. "Remington? Yeah, I believe that's right."

"So not an assault rifle?" I asked.

"No. They're illegal, aren't they?" I nodded. "Well, even if they weren't, I wouldn't let him sell those things to anyone around here. You ask me, they don't belong in civilian hands."

"What about you?" I asked. "Are you into guns?"

"Not at all."

Why would he be? He didn't need a gun. He could just pick you up and throw you out the window. "So you don't know whether the deals he offered were any good," I said.

"No. But Pedro might." Isaiah stood up and walked over to the window. He cranked it open and yelled, "Hey, Pedro."

Pedro, a middle-aged Hispanic man in a denim jacket and cowboy boots, came in. Isaiah asked in fairly decent Spanish what Shane had offered him. He translated for us, though I pretty much got the gist of what Pedro had said. "Shane offered him a Smith and Wesson thirty-eight special. Pedro says it was like new—for two hundred and fifty dollars."

"He showed Pedro the gun?" I asked.

Pedro nodded and said, *"Sí."*

"And it was in good shape?" I asked.

Pedro said in Spanish that it looked brand-new.

Isaiah nodded. "He said it looked—"

I held up my hand. "Got it. Did Pedro buy it?"

Isaiah translated, and Pedro shook his head.

"Did Shane offer to sell guns to anyone else?" I asked.

Isaiah translated, and Pedro replied in Spanish. Isaiah turned to me. "Pedro says he tried to sell to all the other guys, but he doesn't think anyone bought a gun from him. Too much money, and they weren't sure how legal it was."

But just to make sure, we had Isaiah bring in all the other workers, one by one. Pedro was right. No one had bought a gun, though others had seen the one Pedro described and all agreed it looked new. When we finished with them, we thanked Isaiah for his help, said we'd be in touch, and warned him that at some point the media might come after him for a statement. He chuckled. "Don't worry, they won't get anything out of me, ladies." Ladies. Again. Oh, well.

But I wasn't worried about him.

The reporters who messed with him—*them,* I worried about.

35

"Do you realize how much a new Smith and Wesson thirty-eight special costs?" I asked, when we got back into Bailey's car.

"No, but I'm guessing you do."

"Over seven hundred bucks. If that gun Shane was trying to sell to Pedro really was new, his price was ridiculously low. Looks like Shane had a little business going on the side."

"Selling hot guns?" Bailey said. I nodded. "Pretty risky. If anyone ever ratted him out he'd do some serious time."

"He doesn't seem like the type who'd play out those consequences. Like Isaiah said, he's got authority issues."

"Assuming Paul Bunyan back there sussed him out right."

"So you saw it too?" I grinned at Bailey. "He was actually kind of dreamy, don't you think?"

"To me? No. But I noticed you got a little fluttery."

"Fluttery." I gave her a look. "Me. Are you high?"

"S'okay. He looked like he wouldn't have minded letting you do a little more questioning either."

"You can let me out of this car anytime." I folded my arms and looked out the window. The road to the freeway led us past miles of strawberry, Brussels sprout, and lettuce fields. We were out in the middle of nowhere.

Bailey turned on the radio. The opening organ notes of "Light My Fire" filled the car. I usually love the Doors, but the timing right now only served Bailey's obnoxious purpose. And, of course, she was smiling. I glared at her. "I just want you to know I'm ignoring you." She stifled a yawn.

We rode on through the fields in silence. I thought about what we could accomplish while we were up here in farm country. "You want to try and dig up Nancy Findley?"

"That's what I was thinking. Unless you've got a better idea?"

"Not necessarily better, but if we have trouble finding her, we could head back to L.A. and see what Evan and Caleb have to say about Shane Dolan. If Logan was that impressed with Shane, he might've tried to show him off."

"Good idea."

Bailey called in and asked for a location on Nancy Findley. As it turned out, she lived in Thousand Oaks, just a few minutes south of Camarillo, which was on our way back to L.A. And she was in pocket.

"Guess it was meant to be," I said. "So where's 'in pocket'?"

Bailey pulled off the freeway. "You'll see." Five minutes later, she'd parked in front of a tattoo parlor in a strip mall. It was sandwiched between a nail salon and a frozen yogurt place. Kind of a nice combination of services. I could just picture it: "Hey, Mom, let's have a girls' day. We can do mani-pedis, get tattooed, and have double scoops with sprinkles."

Nancy was easy to spot because she was the only girl there. Also because she had waist-length, neon-green hair with a black stripe down the middle, multicolored tattoo sleeves that snaked up her neck—one of which was an actual snake—a double nose ring, a lip ring in the left corner of her mouth, and rows of piercings up each ear. And those were just the things we could see. I forced my imagination away from all the other piercing possibilities both above and below the belt.

Bailey had pulled up a photo of Shane on her cell phone. After we'd made the necessary introductions, she showed it to Nancy. "Do you recognize this person?"

Nancy, who'd been practically catatonic when we introduced ourselves—so much so, I suspected chemical or herbal influences—suddenly woke up. She covered her mouth with her hand. "Oh no!" Nancy's eyes were round with fear. "Is Shane in trouble? Did something happen to him?"

"We just need to ask him some questions," I said. "When was the last time you saw him?"

Nancy wrinkled her nose. "Do you mean actually *saw* him, like in person? Or like on FaceTime?"

"Let's try in person first," I said.

"That would be a little over a month ago. It was at the tree service where he works."

"Did he discuss any plans he may have had to leave the city for any reason?" I asked.

"No." Nancy's brow furrowed. "So he's gone?"

No, I just like to hear about my suspects' vacation plans. "It seems so. Do you remember what you talked about?"

Nancy frowned at the floor and jammed her hands into the back pockets of her skinny jeans. When she looked up, I saw she was blinking back tears. "That…uh…he didn't think it was going to 'happen' for us. That I couldn't keep coming by his job and calling him and…like that." The tears finally escaped and rolled down her cheeks. She gave them a rough, angry swipe.

If Shane had been standing there I would've slugged him. Sure, she was a little strange, and, yes, quite possibly a stalker. But still. Knowing what we did about Shane so far, I'd guess Nancy was one of the many girls Shane had picked up, got bored with, and dumped. Asshole.

"I'm sorry, Nancy," I said. "Did you talk to him again after that? On FaceTime?"

"Yeah. But I called from a friend's phone, so I don't think he realized it was me at first. When he came on, I could tell he thought…"

It was someone else. I might've been channeling some issues of my own with past boyfriends, but seriously, if I ever found him, I was going to mess this jerk up so bad.

"I told him I just wanted to see him one last time. He said his boss was calling him and he had to go. Said he'd call me later. That was a couple of weeks ago. I haven't heard from him since." Nancy heaved a big sigh and swallowed the rest of her tears. "I know he wasn't good for me. My mom says it's for the best and I'll get over it, but it just doesn't feel that way right now."

Oh, Very Young, it never does. "Your mom's right. You won't be over it until you're over it. All you can do is keep reminding yourself that you deserve better. Eventually, you'll believe it."

Nancy nodded. "Thanks."

We gave her our cards and told her to call if she heard from him. She promised she would.

We headed back to the 101 freeway, southbound for L.A. "Feel like killing him?" I asked.

"Nah, killing's too fast. I'd kneecap him. Both knees."

"Nice." When it comes to payback, Bailey and Toni are creative geniuses.

At that weirdly inopportune moment, Graden called. "Rachel?"

"Yeah." I didn't recognize his voice at first, and I think mine was probably still in "I hate Shane" mode.

"You okay? You sound . . . strange."

"Sorry. I'm just a little tired. It's been pretty nonstop."

"I know," Graden said, his tone warm and full of sympathy.

My lizard brain remembered that Graden wasn't Shane or any other asshole I'd ever had the misfortune of knowing. "You okay?"

"I'm fine," he said. "Look, I just got word that a letter addressed to you was delivered to the school."

School? "What school?"

"Fairmont High—"

"Why on earth would anyone send mail to me at—"

"Good question. And there's no return address. It feels bad to me, Rachel. I know this may sound paranoid, but I told them to leave it right there and not touch it. I called in the bomb squad—"

"Jeez, seriously? It might just be someone who recognized me on some news footage or—"

"I'd be glad to be wrong. But I'm not taking any chances. The bomb guys are going to handle it. Assuming it doesn't explode, Dorian's people will check it out. But I expect everyone to move fast, so you should be able to get a look at it pretty quick. I'd suggest you get downtown as soon as you can."

I agreed, ended the call, and told Bailey what he'd said. "I don't know how many people would've recognized us from the news footage though. The shot I saw was maybe two seconds."

"Yeah, but they showed footage from the Antonovich trial that had your face all over it. So anyone could've written that letter. Might just be a weird fan—"

Big cases always brought out the tinfoil-hat brigade. "I'm still getting mail about that trial..."

"Yeah, the only thing that bugs me is no return address. I'm with Graden. If it was an innocent thing, why not leave a return address?"

That was the question. One of them anyway.

36

On the way downtown, I called Principal Campbell to ask him how they'd come across the letter.

He'd been surprised by it too. "The past couple of days we've had mail pouring in from all over the world. There was no way to keep up with it, so some of the teachers volunteered to help sort. But it turned out to be easier than we'd thought. Most of them were addressed to the school, and they were obviously meant for everyone. The rest were addressed to the families of the kids who...didn't make it." He paused to collect himself. "So the one addressed to you stood out. I thought I should call."

"You did the perfect thing, Dale," I said.

By the time we got to the station, the letter had been cleared by the bomb squad, and Dorian had finished processing it. Now it sat alone in a ventilated cardboard box on Graden's desk.

"Did you read it?" I asked him.

Graden nodded, tight-lipped. "I only had the chance to scan it, but..."

His worried expression made me nervous. I opened the box. There was just the letter, no envelope. "They took the envelope?"

Graden nodded. "Yeah, to see what they could do with the postmark. And there were two actually. The outer envelope was addressed to Rachel Knight at the school, and there was one inside it that just had your name. The letter was in that second envelope."

The letter was typed on plain white Xerox paper. I put on latex gloves and took it out.

Rachel Knight, Fairmont High is only the beginning. They say we're Columbine Copycats. They're idiots. We already proved those pathetic losers are nothing compared to us. But we have more, much more, to show the world. Do you realize how lucky you are? You have the privilege of being involved in what will be the greatest criminal legacy of all time. They say you got famous after that case with the Hollywood director, but that was nothing compared to this. I bet that's why you wanted my case. Because you always want the big case. Because you blew it with Romy. And now she's probably dead. I could have saved her. You know why? Because I'm superior to you—to all of you—in every way.

I am the best, the very best you've ever seen or ever will see. Our victory at Fairmont High was NOT luck. It was skill. MY skill.

If you catch me, you'll be a hero. But if you fail, Rachel Knight, like you did with Romy, many, many more will die. So now, it's all up to you. Do your job, you'll stop us. Fail and we will go on. And on.

I felt as though I'd been hit in the chest with a sledgehammer. I reread the letter. It wasn't the fact that he knew about my sister's abduction. That story had been blasted all over the tabloids during the Antonovich trial. Everyone and his dog could know that my sister had been abducted by a man in a pickup truck while we were playing hide-and-seek in the woods near our house. And it didn't strike me as a big leap in logic or insight that Logan figured out I might need to avenge my sister's kidnapping by taking on the gnarliest cases I could find. But that this kid had managed to zero in on my survivor's guilt—that was a little less obvious. It showed me he not only had smarts, but he also knew how to go for the emotional jugular.

Logan's teachers had said he tested at genius level. And strategizing the shooting and escape clearly took some intelligence. What I hadn't counted on was this kind of insidious cunning. Or such grandiose megalomania.

I gave the letter to Bailey. Her face was ashen when she passed it to Graden. He read it, and when he looked up, his eyes were blazing with fury. "This animal needs to be put down, and fast." Graden raked his fingers through his hair. "I've got to take this to the chief ASAP." He looked from Bailey to me, his expression stern. "This stays between us until I say otherwise. If anyone asks, it was just fan mail. Got it?" Bailey and I nodded. If the public found out what was in this letter, the threat of future shootings would cause mass hysteria. And there was no realistic way we could allay the fear. As Bailey pointed out, we couldn't secure every single public building in the city and county of Los Angeles. Graden reread the letter, then put it back in the box. "This was obviously written by the ringleader—"

"Logan, based on what we know at this point," Bailey said.

"And it sounds like a high school kid," I said.

Graden frowned. "Do we know if Shane Dolan is our second shooter?"

"No," Bailey said. "He's looking good, but it's too soon to commit to anything."

Bailey filled Graden in on what we'd just learned from Isaiah Hamilton and Nancy Findley.

"And we're sure no students are unaccounted for?" he asked.

"Checked and double-checked," Bailey said. "All accounted for now. We've got alerts out for Logan and his Toyota, and for Shane and his pickup. And the lab is still sifting through a mountain of evidence."

"We're going to hit up Caleb and Evan and see what they know about Shane," I said.

Graden nodded. "Sounds right." He looked at me closely. "That letter was one hell of a gut shot. Are you okay?"

"Yeah, sure." I'd tried to sound casual, but the words came out a little choky. Graden put an arm around me. That kind of physical display was something we never did at work. Ordinarily I would've appreciated it. Not now. This was my private bête noire and I needed to deal with it on my own. I straightened and leaned away. "It really is okay. I'll be fine."

Graden nodded and stepped back behind his desk, the move as much emotional as physical. "Just a word of advice about your interview with Evan," he said. "You might want to go easy on him right now. He felt bad for not telling you about seeing Logan in the parking lot and, beyond that, for not realizing what was up at the time. Go too heavy and he might just shut down."

"I agree," Bailey said. "He was trying not to show it, but he looked pretty bent about the whole deal."

Graden picked up the box containing the letter. "I sincerely doubt that these guys have the wherewithal to follow you two—"

I shook my head. "We're too small a target. They don't want us. They want a massive hit and they're busy planning it. Right now." Just hearing myself say the words made me want to run outside and start hunting, anywhere and everywhere. Every second we stood there was another second wasted.

"Still, I'm going to try and get you extra security. But in the meantime, be on your guard." He looked from Bailey to me and back again. We nodded.

Graden left to see the chief, and Bailey and I headed out to her car. In the last twenty minutes, the entire complexion of the case had changed. It had never occurred to me that escaping from Fairmont High wouldn't be enough for them. That, far from trying to hide, they'd be brazenly planning another attack. But now that I knew, it seemed obvious, even naive of us not to have anticipated this. Bailey's grim expression as she steered out of the parking lot told me she was having similar thoughts.

"All we can do is push ahead," I said. "The moves are the same." Track down the witnesses, squeeze them for information, follow the leads.

"Yeah, but the moves need to be a lot faster now."

I nodded, feeling my gut tighten with anxiety. I forced my brain to slow down and focus on our interview with Evan. Graden and Bailey had both made a fair point. Evan was pretty frayed around the edges when we'd last seen him. The past few days had given him time to think. Time to feel guilty about not having sounded the alarm when Logan told him to ditch school. Maybe time to wonder whether Logan or the other shooter would remember that conversation—and decide to do something about it.

I still had trouble believing Logan would risk making a move on him. But Evan knew Logan better than we ever would.

37

The sky was turning to hues of purple and indigo when we pulled up to Evan's house. It was downright cold now that the sun had set. I was glad I'd worn my peacoat and cashmere scarf. This time we met Evan's father. John Cutter had that tight, lean muscle and super-groomed, short-haired look that screamed military.

"Did you happen to know Logan, Mr. Cutter?" I asked.

"I met him a few times when he was here to see Evan, but I can't say I formed any strong impression one way or the other. He seemed pretty introverted." He shook his head. "I guess you just never know, do you?"

"You really don't," I said. "Have you ever met a person named Shane Dolan?"

"The name doesn't ring a bell. If you had a picture, I might—" Bailey showed him the photo she had on her cell phone. Cutter shook his head. "No, I'd remember if I saw a man like that in my house."

Like the *k* in *knuckle*, the "he-wouldn't-step-foot-in-this-house-again" was silent. "Do you mind if we speak to Evan in his room?" I asked.

"Not a problem."

Bailey and I followed him down the hall. "Evan has an older sister in grad school back East, doesn't he? Does she come home much?"

"No. Once she moved out to college, it was just Thanksgiving and Christmas."

"So it's been, what? Five years since she lived here?" Bailey asked.

"About that, yes."

We'd let local police back East check with her about Shane, but it was probably a dead end. There were two doors at the end of the hall.

A thumping bass was vibrating behind the door to our left. Cutter rapped his knuckles sharply on that door, and a faint voice replied, "Yeah?"

"The detective and deputy district attorney are here to see you, Evan. Open up." He put his hands on his hips and stared at the door with impatient eyes.

The music got softer right away, but it took a few long moments before the door opened. Evan looked like he'd had a bad night. His eyes were bloodshot, and his face looked drawn and pinched.

"Hey, Evan," I said. "We've just got a few questions for you. It won't take much time, I promise."

He nodded, dipped his head, and stood aside to let us enter. I turned to Mr. Cutter. "Thank you. We'll just be a couple minutes."

Cutter wanted to listen in. I could tell he was fighting the urge to say that it was his house and he'd damn well be in any room he wanted. But his better instincts won out. He nodded and left us. We stepped inside and closed the door. Evan leaned against his desk.

"How're you doing?" Bailey asked.

Evan shrugged. "Okay, I guess."

I guessed otherwise but knew better than to call him on it. "It's a tough time for you, I know. We won't take long. Just a few questions, okay?"

Evan gave a resigned nod.

"Do you know someone named Shane Dolan?" I asked.

He frowned, then shook his head. "No."

Bailey pulled up Shane's photo on her cell and showed it to him. "Do you recognize this person?"

Evan studied the photo. "No." A worried look crossed his face. "Who is that?"

"We think he might be a friend of Logan's," I said. "Did Logan ever talk about someone named Shane?"

"No, not that I remember." Evan's eyes strayed back to the photo. "And I know I never saw that guy with him." He was trying to act cool. But as he said it, he gripped the edge of the desk he'd been leaning against.

"Evan, we're looking out for you," I said. "I don't want you to worry about... anything."

He looked at me briefly, then lowered his head. "I'm okay."

"Did Logan ever talk to you about a guy who had access to guns?" Bailey asked.

"No."

He stared at the floor. His expression was tortured. But it was also tight and unyielding. It didn't matter how much I tried to reassure him. He was scared, and hearing about this Shane character had only made matters worse. We wouldn't get anything more out of him. At least, not now.

I noticed his laptop on the desk near the window. It was closed. But I'd bet it hadn't been before he opened the door. "Evan, I'd like to take your computer for just a few days, if you don't mind."

That snapped his head up. "What? Why?"

"Because Logan must have sent you emails. There might be something in them that gives us a clue as to where he might be. And he may even try to reach out to you."

"You don't have to agree, Evan," Bailey said. "But I'm about a hundred percent certain we can get a search warrant for it. 'Course, if we do that, it might take forever to get it back to you because it'll be considered evidence. That means we'll have to hang on to it until the case is all over. Could take years." Bailey turned to go. "But, you know, your call." It wasn't technically accurate that we'd have to hold it ad infinitum, but she was definitely right that we'd be able to get a warrant.

"If I let you take it now, do you promise to give it back in a week or so?"

"No promises," Bailey said. "But it'll sure be a lot sooner than if we take it with a warrant."

Evan unplugged the laptop and handed it over, looking glum. I felt sorry for him. And increasingly worried. Not so much about his safety—the local cops were keeping an eye on him, and I didn't believe Logan was really a threat. It was his mental state that worried me. "Look, the cops are watching the house, and if you want, we can try and get you extra security, okay?"

"I'm good, really," Evan said. "You don't need to get me any more security."

"You're sure?" I said.

"Yeah, save the manpower for the real problems. I'll be fine."

I wasn't so sure about that. But I was sure that was the answer his father would've liked. We walked out of the room and called out to John Cutter that we were leaving.

Oddly, Cutter seemed more upset at our taking the laptop than Evan. "Why on earth do you need his computer?" Bailey explained that it might have information on Logan Jarvis. He put his hands on his hips. "What's he supposed to use for school?"

"We won't keep it that long," Bailey said. "But I'll check with our Computer Crimes Unit and see if they can line up a loaner for you." She tucked the laptop under her arm and reached out to shake his hand. He frowned and reluctantly gave Bailey's hand a firm single pump. It looked to me like his grip had a little something extra in it, so I decided not to risk it.

"Were you in the Marines, Mr. Cutter?" I asked.

"Seventeen years. How did you know?"

"Just a guess."

38

It was after seven p.m. by the time we got back downtown, and we were both starving. Threat of mass destruction or not, we still needed to eat. I reminded Bailey of Graden's earlier offer to buy us dinner at the PDC. "If he's still up for it, we can eat and keep working."

Bailey nodded. "You make the call. Tell him we'll meet him there. I'll drop the laptop off with Nick."

The sooner Nick got into Evan's computer, the better. "How about if I ask Twan to join us? We could use a little outside perspective."

"That'd be great." Bailey pulled into the parking lot at the PAB. While she went to hand off the laptop to Nick, I called Toni and Graden. Both were on board for dinner. Bailey and I got there first and lucked out with a booth in the Club Car. We'd just ordered Bloody Marys for the table when Toni showed up.

"I'd ask how you are, but why pretend? You all look like hell." She slid in next to Bailey.

"You, on the other hand, look disgustingly gorgeous," I said.

"I love that suit," Bailey said.

"Girl, everyone likes this suit," Toni said. "It's Armani. I scored it at a sample sale."

Toni had fashion sense to spare. I'd never known anyone who managed to look as good as her—and I'm talking twenty-four/seven. She tells me I could do it too. Trust me, I can't.

She held up her tall glass. "To both of you getting some sleep before you keel over." We clinked and took healthy sips of our drinks. "Now catch me up."

We brought her up to speed on the latest developments, ending with the letter. I knew Graden wouldn't mind us telling Toni about the letter. She was family. We'd just finished describing our last interview with Evan when Graden showed up. He slid in next to me, gave me a warm hug, and smiled at Bailey. "How are you, Toni? Anything new?"

"You mean other than some fool in the parking lot telling me she loved my last concert?"

"Your last... what?" he asked.

Bailey and I rolled our eyes. We didn't have to hear the story to know what she was about to say—this wasn't the first time.

"Apparently, Beyoncé and I could be twins." Graden tried to hold back his laugh, but a short bark leaked out anyway. Toni shook her head with disgust. Other than being black, there was no resemblance whatsoever. "She also told me my hair looked better this way, so I guess the answer is, me and my hair are 'good.'"

The waiter came and took our orders. We all got the steak and lobster and decided to share two orders of their fabulous steamed asparagus. And, of course, another round of Bloody Marys. We talked about Toni's case—she was in trial on a kidnap-murder—until the waiter brought our drinks.

We toasted to nailing all of our killers, and then Graden turned to Toni. "I assume they told you?"

Toni nodded, somber. "This case gets crazier by the second."

Graden rubbed the side of his face. One of his tells when he's upset. He took a sip of his drink. "Nick called just as I was leaving. He got into Evan's computer with no problem."

"Anything?" Bailey asked.

"Not so far."

Toni jammed the straw into her drink, now mostly ice. "What do your shrinks have to say about all this—the letter, Shane?"

I interrupted. "We haven't confirmed that Shane's the second shooter—"

"Whoever. You need to figure out where they're planning to strike next. Your shrinks might have some ideas. And it looks to me like Logan is the mastermind. This started with a school shooting. That's all about *his* motive, not this Shane dude's. Unless Shane went to Fairmont High—"

"No," Bailey said. "And I agree. Logan's got to be the lead sled dog. The letter even sounded like a high school kid."

"We do need to get with our shrinks," I said. "But I don't need them to tell me that Shane's photo got Evan pretty rattled."

"Yeah," Bailey said. "But do you blame him? Shane's a sketchy-looking character."

"Can I see?" Toni asked. Bailey pulled up Shane's photo and handed her the phone. Toni raised an eyebrow. "Yeah, sketchy. But hot."

Graden took Bailey's phone, looked at the photo, then shook his head. "You call this hot?" He sighed. "Some things I'll never understand."

Bailey suppressed a smile. "I'll call the shrinks first thing in the morning."

"Let me know what they say," Graden said. "And you'll have the unis ask the rest of Logan's buddies about Shane?"

Bailey nodded. "Already being done. We'll talk to Caleb and Kenny ourselves, let the unis handle the outer circle."

"We've got to get out ahead of this," Graden said. "God knows where they're planning to hit next."

"We do know one thing," I said. "It'll be big."

On that grim note, the waiter brought our dinners. For which we now had zero appetite.

39

FRIDAY, OCTOBER 11

I woke up the next morning with an aching head and a gnawing emptiness in my stomach. I'd barely managed to choke down three bites of my steak, so the Bloody Marys had hit pretty hard. On the bright side, my pants were looser. Hell of a thing, this Mass Murderer Diet.

A pale, gray morning light poured through the gap between the drape and the window. I burrowed deeper under the covers to enjoy the warmth for just a minute more. It was almost as cold in the early mornings as it was at night. Keeping the covers tight around me, I snaked out a hand and called in my breakfast order: two eggs over medium, bacon, and toast with a large pot of coffee. Then I threw back the covers and forced myself out of bed.

After I'd showered, dressed, put on my face, and finished breakfast, I decided to drop in at the office. Bailey had said she'd call when she had our interviews set up. Since I hadn't heard from her yet, I figured I had a little time to go in and talk to Eric. I hadn't spoken to him in a while, and I wanted to get his take on our latest developments.

The sky was heavy with dark clouds that looked ready to open up and pour any minute—which they did, just as I got to the back entrance of the courthouse. I stopped by my office to check my in-box and found it blissfully empty. Maybe I was about to have a good day. Lord knew, I was due.

I went over to the window and looked out at the city. Even on a gloomy, wet day like this the view lifted my spirits. I stretched my arms up and leaned from side to side to work out the kinks that had built up from too many nights of fitful sleep and too few days at the gym. As I brought my arms down, the sleeve of my sweater caught on my earring and pulled it out. I felt my shoulder, but it wasn't there. I looked down at my feet, but it wasn't there either. Damn, it must have fallen under the table.

I got down on my knees to look, but it was too dark to see anything, so I got my phone and turned on the flashlight app. I saw a metallic sparkle against the wall—as far out of reach as possible. Groaning, I crawled under the table, but as I put my hand out to grab the earring, I noticed something stuck in the corner of the wall. At first, I thought it might be a cockroach or a water bug. I snatched my hand back. But then I noticed it wasn't moving. And it looked too square. I shined the flashlight on it. Definitely not a beetle. It was a small, black rectangular box, no more than an inch long.

I pulled at it and it came away from the wall with a ripping sound. It had been attached with Velcro. I clutched it in my hand and backed out from under the table. I turned it over and saw a tiny red LED light and what looked like a USB port on the end. What the...? A bug? It had to be. My heart gave a dull thud in my chest. Who'd planted it? And when? I stood there staring at the object in my hand, trying to figure it out.

I knew it hadn't been there before. My office had been swept regularly during my last trial, and it was clean then. Could it be the press? This school shooting was definitely big enough to make it worth their while. Tabloids were used to spending big bucks to get the "scoop," but this case was hot enough to make even the mainstream press dig into their pockets. I thought about who else would want to keep tabs on me. Vanderhorn? This case could give him a real shot at the governor's mansion—or doom him to a life of obscurity in a midlevel law firm. And what about sociopathic Lilah Bayer? She had plenty of reasons to want to keep an ear trained to find out if we were closing in on her. The list of possible suspects was daunting. The thought of someone sneaking into my office and planting that bug—and eavesdropping on me for who knew how long—made my skin crawl. I left the bug on my desk and quickly walked out of my office and down the hall to the fire escape. I stepped out and let the heavy metal door slam shut behind me. Then I pulled out my cell phone. The street side of the fire escape was enclosed by metal bars that let in all of the traffic noise, which was considerable at this time of the morning. Graden answered on the first ring.

"Rachel? Are you okay?"

I almost never called him during the day. If there was business to handle with him, Bailey usually took care of it. "Yeah. Well, no. Not exactly." I told him what I'd found in my office and listed the possible suspects. "Vanderhorn might be a stretch, though—"

"Maybe not, actually. Like you said, his political future depends on this case. Your list of possible suspects sounds right on." Graden was silent for a moment. "Where are you right now?" I told him. "And where's the bug?" I told him. "Just leave it there for now and obviously don't say anything you wouldn't want everyone to hear. I'm sending someone over there to check it out. For now, I don't want whoever planted that thing to know we're onto them. I'm going to assign a detective."

"Then you want me to do what? Nothing?"

"As impossible as that is for you. Our planter has to be someone with access to your office, so you can't even talk about this over there. Not to anyone."

"Even Eric?"

"Even Eric. For now, the fewer people who know about this, the better. Just let me handle this, okay?" I was silent. Doing nothing really didn't work for me. "Rachel? I'm not kidding. Any move you make could screw things up."

I sighed. "Okay, okay, I get it."

I ended the call and stared out through the bars at the traffic. My world was a study in insanity. Two murderers on the loose and now someone was bugging my office. What was next? Alien invasion?

There was only one thing to do. Go back to work. I had planned to get Eric's input on the case, but there was so much I couldn't share, I didn't feel comfortable talking to him now. I took the back hallway to avoid passing his office and ran to catch an elevator. I'd just stepped inside when my cell phone rang. It was Bailey. "What's up?"

Bailey huffed. A sign she was righteously pissed. "You won't friggin' believe this—"

"Hang on, let me get to a safe place."

I could've told her to hold off till I got to the station, but her tone unnerved me. I didn't want to wait.

40

When the elevator bounced to a stop at the ground floor, I snaked my way through the crowd, out to the stairway behind the courthouse. "Okay, go."

"You won't believe that little punk Evan. He's been tweeting that we've been *harassing* him—"

"What? Are you kidding me?"

"According to him, he keeps telling us he doesn't know anything and we just keep pressuring him. And the best part? The press just got wind of it."

Damn. Just what we needed—bad press. "Stand by for the four o'clock news. You guys doing another presser today?"

"Yeah. And we're putting out that Shane Dolan is a 'person of interest.' That's a bigger deal, so maybe Evan's little hissy fit will fly under the radar. Either way, it's going to be crazy here. Mind if I come over there?"

"No. You stay put. I'm on my way over."

"Uh, okay."

I could tell she knew something was up. I hurried over to the station and found Bailey at her desk. "Mind if we use the interview room?"

She looked puzzled, but led me to the nearest room and closed the door. "What's going on?"

I told her about the bug.

She slammed her hand down on the table. "Are you friggin' kidding me? What's next?"

"No. Do *not* ask that question, okay?" I rubbed my aching neck. "But there's nothing we can do. Graden's on it and we've got bigger fish to fry. Speaking of which, what's the deal with Evan? I get that he might be upset, but why on earth would he *tweet* that crap?"

We walked out of the interview room and headed to Bailey's desk.

"Who the hell knows?" Bailey said. "My guess? Evan's world blew up on him when he found out his buddy was a psycho killer. So now, anything's possible."

"And he's using the tweets to tell Logan he's not talking so—"

"So Logan won't feel the need to come back and shut him up. That's my take."

Which might not be that crazy, now that I thought about it. "From Logan's point of view, all he knows is we've named him as a person of interest. As far as he knows, no one could identify him. He was covered from head to toe. He doesn't know we spotted his tattoo on the video. So who could've pointed the finger at him?"

"The last person he spoke to who's still alive," Bailey said. "Which seems to be Evan."

"I'm not saying I believe Logan would risk coming after him. But I do get why Evan might be worried about it. We've got someone sitting on Evan's place, don't we?"

"We've got extra patrol, but it'll take some doing to get a car permanently stationed. We're stretched pretty thin."

Graden had gotten the chief to discreetly approve extra details for malls, government buildings, and some of the bigger venues around the city. It was a shot in the dark, but we had to do something. Getting an extra body assigned to one house on a full-time basis when there was no specific threat would've been hard under the best of circumstances—and these were the worst.

"I got hold of the shrinkers this morning," Bailey said. "They should be here any minute. And I had Nick print out all of Logan's emails." Bailey leaned in, her voice low. "We're going to tell them about the letter, right?"

I'd given this some thought. "I'd like to, but our conversations with the shrinks aren't privileged—"

"Jeez, don't you think they'd be willing to keep this under wraps?"

"They're probably cool, but we don't know for sure. If we're wrong and they sound the alarm, there'll be riots in the streets." Bailey gave a tight-lipped nod. "Let's at least hold off until we can talk to Graden about it again."

"Okay, but the sooner the better."

"Absolutely," I said. "I'm going to run to the snack bar." When the going gets tough, the tough pound chocolate. "Want anything?"

Bailey opted for a Snickers. I commended her good taste. I went for the Look! bar. I'd just gotten back when Nick sauntered over to Bailey's desk, wearing his usual cowboy boots and sexy smile. He eyed the candy. "Not that y'all need to get any sweeter, but those are some fine choices." He handed me a batch of pages. "Didn't find too many emails from Logan, and they only go back about ten months. That when they met?" I nodded. "Nothing remarkable crime-wise, but there you go."

"What about Otis's laptop?" Bailey asked. "Anything?"

"Not so far. Kid was a major gamer, but from what I've seen, his guns were all digital. And not all that much correspondence with Logan."

"So no weird writings?" I asked. Nick shook his head. "What about other pictures?"

"None that we care about. Some old ones of him and some junior high buddies at a paintball party. That's about as 'hot' as it gets."

"And nothing of interest on Logan's laptop, I take it?" Bailey asked.

"Nope. I printed out all his emails for the past year, though, just to show you." He handed Bailey a thick stack of paper. "Got some from Evan, a few from Caleb and a kid named Kenny. But it was all just routine boy stuff. Girls, school, movies, junk like that."

We thanked Nick. He tipped an imaginary cowboy hat and left. A few minutes later, Drs. Malloy and Shelby showed up. Bailey had managed to snag us a small conference room in a private corner of the building.

"I wanted to ask you a couple of questions about Evan." I told them about Evan's encounter with Logan the morning of the shooting, his reaction to the photo of Shane, and his recent tweeting that we'd been harassing him. I gave them Bailey's theory. "Do you think he's trying to show Logan he's not a threat?"

Michael Malloy nodded. "Seems likely. And probably your second suspect as well. Bailey's right about his world being rocked. If a buddy he trusted can turn out to be a murderer, especially on this scale, then anything's possible."

"And remember, Evan was in that gym too," Jenny said. "He's lucky to be alive, and he knows it. I agree with your assessment of Logan's point of view. From his standpoint, Evan might well appear to be his number one threat. Does that mean I think he would go after Evan? No. It's too big a risk. And it's not worth it. Evan's information wouldn't put Logan away. And much as I understand why Evan might be frightened by the revelation that Logan has teamed up with someone who looks as threatening as Shane, Evan's certainly no threat to Shane. He seemed to be truthful when he said he didn't know him?"

"He did," Bailey said.

"But we're being objective," Michael said. "Evan's psychological state is not conducive to objective thinking. Remember, all of these kids are extremely traumatized."

"Right," Jenny said. "Now imagine that on top of all that, you're the last living person to speak to Logan. And what he tells you strongly indicates he was about to commit a massacre. The emotional conflicts would be massive."

Michael nodded. "On the one hand, Evan feels guilty about not alerting anyone when Logan told him to skip school—"

"He does," I said. "Which is crazy. No one could've known—"

Jenny held up a hand. "Again, we're not talking about rational thinking here. And on the other hand, he's scared for his own safety, for all the reasons we've discussed. Added to that, believe it or not, he probably also feels guilty for telling you about his encounter with Logan—"

Bailey nodded. "For betraying his buddy."

"And they typically overestimate their own importance," Michael said. "To put it bluntly, they're self-centered. Evan's statement isn't huge in the grand scheme of things, but it is to him. And so he believes it must be to Logan—or maybe Shane—as well."

"Still strikes me as kind of paranoid, don't you think?" I asked.

Jenny tilted her head. "Is there such a thing as irrational fear when you're dealing with someone who's so irrationally violent?"

Touché.

I passed them the copies of all the email correspondence with Logan. "We'd like you to read these and get back to us by tonight or, at the latest, tomorrow morning with any ideas you may have about where Logan and his accomplice might be—"

Michael nodded. "I assume your people have already checked for any oblique references to a plan? Or some kind of code that might have been used?"

"Yes," I said. "There was nothing they could see."

Jenny frowned. "That's very, very odd. I've never heard of a case where there wasn't some evidence of preparation or planning. Typically written. Whether it's in the form of poems to a teacher, drawings of some kind, or posting on the Internet or in some kind of journal. This type of killer is usually a copious writer. And it usually begins months before the event. It's a form of ramping up, if you will. For a mass murderer—especially one as young as Logan—not to write or say anything about what he plans to do...it's extraordinary."

"But why would they want to write down their plans?" Bailey asked. "Why take the risk?"

Jenny nodded. "It does seem counterintuitive, doesn't it? But these killers live in their heads a great deal of the time. They get a lot of traction out of their fantasies. Writing, for them, is a way of savoring those fantasies. Plus—and this is an important point—much of the thrill for this type of killer is the sense of power. Power is the ultimate aphrodisiac for them. That's why the killings are almost always set up 'fish in a barrel' style. They want to master the situation and terrorize a captive audience. That's also why writing about their desires is perfect for them. When they write about their desires, they control it all: the means, the location, and the outcome."

"Writing or no, there had to have been a heck of a lot of planning," Bailey said. "They didn't just put that arsenal together over a long weekend."

"Oh, no doubt they'd been planning this for several months, if not a year," Jenny said. "I'm only saying that these killers need some outlet for all this homicidal energy that gets generated every time they think about what they plan to do. Writing usually provides that outlet."

"They had each other to talk to," I said. "Wouldn't that have siphoned off some steam?"

"Some," Michael said. "But they couldn't talk about it whenever or wherever they wanted. Understand that this killing was something they both thought about night and day, every single day. Writing is something one can do at any time. No one overhears it. And if they're careful, no one sees it. Talking is a different story."

"Right," Jenny said. "And given that there are no writings, it's difficult to believe this boy, Logan, showed absolutely nothing out of the ordinary in the months leading up to the crime."

"His friends did say he seemed wound pretty tight," Bailey said. "He'd pop off at little things. But how would that tip anyone off that he was planning something like this?"

"Yeah, exactly," I said. "What *would* tip you off? If a kid doesn't already have a track record for violent behavior—"

"And these killers seldom do—" Jenny said.

"Then what would you expect to see that would make you suspect a kid would do something like *this*?"

Jenny sighed. "That is the classic question in these cases. So Johnny got into a fight, or stole someone's cell phone. Or defaced school property. Why should that make us suspect he's building bombs in the basement?" Jenny shook her head. "We have never been able to answer that."

41

After the doctors left I started to pace. "You were right, we can't put it off. We've got to tell them about the letter. Is Graden still with the chief?"

"I'll find out."

We were about to head out to his office when Bailey's cell phone rang. She looked at the number and made a face. "It's one of the guys manning our tip line."

"That bad, huh?"

"Worse. This one really has the Looney Tunes coming out of the woodwork." She answered the phone and listened. After a few minutes, she pulled out her pen and notepad and wrote. When she ended the call, she held up her notepad. "Want to hear what I'm talking about?"

"Sure." I needed a good laugh.

Bailey read from her notes. "The second shooter is Justin Bieber. He and Logan are lovers." I chuckled. She raised an eyebrow at me. "Oh, it gets better." She continued reading. "The second shooter and mastermind is Alec Baldwin, and his next target is the paparazzi and tabloid reporters—"

"Go, Alec."

Bailey threw me a look and flipped a page on her notepad. "Logan is in a hotel in midtown Manhattan—"

"Ooh, the St. Regis? Maybe we need to go and check this one out ourselves."

"The caller didn't name the hotel. However, he did opine that Logan is a Gemini and that therefore the second shooter has to be a Scorpio. Our next caller swears he saw Logan in Deer Valley, Utah. Skiing." She turned another page. "Shall I go on?"

I shook my head. "I get the drift—no pun intended." Bailey gave me a sour look. I remembered they'd just released the information about Shane Dolan at the press conference this morning. "What about Shane Dolan? Any sightings of him?"

"More of the same. Nothing that makes any sense. But I've got them checking out every lead. At least those on this planet."

"I don't believe they left the state. Though I don't know why I think that."

"Because given what the shrinkers said, it makes the most sense," Bailey said. "They'll want to aim for places they're familiar with, where they can feel in control. And where they know the escape route. That is, assuming..."

They still planned to escape. We couldn't even predict *that* with freaks like this. I started to go through a mental checklist of the evidence we'd collected so far. "What've we got on the guns they dropped at the school?"

"They're not registered, big shock. The assault rifles were SBR AR fifteens. As for where they might've gotten the guns...Ed said it's going to be tough to narrow down." Bailey saw my frustration. "I know. He's moving as fast as he can. But bear in mind, it's entirely possible those guns went through a bunch of hands before Logan and company got hold of them." Bailey looked at me. "And I doubt that any of those hands belonged to law-abiding citizens."

"So beyond the initial sale from the manufacturer to the store, we might not ever figure out who sold to our guys."

"It's too soon to tell. But don't forget, Shane Dolan might be our buyer. If he was buying and selling on a regular basis, he probably has his own connect."

"Great. So all we have to do is find Dolan's connect. Piece of cake. Except we can't even find Dolan. How can it be that a shitbird like him doesn't have a rap sheet?"

"He does, I told you."

"Yeah, a DUI eight years ago." I started to pace again. Another possibility occurred to me. "They dropped two assault rifles and two small-caliber handguns at the scene, and they used up a ton of ammo. Unless they raided an armory, they'll need to buy more firepower if they're going to strike again. Don't you think?"

"Not necessarily. They might have a whole arsenal stashed away somewhere."

"Yeah, but where?" Was I reaching? I didn't think so. "Think about it: any place Logan had access to would pose a risk. Where would he put the guns? Not his house. And he didn't have any friends who seemed likely to hold on to a stash of weapons. If he or Shane had rented a storage locker, we'd know it by now—"

"Unless they used a fake name—"

"Come on, we're not dealing with the Mafia here. Where are they going to get ID solid enough to rent a storage locker? Those places are pretty tough these days." So many of the people in need of storage lockers were in dire shape—the kind of shape that made storage locker payments very low on the to-pay list—storage companies practically required a blood test. "I'm betting they'll need to score more guns and ammo—"

"Or not," Bailey said. "Who says they'll do it the same way next time? Maybe they'll go for some kind of IED or do it Oklahoma City style—"

Too many unknowns. I was making myself—and Bailey—crazy. "You going to check in with Dorian?" We hadn't heard any news about the evidence seized at the school. That probably meant there was nothing to report. But I was edgy with the need to make something happen.

"Yeah, I'll take the hit this time. You're too crazy."

A sign of true friendship. "I'll call Ed. See if he has anything new."

I called Ed Berry and got his voice mail, so I left a message. Bailey had done the same with Dorian. We headed to Graden's office and found out he was still with the chief. They had no ETA for him, so I headed back to my office.

I'd left the door open for Graden's detective so he could check out the bug. Graden had said he was going to have the detective put it back in place so as not to tip off whoever planted it. I looked under the table, and sure enough, there it was. I knew it was the smart thing to do, but it was a drag. My office, my sanctuary at work, had been violated. It seriously gave me the creeps. And I sure didn't want to talk to anyone with that thing listening in, so I put my phone on vibrate and spent the next couple of hours plowing through the reports that'd been generated so far. It was almost five o'clock before Ed called me back.

"Say, slugger, just got your message," he said. "Guess you're looking for some good news."

"Nah, why would I do a silly thing like that?" The bug couldn't pick up his end of the conversation, could it? No, of course it couldn't. But just knowing it was there, listening, drove me crazy.

"Good, 'cause I don't have any. The serial numbers have all been defaced—"

"Defaced? How—"

"With acid. Surprisingly sophisticated for a teenager."

But not so surprising for a gun nut like Shane.

Ed continued. "And to answer your next question, yeah, it is strange that all of them were removed the same way."

"How old are the weapons?" Pedro had said the thirty-eight Shane was trying to sell looked new.

"Not old, but I couldn't say they all looked brand-spanking-new either." He sighed. "I won't lie to you, no serial numbers means life just got a lot tougher for you and me."

Would we ever catch a break in this damn case? Especially with the threat that hung over our heads, the dead ends were making me want to pull my hair out. Ed didn't have anything else to add so I thanked him and dialed Bailey's number, but at that moment, my cell vibrated. It was Dr. Jenny.

"I've read the emails and conferred with Michael," she said. "He agrees with my assessment, so if you like, I can give you our conclusions. We can do it on the phone, or in your office—"

"Uh, can you hang on, Jenny?" Neither of those options was going to work. I called Vanderputz's secretary and asked if we could use the eighteenth-floor conference room. I knew that couldn't be bugged. They swept it twice a day. I got the okay and told Jenny where to meet us; then I called Bailey.

She said she'd tracked down Graden. "Are you in your office?" she asked.

"Yeah, so don't—"

"Got it. He says we should tell the shrinks. I'll be there in ten." She ended the call.

I tossed my phone on the desk and looked over my shoulder. That bug…I swore I could feel it staring at me.

42

Half an hour later the three of us convened around the table in the conference room. Jenny put on a pair of black-framed reading glasses to consult her notes. "We don't have a great deal to go on here. Neither Michael nor I are code crackers"—she looked up and gave a little smile—"but there's nothing we saw that alerted us to any secret language or code being used. The emails were largely about school or girls." She took off her glasses. "None of it struck us as unusual in the least."

"So their relationship was fairly superficial," I said.

"That's the way it looks."

"Now that you've read those emails, do you feel any differently about why he tweeted that we were harassing him?"

"No, we've gone through all the possible explanations and I don't see anything in these emails that would let me narrow it down to any one in particular. Anything else you'd like to discuss about Evan?"

I shook my head. We'd heard enough about him. It was time to get down to the heart of the matter. "We need to share some information with you that you cannot discuss outside this office. Not even with Michael."

I'd made a copy of the letter—just one because I didn't want to risk its getting lost or lifted from my office. Paranoid? Maybe. But better paranoid than sorry.

When she finished reading the letter, she took off her glasses and said nothing for several moments. "I suppose I should've expected that they'd seek out new targets. It's just...I've never seen anything like this before." Jenny put her hand to her forehead.

I gave her a moment, then leaned in. "What we need more than anything is to figure out where they're most likely to strike next. The more you can tell us about him, the better our chances of predicting his next target."

Jenny nodded. "He—and I say 'he' because this sounds very male—appears to be a classic psychopath. Grandiose, manipulative, completely non-empathic." She looked at me. "But you already know that, don't you? I'll bet you were shocked at how he managed to drill down on your particular weaknesses, weren't you?"

I was shocked that she knew that. "Completely."

Jenny nodded. "They're empathically and emotionally stunted, but even so, they often do have an uncanny ability to suss out someone's weak spot. It's a survival skill for them, and they start honing it from an early age. When most children are learning how to get along with others, make friends, and show affection, the psychopaths—who are emotionally incapable of those things—are figuring out how to manipulate others in order to get what they want."

That certainly fit our letter writer to a T. "But if that's the case, then how come no one saw all that in Logan? Wouldn't it be pretty obvious?"

"No, not necessarily. The smarter they are, the better they are at observing how others respond to social cues and mimicking normal behavior. That doesn't mean some people won't figure out that there's something 'off' about them. You can't fool all the people all of the time. And in any case, we can't be sure that Logan wrote this letter. It seems to me that the letter writer was the alpha in this duo, but there are no absolutes."

"So the person who wrote the letter might be the second shooter," I said.

"It's possible." Jenny frowned and picked up the letter. "But about this parting shot, 'Do your job, you'll stop us. Fail and we will go on. And on.' I don't want to overstep my bounds. I'm not your therapist, Rachel. But I want to be sure that you don't get taken in by this effort to blame you for anything that might happen."

I shifted in my seat, suddenly aware that my back hurt. "I'm not."

Jenny observed me silently for a few moments. "I believe you have a particular...sensitivity when it comes to guilt." I started to respond, but Jenny held up a hand. "Yes, I know it's common. Many people—especially in law enforcement—carry the weight of the world on their shoulders. But given your background, I'd guess that you have a particularly acute tendency to believe you're responsible whenever something goes wrong. So please try to remember that you're not to blame for what these shooters do. Only they are."

Her words reminded me of the feeling I'd had when I'd read the letter—an all-too-familiar heaviness in my chest, the coil of anxiety that wound around my gut. But I was in no mood to share. "I don't have any doubt about that, Jenny."

"Not consciously, no. But subconsciously, you might. And that alone I don't worry about. It's not the worst thing anyone's ever had to deal with. But you're under enormous pressure to catch these killers. When that pressure is added to your subconscious motivators, you may find yourself impelled to take undue risks." Jenny gave me a stern look. "And that's what I worry about."

I tried for a smile to lighten the moment. "So I'll move my toaster off the edge of the bathtub."

No one laughed.

43

After Jenny left, Bailey reported on the uni interviews with Logan's outer circle of friends. "None of them ever heard of anyone named Shane, and the unis had zero impression they were holding anything back. We can catch Caleb at home right now. I've got a call in to Kenny to see if he'll meet us there."

I filled her in on my call with Ed. Bailey agreed that the way the serial numbers had been burned off pointed to someone like Shane. Nice to know, but a minor detail that only left us more frustrated and miserable. With no line on either Shane's or Logan's whereabouts and disaster drawing closer with every second, it was all we could do to keep from punching the walls.

We headed back to my office so I could pick up my coat and scarf. I locked the door behind me, though I don't know why. It obviously didn't do any good.

"So we're not going to use your office for the duration?"

"No way. Not until they figure out who planted that thing." It depressed me, so I turned my thoughts back to the case at hand. As we headed out to the elevators, I thought of another question I meant to ask Jenny. "Why do you suppose they addressed the letter to me? Why not you? Or Dale Campbell?"

"Because you're the famous one."

It kind of made sense. The geeky nerd who wanted the world to know he was all-powerful. And Shane, the rebel without a clue, out to thumb his nose at authority in every way possible. Yeah, that could work.

We made it to Caleb's house in record time. His mother, a pleasant-looking brunette on the attractively plump side, greeted us with a worried look. "Has something else happened?"

"No, ma'am," Bailey said. "We're just gathering information. Thank you for letting us impose on you like this—"

"Oh, my goodness, of course. Anything I can do. Kenny just got here. They're in the living room. Can I get you anything?" We declined and she led us to a cozy room, where an inviting fire was crackling in the fireplace. Seeing it made me aware of how bone weary I was. I pushed the feeling aside.

Caleb, the pocket-protector nerd, and Kenny, a tall, handsome boy with shoulder-length blonde hair, were a study in contrasts. But seeing their easy body language, I got the impression they were pals.

We cut to the chase. "Do either of you know a person named Shane Dolan?" I asked.

"No," Caleb said. "Why?"

"Kenny?"

"I know a guy named Shane," he said. "Not sure about the last name. Maybe if you had a picture—"

Bailey held out her cell phone. The boys studied the photo.

Caleb shook his head. His expression said we may as well have asked if he'd been hanging around with Kim Jong Un.

Kenny didn't hesitate either. "No," he said. "The dude I know is my age. Who's this?"

"We think he might be a friend of Logan's," Bailey said. "Do you remember ever hearing him mention the name?"

"No," Caleb said. "Never."

Kenny shook his head. I had no sense they were hiding anything. I had one last question. "Have either of you talked to Evan lately?"

Kenny said he hadn't, but Caleb licked his lips and began to rub his palms on his pant legs.

"Caleb?" I asked.

He looked down. "He called me yesterday. Said you guys took his laptop and kept bugging him even though he told you he didn't know anything."

"How did he sound?" I asked.

"Stressed. Freaked."

"And what did you tell him?" Bailey asked.

Caleb shrugged. "I told him you guys were talking to everyone. Seems like there are cops at someone's house every day. So I told him he's not the only one."

That was certainly true. "What did he say to that?" I asked.

"Not much. I thought maybe hearing about how everyone was getting the same treatment would make him realize it was no big deal. But then I saw his tweets about you guys harassing him, so…"

"Yeah," I said. "Maybe not."

We asked how they were doing—not great, but as well as could be expected—and ended the interview.

Bailey dropped me off at the Biltmore, and I decided a hot bath might relax me enough to take a full breath. The double shot of Dalwhinnie didn't hurt either.

Graden called around nine o'clock sounding every bit as tightly wound as I was. We tried to keep it light, but the conversation kept stalling as our minds wandered back to the case, so we gave up and said good night. For the thousandth time, I thanked the gods that I'd found someone who understood the all-consuming nature of the job.

I set out my clothes so I could jump into them in the morning, and put myself to bed by ten o'clock with a murder mystery set in London. All the descriptions of fog and damp made me slide farther and farther under the covers, till I was practically holding the book above my head. Finally, I got sleepy enough to put it down and turn off the light.

When the hotel phone rang Saturday morning, I looked at the clock. Six a.m. What the hell? I'd told Bailey I'd be downstairs waiting for her at seven thirty. I snatched up the phone. "I *said* I'd be on time—"

"Get dressed and get downstairs!" Bailey sounded tense. "I'll tell you when I see you."

I turned on the news as I got ready, expecting to hear about another shooting, but there was nothing. What could it be? The question whirred through my brain on an endless loop. When I got downstairs fifteen minutes later, Bailey was already there waiting for me. I hurried to the car and got in. It was still dark outside and icy cold.

"What? Tell me," I said, as I pulled on my seat belt. Bailey jumped on the gas, throwing me into the dash before I could get it buckled. "If you're trying to kill me, just use your gun, it'll be quicker."

"Sorry," she muttered. She didn't speak again until we'd merged onto the 101. "I got a call from the Topanga station. Evan's gone."

"Gone…how?"

"He ran away. There's no sign of forced entry or a struggle. His dad knocked on his bedroom door to wake him up and got no answer…"

"You've got to be kidding me!" I put my head in my hands. "Maybe we should have—"

"What? Slapped an ankle monitor on him?"

Bailey was probably right. We couldn't justify a twenty-four/seven tail on him. But that didn't stop me from thinking we should've seen it coming.

Bailey grabbed my shoulder. "I know what you're doing and you can stop it right now—"

"Caleb told us he was getting weird, he was tweeting—"

"So fucking what? Kids bitch and tweet a thousand times a day."

True, but that didn't make it feel any better.

Fog had blanketed the Valley by the time we pulled onto Evan's street. The flashing blue-and-red strobe from a dozen squad cars glowed eerily through the mist, and the officers guarding the house looked almost ghostly. I saw a news truck parked at the corner. The press was here. Already. News of Evan's flight would go nationwide within the hour.

Bailey left her car in the middle of the street and badged us through the crowd. Evan's father was in the front room, standing nose to nose with a uniformed sergeant, poking his finger at the sergeant's chest. "If they'd given him protection instead of haranguing him constantly, this would *never* have happened!"

The sergeant bore the tirade stoically. "Sir, I can understand you're upset. But we need to process this scene for evidence. Every second I stand here is another second wasted. Now, if you'll—"

Cutter spotted us. "This is all your fault! You come here, you disrupt my house, you harass my son. I'm going to sue you and your whole useless department!"

Bailey took a deep breath and spoke slowly in her Jedi voice. "Mr. Cutter, I am very sorry that this happened. It is your absolute right to file a complaint if that's what you choose to do. But right now, we need to gather the evidence as quickly and efficiently as possible so we can find your son. We'll need your cooperation. I'd like you to talk to a police officer and give all the details you can about where Evan might've gone. Can you do that?"

Cutter was still breathing hard, the veins in his neck stretched taut as piano wire, but he stopped yelling. Bailey stood and waited for him to respond to her question. Finally, he gave the barest of nods. As many times as I've seen her do it, it never ceases to amaze me the way she can calm anyone, no matter how rabid. Bailey asked one of the unis to sit down with John Cutter; then we moved down the hall to Evan's bedroom, where crime scene techs were already at work. That was about as fast as I'd ever seen a team arrive.

The sergeant joined us. "The father said he didn't hear anything last night. Didn't know the boy was gone until he came down for breakfast and knocked on his door."

I hadn't noticed there was an upstairs when I was here before. "Where's the staircase?" I asked.

The sergeant pointed to our far right. I walked in that direction and saw a short hallway that led to a flight of stairs. It looked like an add-on. I went back to Evan's doorway—no one but the techs were allowed in right now—and craned my neck to get a glimpse of his room. The only thing that looked out of place was the window screen, which seemed to be missing. The window was cranked open. I pointed to it and asked the sergeant, "That how he got out?"

"Seems so. Mom says he always slept with it open."

The window was fairly large, four feet by three feet, and it gave easy access to the backyard, which was encircled by a high, whitewashed wooden fence. Which meant Evan's escape was perfectly shielded from view. And of course, it had been dark and too early for anyone to be out and about. The unis would door-knock everyone in the vicinity, but the odds of finding any witnesses in a quiet neighborhood like this were lousy. "Is there a side gate that lets out to the street?" The sergeant nodded. "What happened to the screen? Did you find it?"

"Outside on the ground," the sergeant said.

"Did you call Dorian?" I asked Bailey.

"First thing," she said. "Said she'd be here to make sure they didn't miss anything."

"They won't," the sergeant said. "These guys are the best in the business."

"You haven't met Dorian," I said.

"Sure I have. Who do you think trained 'em?" The sergeant headed back to the front of the house.

I scanned the bedroom again. "I can't imagine they'll find anything of use, but I guess we've got to try." I heard the rumble of approaching news vans. "This is going to hit the airwaves in three, two, one—"

"Probably already has."

"Maybe this time we'll luck out and get better tips than 'Justin Bieber did it.'"

Bailey sighed. "Yeah, maybe this time they'll tag Taylor Swift."

44

We found Mikayla Cutter on the front porch shivering under her long down coat, her face swollen and blotchy with grief. I'd expected her to be holed up in her bedroom, where she wouldn't have to see the swarm of cops and reporters, but she was staring past it all, into the farther reaches of the Valley. Mikayla glanced at us, then turned back to her vigil. "He can't be far, can he?" Her voice was small and far away.

"No," I said. I reached out and squeezed her arm. "We're going to do everything we can to get him home as soon as possible, I promise."

Mikayla bit her lip and nodded as tears leaked out of the sides of her eyes. We wove our way through the police line toward Bailey's car. By the time we hit the freeway, the fog had lifted and left behind a fresh, clean blue sky. "We'd better get our shrinks in on this."

Bailey nodded. "And we need to tell Dr. Malloy about the letter."

I stared down the freeway at the sea of red taillights. We'd hit a nasty traffic snarl dead center. With the threat of another shooting hanging over our heads, no clue where to find the killers, and now Evan's disappearance, being trapped in traffic was so agonizing it made my stomach churn. "Can this goddamned case get any more bizarre?"

Bailey winced. "Must you? Really?"

She was right. I definitely should know better than to tempt fate with a question like that.

As we inched along, I thought about where Evan might have gone. "Are the unis digging into Evan's background?"

"Of course."

"God, if anything happens to him..."

"Don't go there. We'll find him. We have to."

"But when Logan hears he's running—"

"I said, don't go there."

Logan knew Evan better than we did, which meant the odds that he'd find Evan before we did were pretty damn good. And he'd never have a more risk-free chance to kill Evan. By running away, Evan had managed to put himself in a thousand times greater peril.

It felt like a knife was twisting in my stomach. I wrapped my arms around my torso and tried to catch my breath. We should have given Evan protection. If we'd had a car posted in his driveway, this would never have happened. I should've insisted on it. This was my fault, all my fault.

Bailey grabbed my arm. "I told you to stop it. We had no way of knowing Evan would pull a stunt like this—"

"The shrinks warned us he was unstable. Hell, all these kids are off-kilter right now. We should've had someone sit on his house."

"We were trying, remember? Besides, it wouldn't have helped. Evan's window faced the backyard. The cop wouldn't have seen a thing." Bailey sighed. "There's only so much we can do."

I could hear the logic in what Bailey said. It just didn't change the way I felt. But I also knew I didn't have the luxury of wallowing in my guilt. We had two killers out there bent on committing an atrocity that might well eclipse Oklahoma City. Finding Evan was a job for the Valley Division, who knew the territory best. Evan couldn't have gotten far. Not on foot. Besides, the biggest threat to Evan was Logan. Capturing him was the best protection we could give Evan right now.

I forced myself to focus on the matter at hand. Even if we were right about Shane being the second shooter, we hadn't had any tips worth diddly-squat regarding his whereabouts. Same for Logan.

"What drives me nuts is, I think we're right about them still being close by." I folded my arms and stared out the window. "With their faces all over the news, and all our manpower, how come no one has seen them?"

Bailey sighed. "I know."

Logan's parents had been questioned ad nauseam about where he might be hiding. Nothing had panned out. Bailey and I tossed ideas back and forth till we were nearly downtown, but the maddening truth was that with no leads of any substance, we were just churning.

I pulled out my cell phone. "I'm going to set up a meeting with the shrinks to give them the update." Though by the time we saw them, they'd undoubtedly already have heard about it on the news. "Maybe they'll have some bright ideas."

"See if we can meet at Jenny's," Bailey said.

The Bradbury Building where Jenny had her office was an iconic landmark. With its old-fashioned cage lift, art deco decor, and zigzagging wooden staircases, it had the kind of historic charm that sadly was rare in Los Angeles. But more important, it was a quieter, more private place to meet.

I made the calls and found both doctors ready and willing to meet there in half an hour.

45

Twenty-five minutes later we were climbing the first flight of stairs. We didn't want to wait for the elevator. The second floor was occupied by Internal Affairs, and Bailey glowered at the door as we walked past it and headed for the stairway to the fourth floor. I was tired after having been yanked out of bed at six a.m., but we'd been cooped up in the car for so long that the climb felt good. The door to Jenny's office stood open, so we walked in.

Jenny had wisely carried through the art deco motif with a mahogany reception desk, a large fern in the corner, and an Oriental rug. She even had a wood ceiling fan. A nice touch. Michael was already there, sitting in one of the comfy-looking overstuffed chairs that surrounded a circular table a few feet away from Jenny's desk. Jenny sat across from him. They both held steaming mugs of coffee. The classic leather couch, complete with headrest pillow and blankets folded at the foot, occupied the wall to our right. "So you guys still use those?" I nodded toward the couch.

"Some patients prefer it, believe it or not," Jenny said. She gestured to a burr-grinding Cuisinart in the bookcase near the table. "Can I interest you...?"

We gratefully accepted, and I thanked them for coming in on a Saturday.

Michael held up a hand. "Please. I think we both knew our nights and weekends would be kaput on this case."

When we were all settled in, Bailey asked if they'd heard about Evan running away. They had.

Michael frowned. "It does and doesn't surprise me. We've spoken about how destabilizing this trauma has been for all the students. But

Evan has the unique burdens of guilt and fear that we've discussed before. Given all of his stressors, that Evan would run away is not that surprising—"

"Or if he'd become completely reclusive it wouldn't have shocked me either," Jenny said. "But this does increase the pressure to find Logan. I agree, Evan's flight could give Logan exactly the kind of free shot he might've hoped for."

"But Logan and his buddy might be too busy with their next hit to worry about tracking Evan down," I said.

"Their next hit?" Michael said. "You have some evidence of future plans?"

Bailey told Michael about the letter. His eyes widened. "My God." He set down his mug and rubbed his face. But when he lowered his hands, his face was still pale. "I've never heard of a thing like this before. It's... incredible." He stared into his coffee mug. After a few moments, he looked up. "These shooters—or at least your writer—obviously wants recognition. He wants to be famous. But if their identity is revealed, they'll be caught. And as you said, they're not done yet. So since he can't get public recognition for himself, he gets it vicariously by attaching to you through this letter. I'd expect that until these shooters are ready to stop, you'll get more such letters. You agree, Jenny?"

"Seems likely. The only reason to write that letter is to make sure they get the 'credit' for future attacks, so no one will think it's the work of a copycat—"

"Well, not the only reason," Michael said. "In writing the letter he also gets to play with your head, Rachel. Torturing and manipulating someone who's famous is a trophy unto itself. So he gets a twofer."

"I agree," Jenny said. "As I said before, this letter writer is a psychopath, and they're typically fixated on power and control—"

"Which only reinforces the likelihood that the other party is the weaker one, the follower," Michael said. "A pleaser who participates in the killing in part to perform for the leader."

I stared out the window, which gave a view of the side of a building. "Is it possible they might choose to stop at some point, just try to escape?"

"Very doubtful," Michael said. "I predict they'll keep going until they see capture is imminent. Then, they'll either commit suicide or force a police officer to kill them. They'll want to go out in a blaze of so-called glory."

Jenny nodded. "I don't believe they intend to survive this."

"That willingness to die," I said. "For me, that's one of the hardest parts to get. You talk about a 'blaze of glory'...but they won't be around to enjoy it. It almost feels like they don't realize that dead is dead."

Jenny and Michael exchanged a look. "Jenny and I have a slight disagreement about this," he said. "I think mortality isn't real to teenagers—particularly boys. It might be yet another by-product of the undeveloped frontal lobe connections. And criminals with a homicidal pathology like these shooters take it one step further. Orchestrating their own death is the ultimate form of power and control. But beyond that, regardless of age, their focus is on the moment. They fill their minds with the thrill of their homicidal plans and all the notoriety they're going to receive. They're not thinking about their own demise."

"I definitely agree teenagers have a tendency to think they're made of rubber," Jenny said. "Until something really bad happens, they don't grasp their own vulnerability. So death is abstract to them. Something that happens to others, not them. But in the case of these killers, I don't think it's just a failure to grasp the reality of their own death. I think they place little value on life in general. Including their own."

"We talked about the fact that this case bears similarities to Columbine," I said. "Obviously, they knew about that shooting, so is it likely they studied other shootings as well?" It had occurred to me they might aim for similar targets so they could keep proving how much "better" they were than those shooters.

"Oh, of course," Jenny said. "I'm sure they studied many others of that ilk: the Virginia Tech shooter, the Aurora shooter, and so forth. Just as Adam Lanza, the Sandy Hook shooter, studied Anders Behring Breivik, the Norwegian mass murderer. And as Harris and Klebold studied other mass murderers—among them, Timothy McVeigh. In this way they're similar to celebrity stalkers." She gestured to the coffeepot. "Refill?" We all accepted.

"Celebrity stalkers?" I asked. "But they don't commit suicide like the school shooters—"

Jenny nodded. "No, not usually. And the school shooters typically write about their crimes for quite a while before committing them, and the celebrity stalkers don't necessarily—though they do often write to their celebrity targets. All that's true. But those distinctions are relatively superficial. At their emotional core, they have some important things in common."

Michael tapped my arm. "That's why the letter was addressed to you, Rachel. You're the one everyone saw on television—"

"Right," Jenny said. "So fame is a motivating factor for both classes of criminals. And in neither instance do the killers really intend to escape. It would defeat a key goal, which is to become famous. Mark David Chapman, John Lennon's killer, remained at the scene reading a copy of *The Catcher in the Rye.* And Robert Bardo, who killed Rebecca Schaeffer, fled the scene, but all he did was run home. He got caught and confessed that same day. By the way, he carried *The Catcher in the Rye* with him when he did the shooting, in imitation of Chapman. No, there's no question these two classes of criminals have some commonalities. Just as those celebrity stalkers are looking for vicarious fame, so too are these school shooters. The big distinguishing factor is that this type of mass murderer is primarily seeking power and control, proof of his superiority. For him, fame is a welcome by-product because it advertises his 'prowess.'"

"But I want to interject here," Michael said. "We're not equating your shooters—or at least the letter writer—with someone like that Aurora shooter. As I recall, there was some evidence that the Aurora shooter suffered a true mental illness—as opposed to your letter writer, who obviously has a personality disorder."

"Right," Jenny said. "It's fairly rare that the mentally ill act out violently toward others. And certainly not in a planned attack like this. That'll be an important point to make for the jury if we get to trial—"

"*When* we get to trial," Bailey said firmly.

We all nodded, but it was more a gesture of faith than belief.

Jenny pulled out a binder that had been lying open on the table. "I've been reviewing the most recent articles published on young mass killers—"

"Including your own?" Michael looked at Bailey and me. "She's published two of the leading articles on the subject." He saw the surprise on our faces and nodded. "Jenny's not the world's greatest self-promoter."

Jenny waved him off and continued. "And if you want to know more about the celebrity stalker mentality, you might want to consult with Gavin de Becker."

I smiled. "I know Gavin, and if you'll pardon the irony, I'm a big fan." Gavin de Becker was the world's foremost authority on stalking, and he'd been incredibly helpful to me when I handled my first stalking murder shortly after I'd joined Special Trials.

"Anyway," Jenny continued, "like the celebrity stalkers, these mass murderers study and copy each other. And, as in your case, even compete with one another."

A wave of revulsion washed over me at the thought of this despicable "competition." "It's amazing to me that two psychos like this wound up finding each other."

"I'm not sure they're necessarily cut from the same cloth," Michael said.

I flashed on the murder case back in the twenties involving Leopold and Loeb. Two very different personalities who'd committed a killing neither one would have done alone. They too were invested in proving their superiority. "Then you think it was the combination of two different kinds of crazy that led to this?" I asked. "That none of this would've happened if the two puzzle pieces hadn't found each other?"

"I think it's very likely," Michael said. "But we'll need a lot more information before we go there."

"And we have more pressing issues right now," Jenny said. "Rachel, I think you were already headed in this direction: I suggest we focus on the sites of other publicly notorious mass shootings as the next possible targets. I'll compile a list for you and note those I think would be most attractive to these shooters. It will be generic since we don't have much personal information but..."

I nodded. "It's better than nothing." I looked down at my half-empty cup of coffee. "You both seem very certain these guys plan to die rather than be captured."

Jenny nodded.

"Most definitely," Michael said.

I'd thought that was fine by me. But now, hearing that's what they wanted, I swore to myself that I'd find a way to make sure they never got their "blaze of glory." I wanted them caught and caged like the rabid animals they were.

46

My cell phone rang on our way back to the station. I looked at the number, then at Bailey, who was navigating the downtown traffic. "You won't believe this. It's Dorian."

"*She's* calling *us?*" Bailey's jaw dropped. "I think the earth just started turning backward."

As I hit talk to take the call, I whispered to Bailey, "I should tell her not to bother me." Bailey clamped her lips together to keep from laughing.

"Knight here."

"Tell who not to bother you?" Dorian's familiar growl was a reassuring touch point in this Bizarro World case.

"Uh, the press, sorry. I was talking to Bailey."

Dorian proceeded without further preamble. "I finished at the Cutter house. The ground under the bedroom window was a muddy mess. Too damp to see much of anything. But I might have something on the concrete walkway leading down the side yard and out to the street."

"Recent shoe prints?"

"That's what I'm hoping they are. Tell you when I know more. But I can say for sure that there's only one set of prints. Consistent with the kid taking a powder. I know we've got to rule it out, but I'm not seeing any evidence of foul play."

Not that there'd been much doubt about it, but the possibility of abduction had to be addressed. "Think you can get some idea of the shoe size?"

"That would be nice, wouldn't it? I'll let you know."

"Thanks, Dor—" Dead air. She was gone. I told Bailey what she said.

"I'd guess Dorian already asked the sergeant to get some of Evan's shoes from his parents, but I'll call the sergeant. Make sure he remembers."

"That reminds me, what about Logan's folks? I know the unis have been getting what they can out of them, but maybe we should try talking to them ourselves—"

"No, kiddo, *we* don't need to do anything with the Jarvises. They wouldn't spit on us if we were on fire." True. Telling them their son was a mass murderer hadn't endeared us to them. "And it hasn't just been unis. I've had Harrellson talk to them too. He found out Logan has cousins in Utah, but we already checked them out. No way Logan ran to them. They'd have tied him to the back of a truck and dragged him to the police station."

"I'm glad you got Harrellson."

"One of the few good things about this case: I get what I want."

Harrellson was a great detective. Light on his feet for a man his size—six feet by three feet if he was an inch, which explained his penchant for suspenders—he was as smart, funny, and quick as they come, and he never missed a lick.

Bailey pulled into the parking lot at the PAB. When we got back to her desk, she called the sergeant in charge at Evan's house. It was Saturday, but you couldn't tell. All hands were on deck, and they probably would be until we had the shooters in custody.

I sat down at a vacant desk nearby and called Eric on his cell. "You heard about Evan?" I asked.

"Yeah," he said. "Terrible, just terrible. They got anything yet?"

I told him what Dorian had so far. "And Bailey's checking on the door-knock. We need to get out ahead of this somehow, but we just keep hitting dead ends. It's making me crazy."

"Rachel, remember, it's always like this until it isn't. We run into walls until we find the door. All you can do is keep digging. In the meantime, don't make yourself any crazier than you have to. I have faith in you. You'll figure it out. You always do."

I appreciated the support. I did. And I'd have found it reassuring but for one tiny fact: Eric didn't know about the threatening letter yet.

A pang of guilt made my throat tighten. I wanted to tell him, but I'd promised Graden I wouldn't. I said nothing. When I ended the call, Bailey was off the phone.

"Just got the report from the unis who covered Evan's 'hood," she said. "Nothing from the door-knock. One of the unis contacted the paper deliverer, who said he thought he saw a white Corolla around the corner from Evan's house around five a.m., but the uni didn't think it was solid. Everyone in that neighborhood knows Logan drove a white Corolla."

"The paperboy didn't get a license plate?"

Bailey shook her head. "Another reason I'm not buying it. If Logan's car had been around, we'd have more than this one sighting. But Nick's got something for us. He's on his way over."

A few minutes later, he appeared holding a printout. He threw it down on Bailey's desk. "There's the reason you haven't seen anything exciting in Logan's emails."

It was a few paragraphs of very fine print. "Enlighten me so I don't have to strain my eyes," she said.

"Sorry. I always set it to eight-point font to save paper."

"You're a tree hugger?" I raised an eyebrow.

"Like to hug lots of things." Nick gave me a sly grin. I folded my arms and tried not to smile. Nick continued. "This email must have been written right when they first met. It was sent about the same time. Logan tells Evan not to put anything in an email he wouldn't want the world to see because there's no way to really hide it. Says the government is intercepting everything and keeping it in this huge storage place under a mountain in Utah. He's got a link to an article that claims the government can intercept everyone's email and that they plan to start real soon. Logan says they've probably already been doing it for a while."

I picked up the printout. "Is that for real?"

"It might be. I know the government wants to be able to grab whatever whenever they want. Now does that mean the government's interested in two high school kids' bullshit? Probably not. But ain't it typical of teenagers to think so?"

It was. And it did explain why nothing incriminating showed up in

Logan's email. After Nick left, we worked on our next move. With no solid leads, it wasn't easy.

"What do we have on Logan's past?" I asked.

"So far we've only gone back to the beginning of high school, but it shouldn't be hard to go back further," Bailey said. "And remember, Shane was in the military. So we've got military records and the records from the VA. They're pulling it all together. We'll have a full report soon."

"But nothing that gave us any leads on where he might be?" Bailey shook her head. "Well, since we've got time and no better ideas, may as well go back further on Logan. Hit middle school and elementary school." I thought about what Jenny had told me during an earlier phone conversation. "The underlying point of these shootings is to feel powerful, superior."

"And to get famous."

"Yeah, but according to the shrinks, power and control is the key. It was all over that letter."

"True," Bailey said. "So if school was a place where he got tweaked about feeling inferior or weak—"

"Then it becomes a proving ground. But it's also a pragmatic thing. Logan knows the layout, and it's a relatively easy place to score a high body count—'fish in a barrel' style. Plus, it's where other shooters staged their scenes. So if they're looking to beat out the other killers, that's the optimal target."

"Then Logan's next target might be one of his past schools—"

"An elementary school. Or even a middle school." Both were the sites of previous mass murders.

Bailey's cell rang. She looked at the number and rolled her eyes. "The tip line, God help us." She answered the call. But this time, she sat up and stared straight ahead, her gaze intense. After taking a few notes, she ended the call and swiveled her chair toward me. "Finally, a real one." She consulted her notes. "Someone who fits the description of Shane Dolan was sighted up in Red Bluff—"

"Where the hell is that?"

"North of Sacramento. Up near Cottonwood."

"Where was he?"

"Filling up at a gas station. They didn't get the plate. But they did give a description of the car." She picked up her notepad. "A blue Volkswagen Jetta with body damage to the right rear fender."

We grinned and bumped fists. "We have ignition."

I couldn't believe how good it felt to finally get a break.

Bailey's cell buzzed. "Text from Nick. They figured out where the letter was mailed." She picked up her desk phone and punched in the number.

I sat up. If we could pin down where Logan—or the second shooter—had mailed the letter, we'd have another area to search. It was a very brief conversation. Bailey didn't look happy. "It was sent from Boulder, Colorado."

"Boulder?" I'd been sure he was still here, in L.A.

"It doesn't necessarily mean they're in Boulder. They might just have someone there who was willing to mail the letter."

And finding that person would be like looking for a needle in a haystack. A haystack the size of... Boulder, Colorado. I sighed. After the tip about Shane, I'd thought we might finally be on a roll. Two steps forward...

47

With no known ties between Logan and Boulder, the letter was a dead end. I'd had enough of those to last me a lifetime. I went back to the sighting of Shane Dolan. "They didn't see anyone with him? Or did the PR say?"

PR, person reporting. "He didn't notice anyone else. But the suspect was pumping gas, so our PR probably only noticed him because he was standing outside the car. I'd guess our tipster didn't bother to look inside the car once he recognized Shane."

"Assuming it *was* Shane."

Bailey sighed and nodded. "But his picture's been everywhere, so we've got reason to hope. I'm sending Harrellson up there with a couple of unis. If it's a righteous tip, he'll run it to ground."

Harrellson was going to have a lot of miles on him before this was over. "Okay."

Bailey hit a key to wake up her computer and pulled up the report. "But there is something we can do in the meantime. I've got the names and locations of Logan's junior high and elementary school. They're both local, so we could—"

"Say no more." I stood up and grabbed my purse. We were looking for personal information on Logan. Something to tell us whether he'd had an experience at either school that might motivate him to stage another shooting there. But the incident we were looking for might only be something a teacher would remember under questioning—it might not have been significant enough to make it into any records. It was probably something a team of unis could handle, but we'd lose our minds if we didn't get out and do something. "We'll have to see if they'll make time for us on a Saturday, but that's a great idea."

Bailey raised an eyebrow. "But first let's see if we can score you a Xanax, so you don't make them hide under the table."

I looked at my watch. "Come on, let's move. It's after two. Let's catch those teachers before they decide to have a life."

Bailey looked like she wanted to stuff a red ball in my mouth, but we both knew every minute that passed brought us closer to another atrocity. It wasn't a matter of if. It was a matter of when. And when was likely to be very soon. She placed calls to each of the principals. The principal of Platt Junior High answered first. She told us to come in to the school. She'd round up all the teachers she could find. We trotted out to Bailey's car, and within seven minutes, we were bombing down the 101 freeway.

Platt Junior High was a low-profile, almost country-looking little school with colorfully painted walls—some with cartoon-style murals featuring flowers, insects, and animals; others in solid vibrant hues of red, purple, and green. The overall effect was cheery, if a little on the young side for middle schoolers.

And Principal Marion Jenks seemed more like someone's cookie-baking mom than the head of a junior high. Short and round, she was dressed casually in slacks and a heavy sweater. She ushered us into her office. "Just call me Marion." Her warm, relaxed smile soothed my frayed nerves. "Logan's teachers were all happy to come in, and they said they'd stay for as long as it takes. So don't feel as though you have to rush through anything."

Not that we would've, but it was nice to hear. "How many of them do we have?" I asked.

"Four. Math, English, Spanish, and phys ed." She opened a file that was on her desk. "He's a brilliant kid, did you know that?"

"We heard he's a math genius," Bailey said.

"He's a genius, period. He scored one hundred sixty-eight on his last IQ test. I'm not a big believer in those things, but that does indicate a fairly superior level of intelligence—by any measure." Marion flipped the pages of the file. "I've never met him myself, but his file shows no indication that he ever gave us any trouble whatsoever." She looked from me to Bailey. "I don't suppose there's any chance you'll find evidence that he wasn't one of the shooters?"

"It seems unlikely," I said.

She shook her head, her eyes sad. "I guess you just never know." Marion closed the file and handed it to Bailey. "I'll need you to cover me with a subpoena, but I made this copy of his records for you. It's under the table, so hang on to it. When you get the official copy you can just shred it." Marion stood up. "Better get started."

She walked us down the pathway that led past the outdoor lunch area and out to the gym. "I set you up to begin with his phys ed teacher, Joe Cooper. When you're done here, he'll take you to Sophia Magana."

Joe was shooting hoops in a gym that was impressively professional-looking for a middle school. He looked like Jimmy Buffett—with the leathery skin of someone who spent a lot of un-SPF'd time in the sun. Joe remembered Logan more for what he didn't do than what he did. "From the first minute the kid walked into the gym, I'm thinking he'll be a basketball star. Tall as hell, long arms, long legs. I was stoked. It's been a while since we had a decent team."

"How'd he do?" I asked.

"He didn't. Wasn't interested, threw bricks like a girl—oh, sorry."

"It's fine," I said. The look on Bailey's face told me we were both fighting the temptation to grab the ball and show him how girls threw. "So he didn't seem to be the aggressive type?" I asked.

"Aggressive? About as aggressive as overcooked pasta, you ask me." He moved the basketball to his left side. "I'm not saying he was a bad kid. He'd dress and do what he had to do. Which, believe me, I appreciate. Half of 'em won't even put on their gym clothes."

"Did he ever get a hard time from the other kids?" Bailey asked.

"Not in my class. I don't put up with any bullying bs. I tell 'em from day one I'll turn 'em in to the principal and call their parents the first whiff I get of any ugly stuff." He held up the basketball and spun it on his right index finger. I'd always wanted to be able to do that. Watching him, I realized for the first time that it might've helped if my fingers had been a little bigger. Then again, maybe I just wasn't a great "ball handler."

We lobbed a few more questions at Joe, but it was clear that beyond his disappointment at not finding star material in Logan, he didn't have much to tell us.

We thanked him for his time, and he dutifully squired us to Señora Magana's classroom. Her interview yielded even less. Logan was a quiet kid who sat in the back of the class, always turned in his homework, and got straight A's, though he avoided speaking the language whenever possible. Señora Magana did not find that to be an issue unique to Logan.

We moved on to Albert Packman, the math teacher. Here, I expected to get a full report. Surprisingly, he didn't have that much to say. "I remember him because he aced every test and his homework was always perfect. But he'd never talk in class. He always sat in the back and never seemed to be paying attention. At first, I'd call on him just to bust him. But he had the answer every single time. I finally realized he was bored, didn't have to give it his full attention. It was just that easy for him. I suspected he helped some of the kids because they'd turn in homework that was pretty damn good and then bomb their exams, but I couldn't prove it."

And no, he didn't see Logan get into any fights or get picked on by anyone. As we were wrapping up the interview, Bailey got a call on her cell and stepped outside. When I caught up with her, she said the elementary school principal had called back. There was only one teacher who had any specific recollections about Logan. "But she's not far. She lives in Westlake Village and she said we could come by anytime."

Excellent. Our last stop at the middle school was Cherry Fournier, the English teacher. Here, at last, we got something. Cherry was an unfortunate name for a teacher of young boys, and she was doubly cursed to have looks that went with it: blonde and blue-eyed, a sweet face, and a heroic bust, which she tried—and failed—to disguise.

"I don't know how he could have gone so wrong," Cherry said. "The Logan I remember was a wonderful boy. Incredibly smart and very soulful. He wrote poetry, and he actually understood Shakespeare better than almost any student I've ever had. That's no small feat for a kid that age. I'd give him extra reading assignments because the work in class was way too easy for him. He loved Voltaire, so I gave him more of the French classics like Balzac and Camus. He flew through them."

With very little hope, I asked, "Did he have any problems with any of the other students?"

"Logan?" Cherry shook her head. "No, not that I re—" She stopped abruptly. "No, wait. I think he did." She stared out the window for a few moments, gathering the memory. "Yes, now I remember. We'd just finished King Arthur and I asked everyone to write a paragraph about Camelot. He wrote a beautiful poem, very romantic as I recall. About Lady Guinevere and Sir Lancelot. I gave him an A, and I wrote a comment about how sensitive and original it was. When I handed the papers back to the class, I accidentally gave Logan's to one of the football players."

"Uh-oh," Bailey said.

Cherry nodded. "Yeah, big uh-oh. The jerk passed it around to his buddies, and they started laughing and making fun of him, and then this really big kid they called Hot Rod waved it in the air and told me he got Sir Pantsalot's paper by mistake." Cherry's face reddened with anger. "His buddies were all hooting about Sir Pantsalot. Poor Logan just sat there like a bug pinned to a board. I felt so bad for him. I tried to talk to him at the end of class, but he ran out. I could hear the jocks out in the hallway calling him Pansy-Ass-Pantsalot...among other things." Cherry made a face. "Anyway, the next thing I knew, I heard someone screaming out curses. A stream of 'fuck-yous' and 'motherfucking asshole' and whatnot. I ran out there, thinking someone must be getting hurt."

"And?" I asked.

"It was Logan. He was screaming at the top of his lungs at Hot Rod and his buddies. Which took some guts, because he was way outnumbered. But what shocked me was the way Logan looked. His whole body was rigid and shaking, and his face was bright red. And he screamed so hard he was spitting. I was worried he might pass out."

"And the jocks? How'd they take it?" I asked.

"That's the strange part. They just stood there and stared. I think they were probably in shock. Logan's reaction was so completely out of character. He'd always been so quiet, so shy. To see him go ballistic like that was just... kind of scary, actually. Like there was another person inside of him and there was no telling what that person might do." Cherry looked from me to Bailey. "Kind of significant, isn't it? I mean, in hindsight."

Which seemed to be the only way to spot this kind of criminal. "So it didn't turn into a physical fight?"

"No. Logan finished screaming, and Hot Rod and his crew walked off."

"The jocks didn't mess with him again?" I asked.

"Not in my class."

48

"I'm almost relieved," I said, as Bailey and I headed out to the parking lot. "Finally, something fits."

"Yeah, but would you ever have thought that would add up to mass murder?"

The point we'd circled so many times before. "No. But I think this is what the shrinks were talking about. Maybe we should set up surveillance at the school. It's a long shot but—"

"No chances taken, not with these assholes." Bailey drove down Ventura Boulevard until she spotted a gas station with a pay phone.

We had to be very careful about what we said on our cell phones, especially about something like this. It was just a theory that Logan might hit his middle school next, but if it got out that we were putting up extra security it would cause a major panic.

When Bailey got back into the car, I shared something that had occurred to me during our interview with Cherry. "Does this story about Hot Rod make you think Logan really was targeting jocks at Fairmont?"

Bailey started the engine. "Nah. I still don't buy it."

I pulled on my seat belt. "Why? I mean, I'm not saying it was the only thing on his mind, but it might've been one of them."

"I guess. But if jocks really mattered, they could've staged their attack at a basketball game."

"Maybe. Then again, a game isn't as controlled an environment. People move in and out—"

"True. But I'm just not feeling this whole jock angle. It feels like bullshit."

Bailey's intuition was worth a lot. And I'd played devil's advocate, but

I agreed with her. Logan had a bad experience with Hot Rod in junior high, but there was no indication anything like that had happened since then. It stretched the bands of credibility to the breaking point to believe that some idiots calling him Sir Pantsalot had provoked him to stockpile an arsenal and go on a killing spree years later. No, the notion that Logan was a bullied kid who finally "snapped" and decided to go after his tormentors fit a nice media picture. But it sure as hell didn't fit the evidence. Not from what we'd seen so far.

Westlake Village was only twenty minutes north of Platt Junior High, and we made it to the home of Logan's elementary school teacher by four thirty. Vera Littlefield, a petite brunette with sensibly bobbed hair, had just come home from the grocery store and was about to start dinner. She led us into the kitchen.

"I'm sorry to bring you in here instead of the living room, but if I don't get this dinner rolling we won't eat until nine o'clock."

"What are you making?" I asked. Dinner sounded good. I couldn't remember when I'd last eaten.

"Fried chicken and mashed potatoes. It's Kevin's favorite. Mine too, actually."

And mine too. Just the words made my mouth water.

The principal had done our intros for us, so we got right down to business and asked Vera what she remembered of Logan.

Vera stood at the sink and washed the chicken pieces. "Such a sweet boy. Very, very smart. Always the tallest boy in his class. For a shy guy like him that was probably a bit of a problem. I believe he has an IQ at genius level."

"He does," I said. "Do you remember having any disciplinary problems with him?"

She put the chicken pieces on paper towels and began drying them. "I've been thinking about that, and no. None. He was a pretty quiet kid. That's why it's so hard to imagine that he was involved in something... like this." A mixture of fear and sadness crossed Vera's face as she washed her hands and moved to the refrigerator. I got the feeling that she was glad to help us, but she'd be just as glad to put this interview behind her.

"Did you ever see him act out in a violent manner with any of the other kids?" Bailey asked. "Or see him get unusually... upset?"

Vera took eggs out of the refrigerator and put them into a bowl. "Violent? No. I never worried that he was a danger to others." She put the bowl on the counter and pulled out a whisk, then gave us a wry half-smile. "And I never saw him start fires or be cruel to animals." The sociopathic checklist. "But what I do remember is that he was a perfectionist. Even at that early age."

"What age exactly?" I asked.

"Ten. I taught fifth grade. It isn't that uncommon to see kids be perfectionists at that age, but Logan took it to an extreme. If every single thing he did wasn't absolutely flawless, he'd have a fit, and I mean that literally. He'd shred the work, clench his fists, and shake. Sometimes even scream and call himself names, like 'stupid idiot' and 'loser.'"

"What did you do?" I asked.

Vera cracked the eggs into the bowl. "I'd try to calm him down as best I could, and eventually, it would pass. But I knew it was a sign that there was a problem, so I told his parents about it and recommended a child psychologist." Vera began to beat the eggs.

"How did they take it?" Some parents didn't appreciate it when teachers suggested their children needed professional help.

"Very well, actually. They started therapy right away. At least that's what they told me." Vera put the chicken pieces into the bowl and coated them.

Bailey and I exchanged a look. "Did Logan seem to get better?" I asked.

"He did. He definitely stopped having those fits."

We fished around for a little while longer to make sure there was nothing else of consequence, then thanked Vera for her time and let ourselves out. The spatter of chicken hitting hot grease crackled behind us as we headed out the door.

When we got into the car, Bailey pulled out her cell. "Someone should check this shrink business out with the Jarvises. See if they put Logan on some kind of medication."

If we got to trial, any possible chemical influences would offer big support to a mental defense. "Damn. I'd like to hear this for myself. What if we got Nick to go with us? Think that would help?" Nick had the kind of laid-back attitude that might soften the parents' feelings toward us. Although he'd been at the Jarvis house during the search, he'd stayed in the background. It was possible the parents never even noticed him.

Bailey chewed the inside of her cheek. "Bonnie'll be less hostile than Brad. I'll have Nick call and see who's home. If it's just her, and Nick's available, we can give it a try, see if she'll talk. But if she gets the least bit hinky, we're outta there. Harrellson can handle it."

"Of course." Logan's parents didn't have a right to refuse to talk to us. And, fortunately, they hadn't lawyered up yet. But if they'd be more cooperative with another officer, there was no sense insisting on doing the interview ourselves. I could only hope that Nick's charm would work its magic. Because I wanted to hear for myself what Bonnie had to say about all this. And why she hadn't given us this information before.

49

The Jarvises had moved since we'd last seen them. From the moment we'd released Logan's name as a person of interest, they'd been under siege. Reporters camped out in their front yard, gawkers and hecklers filled the street, and within twenty-four hours, they'd not only received death threats, but someone had painted graffiti on the walls of their garage and sidewalk calling them "killer breeders." Luckily, a friend had a small rental property available in Santa Clarita, which was about half an hour northeast of Woodland Hills.

Nick toned down the cowboy theme for the occasion. He still wore the boots, but he'd dispensed with the hat, and his sheepskin-lined leather coat looked expensive. He introduced himself with a warm smile, apologized for the inconvenience with convincing sincerity, and told Bonnie he'd take "just a few moments" of her time.

Bonnie's expression had hardened when she saw us on her doorstep, but Nick's easy manner won her over. She stood aside and let us in without complaint. As we got seated in the living room, I saw that Bonnie looked a great deal worse for wear. It'd been less than a week since the shooting, but she'd aged ten years. Her face sagged like a melted candle. By unspoken agreement, Nick took the lead in the questioning. He broached the subject of Logan's therapy gently. "We've learned that Logan's problems were somewhat more…serious than what you mentioned. Tell you the truth, it sounded like the same kind of problems a nephew of mine had a while back. Sure was tough on my sister. I was just wondering what you could tell us about that."

Bonnie's lip trembled. She stared out the window in silence for several long moments. "I-I hate to talk about it. It's embarrassing to Logan, and it's really not relevant anymore. It was such a long time ago. The doctor said he was fine."

Her reaction was understandable...if Logan was in trouble for ditching school. I wanted to grab her by the shoulders and scream, "*Embarrassing* to Logan? Have you lost your mind?" It was a good thing Nick was doing the questioning.

"But you did get him some help," Nick said.

"Yes, we took him to a therapist." She looked up at the ceiling. "What was his name?" After a few moments, Bonnie sighed. "It'll come to me. But he was a wonderful man. He did Logan a world of good. The diagnosis was obsessive-compulsive disorder and anxiety. No hallucinations or voices." She looked at us pointedly. "No indication of any violent thoughts or tendencies. At least, not toward others."

"Did the doctor believe there was a suicide risk?" Nick asked.

Bonnie swallowed and nodded. "But he also said it was something the medication and therapy would alleviate. That and time. The doctor felt very sure Logan's problems would be resolved over time."

"That must have been very hard for you," Nick said.

Bonnie teared up. "The poor little guy was giving himself fits." Then she looked out the living room window and drifted off. No doubt to a happier time, before the "poor little guy" turned into a vicious killer.

"And was the doctor right?" Nick asked. "Did the therapy work?"

Bonnie nodded. "Yes, therapy and the medication. He seemed to calm down considerably."

Shit. I could see it coming already. A mental defense: the drugs made me do it. "Do you remember what kind?" I asked.

Bonnie squinted at the floor for a few moments. "Luv...something. Luvox? Was that it?" She nodded. "Yes, I believe that's it. But after about a year, the doctor said he was over the hump and took him off it."

Nick gave me a look that said he'd take it from there. "Then he wasn't taking anything by the time he got into middle school?"

"Oh, no. By then he was certainly not taking it anymore." Bonnie gave a heavy sigh that seemed to deflate her whole body. She was worn down to a nub. "Now I remember. It's Dr. Bingham. Jerry Bingham."

Nick asked a few more questions to make sure Bonnie wasn't sitting on any other information, and then we left and huddled at Nick's car.

"Thanks for that," Bailey said to him.

He tipped an imaginary hat with a smile. "Always happy to help out lovely ladies." Then he looked back at the Jarvis house, his expression somber. "You know, if I met her on the street, I'd never figure her for the mother of a maniac like this."

True that.

"So how's that nephew of yours doing?" I asked. Nick looked puzzled. "Your sister's kid, the one who had mental problems."

Nick gave a little smile. "Always wished I had a sister." Nick saluted and took off. We got into Bailey's car, and I called Dr. Michael to ask if he'd heard of Luvox.

"Of course. It's a preferred drug for OCD. Just a general question, I assume?"

"Right. A friend of mine asked me about it yesterday." I had warned the doctors not to mention this case on the phone. "What are the contra-indications?"

"There have been some studies that show it may cause suicidal ideation, depression, and violence."

"Even if he's not still taking it? Our information is that he stopped taking it years ago," I said.

"It's possible. The long-term effects are not well documented."

I asked Michael if we could drop by. I had more questions, but I couldn't ask them on the phone.

"Probably better if I meet you at the station," he said. His office was just ten minutes from the Police Administration Building. "There was a shooting across the street this morning, and the reporters are still floating around."

"We'll meet you in the lobby," I said.

When Michael arrived, we took him straight to an interview room.

"Do you know of a psychologist or psychiatrist by the name of Jerry Bingham?" I asked.

"I do," Michael said. "He's a good guy. He was Logan's doctor?" I nodded. "I'm sure he'd have useful information. But of course..."

"Yeah." Dr. Bingham couldn't tell us a damn thing. The information was all privileged. "Would Logan have any way of getting his hands on more Luvox without his parents finding out?"

"Well, I'm not sure why he'd want to. It's not exactly a hallucinogenic, though I guess you never know." Michael sighed. "It would have to be under the table. Maybe he could find it online—"

"Or maybe he could talk the doctor into passing him free samples."

"I really wouldn't expect any doctor to do that," Michael said. "Especially with a minor. And even if he did, I doubt he'd have continued to do so over any extended period of time."

But he couldn't rule out the possibility. We wouldn't know for sure until we got to trial.

"Do you have anything more for us on Shane?" Michael asked.

"We've got reports on his stint in the Army for you," Bailey said. "But from what I saw, there's nothing out of the norm. We're still digging into his earlier stuff." Like crazy, actually. But it'd only been two days since we'd identified Shane Dolan as our likely second shooter, and his pre-military history was a little harder to find than we'd expected.

Shane was adopted, no known siblings, and both parents were dead. We hadn't found his birth parents yet. He hadn't gone to college, his high school records were archived somewhere—we had unis working on it—and his elementary school records had all been on paper (the school didn't have digital records when Shane was a kid) and they'd been purged.

Michael frowned. "That's too bad. What your witnesses have said so far is helpful, but it really only gives us a thumbnail sketch. And there are some...anomalies in terms of Shane being the follower. I have no doubt that Logan chose Fairmont High as their first target. But that doesn't necessarily mean Shane will let him choose their future targets. The problem is, we don't know enough about Shane to make even an educated guess about what target he'd choose." Michael paused. "There's no indication Shane had any problems in the Army? None at all?"

"Not from what I saw," Bailey said. "Honorable discharge, no record of discipline. It was probably the only time anyone kept him close to the straight and narrow."

"Then we focus on Logan's motives," he said. "Given what you've found, I can't say that Shane necessarily has a motive to target government buildings—"

"Other than his time in the service—" I said.

"Which was apparently uneventful," Michael said. "And I don't have enough data to figure out what motive he might have to target any other place."

50

Bailey escorted Michael to the elevator, and I waited for her in the interview room, thinking about what he had said.

"It is weird that Shane would go along for the ride and let this kid call the shots," I said.

"Yeah, it is. But we don't know that he is. It might be more mutual than that. Shane's had a tough life. There's a lot we don't know and may never know. But even if Logan is calling the shots, it wouldn't be the first time a younger, smarter perp winds up being the ringleader."

How could anyone predict what might happen when two complementary psychos connect? It's crazy to think there could be any concrete rules about anything, let alone which one might be the leader and which the follower. "Have we heard back from Harrellson yet about the Shane sighting up north?"

"So far, no dice. At least no credible dice. And our media relations guy is laughing his head off at how the press is getting a dose of his world. The reporters have been complaining to him about all the wing nuts phoning in their sightings. Mostly of Logan, but some of Shane too. He told them to cry him a river." Bailey shook her head, with a little smile.

"But bottom line, no new information on Shane?"

"No," Bailey said. "He's not using credit cards, and I'd guess he's switched cars by now since the Jetta hasn't been spotted again. But we don't have any more stolen reports we can tie to Shane."

The blue Jetta had been reported stolen, but we hadn't connected it to Shane until after our tipster spotted him at the gas station. Now, we had alerts for Los Angeles County and all points north on any cars reported stolen in the past five days.

"Tell you what," Bailey said. "You call Dorian, see if she's got anything else on Evan's room. I'll check on the security setup for Platt Junior High."

I shot her a dagger look. "I can make the calls about security."

"No, you can't." Bailey gave me a smug little smile.

She was right, I couldn't. But that didn't mean she hadn't deliberately set me up to take the brunt of Dorian's wrath. We bought snacks from the vending machine. I got a disgustingly healthy apple; Bailey got Doritos.

While Bailey worked her phone, I pulled out a swivel chair next to her desk, ate her chips, and punched in Dorian's number on my cell.

"Yeah, what?" Dorian said.

"Hey, Dorian, it's Rachel Knight. I was just calling to find out—"

"Whether I've got money on the Raiders' game, right? I do not." Dorian's funny side showed up at the most unexpected times. "I can't say the shoe prints I found near the house were left that night. They might've been, but there was dirt in the impression, so they could've been there from the day before. Bottom line: I can't rule out the possibility that Evan was abducted, but my very educated guess is that there was no foul play here. The kid rabbited on us."

"No hairs or fibers to work with?"

"So far, everything comes back to Evan or his mother."

My line beeped with a call waiting. I signed off with Dorian and took it.

It was Graden. "Hey, what's up?" I asked.

"We've got another letter."

I felt the apple travel back up to my throat. I took a deep breath to force it back down. "At the school?"

"Yeah. The bomb guys are already on their way out there. Assuming it clears, we'll have it in my office within the hour."

"Call me when it gets there."

51

He smiled. It made him happy to see the line of people waiting for the seven o'clock showing of *Hail of Metal.* They'd been right to pick a Saturday night at the Cinemark in Woodland Hills. No matter how crappy the movie, the idiots always had to have their "date night." The place would be packed to capacity. A pimply young man dressed in a black shirt and trousers opened the doors, and the line slowly filed into the theater. Pathetic sheep.

It was hard to wait. The digital clock in the dashboard felt torturously slow. He drummed his fingers on the steering wheel. One minute crawled by. Then another. Then another. Finally, it was time.

Moving quickly up to the doors past the usher, then moving slowly, with deliberate nonchalance, into the theater. The clock above the concession stand read 7:15. Perfect. They'd planned it all so well. The movie would start any minute. This was it. Go, go, go! Up the staircase. Down the hall. To the door on the right.

Knuckles rapped hard, with authority, on the door of the projection booth.

A voice from inside the booth called out, "Who's there?"

You'll see, dickweed. "The manager. It's important. Open up."

The door opened just a crack. It was enough. Slam! The door flew back, throwing the projectionist to the ground. The knife plunged into his gut, right up to the hilt. He exhaled with a grunt. The knife plunged again, this time straight into his throat. Gurgling, choking sounds bubbled out of the projectionist's mouth. It would've been fun to watch, but there was no time.

Ready.

Two assault rifles, locked and loaded, poked through the window to the theater.

Aim.

As the lights dimmed, the guns tipped down toward the audience. One shifted to the right, the other to the left.

The opening scene—a four-car pursuit—began to play. The sound track blasted the screech of tires, the clash of metal on metal as the cars careered through tight city streets, slamming into walls, parked cars, and mailboxes.

Finally, the cue: a long hail of bullets.

Fire!

The projection booth filled with manic laughter and gunshots. *Blam! Blam! Blam!*

Down in the theater below, people began to scream.

52

Graden had the letter brought into his office, so we gathered there. Nick had asked to be included in the meeting because he'd helped trace the postmark on the last letter. Once again, there were two envelopes. I put on latex gloves and took the folded paper out of the evidence box with shaking hands. Bailey and Nick read over my shoulder.

Hey, Rachel, I bet you thought this would be an easy one, didn't you? After all, how hard could it be to chase down a couple of kids? I guess you're finally realizing how superior we are to all you losers. Especially you. You're turning out to be quite the disappointment. Otis—a "person of interest." Ha! He's a lot more interesting dead than he ever was alive.

I know, you think you can figure me out, just like all those head-shrinkers. All you fools with your clichés and psychobabble. You have no fucking clue. You've never seen anyone like me. I'm the best you've ever seen or ever will see. You're not going to get your happy ending this time, Rachel.

Because life is not a movie. Good guys lose, everybody dies, and love does not conquer all.

"So this is the guy who supposedly wrote eloquent poetry?" Bailey said.

"Not exactly Keats," I agreed. "But he's not aiming for an A in English."

"How did he find out that we know Otis is dead?" Graden asked. "I don't remember releasing that information—"

"You didn't," Bailey said. "He screwed up. He thinks he's digging on his own private joke, making fun of us for calling Otis a 'person of interest.'"

"Laughing at how we fell for the decoy," I said. "Back when we first found out Otis was dead, we hit on the possibility that they deliberately framed Otis to throw us off. That the second shooter might've deliberately mimicked Otis's laugh."

"But we weren't sure Otis wasn't in on it, so we kept looking for more evidence to link him to the shooting," Bailey said. "We've found nothing. All we have is what we started with: the weird laugh and Logan's photograph on Otis's computer."

"So we figured they probably did set Otis up as a decoy—" I said.

"And this letter proves it," Bailey said. "I'd bet Shane—or whoever the second shooter is—sent that photo the night before the shooting to frame Otis."

"So the second shooter screwed over his buddy, Logan?" Nick asked. "'Cause that photo dumps Logan out big-time."

"I thought so too at first," I said. "But actually, it doesn't. So what if Logan's holding a gun? We couldn't even prove the gun in the photo was real, let alone that it was his. And the upside for them was huge: it bought them time while we chased a dead boy."

"Then Logan could've sent it himself," Nick said.

Graden looked skeptical. "But how could they be sure they'd be able to find Otis near the library in all that chaos?" he said. "If he'd survived, we would've been able to clear him pretty fast. So how could they know Otis would be close enough to the library at just the right time?"

"Logan was friendly with him," I said. "Remember, Evan said he saw Otis going over to talk to Logan that morning. So Otis might've said he was going to be in the library—or Logan might've told Otis to meet him there. But then again, maybe they didn't know. It's entirely possible they decided to use Otis as a decoy and then just lucked out to find him near the library. I don't think they *needed* him to be dead. It just bought them more time that way."

"True," Nick said. "It was no biggie if they didn't kill him. The mislead would work for at least a little while no matter what."

"Well, at least we can finally clear Otis," Bailey said. "You agree, Lieutenant?"

"Yeah," Graden said. "Write it up. We'll notify the parents right away."

Finally, a piece of good news. I looked back down at the letter. Something else was bothering me. "That last line." I studied it again. "It's familiar somehow. But something's off about it. It's not right."

"I was thinking the same thing," Nick said. He stared at the letter. "Wait, I think I've got it. It's from that movie with Kevin Spacey, *Swimming with Sharks*."

I looked at him, surprised. "You're a movie buff?" Nick shrugged. I considered the line again. "I'll be damned. You're right."

I turned back to the letter and tried to figure out what was wrong with the quote. Then I had it. An icy chill gripped my heart. "It's everybody *lies*. Not everybody *dies*."

53

A theater. I'd figured it out. Just not in time. A movie's take on the human condition. A movie about the movie business. A quote from that movie—with just one word changed. But we were set up to fail. By the time we got the letter, it was already too late. And even if there'd been some lead time, there was no way to know which theater, or even which city. Los Angeles? Or in Shane's neighborhood, Camarillo? Or in Boulder? It was another needle in a haystack.

Bailey got the call within minutes. A shooting at the Cinemark in Woodland Hills. A theater Logan probably knew well, since it was close to home. We broke all speed limits getting to the scene. There were at least twenty squad cars and two fire trucks occupying all of the drivable space in front of the theater. Bailey double-parked next to a squad car at the far end, and we ran toward the police line. She badged us through and tracked down the detective in charge. It turned out to be Detective Gina Stradley—an old friend of Bailey's from their Police Academy days.

"I heard this one's yours, Keller," she said.

"Yeah, lucky me," Bailey said. "What have we got?"

"Same MO as the school. Twisted fucks." Gina gestured for us to follow her into the theater. "And it was so easy for them. It's sickening. They must've bought tickets, because there's no sign of forced entry anywhere. Just walked in with everyone else. Assault rifles were SBR AR fifteens, like last time."

A short-barrel rifle wouldn't be hard to conceal under a coat, and this was coat weather. Gina turned right and led us up the staircase to a wide corridor on the second floor. She stopped just outside the crime scene tape that stretched across the hallway and pointed to a door on our right. Uniformed cops stood guard as crime scene techs worked inside the taped-off area. Most seemed to be grouped near the doorway Gina had pointed out. "They headed up here to the projection booth, got the projectionist to open the door, and stabbed him to death. They fired through the projection window." A sniper couldn't have picked a better spot. I remembered Jenny's words: "'fish in a barrel' style."

"Only two dead?" Bailey asked.

"In the audience," Gina said. "Four, counting the projectionist and the manager, who ran to the booth when he realized where the shots were coming from." Gina shook her head. "He called nine-one-one on his way up. If it hadn't been for him, it would've been a helluva lot worse."

"So they dumped the weapons again," I said.

"Yeah," Gina said. "But it looks like they shot the manager with a nine millimeter. We picked up a shell casing near the body." It was crowded in the hallway with all the cops and techs, and we were three extra bodies that weren't needed at the moment, so Gina led us back downstairs to the lobby. "Our gun expert says it looks like the rifles were rigged to go fully automatic, but one of them jammed."

Bailey nodded. "One of them jammed last time too—"

"But last time they weren't rigged to go fully automatic," I said.

"Where the hell are they getting these guns from?" Gina asked.

"Probably the same person who altered them," Bailey said. Shane checked both boxes. Bailey told Gina we thought he might be the second shooter.

"Well, thank God he screwed up," Gina said. "If that gun hadn't jammed, we would've had a higher body count than Fairmont."

I nodded. "We got lucky." I stopped even as I heard myself say it. This case had mangled all sense of proportion. Anything less than a double-digit body count felt like a blessing.

Bailey stared out through the glass doors at the throng of police. "Worse than Aurora. That's what they were going for."

"Right," I said. I thought about the incident between Logan and the jocks in middle school. "We'd better shut Platt down."

"I'll get ahold of the principal," Bailey said. "In the meantime, Gina, would you mind if I got our firearms guy, Ed Berry, out here? Just to keep things clean and simple?"

"No problem. I'll make sure they don't bag anything up. Your guy can put himself in the chain."

The chain of custody is how we prove evidence wasn't tainted or tampered with. The more hands on a piece of evidence, the more of a hassle it is in trial because I have to call every cop who touched, tagged, or moved something. So Gina was saving us a headache down the line by letting Ed handle the firearms evidence.

Gina moved off to see to it, and while Bailey put in the call to Ed, I called Nick. "Have you had any luck with the postmark on that envelope?"

"Same as the last one: Boulder, Colorado. And it was sent out by expedited mail yesterday."

"I guess they could've sent it themselves—"

"It's physically possible, but if you ask me, that dog won't hunt. Too much exposure bein' on the road all that time."

"Someone's helping them."

"Has to be."

It depressed me almost more than the existence of the shooters themselves to know that there was someone out there willing to help them.

54

Bailey managed to track down the principal of Platt Junior High. Marion was less than pleased at having to shut the school down but smart enough not to argue about it.

We moved out to the front of the theater and talked to the cops who'd interviewed the witnesses, hoping to get some kind of ID on either of the shooters, but it was a bust. The killers had been in the projection booth during the shooting, and afterward they'd melted in with the crowd. Most of the theatergoers had been blinded by panic, and the rest couldn't see past the stampede. The cashier and ticket takers didn't remember seeing anyone unusual. But I didn't expect them to. Even if they'd worn the same kind of camouflage coats, they wouldn't stand out in this weather.

It was almost midnight by the time Bailey dropped me off at the Biltmore, and we were both wrung out. "I'm going to check in at the office in the morning unless something pops between now and then."

Bailey nodded wearily. "I'll let you know."

I started to get out, then paused. "Have you been getting hassled by the press at all?"

"No. I pushed all my calls to our media liaison, and so far no one's tried to get past him. Plus, the chief's been doing pressers every day."

"They haven't gone after me either, other than bombarding me with messages asking for information. But those poor families..." Since the day of the shooting, there'd been nonstop pieces on the news showing the grieving friends and relatives of the victims.

The funerals had begun as early as Tuesday. There'd been eleven, which still left another twenty-two to go. So far, none of the families had allowed the press to cover them. Bailey and I usually make it a point to go to victims' funerals, but we couldn't this time. There were too many.

I got out and patted the roof. Bailey took off.

Being involved in an investigation can block the big picture, the human side of things. We follow clues and focus on the minutiae, nose to the ground. And we don't look up until someone's in custody. But the next morning, as I was getting out of the shower, the disastrous enormity of the case hit me like a sledgehammer. The body count. Shooters still at large. Their bizarre motivations. And their unpredictability, the impossibility of knowing where they'd strike next. Evan somewhere out there, maybe dead already. Or close to it. As the thoughts flooded my brain, I struggled to catch my breath.

I walked out to the balcony. The sun was shining and the sky was a rich brilliant blue. The air was surprisingly warm, but I didn't trust it. I went back inside and pulled out a turtleneck sweater and slacks. I had an idea about an alternate plan of action, and I mulled it over as I dressed. Then I called Bailey. It was Sunday, and she usually spent at least part of the day with her family, but I knew that ritual would be on hold until this case was solved. "Did the chief approve shutting Platt down already?"

"Yes. Why?"

"Because I've been thinking. That school is our only lead right now. If Logan and Shane see that it's empty, they'll just look for another target—"

"It's not going to be empty. I've set up cops to pose as teachers. A few as students too, which for a middle school wasn't easy. Believe me."

That was exactly what I'd been about to suggest. Bailey didn't sound happy about it, and I didn't blame her. It was about as dangerous a duty as it gets. Plus it was a big expense, and there was no guarantee Logan would choose Platt as the next target. But I'd rather be overprepared and wrong than unprepared and right. Besides, this gave us a fighting chance. The only one we'd had since this whole ordeal began. "And I'd like to talk to our shrinks, see what they think about last night."

"It's Sunday, Knight. They might have lives."

"It can't hurt to try."

One hour later we were seated around the table in Jenny's office with steaming mugs of coffee. It was really good. "What is this? I've never had anything like it before."

"It's my own special blend. And no, I won't share the secret, but I will mix up a bag for you."

"The shooting last night," Michael said. "You're sure it was them?"

Bailey nodded. "Has to be."

I told them about the letter we'd gotten that afternoon and filled them in on details of the shooting. "So who do you think picked the Cinemark? Shane or Logan?"

Michael set down his cup. "We think it may have been Shane's choice—"

"Not that Logan wasn't happy to go along with it," Jenny said.

"Because the Cinemark was their chance to beat out the Aurora shooter, right?" I said.

"Yes, there's no question about that," Michael said. "But they failed, so I was thinking that their next target might be another theater."

I told them about our belief that Logan's junior high school was a likely target, and why.

"That's a fair guess too," Jenny said. "Certainly theater owners will be taking extra precautions now, so a theater would be a more jeopardous choice. Plus, the school would be a crossover target. There was a somewhat famous shooting at a middle school in Arkansas. Johnson and Golden set off a fire alarm and then hid in the woods and picked off the students as they came out. They killed five and wounded ten. And they had planned to get away. The car they used was loaded with supplies."

"I remember that. Back in the nineties, right?" I said.

"Right," Jenny said. "Nineteen ninety-eight. They weren't nearly as sophisticated as your killers. The police caught them before they could even get back to the car. So your middle school theory is a sound one from both perspectives: it's a personal target for Logan, and it's a place where they can 'best' another set of famous killers."

Bailey's cell rang. She looked at the number, then quickly stood up. "Excuse me, I have to take this." She walked out to the anteroom, closing the office door behind her.

"Even another high school is possible," Jenny said. "They're staying pretty close to home so far, choosing targets where they know the lay of the land. I expect they'll continue to do so."

"Then you agree it's unlikely they were in Boulder to mail the letter?"

"Highly unlikely," Michael said. "As you mentioned, there's a lot of risk involved in that much movement. It's much more likely someone is helping them." He poured himself another cup of coffee. "I assume you're concentrating on the Valley."

"We are. We're even covering community colleges in case they decide that's a close enough match to Virginia Tech."

"Good," Jenny said. "In the meantime, we've been digging into Shane's military records. We're trying to construct a profile—"

Bailey stepped back inside, radiating nervous energy. "I'm sorry. We have to go." Her voice was tense and urgent. She tapped her cell phone against her thigh as I gathered my coat and purse. We said hurried goodbyes and headed for the elevator. Bailey punched the down button. A few seconds later, she punched it again. "Damn. Screw it." She flew down the hall toward the stairs, and I ran to catch up.

I waited until we were in the car and headed for the freeway to ask. "What the hell is going on?"

"They've found Shane Dolan."

"Is he in custody?"

"No. We got a tip that he's holed up at someone's house. An Army buddy of his."

"And our tipster knows that guy...how?"

"It's a small town. Everybody knows everybody." Bailey headed north on the 101 freeway.

"And we're sure this is a righteous tip because...?"

"Our tipster is a cop."

Doesn't get much more righteous than that. I closed my eyes and prayed that we were finally about to get a real break.

It felt long overdue.

55

Bailey continued north on the freeway.

"But he didn't see Logan?" I asked.

"No. They might've split up to lay low until the next hit."

"I thought you had Harrellson working the Shane angle up here," I said.

"I pulled him off to head up the detail at Platt."

We passed through the Valley and Camarillo. When we kept heading north after Ventura, I seriously started to wonder exactly where this small town was. "Mind telling me where we're going?"

"No, but it won't help. We're going to La Conchita."

Actually, it did help. Graden and I liked to take day trips up to Santa Barbara, and La Conchita was on the way. It was a town tailor-made for a sitcom—a bohemian, beachcomberish kind of place. Nestled into a hill on the east side of the Pacific Coast Highway—the only thing separating the town from the ocean—La Conchita was a tiny burg filled with individually built houses, trailers, and a random assortment of small apartment buildings. The mom-and-pop liquor store just off the highway was the town's main attraction for travelers. Graden and I had stopped there once or twice to get water and sandwiches.

And it was a tight-knit community. When torrential rains caused a major mudslide that buried four houses, the government had proposed evacuating the town—possibly for good. The residents had refused to go. They'd dug their way out, helped one another rebuild, and rescued their little city from oblivion. It made perfect sense that everyone in town would know if a stranger was hiding out there.

Bailey pulled up to a small cottage that had a front walk lined with crushed seashells and a large conch on the front porch. The doorbell was a literal bell that sat on an upside-down barrel near the door, and the hammock suspended from the overhang swung gently in the sea breeze. Something about the decor reminded me of *Gilligan's Island.* I picked up the bell and rang it, because...I just couldn't resist.

A smallish man with a woolly thatch of dark hair, dressed in a faded Hawaiian shirt and jeans, answered the door. He looked from Bailey to me. "Detectives?"

Bailey pulled out her badge and introduced us. "Officer Santos?"

"That's me. Todd." He held out his hand as he gestured to his clothes. "Sorry for the civvies, but Sunday's my day off. Come on in."

Bailey and I settled on a blue denim sofa that had seen better days sometime before the Korean War. Todd welcomed us and set bottles of water on the electrical cable spool that served as a coffee table. It came as no surprise that he didn't wear a wedding ring. It was a rare woman who'd embrace Todd's choice of decor. But Todd himself was charming. Maybe it was his open face and eager smile. Or the way he leaned forward, hands clasped together, with a look that said whatever we needed, he'd be up for it. Plus, he smelled good. His cologne—possibly aftershave—was light, citrusy, and a little like the ocean. The ocean part might've just been the air. Whatever it was, I liked him.

Bailey pulled out her cell and showed Todd the photo of Shane. "This is the man you called about, right?"

Todd took one look. "Yep, that's him. Must have just got in last night because I only saw him this morning. Spotted him out on the balcony of Max's apartment." He tapped his forehead. "I never forget a face. Especially when it's attached to a criminal. You think he's one of your shooters?"

"Yeah," Bailey said. "And he's a gun nut. There's a good chance he's armed."

Todd looked from me to Bailey. "Want me to back you up?" He nodded at us, indicating what the answer should be.

"Maybe," Bailey said. "What do you know about the guy he's staying with? Is he the jumpy type?"

"Max? Nah. But I didn't want to take any chances, so I didn't say anything to him."

"And you're sure Shane's still there?" I asked.

"Yeah. I've been keeping tabs on him for ya, watching the building to make sure no one leaves. It's been quiet." He got up and motioned for us to join him at the window. Todd pointed to a green apartment building across the street with an open carport and units above. "See that old red Mustang? That's Max's car. That bike parked behind it has to be Shane's ride because I've never seen it before."

"You know which unit Max lives in?" Bailey asked.

"Didn't before, but after I sighted Shane, I went and checked. Apartment two B."

"What do you know about Max?" I asked.

"He's a vet. Did a tour in Afghanistan. Works construction when he can. Nice guy. Not the sharpest knife in the box, but a decent sort."

"Which is why he's harboring a mass murderer?" I asked.

"I'd bet you he doesn't know," Todd said. "He doesn't have a television. Got drunk last year and kicked in the screen when the Dodgers lost."

"Is he going to cause us trouble?" Bailey asked.

"I doubt it. But I'll tell you what. How about I go over there and see if I can pull Max out? I'll keep him quiet, and you guys can move in and take your prisoner."

That sounded nice and simple, except that our prisoner was likely to be armed to the teeth. And nothing fights like a rabid animal when it's cornered. "Maybe we should wait for backup."

Bailey shook her head. "We can't afford to. If he jumps before they get here, we'll be screwed. How about this, Todd. You try and get inside and see what's going on, see whether Max is acting weird. Look for any guns lying around. We'll wait right outside. If it looks cool, give us a sign and we'll move in."

This felt like a dumb cowboy move to me, but since I was the least experienced in the arrest department, I deferred. I opened my purse and rearranged my makeup, comb, and other junk so my gun was on top.

Todd looked at my purse, then at me. I could see him wondering how much use I'd be. I wasn't sure myself.

Todd stood up. "Okay then. Let's do this." Todd went to a side table near the door, picked up a small revolver, and tucked it into the back of his waistband. Then he headed out. We followed at a discreet distance, and I tried to act nonchalant, like I imagined a tourist would look. Except I couldn't imagine what any tourist would be doing walking the streets of La Conchita.

Stairs of pebble composite led up from the street to the second floor of the apartment building where our quarry was holed up. Todd, who was wearing desert boots, made a lot more noise than I would've liked as he clomped up them. The units were in a U shape, and there was a courtyard in the center below, where a dwarf palm tree and flowers grew around decorative rocks. I imagined one of us being tossed over the flimsy metal railing that lined the walkway and landing headfirst on those rocks.

Todd turned left at the top of the stairs, then walked around the U until he reached the last door. Bailey and I hung back a few feet. He looked back, gave us a smile, and knocked. I heard a voice answer from inside the apartment, which tells you how flimsy those walls were. "Hey, Max. It's me, Todd. I need a favor."

A few seconds later, the door opened, and a sun-bleached, graying head poked out. "Whadda ya need?"

"I'm painting my bedroom, and I've got to move my dresser out. There're some cold brews in it for ya."

Max held the door partly open with one hand and stood there, considering the offer. If he didn't go for it, then what? Finally, he said, "Okay. Just gimme a sec to put on my jeans." He closed the door, and Todd glanced at us and gave us a thumbs-up. I rolled my eyes, but he waved me off—*Don't worry.* Yeah, why worry? Just because we were about to try to take down a murderer who had access to an armory? Piffle.

A few seconds later, Max emerged—a square body with skinny arms in a tank top, torn jeans, and flip-flops. In fifty-degree weather. What was he, a werewolf? Todd moved to the side as though to let Max lead the way, but when Max started to close the door behind him, Todd grabbed it. He put a finger to his lips and pushed Max against the wall. When Max started to protest, Todd pulled out his gun. Max's eyes got big, and as we walked past him toward the door, they got even bigger. "You stay here," Todd whispered. Max nodded compliantly. "The brews are still yours, bud." Max slid away, his back to the wall, like a man who'd stepped out onto the ledge of a skyscraper.

Bailey and I held our guns down at our sides as we tiptoed single file toward the apartment. The door was a quarter of the way open. I peered inside but saw only darkness. My heart was thudding in my chest. What a weird place for me to die. In a dingy apartment in La Conchita. I listened for sounds of movement. Music was playing somewhere inside, but it wasn't coming from the front room. Todd pushed the door farther open and moved inside, and we followed, our guns now straight out in front of us. We walked into a living room, which looked empty. I slowed down to let my eyes adjust to the dim light and tried to scan every inch of the room for places where Shane might be hiding, getting ready to spring.

On our left was the kitchen and dining area—a tiny square of linoleum. We stopped and looked around. There was no one there, but the music was getting louder. We moved past the kitchen to a small hallway. There was a door on the right. Todd put his ear to the wall near it and listened, then shook his head. He took one side of the door, and Bailey and I took the other. He carefully reached out and tried the doorknob. It turned. My heart was in my throat as he pushed the door open. It was a bathroom. And it was dark. Todd crouched down, gun in both hands, straight out in front of him. It was a half bath, so there was no tub or shower. And no one was in there.

Todd continued down the hall toward the door at the end. Bailey and I followed. The music was louder now. It sounded like "Poker Face" by Lady Gaga, and it was coming from behind that door. This was it. I envisioned Shane standing inside, holding an AK aimed at us. I tried to pull Bailey back. She shook me off and moved in behind Todd.

Todd listened at the door, nodded to us, then twisted the doorknob. It turned, and as he inched the door open, I held my breath and steadied my gun in both hands. If Todd or Bailey missed their shot, mine would have to be the one to take Shane out. Then, in one swift motion, Todd threw back the door, crouched down, and pointed his gun, shouting, "Police!"

There stood Shane Dolan, hair dripping wet, a towel wrapped around his stomach. He froze, then threw his hands up. His towel dropped to the floor. Standing there naked as a jaybird, he screamed, "Don't shoot!"

56

For several long seconds, no one moved. Bailey recovered first. "Uh, Todd, you can stand down. I believe we can safely say he's unarmed." She looked at Shane. "No offense. Feel free to get your towel."

Shane nodded but kept his eyes trained on Todd as he bent down to get the towel and draped it around his waist.

"Where are your clothes?" Todd asked. Shane pointed to a chair. Todd gave the T-shirt and jeans a thorough going-over, then tossed them to Shane one at a time. Bailey and I checked his wallet and license to confirm his identity, then ripped through the room. We found a .38 Smith and Wesson under his pillow, a 9 mm Glock in the top drawer of the dresser, and an SBR AR-15 in the closet. They were all fully loaded. Bailey read him his rights. He waived them in a shaky voice.

We took him into the living room, handcuffed him, and tied him to a kitchen chair with some electrical cord Todd found under the sink. Bailey and Todd hovered over him, guns at their sides. Shane didn't look so good now, trussed up like a Thanksgiving turkey, all pale and trembling. But looking past that, I could see that his photo hadn't done him justice. The wavy brown hair curling over his forehead, hazel eyes, and full, sensual lips that had a rebellious curl made for an undeniably sexy package. I'd always been wary of the type, myself.

Since I was the only one not visibly armed, I was unofficially elected to play good cop. "Where's Logan Jarvis?"

His eyes narrowed with fury. "That lunatic asshole. I don't know and I don't want to know."

This was not the answer, or the attitude, I'd been expecting. "You two just shot up that theater, said adios, and went your separate ways?"

Shane's mouth dropped open. "Theater? Shooting? What the hell are you talking about?" He looked a little green around the gills. Some guys can do a pretty good job of feigning shock, but nausea—that's a toughie.

"Shane, now is not the time to play dumb. We might be able to save you from death row if you help us. But you can't waste our time with this 'who me?' bullshit."

"Lady, I'm not kidding. I don't know about any theater shooting. And the last time I saw Logan was a few weeks before the school shooting."

I folded my arms and gave him my best "give me a fucking break" look. "So you had nothing to do with the shooting at Fairmont High."

He teared up. His lips trembled, and for a few seconds it looked as though he was going to break down. But he closed his eyes, swallowed, and held it back. When he spoke, his voice was ragged. "Why in the hell would I want to shoot up a bunch of kids?" Shane looked at me, his expression tortured. "If I'd known that's what that fucking freak was getting the guns for, I'd have called the cops. I sure as hell wouldn't have sold him any." He dropped his head, and I saw tears fall into his lap. "I had no idea that's why he bought them until I saw the news that day."

"But we didn't release his name for a couple of days."

"Yeah, but I knew what school he went to, and I knew what I'd sold him. The reports all said what kind of weapons they used." He was right about that. "Plus, Logan talked some really weird shit just before...it all happened. He sent me this off-the-wall email the day before about seeing me 'on the other side.' At the time I just thought he was being his usual strange, geeky self. But then, when I saw the news about the shooting at Fairmont, I put it all together."

"And ran."

Shane gave me a hard look. "Bet your ass I ran."

Because he was, at the very least, on the hook for selling guns to a minor, for selling guns without registration, probably for buying stolen guns, possibly for burning off the registration numbers. The list went on and on.

"Where were you at the time of the Fairmont shooting?"

"At the VA hospital in Westwood, getting my meds. Check it out; they keep records."

"Don't worry, we will." Or rather, we'd been trying. The VA records were a mess. When Bailey got the tip about Shane being in La Conchita, she'd told the unis to drop everything else and focus on any records dated on or near the day of the shooting. With a little luck, we'd have our answer soon. "What were you getting meds for?"

Shane tightened his lips for a moment and looked away. Finally, he answered. "PTSD. I'm not saying I was a model citizen before the war, but when I got back..." He shook his head. "I couldn't deal. Couldn't sleep, couldn't think straight. The only thing that made me feel better was getting high. It was the only way I could block out the memories. I couldn't hold down a job, and after getting fired a couple of times, I was totally hosed." Shane looked up at me. "But I'm guessing Luke already told you about that."

"Some, yeah."

Shane nodded. "After Luke moved out, things really went to shit. I fell apart. They denied my disability claims, I lost my job at the garage, so I couldn't pay the rent. The landlord gave me a three-day notice. I was pretty much homeless. That's when I met up with a guy at a gun range out in Agoura Hills."

I figured out where this was heading. "And that's the guy who got you into gun sales."

"Yeah. It was a natural move for me. I was raised in Montana. Learned to shoot before I learned to read. So I knew guns. And the money was great. I got myself out of debt and out of L.A. and got myself a job at the tree service. And I'm practically off the meds. Doing good now." Shane looked at the three of us surrounding him. "Well, I *was.*"

"Good? You call illegal gunrunning good?"

He leaned back and glared at me. "What the fuck do I care? The U.S. government screwed me over. Hard. Used me up and spit me out. The VA takes a year to process my claims. They were worthless when I needed help finding work. So the government wants to regulate gun sales? Fuck 'em. It's my constitutional right to bear arms."

"And to sell them to kids?" Shane looked away. "Where have you been for the past two days?" I deliberately didn't give him the date of the theater shooting. I wanted to see how much of his time he could account for.

"Up north, near Red Bluff."

"When did you get down here?"

"This morning. I dumped the car—"

"The Jetta?"

"Yeah. Figured you guys might be onto that. Picked up the bike—"

"You mean stole—"

Shane glared at me. "*Bought*—just outside Sacramento."

"When?"

"Yesterday."

If that was true, there was no way he could've done the theater shooting. "Who'd you buy it from?"

"Look in my wallet. There's a receipt. Seller was a guy named Trinidad…something. Got his phone number on there and everything. You'll see."

Bailey leaned over and whispered to Todd and he nodded. "Be right back," she said. "You keep going." I knew she was going to check Shane's alibis.

"Assuming your alibis check out and you're not one of the shooters, you're still on the hook for selling the guns to them—"

"Them? I didn't sell anything to 'them.' The only person I sold to was Logan. I never saw anyone else." His voice was firm. "I kept my customer list tight. Never spread my net too wide."

"You didn't deal with any friends of Logan's?"

"Never. Our deals were always one-on-one."

"Didn't it strike you as odd that one kid would buy that many weapons? All those AKs and at least four handguns?"

"No, it didn't strike me as 'odd.'" He tilted his head to indicate air quotes. "I had more guns than that by my thirteenth birthday."

"Your dad gave you an AK for your thirteenth birthday?"

Shane looked away.

"How'd you get your hands on a fully automatic AK?"

"I didn't. I converted it myself. It's not that hard."

"How many guns did you sell to Logan?"

"Two assault rifles and four handguns."

I had an idea, but before I could pursue it, Bailey came back and pulled me aside. "The VA story checks out," she whispered. "He was there at eighty thirty a.m. the day of the Fairmont shooting and he was in the pharmacy getting his script filled at ten forty-five. No way he could've been at the school."

"And Cinemark?"

"We're waiting to hear back about him buying the bike the day of that shooting, but the receipt was in his wallet and the voice on the answering machine gave the name Trinidad. It's probably going to check out."

And in any case, he had an airtight alibi for the school shooting. If Shane hadn't been involved in the Fairmont shooting, then he probably hadn't done the theater shooting either. Which only begged the question: who the hell was the second shooter? I'd never been wild about the theory that a grown man like Shane would be Logan's sidekick. But clearing Shane meant we had no one on the hook.

When I went back to Shane, his head was hanging down and his expression was tortured.

"Logan never brought a friend who talked guns with you? You're sure about that?"

Shane shook his head emphatically. "I don't remember ever meeting any friends of his and I sure as hell didn't talk guns with any other kids. I only talked to him because he was Luke's brother."

I couldn't think of a reason for him to hold back any names at this point. He knew he was on the hook for so much already, admitting that another kid was involved wasn't worth lying about. He really didn't know. But maybe he could help us find Logan. "Did Logan ever tell you about any places he liked to go?"

"You mean places to hide?" I nodded. "No. And you gotta believe me, I'd tell you. I would. You've got to catch that kid, he's a friggin' maniac."

Coming from the man who'd given him the firepower, that was some kind of irony.

57

Shane rolled his head and stretched his neck. "You can take the cuffs off, guys. I'm obviously not going anywhere."

He did look uncomfortable. But I was fresh out of sympathy for gunrunners. "Who's your connect?"

Shane stared straight ahead. "Internet."

He might as well have been wearing a neon sign that said I'M GOING TO LIE NOW.

"Let me help you with those cuffs." I walked around behind his chair and held up my hand to Bailey for the key. She tossed it to me with a smirk. I unlocked the cuffs. Then ratcheted them down two notches tighter and relocked them. Shane let out a yelp of pain. "Not much better, huh? Sorry 'bout that."

I walked back around and faced him. "Let's try that again. Who's your connect?"

Shane lifted his head defiantly. "I told you, I buy my guns on the Internet."

"Is that right? Then why'd you burn off all the registration numbers?" That was a separate charge unto itself, and I could file one for each gun. Shane's sentence could add up to serious double digits real fast.

"That's how they were when I bought 'em."

I stared at him. "Seriously, what makes you think I'll believe such obvious horseshit? Because I'm female?" I folded my arms. "Or is it just that you're that bad at lying?" Shane opened his mouth to protest. "No. Stop it. We don't have time for this nonsense. That kid you called a maniac is out there planning his next massacre at this very moment. So start talking, and this time, go with the truth."

Shane squirmed in his handcuffs, trying to find a comfortable position. I could've told him not to bother. When I first joined the DA's office, I asked a bailiff to cuff me to one of the chairs at counsel table so I could feel what it was like. He was happy to oblige. And then he and the clerk took off for lunch. Such funny, funny guys. For the next hour, I tried to wriggle my way out of them. I learned two things that day: those cuffs are damned uncomfortable and never trust a bailiff.

Shane tried to flex his shoulders, but the electrical cord didn't leave him any room to move. "You can't do this. It's gotta be, like, against the law."

"That's cute. A lesson on the law. From the man who sold illegal weapons to a minor. Do you know how many years you'll get just for bringing those assault rifles into California? Let alone for selling them to a kid? And then we can talk about burning off the serial numbers. By the time I get done stacking up all the charges, you'll be facing close to a hundred years. And trust me, there isn't a judge in the county who won't max you out. Know why? Because you're going to be Public Enemy Number Three. Right behind the two shooters. They couldn't have done it without you, and I'll make sure no one forgets it. In fact, some might even believe you knew that's what Logan planned all along. That makes you a coconspirator. So tell me, who do you think is going to give a shit that your cuffs are too tight?"

"Coconspirator! You've got to be kidding me. I didn't know!" He looked from me to Bailey to Todd. "I didn't! You've got to believe me!"

"Actually, we might. But I can't speak for anyone else. Probably another DA will handle your case. And if they decide to charge you with conspiracy and you wind up in front of a jury? Conservatively speaking, I'd say you're toast. Try to imagine how badly they're going to want to string up anyone who so much as gave Logan directions to the bathroom. Now imagine how they'll feel about the guy who gave him the guns." Shane was shaking his head. "You paying attention? It's important you stay with me here, because I'm talking about hundreds of counts of conspiracy to commit murder and attempted murder."

Shane's breath was coming fast and shallow now. "I didn't know shit! They can't convict me!"

"Well of course they can. And my guess is they will. They'll bury you so deep you'll still be in prison when you reincarnate. So you can talk now and buy yourself a little goodwill. Or you can keep fucking with me and roll the dice with the twelve-headed monster. Your choice."

Shane shook his head slowly. "I can't tell you. I'll be dead."

"Oh, please, Priscilla, spare us the drama. You'll be plenty safe. You didn't think we were just going to take a statement from you and let you trot on home?" I shook my head. "You're going down for those gun sales no matter what—"

"You think they can't get to me in prison?"

"Who's 'they'?"

Shane pressed his lips together. His face looked pinched.

"We'll make sure you're housed in a safe place. Maybe federal custody. Trust me, by the time you finish your sentence, they'll have forgotten all about you."

Shane dropped his head and sagged in his chair for several long moments. No one said a word. Finally, he cleared his throat. His voice was a hoarse whisper. "You got my cell?"

Bailey held it up. "Give me the name."

"Jax. Jax Esposito."

Bailey started to scroll through his contacts. "How'd you meet him?"

"At a gun show. He had a couple of guns that needed fixing. I fixed them and he paid me in cash on the spot. After that, he asked me if I wanted to help him get rid of some extra inventory. I thought, what the hell? Sell a few guns here and there, but man, I had no idea. Crates of the shit."

"What kind of guns?"

"All kinds. You name it, he had it. Rifles, shotguns, AKs, revolvers, semi-autos. Dude even had a flamethrower. It was crazy."

"So how did you wind up buying enough to make a living?" Bailey asked.

"Because I wound up providing…extra services. He was looking for a drug connection in the States—"

"The States?" I asked. "Where's he from?"

"Mexico."

"And he was looking to buy?" Bailey asked.

"No, to sell."

"What kind of drugs?" I asked.

"Weed, *yayo.* I think pills too, but I'm not a hundred percent. Drugs aren't my thing." I raised an eyebrow. "Anymore."

"Yayo?" Todd asked.

"Cocaine," Bailey said. "Slang, taken from the Spanish word for ice, *hielo.*"

"So what was the deal?" I asked.

"I'd hook him up with a buyer in the States and he'd give me a sweet deal on guns."

"Sweet enough to let you resell for a fat profit."

Shane nodded. "I've been saving up to buy a place in Camarillo. I've almost got enough for a little two-bedroom near the airport."

"*Had,* Shane," I said. "You mean *had.*" Shane sank in his chair and nodded. "How did Logan meet up with this Jax guy?"

"How'd you know he met Jax?"

Because Logan and his buddy had dropped the assault rifles Shane sold them at the school. Because they'd had two more when they did the theater shooting. Which meant Logan had to have bought two more after the Fairmont shooting. If Shane was telling the truth and he hadn't sold Logan any more guns, then Logan had to have had his own connection. And being a Valley boy, as opposed to the son of a Mafia don or Yakuza oyabun, his opportunities to find gun connections were pretty limited. "Just answer the question. How did Logan meet this guy?"

"The first time I met up with Jax to make the exchange—"

"Guns for you, the name of a buyer for him," Bailey said.

Shane nodded. "I was nervous. I mean, I'd done some repair work for the guy, but this time we were making a deal, and it was pretty big, so I wanted backup. Someone else around just in case..."

In case Jax decided to take the name and blow Shane off—or blow him away. "You brought Logan," I said.

"Yeah. Logan knew about my gun business already so I wasn't worried about him going to the cops or anything. Plus, he was real tall, and with shades on he looked older—and kind of scary." Shane stopped and shook his head. Even he couldn't miss the irony of that statement.

"Weren't you worried Logan might cut you out? Get rid of the middleman and make his own deals with Jax?"

"Of course. That's why I never left them alone."

"Never? Your back was never turned? Logan never had a second to slip Jax his phone number, or vice versa?"

Shane frowned. "No... well, I guess I can't say for sure."

Bailey and I exchanged a look. Logan was a lot smarter than this nimrod. Plus, he knew that he'd need to restock his arsenal after the school shooting and wouldn't be able to go back to Shane. "Whose idea was it to bring Logan to that meeting with Jax?"

"Uh, mine. And his. I told him I was about to score the guns he wanted but that I needed some backup, because the guy was kind of shady."

"And Logan said he could be that backup."

Shane nodded. "Yeah."

I inclined my head—*Get it?*

He expelled a long breath and turned his head away as he muttered, "Fucker played me."

Big-time. I took Shane's phone from Bailey and looked at the entry for Jax. The area code was for Riverside, a few hours south of La Conchita. "You know what, Shane? You need more guns. And right away."

58

Bailey tapped me on the arm. "Can we powwow for a minute?"

"Sure." I turned back to the bound-and-cuffed Shane. "Don't go anywhere. I'll be right back."

"'Don't go anywhere,'" Shane said. "That's a real knee-slapper. Who knew you DAs could be such a laugh riot."

Bailey pulled me into the bedroom. "I like your idea of a setup with Jax, but I think we need to take a minute and decide what we want to do with him, assuming Shane can arrange a meet."

"My guess is that Logan has to hook up with him again to restock. So, we put a bug on Jax and follow him until they meet."

"But what if Logan's already met with Jax?"

Then the next shooting couldn't be far off. That was probably true regardless. I knew that. We all did. But somehow, Bailey's words brought the urgency home in a way that made my chest tighten. "Then we'll need to squeeze the guy. Find out everything he knows about Logan. See if he knows what Logan's planning."

"And Logan would tell him because...?"

I exhaled sharply and shook my head. "You're right. He wouldn't necessarily." I started pacing. "But this Jax guy's the most solid lead yet. We've got to do something with him. And thanks to Shane, we've got leverage." I stopped pacing and looked at Bailey. "But Shane's got to be the one to talk to Jax, find out whether he's met with Logan."

Bailey frowned. "I really hate to rely on him for something like that. Why don't we just bust Jax and force him to cooperate? Like you said, we've got the leverage. Shane's testimony alone will nail him—and he'll probably be carrying something we can bust him for."

"What if he won't deal?" Criminals aren't the most logical bunch. You can't count on them to act in their own best interest—let alone figure out what that is. "Besides, setting up Jax as a decoy is our best shot at catching Logan. And we have to use Shane to do that." Bailey didn't look entirely convinced. "How about this: if he tells Shane there's no plan to meet up with Logan again, we bust him. I know it's risky to let Shane set this up. But if it pays off, it's more than worth it."

Bailey reluctantly nodded. "But we'll need serious backup," she said. "This Jax character might bring friends. A lot could go wrong. How about I call Graden and get him to give us Harrellson and a couple of others?"

I thought about it for a moment, then shook my head. "I'm not sure that's such a great idea."

Involving Graden was a good news/bad news proposition. If he liked our plan, it meant we'd be covered both physically and politically if anything went wrong. But if he, or more likely someone above him, didn't like it, we'd be shut down. And there were some pretty obvious reasons for the brass to nix the idea. It was a risky gambit, planting a bug on a known drug and gun seller. If we lost him, or if he found the bug before he met with Logan, he'd be in the wind. In which case we—or at least LAPD—would be on the hook for losing a major player. The potential shitstorm of blame was incalculable.

So odds were, we wouldn't get approval. But this was the only move we had. We needed to make it, and make it fast. Bailey and I and the shrinks agreed that Logan wasn't about to end his siege on a dud like the Cinemark theater. He was gearing up for another, and probably bigger, round. This might be our best—and maybe only—chance to prevent it. If we asked for permission, we'd be shut down. We couldn't afford that.

If it all went south and I wound up fired, so be it. Better that than knowing I blew a chance to stop more carnage. "We could get some… unofficial backup. Let me make a few phone calls."

Bailey raised a suspicious eyebrow. "Hurry."

"You know, *mija,* at some point a debt is paid. Done with. I can't always be bailing you out of shit." Luis Revelo, shot-caller for the Sylmar Sevens gang, spoke patiently, as though explaining the facts of life to a dim-witted younger cousin.

We'd met when he was suspected—wrongly—of having raped the daughter of a wealthy doctor and businessman who turned out to have unfortunate "associations" that linked him to child pornography and murder. I cleared Luis of the rape, and in return, he tricked out my Honda, which had been badly vandalized during the case. Luis planned to go into marketing and give up the gang life. He was aiming for an MBA and had just finished his second year of community college with a 4.0 average. He looked like a shoo-in for acceptance to the University of California in Los Angeles. But he still had to pay the rent. For himself, his mother, a few cousins, and assorted others.

So for now, he was still the gang leader. Which had made him a great source of information for me in past cases. Right now, it meant that he had the firepower and the manpower to provide serious, if potentially overzealous, backup.

"What do you mean *always?*" I said. "I ever ask you for backup before? And besides, I saved your life. Remember? I'd say that means you'll be owing me for a while."

"Aww don' zaggerate. No jury woulda convicted me. Susan woulda told 'em I din't—damn, I mean *didn't* do it."

This is so typical. Win a case, it was a no-brainer anybody could've won. Lose a case, it's *all* you. No matter how you slice it, we never get credit.

"You didn't seem so sure of that when you *kidnapped* me just so you could beg me to help you." Luis had had a couple of his soldiers scoop me off the street so he could plead his case to me privately. Lucky for him, I was open-minded enough to listen. Also, they had guns.

"I *said* I was sorry. An' we jus' snatched you for a little bit. You gonna keep bringin' that up forever?"

Why stop when it worked so well? "You know, Luis, another prosecutor, who didn't have such a highly developed sense of humor, might have actually filed charges for that 'little bit.' You don't realize how fortunate you are that it was me and not some hard-ass."

"Yeah, you're cool, I know that. But look, it's bad for my rep to be hanging around with a DA. I got my name to think of. I got to keep re-speck in the ranks. You feel me?"

The burdens of leadership could be daunting. "*Respect,* Luis. Anyway, this is for the shooting at Fairmont High. You hear about that?"

There was a long pause. "Shit, everybody heard about that. Why din't you say so? Those *pendejo* motherfuckers. Whadda you need?"

59

When I came out of the bedroom, Shane was complaining loudly that he had to use the bathroom. He'd been stuck in that chair for more than an hour. It was possible he was telling the truth. I looked at Bailey. "Do we let him?"

Bailey shrugged. "Your call. Just keep in mind, we're taking him to this meeting with Jax, and it's a very long ride. And I don't intend to make any rest stops."

Todd spoke up. "Since we're going to have to use my car"—Todd looked at Bailey—"we can't use your cop car. I vote we let him answer nature's call before we leave."

"It's unanimous, Shane," I said. I opened my purse and pulled out my gun. "But no one's going to mind shooting you if you try to run."

"I can count. I know I'm outnumbered."

Bailey untied him, cuffed his hands in front of his body, and let Todd escort him. When the bathroom door closed, she whispered to me, "So what'd you work out for backup?" I told her about Luis. She reared back and stared at me. "Are you out of your mind? Bangers? Who's going to protect us from *them?*"

I was saved from having to answer that rather excellent question by the emergence of Todd and Shane from the little boys' room. Todd got him reseated and cuffed in the kitchen chair.

Shane gave Bailey a pleading look. "Can we do without the cord? I'm obviously not going anywhere. Besides, I'm kinda working for you guys now."

We had to trust him eventually. Bailey gave him the evil eye, but she left the electrical cord on the kitchen counter. "Here's the plan, Shane.

You're going to set up a meeting with Jax. Tell him you've got a big buyer on the line who needs guns yesterday—"

"Won't work. He doesn't give a shit about the guns. He only cares about a buyer for the drugs. Jax won't move off his couch unless I promise him a name."

"And where is Jax's couch?" Bailey asked.

"Ensenada."

"Where do you two meet when you do business with him?" I asked.

"Usually Joshua Tree Park. He's got family near there, I think."

That was within reasonable driving distance. "Tell Jax you've got a big drug buyer on the line for him, but he needs to move now. The guy wants his product by tomorrow. Then you tell him you need to get a couple of AKs for someone, and you need them by tonight—"

"Tonight? There's no way—"

"Trust me, there is. But make it late. Around midnight. And set the meeting for Riverside. Got it?"

Shane swallowed hard, but reluctantly nodded. I pressed the number for Jax and held the phone to his ear. The conversation was short and sweet. Jax gave him a little grief about the short notice, but he eventually capitulated. The meeting was set for one a.m. at their usual meeting place in Joshua Tree National Park.

Todd squinted at Shane. "Where in Joshua Tree? That place is a ginormous desert."

"Don't sweat it," Shane said. "I'll get us there."

But I knew that's not what Todd was worried about. Joshua Tree was flat and wide-open. Finding a way to hide our backup was going to be a problem. I nodded at Todd. "We'll see what it looks like, and if we don't like it, we'll suggest a change of plan. We've got his cell."

Shane took a deep breath and exhaled as he closed his eyes. "Jax might bail on you if you change the meeting place at the last minute."

I had a feeling about Jax and his business with Shane. "I don't think he will. Let's get going."

We raided the kitchen for water, soda, and snacks, left some money for Max to pay for it all, then packed up Shane's belongings and piled into

Todd's car, a black Camry. Todd volunteered to ride in back with Shane. It wasn't until we were heading south on the Pacific Coast Highway that I remembered to ask what had happened to Max.

"I called my partner and told him to keep a close watch on Max," Todd said. "I'm betting he didn't know Shane was on the run—"

"He didn't," Shane said.

"—but we'll hang on to him until we know for sure."

The sun hung low on the horizon, and the burnt-orange rays spread across the ocean, giving the water a warm glow. We were all tired and for a while we rode in silence.

Shane cleared his throat. "Uh, Ms.... what did you say your name was again?"

"Rachel Knight."

"Right. Mind if I ask you a question?" I shook my head. "You seemed pretty sure Jax wouldn't get pissed off about a change of plan. How come?"

"Did you ever wonder where Jax was getting all those guns, and all that dope?"

"Not really."

"So you didn't think it was strange that this guy leans on you to get him connects to sell drugs?" Shane shrugged. "Look, no offense, but you don't exactly seem the drug kingpin type. I mean, you guys only hooked up because you knew how to fix guns, right?"

"Yeah. So?"

"It's just a guess, but I think your buddy works for a cartel and he's skimming. It's probably a big enough operation that whatever he's taking—drugs, guns—hasn't been missed. At least, not yet. But he can't let that stuff hang around. He's got to move it fast. So he needs you every bit as much as you need him. Maybe more."

Shane was silent for a few moments. "Man, if you're right, he's out of his friggin' mind."

No argument there. I got on the phone and coordinated with Luis. We'd stop in Sylmar so he and his crew could follow us. I told him the meeting place was in Joshua Tree and that it might be hard to find cover.

"We know what we're doin'," Luis said. "You jes' worry 'bout you."

His certainty was comforting. Sort of.

I had just ended the call when Bailey's cell rang. "Want me to get it for you?" I asked.

"Check who it is first."

It was Harrellson.

"Take it."

"Hey, Skipper."

"I told you never to call me that," he said.

"I forgot."

His parents named him Skipper Don Harrellson. He tried to keep it a secret, but cops are always on the lookout for needling material, and this one was low-hanging fruit.

"They just found a body out in Box Canyon," he said. Box Canyon was west of Chatsworth in a remote corner of the San Fernando Valley. Charles Manson once freeloaded off a religious cult there. "Young white male, approximately sixteen years of age."

A lead weight dropped to the pit of my stomach. "Evan?"

"That's what they thought, but...I'll get back to you when I know more. I'm on my way out there. You'll let Bailey know."

"Yeah."

"Sorry, Knight. I'll be in touch as soon as I know more."

60

I whispered the news to Bailey. She gripped the steering wheel but said nothing for several moments. When she spoke, her voice was tight. "Do we know what happened?"

"No. Harrellson wasn't about to say anything on the phone. But it might've just been an accident. He could've fallen, been hit by a car."

"Be a hell of a coincidence, though, wouldn't it?" I didn't need to answer. Neither of us believed in them. "How do you think Logan found him?"

"No clue," I said. "But we know Evan hasn't been using his cell phone—"

"Probably bought a burner. But I just don't see him reaching out to Logan."

I didn't either. And I didn't know how else Logan would find him. In a city as vast as Los Angeles—hell, even in the Valley—it's pretty hard to run into someone who's trying to run away. I couldn't figure this one out with what little information we had. And for all we knew, it might not be Evan at all. I held on to that hope and turned back to the matter at hand.

The traffic got heavy when we hit Thousand Oaks, and we didn't reach our meeting place in Sylmar until almost nine at night. Subtlety wasn't Luis's style when it came to cars, so I scanned the street for glitter and shiny chrome. Nothing like that was parked on either side of the block. I called Luis. "Hey, we're here. What street are you on?"

Luis chuckled. "You jes' rolled right by us. Turn around." I did, and saw a dark blue, nondescript sedan flash its headlights.

What was I thinking? Of course he was smart enough to know when he needed to keep a low profile. It's how he stayed out of prison. I put my hand out the window to give a thumbs-up.

Luis gave an exasperated sigh. "Don' do that no more."

When we got back on the freeway, the traffic had eased up considerably. We had smooth sailing all the way down to Riverside and pulled into Joshua Tree National Park by midnight. The abrupt shift from all the lights, noise, and motion to pitch-black desert was stunning.

The air felt hushed. Huge rock formations stood out against the black night, and the sky was thick with stars usually hidden by the lights of civilization. Barren, blanketed with the cacti that gave the park its name, Joshua Tree Park stretched out for miles before us. It had an austere beauty, but it conveyed a sense of isolation that made it feel as if we were the last survivors of a nuclear holocaust.

Bailey pulled over to the side of the road just outside the entrance and turned toward the backseat. "Where exactly is your meeting place?"

"It's about two miles in, over there." He gestured with his chin—since he was still handcuffed—to the right side of the park.

The area was bordered by rocky hills that had a sparse covering of withered-looking trees. Plenty of hiding space for Luis and company. So far, so good. I called Luis and told him where we were headed.

"Good," he said. "Now don' call me no more. And don' worry. I got this."

I was about to meet with a gunrunner/drug dealer who was probably an errant cartel member, and my backup was a car full of gangbangers who probably had a bigger arsenal than he did. What on earth could I be worried about?

"Probably best if we uncuff this guy and let him ride up front now," Bailey said.

This was where we knew everything could go south on us. We had to let Shane out, find a place to hide, then hope he'd do his part. The only thing that gave me confidence was the fact that Shane was more afraid of Luis than of us. Todd didn't love the plan, but he hadn't been able to come up with anything better. He reluctantly uncuffed Shane, and I got out to trade places with him.

Shane rubbed his wrists. "Man those things hurt." Todd pulled him out of the car, and he swung his arms and stretched before Todd pushed him toward the front seat. "Hey," Shane said. "Gimme a sec, here. I gotta loosen up for the big play."

Todd had zero patience for Shane's plight. "Move it, Lefty, we don't have all night."

Shane slid into the front seat, and Bailey drove slowly down the dark road. Shane leaned back and studied the scenery. But after a couple of minutes, he sat up and began to rub his hands on his thighs. It was cold, probably no more than forty-five degrees at most, but the moonlight revealed beads of sweat gleaming on his forehead. Shane cleared his throat and pointed to a small body of water to our left that was just below an outcropping of rocks. Perfect cover for Luis and us. Unfortunately, also for whoever might have tagged along with Jax.

Bailey parked facing away from the outcropping and left the headlights on. It was so dark you could barely see your own hand. We climbed up and hid behind the nearest grouping of rocks. Shane sat in the driver's seat—sans keys, of course. We had a good half hour before Jax was due. I pulled out my cell to see if I could get any signal. Only two bars, but it was better than nothing. I could probably reach Luis if I had to, and if things got bad enough, I'd just yell.

Todd looked over my shoulder. "You playing Angry Birds?"

"Gotta keep my score up. Or...whatever people do."

"Not my thing either—"

Bailey, who'd planted herself just ahead of us, turned back. "Shut up. Both of you."

I wanted to call Shane—we'd given him Bailey's cell—just to do a test run, but at that moment I noticed a moving dust cloud to the left of the outcropping where we hid. Then I heard the engine. A black Escalade came into view. Jax had arrived. He pulled up next to Todd's car, peered in through the passenger window at Shane, and got out. I couldn't make out a lot of detail in the darkness, but Jax looked to be in his fifties, about six feet tall and paunchy, in a black leather jacket and khakis. As instructed, Shane walked around to the front of the car and stopped. If Jax joined him there, we'd hear every word. Shane fished a cigarette out of his shirt pocket, leaned back against the hood, and asked Jax for a light.

Jax sauntered over and flicked his lighter. "Got another one?"

"What? You can't buy your own?"

"Wife's trying to get me to quit." Jax shook his head. "S'only been two days and I'm goin' crazy."

Shane shook his head and chuckled, then pulled out another cigarette and gave it to him.

Jax leaned back against the car next to Shane, took a deep, appreciative drag, and blew it out. "So what you got for me?"

"Big name. This guy's serious. Needs five kilos of *yayo.*"

"By tomorrow morning?"

Shane nodded.

Jax shook his head. "I can't get that much. Not that fast. Get him to take two."

Now I was more convinced than ever that Jax was skimming. Five kilos was big, but not that big. Shane shrugged. "Do what I can. You got the AKs for me?"

"Yeah, no problem."

This was it. Time to pop the question. Shane took another drag of his cigarette. "Say, you remember that guy I brought with me last time?"

I stopped breathing. Jax paused, flicked the ashes from his cigarette. "Tall, skinny *güero* in the shades?"

Shane nodded. "That's him. You see him lately?"

"Nah. Ain't seen him since that day he came with you."

How could that be? Shane said he only sold Logan two AKs. So how could Logan have gotten hold of the other two they'd used in the theater shooting? Unless Logan had a second gun connection?

Shane was working it pretty well, but I could hear the strain in his voice. I prayed Jax wouldn't. "Reason I'm asking is he told me he needed to get in touch with you, and I gave him your number."

Smart. Shane was putting Jax at ease in case he thought Shane was pissed off for meeting behind Shane's back.

"No, I din't see that guy. But I did run into a buddy of his." Jax pushed off the car and turned toward the Escalade.

"No shit. When was that?"

"Three, maybe four days ago?" Jax took one last drag, then threw the cigarette down and crushed it under his boot. I appreciated the fact that he observed fire safety measures. "I was visiting family, had a bunch of product left over 'cuz another dude stiffed me. Din't want to take it back over the border. So when the kid called me, said he needed a couple AKs and a forty-four, I figured, what the hell? Green's green, you know?"

"Hell, yeah. But I just need to know, he was a young dude, right?" Shane asked. "I want to make sure it's the right guy. 'Cuz if it is, he owes me for the connect."

Jax started to move toward the Escalade. "Shit, I don't know. He seemed like maybe twenties. Told me that tall, skinny guy who's your buddy sent him. Loman...Lofin—"

"Logan?" Shane asked.

"Yeah, that's it. And the dude gave me your name too, bro'."

"Huh. Dude give you his name?"

Jax stopped and turned back to Shane. "Said it was...Tim...Timothy something. Don't remember the last name. What's up, man?" Jax peered at Shane. "You telling me you don't know the dude?"

Timothy? I racked my brain, but as far as I knew, the case hadn't turned up any Timothys.

Shane threw down his cigarette and ground it out. "Probably a phony name. I don't know any Timothys. What'd he look like?"

"Fuck," Jax said. "I don't know. Kind of medium. Not tall like that other dude."

"What about his hair?"

Jax stiffened. "Man, I don' know. Dude wore, like, a baseball cap and shades." He peered at Shane. "What's with all the questions?"

Shane was doing a hell of a nice of job of this, but Jax was getting suspicious. And pissed. If Shane didn't pull the plug soon, this could turn very ugly, very fast. There was a trunkload of weapons in that Escalade, and Jax was just steps away from it.

"Just making sure who it is, 'cause the dude owes me, and now it looks like he's in the wind. I don't put up with assholes like that. You got any plans to meet up with him again?"

"No." Jax was getting edgier and edgier.

"You remember his ride? 'Cause I find this guy, I'm gonna fuck it up."

Jax stubbed the ground with the toe of his boot. "Some old junker. Chevy, I think." He turned back and moved toward the rear door of the Escalade. Shane needed to get out of this fast and let us take over. Before Jax put his hands on the guns. "Let's get this done. I got to be someplace."

Jax opened the rear door. This was it. I pushed Luis's cell number and punched in 5—our code to move in fast. Within seconds, Jax was surrounded by three of the biggest, meanest-looking Hispanic guys I'd ever seen, plus Luis. And all of them were pointing nine millimeters. I thought I recognized one of the guys from my kidnapping, but it might've just been the size. And did I mention the meanness?

Jax raised his hands high into the air, and I noticed they were shaking. Then I saw a stain spread around the crotch of his pants. Bad day to wear khakis. He looked at Luis, and in a trembling voice, asked, "Who the fuck are you?"

Luis smiled. "Friend of a friend."

Jax's eyes were wide with fear. "Carlos?"

Bailey, Todd, and I stepped out from behind the rocks with our guns drawn, Bailey in the lead. "No," she said. She whipped out her badge and it flashed in the moonlight. "Police. You're under arrest."

Jax dropped to his knees, hands still high in the air, and sobbed. "Oh, *Dios mío,* thank God."

61

While Todd put in a call to the local police, I walked Luis and company to their car.

"You guys were perfect, Luis," I said. "Thanks."

He blew out a disgusted breath. "For what? We din't do nuthin'." He muttered to himself. "Shit—*anything*."

I shoved a couple of twenties through the driver's window. He looked at the bills with disdain. "What's that for?"

"Gas money. It's only fair."

Luis started to push it away, but a voice from the back protested. "Luis, I'm kinda low..."

Luis rolled his eyes, took the cash, and passed it to the backseat. He tilted his head and squinted at me. "Try an' stay out of trouble," he said. "I can't always be here to watch your back, you know." He peeled out, leaving me in a cloud of dust.

I was still coughing when Bailey walked over to me. "All set." Jax was bent over the hood of Todd's car, hands cuffed behind his back. Shane was in the backseat, facing out with the door open. He was cuffed too. Todd was holding a cigarette to his lips, giving him one last smoke.

"We can go over everything with Jax again when we get to the station," Bailey said. "But I have a feeling our buddy Shane got all he has to give."

"Yeah," I said. "Shane did a nice job. Sounds like Jax met with our second shooter, but good luck figuring out who that is. That description could fit about five million guys."

Bailey sighed and nodded. "Virtually useless. And the car—not much better."

I nodded, glum. "Interesting that he bought another forty-four, though."

"Yeah, even considering the cut-rate deal he got from Guns R Us over there." Bailey nodded toward Jax. "That's a lot of money."

Four squad cars showed up, lights blazing and sirens wailing. When the sergeant in charge saw that both suspects were cuffed and peaceful, he cracked a wry smile. "Always appreciate it when visitors pick up their own litter."

I introduced myself and shook his hand. "It's important to preserve the natural beauty of our parks and recreational grounds, don't you think?"

He chuckled. "Want to tell me what we have here?"

While the unis loaded Shane and Jax into their cars, I brought him up to speed—sort of. I didn't tell him how we'd pressured Shane into setting up the meeting with Jax, and I soft-pedaled the real reason for the meeting: to get a lead on the school shooters. Everything having to do with our case had to stay quiet until it was cleared with Graden.

"We'll keep them here for tonight, but we're short of bed space, so—"

Bailey held up a hand. "No problem. We appreciate the help. I'll have them off your hands tomorrow morning."

We followed them back to the station. The paperwork took a while, and by the time we headed back to L.A., it was almost four in the morning.

"Hey, you guys know of a place I can crash for the night?" Todd said between yawns.

"I can get you a room at the Biltmore," I said. It wasn't crowded this time of year, and when I explained why I needed the room, I had a feeling they'd let him have it for free.

"And if you don't mind, I'll have a uni ride up with you in the morning to pick up my car," Bailey said. "Rache, okay if I crash with you?"

"Only if you promise not to wake me up at the crack of dawn." Bailey was a morning person times ten. For me, mornings work best when they're the end of my night.

She gave me a tired smile. I don't know how she managed to keep her eyes open. Bailey had done most of the driving since yesterday morning.

And now that I thought of it, she really had no choice. She had to spend the night with me. We needed to get our stories straight.

MONDAY, OCTOBER 14

The next morning over breakfast we agreed on our official story about last night: Harrellson had forwarded us the tip from off-duty officer Todd Santos about seeing Shane in La Conchita. We followed up, and Shane agreed to help us out by setting up the meeting with Jax. All true, except for the bit of arm-twisting we'd needed to persuade Shane to join up with the good guys. But that bit of fudging only helped make him look better, which would come in handy when his lawyer tried to negotiate a deal for him. When we told him how we were going to play it, he was happy to go along.

We watched Shane give his statement on a monitor outside the interview room. It was a little scary how well he sold it.

We still hadn't gotten any updates from Harrellson about the body they'd found in Box Canyon. A part of me didn't want to hear from him. I didn't want confirmation that it was Evan. But we needed to find out whether they'd recovered anything from the body or the scene that might help us find Logan and company. "You want to give Harrellson a call?" I asked.

"Yeah, I've been wondering what the holdup is." Bailey picked up her office phone and punched in the number. Then she frowned and hung up. "I got his voice mail." Her tone was aggravated.

"So? I'm told it happens in the best of families. Why not leave a message?"

"Because I called his private cell, and he always answers it." She used her cell and tried again. This time, he answered. "Hey, what gives?" Bailey asked. She listened, then finally said, "Okay, got it," and ended the call. She didn't look happy. "Said he got my first call but didn't want to answer because it was the station number and he wasn't sure it was me. He wouldn't talk on the phone. He's at the morgue. Said he'll get in touch when he's done. I know we need to be careful and all, but seriously? It's going be on the news in about ten seconds anyway."

"Yeah, this radio silence shit is getting pretty old," I said. And to be honest, we weren't in the best of moods. The Shane–Jax connection had only confirmed our working theory: there was a second suspect—*still* unknown—who'd scored more guns after the school shooting. Since there was no indication when or even *if* the shooters ever intended to go back to Jax, we were basically back to square one. "We need another move."

"I know," Bailey said. "I've been thinking about those letters. We figured someone must be helping them because it's not likely our shooters mailed them from Boulder, right?" I nodded. "I was thinking that person might be a weak link."

And therefore our best lead. "And what's cool is they'll be so easy to find. After all, there's only about twenty-seven million people living in Boulder, Colorado. We can just start knocking on doors. Hell, by twenty twenty-five we might get through a good ten percent of them." We'd already checked all of Logan's phone records—both the family phone and his cell—for calls to or from someone with a Boulder area code. Zilch.

Bailey sighed and leaned back in her chair. "We need to smoke that person out. Make him come to us."

"Maybe our headshrinkers can help."

"Can't hurt."

Michael picked up on the first ring. I told him we needed a strategy meeting. One hour later we were in Jenny's office.

Bailey laid out our idea to smoke out the letter mailer. Jennifer liked it.

"And bear in mind, this helper may not even know what he's helping *with,*" Jenny said. "As I recall, you said you received an envelope within an envelope?" I nodded. "If the shooter sent these letters out to the helper in a sealed envelope with instructions not to open them and to mail them to you at a given address, the helper might never have seen what was being mailed."

It was a good point, and one I hadn't thought of. "So how do we lure that person out?"

"By getting on camera and telling the truth," Michael said. He saw the look on my face and shook his head. "Not the whole truth. You don't have to say what was in the letters, you only have to say that the content of the letters made it abundantly clear—"

"Okay, I'm not going to say 'abundantly'—"

Michael smiled. "Yes, of course—sound-bite English. But in essence, say that you have proof the letters were written by the shooters, but you also have proof they were mailed by someone else. Someone who may not know they've been helping the killers."

I wasn't sure about that strategy. "That might motivate a decent person to wake up and realize what they were doing, but..."

Bailey finished my thought. "But since Logan's name is already out there, don't you think that person already knows he's been helping the shooters?"

Jennifer nodded. "If Logan is the one they're helping, then yes. You're right. But if it is the second shooter—the one whose identity hasn't been publicized—then maybe not."

Bailey nodded. "I guess I just assumed that since the shooters were buddies, the person doing the mailing would know them both and make the connection."

Michael reached for the pot of coffee and poured himself another cup. "And you may be right. But Logan did have more than one friend. Even if your helper knows the letter writer is a friend of Logan's, that wouldn't necessarily mean he's the one who was involved in the shooting."

Jenny nodded. "And if the helper isn't following the case daily, the name Rachel Knight may not mean anything to him. In any case, we have to proceed with the possibility that our helper is an innocent third party."

Because if it wasn't an innocent third party, it wouldn't matter if we put on tiaras and waved a magic wand—he wasn't coming forward.

Bailey nodded. "I think Graden will be able to persuade the chief to go along. The only real downside is that the press will go nuts trying to find out what's in those letters."

Bailey's cell phone rang. She looked at the number and took the call.

After saying little more than "yeah" and "got it," she ended the call. "That was Harrellson. He's on his way back to the station."

Time to find out what he was keeping so close to the vest. We thanked the doctors and hurried out.

Harrellson was waiting for us in the bull pen when we arrived. He waved us into a witness interview room and closed the door. "You better sit down." We all took seats around the small table. "The body they found in Box Canyon isn't Evan's."

That should have been great news, but Harrellson's face said otherwise. "So who is it?" Bailey asked.

"Logan Jarvis."

62

I felt like I'd taken a lead sap to the head. Bailey looked just as stunned. We sat in silence for a few moments.

"From all indications, it was suicide," Harrellson said.

It dimly penetrated the haze of shock that our shrinks had said Logan seemed the suicidal type.

"Ready for more?" Harrellson asked. No, I really wasn't. I nodded anyway. "According to Dr. Shoe, he's been dead for days."

I put my hands on the table. "What?"

"How many days?" Bailey asked.

"At least three. Cause of death is a gunshot wound to the head."

I stared at the wall. Three days. I slowly absorbed the ramifications. "If Logan's been dead for three days, then—"

"He couldn't have done the Cinemark shooting," Bailey said.

"But there were two assault rifles," I said.

"Yeah." Harrellson rubbed his neck. "This is crazy. So now what? We have a third shooter?"

Bailey frowned. "But the kids in the school only saw two."

"And all the cell phone and video surveillance footage only showed two," I said. "There's been no evidence of a third party anywhere."

"Unless a third party's been in the background all along," Harrellson said.

"I don't know...that just doesn't feel right." This wasn't the Bling Ring, a bunch of idiot teenagers looking to burglarize movie stars for shits and giggles. These were two deranged sickos bent on mass murder. The fact that they'd even managed to find each other stretched the odds, but finding a third? One who could be trusted not to fall apart at the last minute and get them all busted? That stretched the odds to the breaking point. Or, as Nick would say, that dog wouldn't hunt. And I'd never heard of a school shooting that involved more than two killers.

When pieces don't fit, it means you're forcing them. I leaned back and stared at the table. I had to let go of every assumption we'd made about this case. We knew there were two gunmen at Fairmont—we'd seen them on the videotape. We'd assumed the same two gunmen had done the shooting at the Cinemark. But now we knew Logan couldn't have been one of them. I mentally played out the sequence of events described by Gina. Then did it again. Slowly, an answer began to take shape. "What if there was just one shooter at the Cinemark? Think about it. The projectionist gets stabbed: that's a one-man job. Then shots are fired into the theater. We found two assault rifles, but one guy could have pulled both triggers—"

Bailey nodded slowly. "And it would only take one guy to kill the manager."

"He dropped two guns to make us think there were two shooters?" Harrellson asked.

I shrugged. "Why not? The mislead seems to be his MO. He did it with Otis..."

I watched Harrellson play it out for himself. He nodded. "Yeah, I guess that's possible. But one guy or two, we still don't have ID—on either."

That pretty much summed up what we didn't have. So I focused on what we did have. That gave me a lot less to think about. "Evan's still in the wind—"

"Yep," Harrellson said. "I've got every available officer out there looking for him."

"What's it been now," I asked, "two days?" He nodded. "It's weird he hasn't even called his parents. Just to say 'Hey, I'm okay.' Don't you think?"

"Yeah," Bailey said. "My guess is he's got friends no one knows about. But you're thinking Evan might be involved—"

"Not necessarily," I said. "But I'm starting from scratch. Trying to see if we've missed anything. Maybe Evan knew more than he told us. And maybe that's why he ran. Did his story about being in homeroom the day of the school shooting check out?"

"Yeah," Harrellson said. "From what I remember, his teacher verified."

"Anyone see him in the gym at the time of the shooting?" I asked.

Harrellson squinted up at the ceiling. "I'm pretty sure I saw that in one of the uni reports. But I've been through at least a hundred statements. I'll go back and make sure."

I considered another angle. "We should tell Evan's parents about Logan," I said.

"You're thinking if he finds out Logan's dead, he'll come home," Bailey said. I nodded. "The parents haven't had any contact with him. Unless they're lying—and I don't think they are—that won't work. If we want to make sure he knows the coast is clear, we'll have to go public with it."

"Any risk that'll push your second shooter further away?" Harrellson asked.

"I wish," I said. "No, that psycho isn't looking to escape. He's looking for his next big hit. I don't see a downside." I looked at Bailey. "You?"

"No. But I'll run it by Graden first just to be on the safe side. In the meantime, let's catch Harrellson up."

We swore him to secrecy and told him about the letters and our plan to try to smoke out the sender.

"I like it," he said. He shook his head. "Friggin' incredible. I always knew they were psychos, but jeez..."

"Just one more thing, Harrellson," Bailey said. "I hate to do it to you, but I need you to notify the Jarvises. I'd do it myself, but we're not exactly popular over at that house anymore."

"You mean, since you told them their son was a mass murderer?"

Bailey sighed.

Harrellson moved toward the door. "That's why they pay us the below-middling bucks." He gave a mirthless smile. "I'll take care of it, but give me enough time to get to them before the chief announces."

"Make it fast. The press is on full swarm, and they probably already know a body was found in Box Canyon." Harrellson opened the door. "Oh, and hey, I owe you for this."

"You sure as hell do." Harrellson turned to go and wiggled his fingers over his shoulder. "Ta-ta, my rose petals." He walked out.

Next stop, Lieutenant Graden Hales. Logan's death hit him hard too. It took him several seconds to recover enough to ask, "Suicide? But I thought Logan was the mastermind."

"Our shrinkers were always skeptical about that," I said. "Anyway, mastermind or not, the second shooter's still out there."

"And we have no clue who he is." Graden raked his fingers through his hair and sighed. "What we do know is that he's getting ready to make up for his failure at the Cinemark."

Unfortunately true. Bailey and I told Graden our plans.

"With the press buzzing around like crazy, the chief will have to announce Logan's death in a couple of hours anyway," Bailey said. "And if you frame it right, he can make it sound like asking the letter mailer to come forward is based on a new lead we've developed."

Graden nodded. "Good idea. I don't know if it'll work, but it won't hurt to try."

With Graden's backing, we could count on the chief's approval. I'd have to tell my office what was going on pretty soon, and I wouldn't mind having Vanderhorn ask the letter mailer to come forward. The more the merrier. But I didn't want to give him the chance to steal the chief's thunder. I waited until it was just fifteen minutes before the press conference to call Eric.

When I finished recapping, Eric gave a low whistle. "All that in just the past two days? That's insane. But Rachel, Vanderhorn's going to want you to come in and give him the full report in person. You really can't avoid it anymore."

"Yeah, I know. But I've got to stick around until the chief does his press conference—"

"Wait, what? The chief's doing a presser? Get over here now—"

"Oh, wow, Eric, it's about to start. Gotta go! Call you later."

I knew I was going to catch hell for this. But there'd be plenty of time for Vanderhorn to have his media moment after the chief made his bid to the letter mailer.

The reporters barely had an hour's lead time, but even so, the place was packed to capacity a full ten minutes early. I wondered how many speeding tickets got handed out that day. Bailey and I decided to watch on a monitor in Graden's office. Graden had been drafted to stand next to the chief as backup, and he was all spiffed up in his dress uniform. He always looked hot, but in that uniform, with all those medals... well, words fail me. I got a rare chance to enjoy the view without his knowing and I took full advantage of it.

The chief kept it short and sweet. Vanderhorn could take a few lessons. Not that he ever would. The statement took only five minutes, but the questions came in hot and heavy for half an hour.

Logan's death was the bombshell of the day. The top of the story was Logan's suicide, but the question "What was in those letters?" ran a close second. When the chief refused to elaborate, the press quickly moved on to "Who's been mailing them?" We couldn't have hoped for better coverage.

"We can wait for a few hours to see if Evan surfaces," I said. "But I hate—"

"Waiting," Bailey said.

"The waste of time. It bugs me that no one's heard from him. Besides, it's the only thread we've got to pull, so let's work it—"

"I'm on board." She paused. "But first, I've got one other move. It won't take long."

There was no such thing as too many moves in my book. "Hit me, I'm all ears."

63

"Unless the shooter found another connection, he's going to need more guns," Bailey said. "And we know he called Jax on his cell phone last time—"

"And we've got Jax's cell phone," I said. Bailey nodded. "Did you book it into evidence yet?"

"Not yet. I was thinking we might want to get a search warrant for it and try to find the call from our shooter."

I looked at my watch. It was almost five o'clock, but if we hurried, we could just make it to the jail where Jax was being held. And I had a feeling the jail deputies would stretch visiting hours for us on this case.

"Maybe," I said. "But it'd be faster to get Jax to give consent and help us narrow down the list of calls."

"He won't even say *hola* unless we give him a deal."

Which neither of us wanted to do, but time was running out. Now that Logan's death was public knowledge, the second shooter might start to feel the pressure. And if he was getting nervous that we were about to catch up with him, he'd want to stage his final coup. "What would you rather do? Deal, or be too late to stop another shooting?"

"Fine," Bailey said. "Let's go see our cartel thief."

"My, my. So judgmental. You've got Jax's phone?"

"In my glove box."

It was a smooth move to keep the phone handy. Since we weren't worried about lifting prints or DNA, it was a good idea to hang on to that phone—just in case our shooter tried to reconnect with Jax to get more weapons. We left the station and headed for the Men's Central Jail on Bauchet Street. It's the largest county jail in the world. And the epitome of institutional dreariness and misery. As we entered the squat concrete building, the familiar odor of disinfectant mixed with sweat, urine, and despair made my empty stomach seesaw.

Bailey and I checked our guns, passed through the metal detector, and asked for an attorney room. Unlike the usual setup, with a row of seats and a glass partition with phones, the attorney room is a windowed cube with a table and chairs. It affords sound privacy, but the air barely circulates and the glass walls are always filthy. It makes me feel like a hamster in a cage.

After ten minutes, a room opened up and the deputy escorted us inside. Not long after that, Jax, his wrists chained to his waist and his feet connected by more chain, was escorted in. We'd pulled his rap sheet the night we busted him and found only two arrests, both for possession of cocaine, but no convictions. It was a miraculously clean sheet, all things considered. His lips stretched into a wide grin when he saw us, and it wasn't because he'd been lonely. Clean sheet or no, Jax was savvy enough to understand that when cops come to visit, it probably means a deal is in the offing.

I got right to the point. "Just so you know the lay of the land, Jax, you're facing charges for possession and sale of illegal weapons. If you decide to help us out, we can make some of those charges disappear, but not all of them."

Jax tried to fold his arms across his chest, but the chains wouldn't stretch that far and his hands fell back to his lap. He leaned back in his chair and looked at us through half-closed eyes, trying to recover some cool. I had to bite the inside of my cheek to keep from laughing.

"I want probation."

They always do. "Won't happen, Jax. The guns you sold were just used in two shootings. Lots of people died—"

Jax gave me a hard look. "I don't believe you."

"You know better than that," Bailey said. "We can't make this shit up. Either the bullets match the guns or they don't." Jax set his jaw. "So you didn't hear about it?"

He shook his head. "I didn't hear about nothin'. I don' live in the States."

"Okay, well there's no way you're getting a straight walk," Bailey said. "To tell you the truth, we're going to have a hell of a time getting anyone to agree to any kind of deal for you."

Jax looked from me to Bailey, then blew out a long breath. "Well, I ain't talking for free." He rolled his head from side to side, sending out a ripple of impressively loud cracks. "Got arthritis in my neck. Doc says cortisone shots might help me." He looked from me to Bailey. "I want a prescription. Some physical therapy maybe. And you got to dump some of the charges."

I shrugged. "We don't 'got to' do anything. We've got you by the nuts, Jax. This is your only chance to beat *any* of the counts."

Jax worked his jaw from side to side. It cracked too. The man was a mess. "Okay, I'll deal. But you gotta move my cell. Guy I'm with is a damn junkie who don' believe in showers. And he passed gas all night long. It's disgusting."

I bit down on my cheek again. "I'm pretty sure we can arrange that. Bailey?"

Jax looked at Bailey. Her expression was completely blank. No one could top her poker face. After a few moments, she nodded slowly. "I'll take care of it."

Jax gave a short nod. "Okay. What you want?"

Bailey pulled out Jax's cell phone, which was in a baggie. "I need you to show me which call came from the last guy Shane sent to you."

"Young *güero* bought the AKs?"

"Right." Bailey took the phone out of the baggie and pulled up the list of recent calls. "I'm going to start with the day before yesterday and work backward."

"It was before that. Day before yesterday I was in Ensenada."

Bailey nodded. "Yes, Jax, I know. I'm just making sure we don't miss anything."

Jax studied the list for a couple of seconds. "Keep going." Bailey scrolled down the list. When she got to one day before the theater shooting, he told her to stop. Jax pointed to the number at the top of the screen. "I think it's this one."

"Are you sure?" I asked.

Jax frowned and shook his head. "Pretty sure. Thing is, I don' remember whether it was an eight-one-eight area code or a nine-five-one."

Eight-one-eight was the San Fernando Valley. Nine-five-one was Riverside. Unfortunately, there were a bunch of both. "Do you remember what time you got the call?"

"Early. I was staying with *mi familia* and the little ones get up at, like, six o'clock, make a lotta noise. He called before that. And I met him in the daytime. I'm sure about that."

That would help. Bailey copied the numbers to her phone while I tried to squeeze Jax for a better description of the *güero,* but the guy had been smart enough to cover up with a hat and sunglasses, and Jax really wasn't looking.

"Now here's the deal, Jax," I said. "We're going to hang on to this phone. If the guy calls you again looking for more guns, we're going to need you to set up a meet with him."

"And we might even have you come," Bailey said. "You down with that?"

"Yeah." He sighed. "I guess."

I signaled that we were finished. As the deputy stood him up, Jax looked at us. "Wait...this guy, who'd he kill?"

I nodded. "High school kids. A lot of them. And some people at a theater."

"Kids? He killed kids?" With a disgusted look, he spit out, "*Pinche cabrón.* Tell you what, you find him, just get him in here. I'll take care of him."

Bailey looked at the waiting deputy. "You didn't hear that."

He gave her a deliberately blank stare. "Hear what?"

64

It had been a lot of hard-and-fast running in the last forty-eight hours, and by the time we left the jail, Bailey and I were both beat. Plus, I was starving. "I don't know about you, Keller, but I'm about ready to eat my own hand."

"Yeah, me too. So let's make it someplace close. And quiet."

"Checkers?" The restaurant on the ground level of the downtown Hilton had a peaceful, comfy dining room and great service.

"Sold."

We pulled up in front of the restaurant in less than ten minutes and scored a table next to the glassed-in patio. I looked out at the skyline. The night was clear, but the ambient light from all the office buildings shrouded the stars from view.

I picked up the menu. "Think we can risk a glass of wine? I could sure use one."

"No, but I'm getting one anyway."

We both ordered the sea scallops with baby bok choy and a glass of white, which we decided felt less alcoholic than red.

I held up my glass. "Here's to Jax getting a phone call from psycho boy." We clinked and sipped.

"Pisses me off about the suicide," Bailey said.

"Yeah, there's no satisfaction in it. We can't get our pound of flesh and we can't get any answers." Which was why shrinks usually had to rely on what these shooters left behind. Like the Columbine basement tapes or letters or journals. "We should let Michael and Jenny know."

"Won't be any surprise to them."

True. They'd pegged Logan as suicidal right off the bat.

Bailey continued. "Tomorrow we dig into Evan's background. His parents have been calling the chief about ten times a day—"

"Can't say I blame them."

"Me either. But we're doing all we can. And I got Nick to do a computer search on Evan's background since the family bounced around so much."

"Do we know where he lived before they moved to the Valley a year ago?"

"Yeah, Texas."

Our dinner arrived, and the delicious aroma brought all conversation to a halt. We didn't speak again until we had forked up the last of the scallops.

Bailey patted her mouth with the napkin and sighed. "What do you make of that car Jax described?"

An old Chevy junker. "My first guess was Rent-A-Wreck. But even they require a credit card, don't they?"

"Probably. But we can't do much without a license plate. Or at least a better description." Bailey's cell rang and she looked at the number. "Van Nuys Division." That was in the San Fernando Valley, but not the West Valley, i.e., Woodland Hills. With a puzzled look, she answered the call. "Keller."

I took out my cell phone and found seven messages, all from the same number, marked urgent. Vanderhorn. I didn't need to listen to know what they said. Vanderhorn had heard the press release about Logan Jarvis's death and was on the warpath. I'd have to call in and face the music tomorrow. Bailey sat up in her chair.

"What? When?" she said.

My chest tightened as I watched her make notes on her small pad. I motioned to the waiter that we needed the check. Whatever Bailey was hearing, it wasn't good.

When she ended the call, I said, "The check's coming. Do I want to know?"

"No—"

"Tell me it's not another—"

"Shooting. At the Target on Ventura near De Soto. Three wounded, one dead. So far."

"Do they have him?"

"No. By the time they called the cops, he was out of there."

"Any descriptions of the guy? His car?"

"Don't know yet."

We could only hope. I paid the check, and we were on the road in less than two minutes.

Bailey flew down the freeway with grim determination, weaving through the last of the evening's commuters. For both our sakes, I decided not to distract her. And I didn't have a thought worth sharing anyway. All I could think about was the fact that we were always playing defense, always too late to do anything more than witness the carnage.

When we got to the scene, I saw that this Target was a freestanding building fronted by a huge parking lot. Right now, at least half of the lot seemed to be filled with squad cars, fire trucks, and ambulances. Bailey parked as close as she could, and we jumped out and hurried toward the store. Then it occurred to me that this location should have been considered West Valley. "How come Van Nuys Division called you?"

"Everyone and his brother responded. I'd guess they put Gina on this and she told someone to call me."

Bailey was right. After she'd badged us past the line of patrol officers holding back the crowd—the curious and the reporters—we found Gina talking to a man in a sport shirt and tie just outside the store. She waved us over. "This is the manager, Enrique Sosa." Gina pointed to a double row of registers near the front of the store. "Enrique was walking toward the cashiers when it happened." He was still breathless and sweating in spite of the cold night air.

"Is that where it happened? Near the cashiers?" Bailey asked.

"No, it was in front, just inside the entrance." He pointed to the three sets of double doors. The area was guarded by another set of officers. Behind them I saw paramedics huddled around a body on the floor. Torn, bloody pants that'd been ripped off the body lay a few feet away. Next to them was a purse, its contents strewn across the floor. "He walked in and just started shooting."

"Could you see his face?" I asked.

"No, he was wearing a ski mask. One of those kinds with just eyeholes. And he had on a coat, like an Army jacket—what do you call it—"

"Camouflage?" I asked.

"Yeah."

"Could you tell how tall he was? Anything about his size?" Bailey asked.

Enrique swallowed and wiped his forehead. "Uh, I think he was kind of tall." But Enrique wasn't much taller than me—five feet seven, tops. Most men would seem tall to him.

"Could you show us how much taller than you?" I asked.

"Maybe about this much?" Enrique gestured about three inches above his head. That would make the shooter about five feet ten. "And he looked kind of stocky, I think. Not fat. Just...not thin."

It was possible the coat made him look bigger than he really was. This type of eyewitness description could be notoriously unreliable. One man's idea of big was another one's idea of medium.

"Did he say anything when he was firing the guns?" I asked.

"No. He just started shooting at everyone around him. Then he ran out."

"Did you see him throw anything down before he ran?" I asked.

"Yeah, I think he dropped the guns."

"Did you see him do that?" I asked.

He frowned. "No, I guess not, but I heard the police saying that."

We wrapped up with the manager and stepped away to talk to Gina privately.

"Have they found any decent witnesses?" I asked.

"I don't know," Gina said. "You might check with Jay Rollins. He took the people in the parking lot." She pulled out her cell and punched a number. "Hey, Jay, where you at? I've got the lead IO here." She listened, then said, "Okay, I'm sending them over." Gina ended the call. "I've got to stay here and coordinate." She pointed to a black man in a detective uniform—sports jacket, tie, and slacks—in the parking lot, standing next to an unmarked car. He was talking to a squat woman in a long skirt and hooded parka.

"Thanks, Gina," Bailey said.

I couldn't remember when I'd seen Bailey look so miserable, so defeated.

Gina gave her a sympathetic look and slapped her on the back. "Don't worry, Keller, you'll get the son of a bitch. You always do."

We headed for the parking lot. "Yeah," Bailey muttered under her breath. "The question is, when?"

When we got to him, Jay was still listening to the woman, and she didn't sound as though she was inclined to be finished any time soon. He nodded in our direction and held up two fingers to let us know he'd wrap it up.

"I mean, it was just a blur," she said. "But I know I saw a guy running. I know I did."

From Jay's expression, I could tell this was probably the fifth time she'd repeated that amazingly unhelpful statement. But there was something about him that told me he was pretty good at dealing with people like her. He couldn't have been much past his forties, but he had a kind face and a relaxed attitude. Jay let the woman run through it all again, then thanked her and motioned for us to follow him.

He headed toward a circle of squad cars at the far west side of the parking lot. As we fell in next to him, we exchanged introductions.

"I don't envy you this one, Detective Keller. But I think I may have the break you were looking for."

A break. At last. I didn't know whether to laugh or cry.

Jay stopped and pointed to a squad car ten feet away. "We've got a witness over there says he saw the guy get into a car. Got the description of the car and the license plate."

Bailey looked from the car to Jay. "No shit."

"No shit. He's—well, I'll let you see for yourselves. But I think his story's solid."

"Someone ran the plate?" Bailey asked.

"Of course. It's registered to a woman. Angelica Freeman. Address in Canoga Park."

"What kind of car was it?" I asked. Please let it be an old Chevy.

"Pontiac sedan. Nineteen eighty-six. Our guy said it was a screwed-up junker."

Close enough. I could feel my heart beat faster. "It wasn't a stolen?"

"No. But we're checking on the insurance. Might just be that the woman wasn't driving it so she didn't realize it was gone."

Jay led us to the squad car and pointed to the backseat, where a young man in his twenties was bopping to the sound coming from his earbuds. His shoulder-length brown hair looked like a combed-out Brillo pad, and probably would've been flying all over the place if it hadn't been for the knit cap pulled down to his eyebrows, one of which was pierced. He wore a frayed, dirty-looking blue puffer coat and sneakers that were coming apart where the rubber met the canvas. The overall look told me indoor plumbing wasn't a regular experience for him. His home address was probably the seven hundred block of Ventura Boulevard.

Jay leaned down and tapped his arm. "Hey, Forest, got a couple more people for you to talk to."

"Oh, sure thing, Detective!" Forest jumped out of the car, tugged on his cap, and gave us an anxious smile.

He didn't offer his hand for a shake, so I didn't offer mine. Some of the homeless have issues with physical contact. "Hi, Forest, I'm Rachel Knight and this is Detective Bailey Keller. You saw something tonight?"

He gave us both a little wave. "Hi. Uh, yeah." Forest bounced from side to side. "I heard people screaming, you know? And I was, like, right over there." He pointed to an area behind us, stretching his arm as far as it would go.

"Like where that red Prius is parked?" I asked.

"Yeah, that's it!" Forest shifted into hyperdrive. His words came flying out as though they'd been spring-loaded. "So then, I noticed this dude. He was, like, wearing one of those Army jackets, you know? And he wasn't screaming or nothing like the others. I seen him walking fast, but not running like everyone else. So I, like, ducked down behind that car there"—he pointed to a blue Ford Explorer twenty feet away. "I saw him get into this banged-up old green car. And I memorized the license plate 'cuz, like, I knew. I knew something was up with that dude."

"Could you tell how tall he was?" I asked. "Was he as tall as you?"

Forest was at least five feet ten, maybe six feet. "Nah. He was like maybe so tall." He held a hand about three inches above my head.

"What size body did he have?" I asked. "Skinny? Medium? Fat?"

"Nah, not fat. Not skinny. Well...I guess I couldn't really tell under that coat. But I'm sure he wasn't fat."

"Could you see his face or his hair?" I asked.

Forest shook his head. "He was wearing one of those things." He put his hand in front of his face. "Like in the movies, where you can only see the eyes. Except I couldn't see his eyes. He was too far away." Forest shoved his hands into his pants pockets and looked down. "Sorry. I'm sorry. I wish I could've seen more."

"Forest, don't be sorry. You did great." I waited for him to look up. When he made eye contact, I smiled at him. "Really. You've helped a lot and we so appreciate it."

He dipped his head and looked at me shyly through his fringe of woolly hair. "Always try to help." He nodded to himself. "I try."

I smiled again. "I know you do." His sweetness was heartbreaking.

Jay stepped in. "Forest, I don't know about you, but I'm really hungry. Want to grab a bite with me, my man?"

Forest looked from Jay to me and then to Bailey. "You don't still need me here? I'm done?"

"You're done for now," Jay said. "So what do you say we grab a couple burgers?"

"Well, uh…sure!"

"Just give me a minute and we'll head on out." Jay motioned for us to join him a short distance away. "There's a burger joint just a couple of blocks away. I'll take him there. But I'm going to be around for the duration. I'll call you the minute I hear anything."

"Dynamite witness," I said, nodding toward Forest.

Jay smiled. "He really is. But I don't know if we'll ever find him again."

We probably wouldn't. If I needed him for trial, I'd be shit out of luck. But I'd drive off that bridge when I came to it. "Right now, I'll settle for just finding this asshole."

"I heard that." Jay gave us a mock salute and headed off with Forest.

Bailey scanned the parking lot. "I guess we could go back in there and find out what the rest of the witnesses said."

"But I doubt it'll get much better than that."

"Probably not."

I was freezing. The clear night meant no cloud cover, and in the dry semi-desert of the Valley, that meant pretty damn cold. "You mind if I go sit in the car for a few?"

Bailey took in my shivering. "Swear to God you're like a lizard. You have zero body heat."

We went back to the car. "Mind turning on the engine? It's an icebox in here."

Bailey made a face. "Come on, Knight. We're inside, what more do you want?"

"Heat. Feel this." I put my frozen hand on her cheek.

She pulled back. "Are you kidding me?" She turned on the engine. "Keep those things to yourself."

"Told you." I cranked up the heater and put my hands next to the vents. "We didn't get a letter this time."

"Yeah, I thought about that. But I figure he either got nervous and decided to stop writing, or the person who was mailing the letters decided it was over between them."

"Right. Did you happen to hear what kind of guns he used this time?"

"No, that's one of the things I want to go back and ask Gina," Bailey said. "You can wait here."

"No, I'm okay." I wasn't. My hands still felt like blocks of ice, but I wanted to hear what Gina had to say.

We found Gina inside the store, talking to some unis. She peeled off when she saw Bailey and me. "I heard about that witness," Gina said.

"If the shooter doesn't ditch the car, we'll have him by morning," Bailey said. "What kind of guns did this guy use?"

"We've got casings that look like he used a twenty-two and a thirty-eight."

"No assault rifle?" I said. Gina shook her head.

"He must be out," Bailey said. "Did he drop the guns?"

"Not this time."

I scanned the store. "I thought the manager said he heard officers talking about finding guns."

"He probably heard them talking about the last two shootings. But no, we didn't find any guns this time."

Bailey sighed. "Thanks, Gina. Guess we'll go see what they got from the other witnesses."

We checked with the officers who'd taken statements. After an hour of hearing nothing new, we decided to call it a night.

It was past ten o'clock by the time we headed for home, and we were both thrashed. "So he's hanging on to his guns now."

"Seems that way," Bailey said. "Guess it was to be expected. He's got to be running out of money."

"Which makes it less likely he'll try to find Jax." Bailey nodded, glum. "But where did he get the twenty-two? Shane never said anything about selling any small calibers like that."

"He must've scored it from someone else."

"*Another* connection?" I said. "Whatever happened to consumer loyalty?"

I turned up the heat and held my hands in front of the vent, but the only thing that would warm me up now was a hot bath.

Or a call saying they'd found the shooter.

66

TUESDAY, OCTOBER 15

My landline rang at six twenty-three a.m. These way-too-early mornings were really starting to get to me. I opened one eye and glared at the phone. Knowing it had to be Bailey, I snatched it up. "This better be good."

"Ah, I believe it is, but I suppose you'll be the judge. This is Rachel Knight, isn't it?"

It was Jay, the detective who'd found our best witness. I sat up and rubbed my eyes.

"Yes, it is. Sorry, I thought it was Detective Keller."

"She's the one who told me to call you. I thought it was a little too early, but she said you were an early riser." Jay chuckled. "I'd say you're entitled to payback for this one."

"Oh, count on it. What's up?"

"The unis talked to the owner of the getaway car about an hour ago. She knew her car was gone, but she didn't report it because her son has a habit of taking it without telling her."

Her son. I sat up farther. "What do you have on him? Does she know where he is?"

"His name is Francis Spader. Spader's the dad's last name, but Dad's been in the wind since birth. Francis's stats fit the description: he's twenty-four, five feet ten, one eighty—though he might be thinner than that now. He's a meth head. Lots of busts for possession and theft. Fell off his last diversion program, violated probation for testing dirty. Mom hasn't seen him since yesterday morning, but she claims he always winds up back at home."

And smelling great, I'd bet. "You've got units sitting on Mom's house?"

"Yep. Five bucks says we pick him up within the next twenty-four hours."

"A ten-spot says you get him by the end of the day."

"Huh, done. And I won't mind losing."

"Does Mom know Francis is wanted for the shooting at Target?"

"No. I just told her we were looking for him on the probation violation. I didn't want to take the chance she'd help him run."

Smart. "So she's cooperative?"

"For now. But I told Bailey you guys should probably stay away from her for the moment. If you show up on her doorstep, she might recognize you from the news—"

"No problem."

"I'll be in touch."

I hung up and headed for the shower. We might have our psycho in custody very soon. I prayed it would be soon enough. I splurged and celebrated with pancakes for breakfast. After I finished sopping up the last bit of syrup, I poured myself a fourth cup of coffee and thought about Francis Spader. I wondered what connection he had to Fairmont High. Did he go there? Did a kid from that school diss him? And he was a meth head. Crystal meth turned brains into Swiss cheese. And it wasn't at all uncommon for some addicts to get crazy violent. But it was usually spur-of-the-moment, an explosion. Not planned violence. I called Bailey.

"Keller."

"So Jay called..."

"Just now?"

"A few minutes ago." It was eighty thirty. Let her think her little plot to mess me up with that six-thirty call hadn't worked. "I was thinking about the possible connection between Francis Spader and Logan."

"As in, where is it?" Bailey said. "I know. We've already been through Logan's history, and I don't remember seeing any mention of this Spader guy."

"Did he go to Fairmont?"

"No, but he might've been buddies with Logan and just used a different name. I saw a few aliases on Spader's rap sheet."

"Logan's got family in Utah. Where's Spader been?"

"Hang on." I heard the tap of computer keys. "He's got busts in Arizona…Nevada…and—"

"Utah. Tell me it's Utah."

After a few seconds Bailey said, "Yep, Utah. So that's something." I heard Bailey's desk phone ring. "Hang on a sec."

Bailey put me on hold, and I got up and paced, thinking about how to find the connections between Spader and Logan. Utah was a big state. The fact that Logan had family there and Spader had a bust there might not amount to anything. But it was a place to start.

Bailey came back on the line. "They've got him. Get downstairs. I'm on my way."

I ended the call and pumped my fist in the air. "Yes!"

And I'd won my bet with Jay.

67

Spader was being held at the local jail in the West Valley Division. Jay escorted us to his desk.

"First things first." I held out my hand.

Jay grinned and fished out a ten-dollar bill. "Happiest payoff I've ever made." He filled us in on how they'd caught Spader.

A couple of unis had spotted his car—or rather, his mother's car—under a freeway overpass, what we euphemistically call a "bridge" in L.A., on Canoga Avenue just north of the 101 freeway. They'd immediately called for backup, and within minutes, the car was surrounded. Spader was still wrapped up in his camouflage coat and fast asleep in the backseat. When they'd called him out with a bullhorn, it took a good five minutes before he emerged from the car. And even then, he was still so wasted, he had to hang on to the door to pull himself out. When they ordered him to put his hands up, he lost his balance and did a face-plant.

"They had to carry him to the patrol car," Jay said. "We couldn't even get the booking done. He was too messed up to give us anything besides his name."

"Where is he now?" Bailey asked.

"Sleeping it off in his cell."

"Since?" I asked.

"About eight thirty this morning."

I looked at my watch. It was after ten. "Think we can get Sleeping Beauty out here for an interview?"

"Definitely. I just figured I'd wait until you got here."

Jay escorted us to the interview room, aka, a box. One so small there was barely room for the standard metal table and chairs. A few minutes later I heard Jay speaking in a low rumble that sounded like "Come on now, come on now." The door opened and two officers escorted in a human scarecrow. The Pendleton-style shirt Spader wore looked like a reject from Goodwill, and I could see his last three meals in the stains on his gray Dickies. The smell coming off him made the Men's Central Jail seem like a perfume counter at Neiman Marcus.

Jay took a seat as the officers parked Spader in the chair across from us and cuffed him to a ring on the table. He slumped down, and his head rolled onto his right shoulder. He gazed at us through half-closed eyes.

This was the mastermind of the massacre at Fairmont and a near mass murder at the Cinemark? *This* was the grandiose psychopath who'd written those taunting letters? A glance at Bailey told me she was having a similar reaction.

"Is your name Francis Spader?" I asked. He widened his eyes at me—not in shock, in an effort to keep them open—then they drifted back down to half-mast. I repeated the question. This time he nodded, but said nothing.

Now that I'd had the chance to see his eyes, I noticed that they were not only red but also permanently crossed—or he was so trashed he couldn't make them move in the same direction. If this was an act, it was a damn good one.

"Do you know where you are?"

He spoke in a hoarse whisper. "In jail."

I introduced myself and Bailey and said we wanted to talk to him about something that happened last night. "Do you feel able to talk to us about that?" Spader widened his eyes and wiggled himself upright. He worked his mouth, and it made that sticky sound that comes from being too dry. "Would you like some water?"

He nodded. Jay motioned to one of the officers standing behind him to go get it. If I got a confession out of him, there'd be a bloody battle over its admissibility. His lawyer would argue he was too non compos to know what planet he was on—let alone give a knowing waiver of rights. Unless Spader started looking a whole lot better in the next few minutes, I wouldn't even bother trying to talk to him. I decided to start by explaining his rights and see what happened.

I checked the camera in the corner of the ceiling to make sure the red light was on and waited for the officer to bring him a bottle of water. I let Spader take a long slug. He looked at least marginally more awake. "We'd like to talk to you about last night, but before we do, I have to advise you of your rights. Have you ever been advised of your rights before?"

Spader had been arrested plenty of times, so he'd definitely been through the drill. If he could remember that now, it'd go a long way in proving he was able to give us a valid waiver.

"Yeh." Spader quietly burped and swallowed.

"You have the right to remain silent, Francis. Do you know what that means?" He nodded. "Why don't you tell me?"

He nodded dully. "Means I don't have to talk to you guys."

I went through each of his rights with him this way, having him explain what each one meant. By the time I got to the end, I was convinced he was all there. Well, as "all there" as he'd ever be. "Okay, Francis, having all of these rights in mind, do you want to talk to us now without a lawyer?"

He nodded. "Yeah. I guess so. Yeah, I do. If it really happened."

"If what really happened, Francis?"

He swallowed several times, and I watched his Adam's apple bob up and down. "The…the thing. At the store."

"Tell me what you mean by that." Spader gave me a measuring look, as though gauging the possibility that I didn't know about the shooting. He was looking more alert by the second. I prompted him again. "Do you remember the name of the store?"

"I think it was Target."

"Which one? Do you remember what street it was on?"

"Ventura."

I nodded. "Tell us what happened."

Spader's eyes finally seemed to focus. "Oh, God." He dropped his head and began to cry. He spoke through choking sobs. "It happened. It really happened. I thought it was all a dream. Just a weird thing playing in my head where I was one of those guys..." Spader trailed off, and his shoulders shook as he wept.

And with those words, I knew. But I had to get him to say it. "One of which guys, Francis?"

It took him a few seconds to find his voice. When he did, it came out ragged. "One of those guys at the school. At Fairmont."

"Do you know those guys?"

"Yeah." Spader looked up, his mouth slightly open. "I saw the news about them."

"No, I mean know them as in being friends with them."

Spader looked perplexed. "I...how could I be friends with them?"

"So you don't actually know them." Spader shook his head. Just as I'd feared. But I had to make sure. "Can you tell me where you were for the past two weeks?"

Spader took a deep, somewhat jerky breath and blew it out. I turned my head to avoid the blast. "Vegas. I just got back." He looked up through reddened, tearstained eyes. "I think it was a couple of days ago, but I'm not sure. You could ask my mom. I went to see her first when I got to L.A."

I got enough details out of him about where he'd been in Las Vegas—who he'd seen and what flophouse he'd stayed in—to establish an alibi. Even flophouses keep records, and we only needed to go back eight days.

Even before seeing him, I'd had my doubts, though I'd squashed them down with hope. Nothing fit. The MO was all wrong. Spader stood right in the middle of the store and fired around himself. He had no physical advantage at all, other than surprise. In fact, it was a miracle he hadn't been taken down right then and there. This wasn't the "fish in a barrel" scenario our shrinks had said these shooters go for. Spader hadn't used an assault rifle, and he hadn't dropped any weapons at the scene.

The truth was, Spader's meth-addled brain had obscured the line between fantasy and reality. He'd had some warped dream about being one of the Fairmont shooters, and in the throes of his speedy high, he'd made it come true. He was just a copycat. He was good for the Target shooting, but nothing more.

It only took a few phone calls to verify Spader's alibi. He was not our guy.

68

We headed back downtown. "What's up with Evan?" I asked. "It's been long enough for him to hear that Logan's dead."

"Yeah," Bailey said. "He should've surfaced by now. And if he hasn't heard about Logan, something's really wrong."

What we didn't say out loud: Evan knew who the second shooter was—and the second shooter knew it too. I pictured Evan's body at the bottom of a ravine, or in a Dumpster, or lying in a shallow grave in the hills of Griffith Park. "And his cell phone's still off?"

"Yeah. I get that he didn't want us to be able to track him at first, but now..."

"Right," I said. "You've put out enough manpower to find Hoffa's body. So now what?"

"The only thing left to do is dig into his past, see if there's someplace or someone he could've run to. I had a uni get a list of his past addresses and schools from the parents. The report should be waiting for us when we get back."

"We haven't had any luck on whoever mailed the letters in Boulder yet, right?"

"No, but it could still happen." She sighed.

Luck hadn't been our strong suit lately.

When we got back to the station, we found Harrellson with his feet up on Bailey's desk, talking on his cell. Given his size, that was a fairly acrobatic move. Bailey pointed to his shoes. "Get those things off." She looked at me. "What is it with men and my desk lately?"

Harrellson ended his call and reluctantly dropped his feet. "This is the thanks I get for doing your dirty work?"

"What dirty work?" Bailey asked.

"A uni dropped off the list of past home addresses and schools from Evan's parents. I took it upon myself to get the phone numbers of principals and counselors." He handed Bailey a stapled batch of pages. "You're welcome. And yes, I am a gem."

Bailey handed back half of the printouts. "Okay, Ruby, you want to earn my undying gratitude, why don't you help us make the calls?"

"Ruby. Bullshit. This here"—he gestured to his bulk—"diamond, baby. Several carats, set in platinum." He took the pages back from Bailey. "I'll make two copies so Ms. Daisy over here can join in the fun."

I glared at him. "It's not my fault. She won't let me drive."

Harrellson raised an eyebrow. "Not what she says, but whatever." He hefted himself out of the chair and trundled out to make the copies.

I pulled up a chair next to Bailey's desk. "What are we looking for? Names of friends? Connections to Boulder? To Utah? What?"

"All of the above. And of course, if you come up with any link to our second shooter along the way, that'd be nice—"

"And how do I go about getting all that stuff?"

"I don't know. Fish around."

I looked at Bailey. "Fish around? That's your plan?"

"You got a better one?"

"Be hard to do worse."

"Then let's hear it."

The truth was, I hadn't had anything like a plan, but in that moment, something did occur to me. A way to get at the second shooter. "Get someone to check out where there were gun shows that Logan and the second shooter could have gotten to. If they had another source besides Jax, it most likely came from someone at a place like that. And that's who the second shooter might go back to now."

Since Logan wasn't eighteen, he couldn't have legally scored a gun on his own. If the second shooter was in the same boat, his options were similarly limited. But security at gun shows was notoriously lax. If Logan and his buddy had scored at a gun show, that seller might be the second shooter's other connection.

"Not bad. I'll get someone on it." Bailey picked up her phone. "Nice, the way you pulled that one out of your ass at the last minute."

"What are you talking about? I've been meaning to talk to you about it. I thought of that, like...yesterday."

Bailey gave me a look and sat down at her computer.

Harrellson came back with the copies. "The list goes back to elementary school," he said. "First grade, I think."

We got down to work.

Evan had moved around even more than we'd originally thought. Before Texas, his family had lived in New Mexico, Wyoming, Louisiana, and Arizona. This little fishing expedition was turning into a global sea hunt.

Harrellson scanned the list and blew out a breath. "Damn, this is crazy. Tell you what. You take New Mexico and Texas. Since those were his last addresses before he moved here, they're the most likely to pan out. I'll take the rest."

I nodded toward Bailey, who was on the phone. "Her Nibs over there can do some too."

"Oh, don't you worry your pretty little head about that. The minute she's off that phone, she'll take Wyoming and Arizona."

"I notice you're keeping Louisiana."

"Because even over the phone I can smell the gumbo."

The principal of Evan's high school in New Mexico was a sweetheart. I explained about Evan having run away. "Oh, that poor dear. He must be terrified. How can I help?"

I decided that while I was hunting for Evan, I'd ask about any kids he hung out with who might've moved to California—someone who might be our second shooter. I asked the principal for a list of kids who'd transferred out of the school during the year Evan was there, and for six months after that. "And if you could also tell me whether any of them had been in Evan's classes, that would be a big help."

"That should be easy enough. Can you hang on a sec?"

"Sure."

In less than two minutes she was back. "I had a feeling. There were no transfers during that time frame. We're a pretty stable population here."

Damn. I asked if there was any indication of who his friends were, what clubs he might've joined. Nothing. I thanked the principal and moved on to the high school in Lubbock, Texas.

The principal there recommended I talk to Evan's counselor, a Mr. Greg Kingsley. Greg was more than happy to help, but his drawl was so heavy it was like listening to a foreign language. "Can you find out whether any of the students who were in school with Evan transferred out—say within six months after he left?"

"Yeah, but it'll take me a bit. You don't mind hangin' on?"

I heard computer keys being tapped as Greg hummed to himself softly. "Oh, yeah, I plum forgot about that. Evan did get into a bit of trouble. Nothin' big, mind you, but I s'pose that's what bein' a teenager's for."

"What kind of trouble?"

"Just a bit of petty stealin', from what I recall. But you folks probably have more access to that information than I do."

"Was it out there in Lubbock?"

"Yeah. Evan and a couple other boys stole a cell phone out of a truck parked alongside the road. From what I remembah, they all got probation and had to do some community service. Freeway cleanup? Somethin' like that."

Theft from a car. That really was small-time. "Did Evan have a probation officer?"

"Yeah. Let me finish this search and I'll get that for you."

The probation officer would have the names of the other two culprits. Maybe I'd get lucky and one of them would turn out to be our second shooter. And maybe the Easter Bunny would show up with a basket of chocolate eggs too. Finally, Greg came back.

"Okay, the PO's name is Stanley Addison." He gave me the phone number. "As I recall, he was pretty impressed with Evan. But you give him a jingle, he'll tell you hisself. I looked at all the transfers out of the school durin' the year Evan was here and for six months after he left, like you asked. Only got twelve transfers total. One of 'em did have a class with him. A girl. Transferred out just before Christmas break. Want her name?"

What the hell, may as well. "Sure."

"Amanda Kozak."

The name pinged. "Do you have any contact information for her?"

"I don't know how good it is now, but I've got cell phone numbers for her and her mom." He gave them to me.

"Do you have any idea where she transferred to?"

"Yeah, says here she moved to Boulder, Colorado."

And that's when it hit me. Amanda. The name of the girl in Logan's writings. The one he was in love with. In Boulder, Colorado. It couldn't be a coincidence. I got her address. Then I called Stanley, the PO. He wasn't in, so I left a message. I found Bailey and filled her in.

"Well, what do you know," she said. "An actual, bona fide lead. So *that's* how it feels." Bailey sat down at her desk. "I'll follow up on Amanda. We should see her in person. Hell, Evan might even be with her."

"Yeah, but let's wait to hear back from the PO first. He might have something for us, and I think he'll call back soon."

"Okay, but if he doesn't pan out, go pack your Skivvies. We're heading for Boulder."

69

I was right. Five minutes later, I got a call back from Stanley, the PO. I asked him about the other two suspects in the car burglary. "Were they juveniles too?"

"Yeah. Coupla goofball stoners. High as kites when they did it."

"And Evan? Was he high?"

"Didn't test dirty, but I'm not sure what they tested for, so I wouldn't swear he was clean. Probably wasn't. The whole thing seemed like a stoner kid prank to tell you the truth. But Evan Cutter got the message. He was the only one who completed his community service on time. Matter of fact, he was a model probationer. Even wrote a letter of apology to the victim all on his own. Don't see that very often." Stanley sighed. "You gonna find him, you think?"

"We're trying. Where are the other kids who did the car burg with him?"

"Hold on, lemme check." A few moments later, he came back on the line. "One of 'em's in juvenile hall for drug possession. Been there for the past three months. Other one…let me see. Mark Unger. Looks like he moved. Yep, got a forwarding address out in San Diego. Want it?"

I sure as hell did. "Do you know whether that address is still good?"

"Nope. He's San Diego's problem now."

Or maybe the San Fernando Valley's. "You have a description of him?"

"Hang on…five ten, one sixty, brown and brown."

It fit. "Thanks for your time, Stanley."

"Not a problem. Anything else I can do, you just let me know. Damn shame if something happened to Evan. Seems like it's always the good ones."

In the immortal words of Billy Joel. When I hung up, Bailey was typing on her computer. I told her about Mark Unger. "It may not pan out but—"

"But it just might," Bailey said. "I think we need to divide and conquer. Harrellson's got connects in San Diego—"

"Harrellson's got connects on the moon—"

"How'd you find out? Anyway, he'll get faster answers down there than we will. We should head out to Boulder. This girl might be a link to our shooter. And if Evan's with her, I don't want to give him the chance to move on."

"But what if—"

"The shooter strikes again? What more can we do here?"

I shook my head. Nothing. And we hadn't had a letter. Maybe now that he'd lost his partner in crime, the killer had to fall back and regroup. It was our only hope.

"I assume this means you found Amanda?" I asked.

"Yep. She's been in school every day." Bailey resumed typing. "I'm banging out our request for travel authorization."

Five minutes later, we headed to Graden's office, paperwork in hand. He had a new secretary, Cherie, who was a little too young and flirty for my taste. She was staring at her computer screen and barely glanced up when we said we needed to see Graden. "I don't think he's available right now." She went back to her monitor as she said, "Have a seat. I'll let him know you want to see him."

Bailey raised an eyebrow. "You do know we're working the Fairmont case, right?"

With an irritated sigh, Cherie looked up from her computer screen. "Yeah, I know. And I also know he's busy right now. So if you can't wait, I suggest you come back in half an hour."

Sure, why don't we, honey? Another fifty people might be dead by then, but, whatever. Bailey's expression should have warned Cherie that she'd taken the wrong tack, but it didn't. Cherie blithely went back to her computer.

"Uh, Cherie? We can't wait half an hour. Matter of fact, we can't wait five minutes. Now you can either call and tell him we're here, or you can call the hospital and book yourself a bed. Right friggin' now."

Cherie's eyes narrowed. "You don't want to threaten me, Detective."

"No? That's funny, I thought I just did."

"We'll see what Lieutenant Hales has to say about this." Cherie glared at Bailey, but her hand trembled as she picked up her phone and pressed the buzzer. "Sir, I need to see you for just a moment." She got up and went into Graden's office.

I pulled out the ten-spot Jay had given me. "Ten bucks says she's canned by tomorrow."

"Two to one she's canned in three minutes."

I looked at Bailey. "Getting a little cocky, aren't we?"

"You know how we've been feeling?"

"Yeah." Pissed off, freaked-out, and frustrated beyond speech.

"And Graden's stuck behind a desk." Bailey looked at her watch. "In three-two-one—"

Cherie burst out of Graden's office, beet red, eyes shooting sparks. She refused to even glance our way as she yanked open her desk drawer, pulled out her purse and her thermos, and snatched her coat off the back of her chair.

Bailey gave her a fake smile. "Have a nice day."

Graden appeared at the door and motioned for us to come in. The glint in his eyes showed just how right Bailey had been. This was no time to whine about a detective who was running down the biggest case in the city.

Bailey filled Graden in on all the latest developments in one long breath.

Graden didn't hesitate when she'd finished. "You're good to go on the travel request. You want local backup, just in case?"

"Not yet. We can't afford a leak right now. The fewer people who know where we're headed, the better. If Evan's with her, he might run. And there's no reason to think she poses a threat at this point."

"Not even if she's knowingly helping our shooter?"

Bailey set her jaw. "It's a chance we'll have to take. We can't afford to have either one of them slip through our fingers."

Graden looked at me. "Is your carry up-to-date?"

Meaning, my license to carry a concealed weapon. I'd resisted getting one for years until Bailey finally put her foot down. "Yep. I'm locked and loaded."

Graden came around the desk. "Now listen, any trouble at all, you call for backup immediately. No cowboy antics." We nodded. "I'll have them put you on the first available flight."

We headed for the door, and then I remembered what I'd been meaning to ask him. "Any progress on finding out who planted the bug in my office?"

"Nothing yet, but we're moving pretty fast. Your investigators are helping out."

"Okay, thanks."

"And text me when you land. There and here. Please." I had a habit of forgetting to do that. I nodded and gave him a reassuring smile. Graden did not look reassured. "Be safe."

Bailey picked up the murder book on our way out. "I'll drop you at the Biltmore. Pack fast—they'll probably get us an early evening flight."

I was sitting on my suitcase, trying to get it zipped, when Bailey called to say she was downstairs. "We've got a six o'clock flight and the traffic's going to be a bitch. Get the lead out."

They say you should wear layers when traveling to a colder climate. I took the advice to heart: long underwear, jeans, long-sleeved T-shirt, turtleneck sweater, down vest, wool scarf, and my long down coat. I waddled down to the lobby as fast as I could, and by the time I got there, I was starting to sweat.

Angel raised an eyebrow when he saw me. "I didn't know you skied."

"I don't." Actually, I used to. I liked the speed, loved carrying the schnapps-filled bota bag, but—big surprise—I couldn't handle the cold.

"You flying up to Alaska or something?"

"No."

Angel mouthed "okay" as he held the door open for a group of twentysomethings who had that giddy "I got off work early and I'm ready to party" look. I rolled my suitcase over to Bailey's trunk and motioned for her to pop it open.

"Here, let me help you with that," Angel said. He reached down and hefted it up with a grunt, then swung it into the trunk.

The moment I got into the car, Bailey said, "What did you put in that thing? I can hear my back tires going flat." Then she glanced at me. "Nice look, Nanook. Should only take you three hours to get through security."

The traffic was the worst kind—barely moving, but people were still trying to dart and weave through it. I'd rolled down the window to cool off, but the heavy exhaust fumes made me feel like I was inhaling cancer. Better to sweat than die. I closed the window. "Think it's too soon to call Harrellson?" We were praying that Mark Unger, the kid in San Diego, was our second shooter, but Harrellson had threatened to strangle us if we called and bugged him about his progress.

"Probably. Do it anyway."

I called him at the station and got his voice mail. I called him on his cell...and got his voice mail. "Damn."

"Yeah, it's a pisser. We'll try him again after we get checked in."

But when we got to the airport there was no time to spare. Luckily, the security line moved fast. Even so, we had to run all the way to the gate and only just made it before they closed the door to the Jetway.

"What've you got on Amanda so far?" I asked, as we fastened our seat belts. Bailey had asked one of the unis to dig into her records.

"Nothing that stands out. Average student, never in trouble. Driver's license shows no outstanding tickets. No juvenile history."

Bailey pulled out a print of a photograph and passed it to me. A serious-looking young girl with long, straight brown hair parted down the middle stared back at me. She had the kind of features that could be prettied up with makeup and a little confidence, but even in this photo I could see the insecurity in her eyes. "Anybody in her family into guns?"

"Dad owns a hunting rifle and a handgun, but he doesn't have a carry."

Colorado was big hunting country, so that wasn't unusual, but it did mean she had some connection to guns. "You find any gun shows near Boulder?"

Bailey gave me a little smile. "Funny you should mention it. I found a pretty big one in Colorado Springs."

"When was it?"

"April."

Six months before the shooting. "The timing works," I said.

"And it's only an hour and a half away from Boulder."

The edges of the puzzle were starting to fall into place. I sighed. Now if we could just find the center piece.

70

By the time we landed in Boulder it was almost nine thirty. Too late to drop in on Amanda. Bailey rented a car and we drove straight to our hotel, the St. Julien, a fairly nice place with a spa we'd never get to use. Bailey called Harrellson again. And got his voice mail. "Shit," Bailey said. She threw her cell phone on the bed.

"On the bright side, this must mean Unger's still in the running," I said. If he'd been ruled out, Harrellson would've let us know by now.

"Yeah, I guess."

The restaurant was closed, so we showered and ordered room service. I got the chef's salad, Bailey ordered a hamburger, and we both decided we deserved a bottle of Pinot Noir. When our dinner came, I poured us each a glass and we toasted. "To a cooperative Amanda," I said.

"And to finding a healthy and breathing Evan." We clinked glasses.

"I've been trying to figure out why she'd do it," Bailey said. She shook out some ketchup on her fries. They smelled so good—too good to resist. "Wouldn't you be suspicious if someone told you to mail some letters? I sure as hell would be. And I'd tell him to go mail them himself."

"You're assuming she doesn't know what she's mailing—"

Bailey picked up her hamburger, and I snuck a couple of fries off her plate.

"Well... yeah."

"If you're right, then either she's kind of dim or this guy has something on her—"

"Or he knows how to charm her," Bailey said.

As she took another bite of her hamburger, I snaked my hand up to cadge another couple of fries. Bailey sighed, took a fistful of them, dropped them on my bread plate, and passed me the ketchup.

"If she's shy, insecure, and not particularly streetwise, and he's kind of a hottie, I can see it," I said. "No one's ever paid much attention to her, and then suddenly there's this charming guy who's telling her how great she is—"

Bailey sipped her wine. "It fits with what our shrinkers have been saying about psychopaths. How they can be charismatic and really good at manipulating people."

It did. But if Bailey's hunch was wrong, if Amanda knew what she was doing in sending those letters—assuming she *was* the letter sender—our chances of getting her to cooperate with us weren't good. In fact, I could envision her being like the Manson girls: martyrs to the cause of protecting their "hero."

"We should figure out what we can threaten her with, just in case she hitches up on us," I said. "Maybe some federal charges for helping to send those letters across state lines or something."

Bailey ate the last of her fries. "Let's not go there yet. We have at least a fifty-fifty chance she'll be cooperative." She stood up and yawned. "I'm beat, and I'm warning you we're getting an early start. I want to get to this girl's house before she leaves for school."

I was dead tired myself and it was already close to midnight. "But that means we'll have to be at her house before seven thirty." Bailey stared at me. "Fine."

But as it turned out, I was so keyed up my eyes flew open at six a.m. Neither one of us wanted to bother with breakfast. We made coffee in the little two-cup machine in the room and drank it while we got ready. I piled on my thermal underwear, sweater, down vest, and coat, slipped on my gloves, and wrapped my wool scarf around my neck.

Bailey's lips twitched when she saw my getup. "We're not doing the interview on an ice floe." She was wearing a crew neck sweater and a parka. No vest, no scarf, no gloves.

"Okay, I'll make you a deal. I'll peel off a few layers if you fire up the car heater."

"Want to borrow my parka?"

"Yeah. That's what I thought. Let's go."

The city of Boulder isn't big—just under thirty square miles—and the population is just over one hundred thousand. Surprising, because it's a beautiful place. It lies in a valley with the Rocky Mountains on one side and the Flatirons on the other. Nothing but spectacular views wherever you look. And we happened to hit a particularly gorgeous day, the sky a kind of deep, limitless blue you'll never find in a big city. The air had that crisp, green mountain smell. "Where's the snow?"

"They don't usually get any until later in the year."

How Bailey knows stuff like this is beyond me. It only took us ten minutes to get to Amanda's neighborhood. It was pleasant and typically suburban—lots of basketball hoops in driveways and cars with bumper stickers for the kind of hip radio channels and liberal causes that showed they belonged to teenagers. But unlike suburbia in Los Angeles, the houses weren't crammed on top of one another. Here, there were only a few houses on each side of the street, and evergreen and pine trees filled the space between them. The houses were all ranch style, and Amanda's had a long front walk lined with yellow flowers. A beat-up skateboard on the front lawn told me Amanda probably had a younger sibling. My heart began to thud as Bailey parked in front of the house. A lot could be gained—or lost—in this meeting.

Bailey pulled her coat closed to hide the gun in her shoulder holster. I left mine in my purse. As she joined me on the sidewalk, she said, "Here goes nothin'."

"Yep." I put on a confident smile. So did Bailey. Neither of us was fooled, but we weren't the audience that mattered.

I followed Bailey up the front walk, feeling my palms sweating inside my gloves. We'd just reached the front porch when the door opened and a little boy, who looked no older than eight or nine, came hurtling out, the hood of his parka pulled up over his head, with the rest of the coat flying behind him like a cape. "Bye, Mom!" he yelled, then "Oops!" as he ran smack into Bailey and bounced back.

"Hey, big man, where's the fire?" Bailey laughed. Moments like these reminded me that she came from a big, healthy, loving family. I'd had the opposite. It made me wonder what that was like. The pang of loss for something I never had—and never would have—hit me every single time.

A tall, slender woman in a business suit with brown hair twisted in a low bun appeared in the doorway. "Zip up, Petey, it's cold!" The boy reluctantly put his arms into his coat and zipped up, then continued on his way. The woman looked at us. "Can I help you?"

Bailey pulled out her badge and cupped it in her palm so only the woman could see it. "Janice Kozak?"

The woman looked perplexed. "Yes."

"We're looking for Amanda."

"Why? What's happened?"

"It might be better if we discussed this inside," Bailey said. "If you don't mind."

"Yes, of course." She stepped back and held the door open. "Come in."

We followed her past the kitchen and into a cozy living room. Bailey and I sat on the plaid chenille sofa, and Janice sat on a matching wing chair across from us. I introduced myself and showed her my badge. "I know this is inconvenient. Please understand, we wouldn't be here if it wasn't urgent." I told her we were investigating the shootings at Fairmont High and the Cinemark theater. When she heard that, her eyes widened. And then I told her we had reason to believe Amanda might know someone connected to them.

She put a hand to her throat. "'Connected'? To one of the shooters? That's impossible! Amanda doesn't know anyone who—"

"Mom?"

And there she stood, at the end of the hallway that led into the living room. Amanda—in jeans, boots, and a blue hoodie, looking very much like her photograph.

Janice beckoned to her daughter. "These are police officers from Los Angeles, honey. They think you might know someone connected to the shootings." Janice kept her eyes on Amanda, and I had the feeling she was waiting for her daughter to insist that was impossible. Amanda stood frozen and looked from her mother to us with wide eyes, but said nothing. Janice studied her daughter for a moment, then said, "Is that true, honey?"

"N-no, no, it can't be."

Janice turned back to us. "Is she in trouble?"

"Not necessarily," I said. "But we can't be sure until we talk to her." I didn't want to mislead anyone. Amanda might be in a lot of trouble. We just didn't know at this point.

Janice's hand shook as she tucked a strand of hair behind her ear. "Then m-maybe I should call a lawyer."

I couldn't let this happen. We needed the information a lot more than we needed to arrest Amanda. And we didn't have time to haggle with lawyers. "Tell you what. I'll make you a deal. Nothing she says to us right now will be used against her. And if we get to a point where we can't honor that promise anymore, we'll stop talking and let you call a lawyer. Okay?"

Amanda finally found her voice. "Somebody tell me what's going on!"

"We're investigating the shootings at Fairmont High and the Cinemark theater, as your mother said. Bailey Keller is the detective on the case, and I'm the prosecutor. My name is Rachel Knight."

Amanda's mouth dropped open. She took a step back. "*You're* Rachel Knight?"

I nodded.

I pulled out my badge in its case and held it out to her. She moved toward me as though she were sleepwalking and slowly took the badge from my hand. When she looked from the badge to the photo ID on the opposite side, she sank down on the ottoman near Janice. Her expression told me we'd found our letter mailer.

"Who was it, Amanda?" I asked. "Who gave you the letters to mail?"

Amanda's lips moved, but no sounds came out at first. Then, finally, she managed a low whisper. "Evan. Evan Cutter."

71

I felt all the blood leave my face as her words washed over me. It couldn't be. A buzzing filled my brain as I fought to make sense of what I'd just heard. Evan Cutter, the second shooter. The frightened runaway, the reluctant witness was...the suspect? A thousand questions sprang to mind. "What did he tell you about me and why he wanted you to mail those letters?"

"H-he s-said Rachel Knight was a school counselor who was coordinating the grief therapy sessions. He said the letters were condolences. He felt bad for the kids because he used to go to Fairmont High."

"So he told you he wasn't going to Fairmont High anymore?" Amanda nodded. "Did he say where he was going?"

"He said he was getting a GED."

"And you never wondered why he didn't mail the letters himself?" She shook her head again. "Amanda, I have to tell you, the letters he gave you were not condolence letters."

"Th-they weren't?"

"No." She dropped her gaze to the floor and fell silent. I waited for her to absorb the news.

Finally, she looked at me. "What were they?"

"Threats. Written by one of the killers."

She jumped to her feet. "What? No way! That's impossible!"

"I'm sorry, Amanda." I pulled the copy I'd made of the letters from my purse and held them out to her.

Her breath was coming fast and shallow. She stared at the pages in my hand as though they were poisonous snakes. "That's impossible! I know it is because...because didn't the same guys do the theater shooting?"

"Yes. So?"

"So, there's no way! He couldn't have done the shooting at that theater."

"Why not?"

"Because he was gone! He ran away; it was on the news!" Tears sprang to her eyes.

I didn't bother to argue. "Then you haven't heard from him since he gave you the last letter?"

"No."

"Please read these letters, Amanda. It's important that you know the truth."

Amanda took the letters and sat down on the ottoman. Her mother leaned in and read with her. I watched as the horror spread across their faces.

Everything we'd believed about Evan was a lie. The distraught, conflicted friend, the frightened witness—all of it was an act.

Harrellson had said Evan was present in homeroom the day of the shooting. But now that I thought about it, he could easily have slipped away when the class headed for the gym. The gym. Didn't Harrellson say he thought he'd seen a witness statement putting Evan in the gym at the time of the shooting? But I couldn't remember him ever saying he'd confirmed it. I'd bet there was no such statement.

Then I remembered how Evan had talked about Otis during our first interview. What he said, the way he'd said it. Just enough spin to build suspicion, but not so much that it seemed pointed or vindictive. And Evan and Otis were close enough in size. Otis, the loner loser—and the perfect patsy. I thought about the timing of the second letter. If Evan got the second letter to Amanda on Thursday, it could easily have gotten to me the day of the Cinemark shooting. The timing worked.

As for the logic...that did too. There was no doubt that the same shooter who'd done the Fairmont High attack had done the Cinemark shooting. And we now suspected there was only one shooter at the Cinemark. Evan was never "on the run." He was just gearing up for his next massacre.

In fact, now that I thought about it, all his tweets about "police harassment" were nothing more than window dressing, meant to set us up to believe he was scared so we wouldn't get suspicious when he took off.

"Oh, God!" Amanda dropped the letters, covered her mouth, and ran out of the room. From down the hall, we heard the sounds of violent retching. Janice picked up the pages and stared at them, pale and speechless.

A few minutes later, Amanda stumbled back into the room clutching a wad of Kleenex, her face clammy. She squeezed into the wing chair with her mother and put her head on Janice's shoulder. Janice wrapped her arms around Amanda and stroked her hair.

Did it occur to me that this might be an act? Of course. After Evan's successful feint I was ready to second-guess gravity. But this time I was prepared. "Amanda, I showed you those letters because I need you to understand how important it is that you be completely honest with us. We have every reason to believe he's going to commit another mass murder. We don't know where or when, but we know it's coming. And soon. Whatever information you have, anything you know about him, it's critical that you share it with us."

"But I don't have any information! I don't know what he's going to do. He never told me anything!"

He probably didn't tell her what he intended to do. That much I believed. But she had to know *something.* She'd mailed those letters and apparently never thought to question it. Why? I knew there was more to that than just blind trust.

I wanted to think about it before I pushed the issue any further. For the moment, I turned to Janice. "Did you meet Evan?"

"No, but Hank did."

"Your husband?" Janice nodded. "How did that come about?"

Amanda looked up and darted a glance at her mother out of the corner of her eye. "My dad took us to a gun show," Amanda said. "He hunts. I don't. But I like to go to the range and do target practice."

I smiled at Amanda. "Me too. When was it that you all went to the gun show?"

Amanda fidgeted with a spot on her jeans. "I don't know. A while ago."

She seemed uncomfortable. I had a feeling it had to do with her mother being there. "Janice, do you think I can impose on you for a glass of water? All this clean air is starting to get to me."

Janice patted Amanda's arm. "Of course. Detective Keller, can I get you something as well?"

"Do you have tea?" Bailey asked. Janice nodded and stood up. Bailey joined her. "Let me help you."

Bailey hated tea. But that was her signal that she was buying me time alone with Amanda. When Janice and Bailey left the room, I leaned toward Amanda, who'd reseated herself on the ottoman, and kept my voice low. "You're not in any trouble, Amanda. I'm going to tell your mom that you won't need a lawyer. But I think it'd be better if we talked privately. What do you say?"

Amanda nodded and swallowed hard. "Only, can you promise not to tell anyone what I tell you?"

"I can promise to try. Okay?"

She sighed and looked away. Her hair fell forward, cloaking her face like a blanket. Eventually, she nodded. Bailey came in carrying a cup of tea and raised her eyebrows at me in a silent question. I nodded. Janice followed, carrying two bottles of water. I took one of the bottles and thanked her.

"Amanda is not going to need a lawyer. She's not in any trouble and she's not going to be."

Bailey took over. "But we will need to talk to her for quite a while. So if you wouldn't mind calling the school..."

Janice nodded and turned to look at me. "You're sure?"

"Absolutely. I'll put it in writing and on tape if you like."

"No, that's okay."

"But it would help if we could talk to her alone," I said. "We need her to try and remember a lot of details, and having someone else listening can be a distraction." I wasn't sure that was true, but it was the best I could come up with off the cuff.

Janice looked uncertain. "I think I'd rather—"

"Mom, it's okay. I'm not a baby. Let me do this. And you need to get to work anyway. These guys can take me to school when we're done."

Janice studied her daughter. "No, I'm staying here. Work can wait. But I won't sit with you, okay? I'll just be in the den..."

Amanda sighed. "Okay."

Janice scanned us all with one last look of concern, then left the room. Amanda moved to the wing chair and tucked her feet under her. I picked up where we'd left off. "When was the last time you went to a gun show?"

"Last spring. I wasn't that interested, but Evan wanted to go."

"Was that out here in Colorado? Or in Texas?"

"Here, in Colorado Springs."

"So he traveled out here to see you?"

"Not just me. He said they were going to visit family out in Utah."

"So he didn't come alone?"

"No, he brought Logan." Amanda swallowed, her expression wary. "He's the guy...the other shooter, isn't he?"

"Yes. Was he friendly with you?" Amanda let her hair fall all the way across her face. The gesture couldn't have been more obvious. "It's not your fault, Amanda. There was no way for you to know."

After a few moments, she nodded. "He...sorta had a crush on me. But I got the feeling it was mostly because he always wanted what Evan had."

"And were you Evan's girlfriend?"

Amanda nodded shyly. I saw a faint tinge of pride before she dropped her eyes. "We got together just before I moved out here. Back in Lubbock, we saw each other every day, but we didn't really get, like, involved until about a month before I left." Amanda gazed off into the distance of her memory, a happier place. "Evan could get any girl he wanted. Even last year's junior prom queen. She was a model. And he was just a sophomore."

Wow. Imagine. "So he was pretty popular?"

Amanda stared at the floor. "Yeah. I figured he'd never be into somebody like me."

He never was. But I wouldn't be the one to give her that painful news. "Was that gun show the first time you met Logan?"

"Yeah. Actually, that was the only time I ever saw him. After that visit, Logan wrote to me for a little while, but then he stopped."

"Letters? Or emails?"

"Letters."

"Did you answer him?"

"Sure. I felt sorry for him. He seemed kind of…sad, you know? He wrote a lot about how he'd always felt so alone, how no one 'got' him—"

"Not even Evan?"

"No. But I never thought he and Evan were that tight. Evan never talked about Logan, and Logan hardly ever mentioned Evan in his letters. That's why when I heard Logan might be a suspect, it never occurred to me that Evan could be…" Amanda stopped and bit her lip. She blinked rapidly, then continued. "Anyway, I got the feeling Logan just liked being able to hang out with someone that cool. Someone who wasn't afraid of anything."

"And Evan wasn't afraid of anything?" I'd never seen him show that kind of swagger. But I'd only seen the act. Not the real Evan. I'd bet the guy Amanda saw was closer to the truth.

"Yeah. Nothing scared Evan. Logan thought that was amazing." Amanda's face crumpled, and she wiped away a tear that escaped from the corner of her eye. "I did too."

I knew where her thoughts were taking her. I tried to nip it in the bud. "It makes perfect sense for you to be sad that Evan isn't the person you thought he was. But if you're feeling guilty about it, you have to stop." Amanda bit her lip. The pain in her eyes was heartbreaking. "Evan's a very good actor. He fooled a lot of people for quite a long time—us included. And it's our job to spot guys like that. So let yourself off the hook, okay?" Amanda nodded without looking up. I hoped my words would sink in eventually. But right now, I had to move on. "So Logan confided in you about feeling lonely and depressed. Did he ever say anything about suicide?"

"Never, like, 'I'm gonna do it.' More like it was something he used to think about when he was a kid." Amanda pushed her hair back. "If he'd said something about wanting to kill himself right then, I'd have told someone. For sure."

Talk of past suicidal thoughts could just be typical melodramatic teenage posturing. Or it could be an oblique way of talking about serious *current* suicidal ideation. Obviously, Logan's talk was the latter. But there was no way for Amanda to have known that. "You say he wrote to you for a while, then stopped. How come?"

"I think he could tell from my letters that Evan and I were together, and I wasn't into anything more than being friends."

"Do you still have those letters from Logan?"

"No, I'm sorry."

I was too. They might not have been terribly illuminating, but any little bit of information would've helped. The more we could learn about these shooters, the better we'd be at spotting them in the future. Maybe. "Let's get back to the gun show. Did he or Logan buy any guns?"

"They couldn't. But I remember they went off on their own for a while." Amanda tucked a strand of hair behind her ear. "I couldn't find them, and my dad was, like, 'Where are they?' It was so uncool. He was pissed."

"Did you see either of them with a gun after the show?" I asked.

"No. But that doesn't mean they didn't have one. They could've found someone to buy a gun for them. That happens sometimes."

Yes, it does. The picture was becoming clearer. I'd bet Evan had sized up Amanda right from the jump as someone he could use. I doubted he knew exactly how she'd be of use to him when she moved to Colorado. But he was obviously capable of long-range thinking and he knew a valuable asset when he saw one. So when he found out she was moving, he made Amanda his girlfriend. After all, what did it take? A bit of romancing before she left, some phone calls now and then after she'd moved. And it had paid off. I had no doubt that by the time he and Logan went to the gun show with Amanda, their plans for Fairmont High were well under way.

So now I knew why Evan had trusted her to mail the letters to me. What I still didn't get was why she'd done it.

72

I had to be careful how I segued back into the subject of Evan's letters to me. A sharp turn into serious territory like that could push Amanda into panic mode and make her clam up. I decided to approach it from the relationship angle. "Did Evan say he still wanted to be a couple after you moved? Or did you guys become just friends at that point?"

Amanda blushed a little. "He said he didn't want to give me up." She floated away for a moment. "Evan always told me I was special. That he could really talk to me—not like the other girls. He said they were lame, that they only cared about their clothes and their makeup and who was sleeping with who..."

"He made you feel special." Amanda nodded. "What did you and Evan talk about?"

"Everything. How stupid politicians are and how the sheeple keep voting for them because they get taken in by campaign promises that're obvious lies—"

"Any specific politicians?" The sheeple. Stupid. Lies. A grandiose indictment of both the voters and the candidates. Typical of a psychopath. And Amanda's delivery sounded like it came straight from the horse's mouth. If that horse was a sociopath.

Amanda frowned. "Probably, but I can't remember. He said he wanted to go over to Iraq. He'd kill the bad guys and end this thing fast."

No, he wouldn't. It was too dangerous. Evan was no hero; he killed like a coward. "So you guys stayed close after you moved?"

"Definitely. We Skyped or talked on the phone."

"You didn't email?" I asked.

Amanda shook her head. "Evan had a thing about emailing. He said he didn't trust it."

"Did he stay with you during the gun show?"

"No. They drove out in Logan's car and took off afterward. Evan said Logan had to visit his relatives in Utah."

Or something. We knew that was a lie. The family in Utah said they hadn't seen Logan in years. "Was that the last time you saw Evan?"

"Yeah."

Time to get to the point. "And you guys never wrote letters to each other?"

"No, never."

"So what did you think when he sent you those letters and told you to mail them to me?"

Amanda shrugged. "I guess I didn't think anything. It was just a favor he needed, so I did it. I mean, it wasn't that big a deal. He sent the letters along with his other stuff."

Bailey and I exchanged a look. "What other stuff?"

"Um, notebooks."

My ears perked up. "Notebooks? What was in them?"

"I don't know. When he sent them to me they were all sealed up, and he told me not to open them."

"Did he tell you why?"

"He said they were poems and stories and stuff like that. He was going to send them to an agent, to get published. But he didn't want anyone to see them because they might steal his ideas."

"What did he want you to do with them?"

"Just keep them safe where no one could see them."

"Did he just recently send them to you?"

"Not all of them. He started sending them to me a while ago. But the last two he sent were recent. Those were the ones that had the letters with them."

"And you never thought to question why he needed you to forward those letters for him?"

Amanda shook her head. "I know it sounds stupid." New tears gathered in her eyes. "I—he was my boyfriend. I trusted him. So I went along with it. And now I don't know why."

I gave her a sympathetic nod. "Those notebooks, do you still have them?"

Amanda tucked her hair behind her ear and began to play with the drawstring on her hoodie. "Yeah, but... I promised him."

We could probably justify a search warrant and tear the place up looking for those notebooks, but that would take time. And time was exactly what we didn't have. "Amanda, no you didn't." She looked at me, startled. "You made that promise to the person you *thought* was Evan. But that person doesn't exist. The *real* Evan is a murderer. The real Evan lied to you about what was in those letters he gave you. And I have no doubt that he lied to you about what's in those notebooks. You know what I think is in them?"

Amanda looked at me warily. "N-no."

"Plans for the shootings. For Fairmont, for the Cinemark theater, and probably for the ones he's about to do. You saw what he wrote in those letters to me. He's going to keep doing it until we stop him. If you don't give us those notebooks, you'll be helping him kill more innocent people."

She squeezed her eyes shut and began to sob. Bailey and I exchanged a look. We'd told her to forget what she'd believed—and wanted to believe for more than a year, that Evan Cutter was her Prince Charming—and believe what she'd just learned in the past hour: that he was a mass murderer. It was a hard turn for her to make. But after a few moments, Amanda swiped the back of her hand across her cheeks and stood up. "Come on."

We followed her into a bedroom that was surprisingly austere for a teenage girl. You could bounce a quarter off the perfectly made twin bed, and the two navy-and-red decorative pillows looked like they'd been positioned against the headboard with a T square. A few posters of bands I didn't recognize were taped—not tacked—onto the wall. The oak dresser was bare of any cosmetics or jewelry, and there were no clothes on the floor or the bench at the foot of the bed. In fact, there wasn't a hair out of place in the entire room.

Dating Evan—if you could call it that—seemed to be Amanda's only wild move. But talk about hitting a home run right out of the box. Amanda pulled the chair away from her small desk and dragged it to the shelving against the wall in the far right corner of the room. She climbed up on it, reached behind some tall books on the top shelf, and started to pull down manila envelopes completely encased in heavy wrapping tape.

"Hold on," Bailey said. She grabbed a box of Kleenex and covered her hands, then reached for the first envelope. I covered my hands and took it from Bailey, and placed it on Amanda's desk. When we'd finished, there was a stack of nine envelopes.

"Is this all of them?"

Amanda nodded. "You can look around if you want to." She swept her arm out to indicate her room.

"And he didn't send you anything else? Pictures? Books?" Amanda shook her head.

"We'll just check the rest of these shelves to make sure you didn't miss anything, okay?"

Amanda nodded. "Go ahead. But he only sent me the nine envelopes. I'm sure."

I felt reasonably certain she was telling the truth, but Bailey and I took a few minutes to look through the room anyway. We'd have officers do a more thorough search, just to check for any small things Amanda might've forgotten about. But right now, we needed to dig into those notebooks, and fast.

If these were the writings the shrinks had talked about, they might tell us where Evan was planning to strike next. And if there was a third party involved—I thought of the lead Harrellson was working in San Diego—they might give us that person's name. I was eager to get going, but I had just a couple more questions for Amanda. "When did Evan start sending you these envelopes?"

"About a month after we moved here, I think."

"And when did you get the last one?"

"Um...about a week ago?" Her brow furrowed, then she nodded. "Yeah, about a week ago because I asked him if he could come out for

Homecoming, and he sent me a note with the last package saying he was going to be busy."

Boy, was he ever. "Did you keep that note?"

Amanda nodded and went to her nightstand. She picked up a book—*Girls: A Guy's Perspective.* I wanted to tell her that if she was trying to understand Evan, she'd have to get *American Psycho.* Amanda pulled out a piece of lined paper that had been folded and tucked into the middle. Bailey took the paper from her using the Kleenex. "Can you tell me where your mom keeps extra grocery bags?" Amanda told her, and while Bailey went to get them, I asked her my last few questions.

"When Evan sent you the letters to mail to me, did he send a note to you with them? Or did he call you and tell you he was sending them?"

"He called." Amanda knew what the next question would be, and she didn't wait for it. She pulled her cell phone out of the pocket of her sweatshirt and scrolled. She pointed to a number. "This is it. It's around the right time, and I know all the other numbers on here."

"You don't have a number for him?"

"No. He uses burners. He says the government can track you on a cell phone, so he never uses a phone more than twice."

A lie to keep Amanda from having access to him? Or true? Given his distrust of emails, it might well be true, which meant the chance that we might be able to track him with this number was very slim. But slim or not, it was worth a try. I copied the call history on Amanda's cell phone for the past two weeks and emailed it to myself.

Amanda gestured to the notebooks piled on her desk. "Do you really think the plans for the Fairmont shooting are in there?"

"Yes." I took in Amanda's pallor. "Do you feel well enough to go to school?"

"I...yeah." She turned away from the envelopes. "I want to be with my friends."

I got it. She needed to reassure herself that she'd made some good choices too. And that there was a normal world out there. "Okay, we'll take you."

Bailey returned with paper grocery bags, and we put the envelopes into them, packing the note to Amanda separately to preserve prints. We told Janice we were done and that we'd take Amanda to school. She and Amanda held each other in a long hug.

We all trooped out to Bailey's car. Amanda gave us directions to her school. It was past ten o'clock by the time we dropped her off.

I got out of the car with her. "Remember to call us immediately if you hear from him, okay?"

I didn't think Evan would make contact with her now. He was in full attack mode. But you never know. If he got desperate, he might show up with some cockamamie story about how the psycho killers were after him. The kind of story she might've believed just a little over an hour ago, but surely wouldn't now. I hoped.

Amanda nodded. "I will. I promise."

I watched her move slowly up the front steps, bent forward under the weight of her backpack. She looked like the same girl who'd woken up that morning. But she wasn't. She'd just learned that the boy she'd loved and trusted was a soulless monster who had used her and lied to her. The world would never look the same to her again.

73

Bailey put out the alert for Evan Cutter. When she ended the call, I gestured to the notebooks that were now packed in grocery bags in the backseat. "We can't wait for Dorian. We need to tear into those things."

"Definitely," Bailey said. "And we've got to let Harrellson know—"

"I'll try him now."

I couldn't get any signal. When we got back to the hotel, I got Harrellson's voice mail and left a message—no details, just saying it was urgent. I hoped he'd cleared Mark Unger. One missing psychopath was plenty. Bailey called Graden and filled him in, while I found us a three o'clock flight back to L.A. Then Bailey took out her Swiss Army knife and sliced through the tape on all of the envelopes.

At Graden's request we headed straight to his office with the notebooks. Now we reread them over his shoulder. The first line encapsulated the running theme throughout all of them.

"The world is filled with stupid, pathetic, inferior worms. They're all a waste of precious resources."

Evan, the brilliant, the amazing, had no use for the "shrimp brains" of the world. Except as fodder for his sadistic fantasies.

"I saw a movie once where they tied a guy's arms to the bumper of one car and his legs to the bumper of another, then drove the cars in opposite directions. Just tore him to shreds. I loved it."

Graden finished the fourth notebook. "Jesus," he muttered. Bailey and I exchanged looks. We'd had a similar reaction. It was a bird's-eye view into the mind of a raving psychopath. But these pages explained something that had always bothered me about the letters I'd received. Back when I thought they'd been written by Logan, I'd had a hard time squaring them with the eloquent writing style Logan's teachers had described. I'd supposed Logan's fury had stripped his prose of its usual poetry. But now, knowing that it was Evan who'd written the letters, and seeing the writing in these notebooks, it all made sense.

In Notebook 6 we found a mention of the car burglary charges in Lubbock, Texas. It was a chilling example of Evan's skill in presenting a facade that was a hundred and eighty degrees from the truth.

"Dumbass fools! Not one of those stupid fucks in juvenile court has a fucking clue. I wrote that bullshit letter to that loser victim yesterday and my PO was all like, 'Oh, Evan, y'all are doin' so well. I wish all my probationers were like you.' Really, rat face? Do you? Do you wish all your probationers were a thousand times smarter and better than you? And that dumb fuck victim. He DESERVED to have his shit stolen, leaving it on the dashboard in plain sight. STUPID chump-assed motherfucker!"

Stanley, the PO, had no clue. He'd been completely taken in by the act. As the PO put it: "He was a model probationer." And all the while, Evan was laughing at the "chump-assed motherfucker" he'd duped so easily.

There was a mention in Notebook 7 of James Holmes, who'd done the shooting in the theater in Aurora, Colorado.

"Pathetic fucking loser, with that stupid orange hair. Fucking clown. It's all in the execution, asshole! If you'd done it RIGHT, you could've taken out at least a hundred. Fool."

In Notebook 8 we found a sneering reference to Timothy McVeigh and Oklahoma City. *"He sets up a bomb and hides like a little bitch. Where's the art in that? Where's the joy? The world is going to see how it's done by the BEST. And when we get through, everyone will know we're far superior to that little punk-assed bitch McVeigh."*

I pointed to the line. "That's the first time I've seen him say *we*. So at this point he must've hooked up with Logan."

"And started some actual planning," Bailey said.

Evan made it clear that he didn't intend to get caught "like that stupid clown douche in Aurora," and that he wasn't afraid to die. In fact, he planned to go out in a "blaze of glory." Just as our shrinks predicted. But there was no mention of any plans for future shootings. Not even a specific mention of the plans for the Fairmont shooting.

When he'd finished reading the last notebook, Graden looked up at us. "I have never seen anything like this."

"Who has?" Bailey said.

"But I don't get this," Graden said. "For a kid this young, with his background, to be such a cesspool of hate. I'm not saying his parents were necessarily perfect—we never know the whole story when it comes to family dynamics. But they didn't seem *that* far off the beam. Where did it come from?" I shook my head. That was a question no one seemed to be able to answer. "And why didn't he put his plans for Fairmont or the Cinemark in these notebooks? You think he didn't trust Amanda?"

Bailey began putting the notebooks back into their manila envelopes. "Yeah. He couldn't take the risk. If Amanda read about those plans, she'd have called the cops—"

"And also, he probably wanted to keep those plans close," I said. "The shrinks did say these mass murderers get off on writing and reading their own master plans." My eyes were gritty and my shoulders ached. I looked at my watch. Nine o'clock. I hadn't realized how long we'd been at it.

"Guess we can pull back on the Platt Junior High security," Graden said.

"Yeah," Bailey said. "That was Logan's thing, not Evan's. We should probably keep a detail on it just in case, but I doubt Evan will hit there."

Graden looked more than just tired. He looked drawn, spent. "You okay?" I asked.

"Yeah." He sighed. "I went to another one of the funerals today."

A lead weight pulled at my heart. I was no stranger to depravity—none of us were—but this case was enough to shake what little faith I had in humanity. I thought about naive, unsuspecting Amanda, all the innocent children and teachers at Fairmont High, the victims at the Cinemark, and all the others who were such easy pickings for monsters like Evan. Good people didn't stand a chance against this kind of random evil.

74

Graden drove me home. I invited him to come up to my room even though we were both fried. I needed to connect with something positive. The insanity I'd been immersed in for the past week had reached a crescendo with those notebooks.

I poured us each a glass of Ancien Pinot Noir. "Do you want to order room service?"

Graden studied his glass. "No, I don't want anything to get in the way of the buzz."

I turned on the CD player and we sat on the couch. The lazy-sweet strains of Stanley Turrentine's "Little Sheri" softly filled the room. Graden clinked his glass against mine and we took a sip. He put an arm around me, and I kicked off my shoes and curled up next to him. "You know, it's funny," he said. "I've seen you more during this case than I ever do, but it sure doesn't feel that way."

We hadn't had the chance to really connect because we were always running ninety miles an hour. "It is kind of a tease."

He smiled. "Well, I don't think I've ever been accused of *that* before." He put down his glass, lifted my chin, and kissed me. A long, slow kiss. "Better?"

I was a little breathless. "Even more of a tease."

He took my glass and put it down on the coffee table, then stood up and pulled me to my feet. Ten minutes ago, I'd have bet serious money that nothing could put me in the mood. But all it took was five minutes alone with Graden to completely change my mind. I followed him into the bedroom and we fell into each other as though we'd been apart for months.

I woke up Thursday morning feeling rested for the first time since I'd caught the case. Graden was already out of the shower and trying to dress quietly. "It's okay, I'm up." My voice was still hoarse with sleep.

He smiled and came over to sit next to me on the bed. He pushed my hair out of my eyes. "What's on tap for you today?"

"We've got to meet with the shrinkers about those journals."

"Did you get a look at that note he wrote to Amanda?" he asked.

"The one asking her to keep the notebooks for him? No."

Graden shook his head, his features stony. "He worked her but good. Said, 'You're so special. You're the only one who gets me. That's why I trust you with these. They're the most important things to me—other than you, of course.' It's incredible how that monster can mimic human behavior." Graden picked up the remote. "Since you're up, mind if I turn on the news?"

"Nope. And you can order us breakfast while you're at it. Two eggs over medium and a bowl of mixed fruit."

"I'll go rattle some pots and pans."

I kissed him and headed for the shower. I'd just finished drying my hair when I heard my name coming from the television. I ran into the bedroom and saw a news reporter standing in front of the St. Julien, where Bailey and I had stayed in Boulder. I turned up the volume.

"...and now we've learned that prosecutor Rachel Knight and Detective Bailey Keller paid a visit to someone here in Boulder yesterday. Officials have refused to answer questions about why they were here or who they saw, but it had to be something big to take them out of Los Angeles with at least one killer still at large. Back to you, Andrew."

Graden had walked in during the newscast. He looked at me, worried. "How the hell did they find out about your trip?"

"Could be someone at the airport, or at the hotel. Who knows?"

Room service arrived. Graden started toward the door, then abruptly stopped. "Wait...Evan—"

"Will know we were talking to Amanda."

Graden pulled out his cell. "Yeah, Sandy, get me Boulder PD right now."

The captain of the Boulder Police Department took about ten seconds to guarantee immediate, round-the-clock protection for Amanda and her family. We barely spoke as we ate, each of us consumed by our own thoughts. When we'd finished, I brushed my teeth and grabbed my raincoat and scarf. The sun was shining, but I didn't trust it—the trees were swaying in a strong wind.

Graden pulled me in for a quick hug before we went out into the world. "Let me know what the shrinks say."

"I will."

He gave me a little smile. "And hey, thanks for last night."

"No, thank *you.*" I wrapped the scarf around my neck and opened the door. "Your money's on the nightstand."

Graden gave me a shove. "Get out."

We headed downstairs. Graden, unlike Bailey, always had Rafi park his car, and he tipped well. His car was waiting at the curb. Bailey pulled up, and Graden waved as he drove off. She raised an eyebrow at me as I buckled up. "I see you've been putting in some overtime."

"How original of you." I told her about the newscast and getting protection for Amanda.

"I'd be surprised if Evan bothered with her at this point, but we should ask the shrinks about it."

I intended to. "Did you get a copy of Evan's journals out to Jenny and Michael?"

Bailey nodded. "Made them myself last night. Sealed them up and had them hand-delivered early this morning."

"Do you ever sleep?" Bailey gave a grim smile. It was a drag of a chore, but she was wise not to trust anyone else with it. If those journals leaked, there'd be mass panic. "You talk to Harrellson yet?" I asked. "Hear anything about that San Diego kid, Mark...?

"Unger, yeah. He's got a solid alibi. Kid's been in school and at work at the local Jamba Juice every day for the past month. So at least we know we're only looking for one psycho."

"Good," I said. "Did you ask Harrellson if he ever found that uni report saying witnesses had seen Evan in the gym?"

"I did. He can't find it, and now he thinks he must've been hallucinating."

"But Evan did go to homeroom," I said.

"Yeah. But if they had all their stuff stashed close by, he could've ducked out when everyone else headed to the gym. It's not that hard."

Exactly what I'd figured. Now that I thought about it, I'd snuck into the girls' room to ditch assembly a time or two myself. "I assume by now someone's told Evan's parents that we've got an arrest warrant out for him?" Bailey nodded. "How'd they take it?"

"The mom fell apart, but the dad refuses to believe it. Said Evan was never violent and never showed any interest in guns."

"Did anyone ask them how Evan was acting just before the Fairmont shooting?"

"Yeah, and they said he acted completely normal. A little busier than usual; he wasn't around much. But that was it."

I had a hard time believing it. How could he possibly be that well controlled? Maybe later, when the shock wore off, his parents would be able to sift through their memories and find the clues that were escaping them now. But those clues had to have been fairly subtle for the parents to have missed them to begin with.

"Has the tip line blown up?" I asked. Now that we'd identified Evan Cutter as the shooter and released his photo, I expected a flood of calls.

"Of course. But nothing solid yet."

Releasing Evan's identity was a double-edged sword. The upside was that people would be on the lookout. The downside was that now he'd know he had to act fast to put on his big "finale." And that meant the pressure was on like never before.

I put in a call to Eric to bring him up to speed.

"Hey, Rachel, I just heard about Evan being your suspect. What the hell?" I gave him the whole story in abbreviated form. "I have never seen a case like this in my life." Eric gave a long sigh. "I hate to be the bearer of bad news, but Vanderhorn wants you in ASAP for a debriefing."

"Tell me he didn't actually say 'debriefing.'"

"Unfortunately, he did. I wouldn't push you on this, but there's a big memorial planned for the Fairmont High School victims, and he's planning to attend."

"Of course he is. There's bound to be a ton of press."

I could hear Eric smiling. "So Vanderhorn wants to know as much as possible, just in case he has to give a statement."

Just in case. He'd chase them down and tackle them if they didn't ask for a statement. This was one of the few moments when I really hated my job.

"Okay. But I've got a meeting with the shrinks first."

75

We found Jenny and Michael already starting on their second cup of coffee. This coffee-meeting ritual had grown on me. There was something comforting about it, although given the reason for these meetings, I didn't know why. The photocopied pages of Evan's journal were spread out on the table between them. Jenny held up the pot. "Want some?"

"Sure, thanks," I said. Bailey took a cup too, and we settled in around the table. Bailey brought them up to speed on the latest events, including the press release identifying Evan Cutter as the shooter and the leak that we'd been in Boulder.

Michael and Jenny exchanged a look; then Michael cleared his throat. "Before we get to these pages"—he gestured to the copies of the journals—"we think you should be aware that the press releases are likely to speed up his timetable. I guarantee he knows that he's been identified."

"So the net is tightening quickly," Jenny said. "As we've surmised, he never expected to go on indefinitely, and this journal confirms what we've said all along: he plans to continue these rampages until he's stopped—"

"And that means when he dies," Michael said. "Evan Cutter has no intention of being taken into custody."

And I had no intention of letting him have his finale of choice. Death was too good for this subhuman. I wanted Evan Cutter taken into custody alive and kicking. "We agree. What'd you think of his journals?"

Jenny led off. "This boy is a classic example of a psychopath—"

"No big shock there," Bailey said.

"No. But I've seen what many would have called the most extreme psychopaths in the world, and Evan Cutter is right up there. And unlike some of the other, more prolific killers, he doesn't even pretend to be serving a political ideology. He simply hates the world. And loves power. The combination of that hatred and thirst for power is what fuels his desire to kill. Murder for him is the epitome of power." Jenny pushed a few of the pages around, then pulled one out and pointed to the bottom of the page. "See here, where he rails against his father for moving the family around so much? For a normal child that might be tough, but for Evan Cutter it was torturous because it undermined his power. His father said go, and like it or not, he had to go. That infuriated him. You said his father is a military type, a former Marine, correct?" I nodded. "And I'd guess fairly strict?"

"I got that impression," I said.

Jenny shook her head. "You couldn't hope for a worse combination. In general, psychopaths can't tolerate any form of restriction. But Evan in particular has a very low threshold for frustration. What is apparent in these pages is that any obstacle, no matter how small, sends him into a rage."

"Because it's a threat to his power," I said. Michael nodded. "But he doesn't fit the profile you guys gave us. Evan didn't complain about feeling persecuted or even do a lot of yakking about guns. And neither did Logan."

"We had to go with generalities," Jenny said. "But when it comes to specific individuals"—she sighed—"there just are no concrete rules. And this is a big part of the problem when it comes to spotting a potential psychopath of this ilk. As we said from the start, they're heterogeneous. There is no single profile."

"True," I said. "But Logan...he doesn't fit any mold."

Jenny nodded, reached into an accordion folder that was on the floor next to her chair, and pulled out some photocopied pages. I recognized them as the pages from Logan's journal. I'd forgotten we'd given them a copy. "After hearing that Logan was dead, I took another look at these pages. I'd always had the sense that Logan was a follower, not a leader. I think Amanda probably had it right when she told you she thought Logan had a crush on her primarily because he wanted to emulate Evan.

And Logan clearly had some serious psychological problems—certainly he was severely depressed. I don't think, given what he ultimately did, that it's a big stretch to say Logan also had a great deal of anger boiling inside him. In that regard, he and Evan had something important in common. But the difference is in how they dealt with that anger. That difference is what made Evan so attractive to Logan. Evan's aggressive energy, his apparent power, was revelatory for Logan. Here was someone who channeled his rage outward, who punished others rather than what Logan did—"

I nodded. "Punish himself."

"Right," Jenny said. "I doubt Logan, on his own, would ever have harmed another person. He might've fantasized about homicide in his darker moments, but I doubt he would ever have acted on it. It was the introduction of Evan into his life that induced him to turn his rage outward—"

"You think he committed suicide out of guilt?" I asked.

"In part, yes," Michael said. "He was suicidal in general, so he might've killed himself eventually no matter what. But Logan was not psychopathic, so it's highly unlikely he derived the pleasure from killing that Evan did. In fact, it wouldn't surprise me if Logan suffered terribly in the aftermath of the Fairmont shooting."

"And what about the reverse?" Bailey asked. "Would Evan still have done these shootings if he hadn't met Logan?"

"In light of the fact that he did carry on after Logan killed himself, I'd say probably yes, he would have," Michael said. "Now, would he have done the Fairmont shooting if he hadn't met Logan? That I can't say. But I can say that connecting with Logan made Fairmont a more likely target."

I had a question that'd been in the forefront of my mind since our meeting with the Cutters. "Sorry for the dogleg, but I've been meaning to ask you, how come none of the parents—not the Jarvises or the Cutters—saw anything wrong, nothing out of the norm, before the shooting? The parents seem like responsible people. The type who pay attention. These guys were planning the Fairmont murders for almost a year. How can it be that they didn't notice anything was wrong?"

"The only thing the parents said was that the boys weren't around much in the last month," Bailey said.

Jenny nodded. "Of course, they were busy getting ready. Or they might've been keeping themselves away to make sure no one could see any difference in their behavior. But that wouldn't register with any parent as 'something wrong.' As for Evan, I wouldn't expect to see any gross manifestations of unusual conduct by the time he was planning the shootings. He had no moral compunctions about it, so there was no reservoir of guilt to trip him up. These shootings were something he eagerly anticipated. He would've made sure not to do anything that might raise concerns."

"Logan would have been the one more likely to show visible signs of something amiss in the last few weeks," Michael said. "He had a conscience."

"But even if Logan wavered, or started to act out, Evan was there to keep the lid on," Jenny said.

"Right," Michael said. "And it's even likely that Logan was in a bit better mood than usual in the last month. Once a suicidal person has made the decision to end his life, he feels a sense of relief, even euphoria. Logan knew the killing spree couldn't last forever. So for him, the shooting marked the light at the end of the tunnel."

"Bottom line, by the time their plans were under way, it was way too late," Jenny said. "They were old enough to manage their behavior. The time to catch signs of homicidal pathology like Evan's was much earlier, in childhood."

"And what would those have been?" I asked.

"The early signs of psychopathology are varied. There was a study that showed infants who turned out to be psychopathic had a pronounced tendency to stare at objects out of their reach. They theorized that the infants stared in an effort to exert control; that the space between the infant and the object was a threat to the baby's control—"

Michael shook his head. "I'm not sure how much stock I put in that one—"

"It may be a bit far-out," Jenny said. "But generally, psychopaths show a greater attachment to objects than to people from a very early age. Some believe that may be caused by mothers who have difficulty bonding with their babies. Personally, I think the child has to already have a tendency toward psychopathology for maternal detachment to have that kind of impact. My own mother suffered severe postpartum depression for a solid year after I was born. Refused to even touch me. She eventually recovered—enough to go back to work, anyway. But she never became anything close to a 'loving' mother."

"How *did* it affect you?" I asked.

"From about the age of six I knew I wanted to help children—"

"So it had a positive effect?" Bailey asked.

"Well…I also vowed never to have any children of my own. But it certainly didn't make me a sociopath. And, diagnostically speaking, that's the problem we face. Family trauma or even abuse is not a predictor. As I'm sure you've seen, there are plenty of kids who suffer devastating abuse who have no violent tendencies whatsoever."

I nodded. I'd been assigned to juvenile court for a year. It was sadly common to find that the kids had been abused, but most were charged with drug crimes or theft. The few who were in for violent crimes were usually involved in gangs.

"Anyway, as for the early signs of psychopathology, you've heard of the classic ones: cruel, sadistic behaviors toward animals or smaller children—"

"And younger siblings are often targets," Michael said. "But in this case, neither Logan nor Evan had them."

"And not all children will behave in such obvious ways," Jenny said. "While they lack empathy and do not have normal attachments to family and friends, their behavior may not initially be overtly abnormal. A child may merely appear to be less demonstrative than others or a little less empathic. But if the child is a fast learner, he'll pick up on the appropriate social cues at a young enough age to avert detection. Destructive behavior is common. Such children often have a penchant for setting fires. Deceptive behaviors, lying, cheating, stealing. For them, the ends always justify the means, and no value is placed on honesty—"

"Which is why they can be very glib," Michael said. "They have no regard for rules or for the truth. Evan had that juvenile arrest for car burglary?" I nodded. "I'd bet he was the ringleader. And I'm sure there were other such instances for which he never got caught. I'd also imagine Evan committed noncriminal acts as a child that showed a cruel, sadistic side, but weren't big enough to force the parents to put two and two together."

"How on earth could a parent see *any* kind of sadistic behavior and not know that there's something seriously wrong?" I asked.

"A combination of denial—we don't see what we don't want to see—and a failure to grasp the significance of what they're seeing," Jenny said. "It's not uncommon for parents to view each incident as an isolated event and explain each one away, rather than see the whole picture. And if the behavior surfaces during adolescence, well...even the most normal teenagers can be unlovely." Jenny gave a brief smile.

Memories of our interviews with Evan flashed through my mind. "I just can't believe Evan gamed us so well," I said.

Jenny nodded. "I understand. It is upsetting. But remember, your contacts with him were relatively limited. And even trained professionals have been deceived by psychopaths. They can be excellent actors. After all, they've been studying normal behavior practically since birth."

"Where does it come from?" I asked. "Psychopaths are born, not made, right?"

Jenny nodded. "Biology plays a part, of course. There are studies of monozygotic twins that show psychopathology has a genetic component."

"But environment, upbringing, they matter too," Michael said. "Though, as this case has shown you, socioeconomic factors really don't matter. You can find psychopaths in Beverly Hills or on skid row."

"And to complicate matters further," Jenny said, "this pathology is not a black-and-white issue. On one end of the spectrum you have narcissists, who are most certainly empathy-challenged and self-absorbed, but not usually physically dangerous. And on the other end of the spectrum, you have the most severe psychopaths—who are extremely dangerous in every way."

"Like Evan," Bailey said.

"Yes," Michael said. "And you have everything in between those two extremes."

"But studies do show that psychopathology is on the rise," Jenny said. "I'm not sure whether that's because we're better at spotting the disorder or the incidence has truly increased."

"If it really has increased, wouldn't that explain why there seem to be more of these mass shootings?" I asked.

"It might," Jenny said. "But remember, not all of these shooters are psychopaths. Logan is a prime example. His pathology might never have resulted in harm to another person had he not met up with Evan."

"You mentioned these killers live through their writings," I said. "Then why did Evan give his writings to Amanda?"

"For posterity," Jenny said. "Remember, he doesn't have any illusions about his longevity on this planet, and in addition to satisfying his homicidal desires, he wants recognition, fame. By secreting those notebooks with Amanda, he was ensuring that they would survive him. He plans to die in a spectacular way, and once he does—"

"Amanda would bring out the notebooks, and everyone and his brother would want to see them," I said. It was disgusting, but true. "You also said they love to write about their killing plans, but there aren't any in these journals. Is it possible he did write out his plans but didn't want to risk leaving them with Amanda?"

Michael sat forward. "Yes, that's what we believe. He took a big risk even leaving those journals with her."

Jenny nodded. "We think he's keeping his plans close at hand, wherever he is."

"Now if we just knew where that was," Bailey said. "The problem is, he could be anywhere. Sleeping in his car, camping out under a bridge—"

"Even staying in a motel if he has a fake ID," I said.

"But now that we put his picture out there, he's going to have a much harder time with that option," Bailey said.

"You have an alert out for his car?" Jenny asked.

"Of course," I said. "And we still have one out for Logan's car too."

"Those cars have got to be where they stashed their weapons," Bailey said. "If they'd been anyplace else, we'd have found them by now."

I nodded and took a sip of coffee, though my stomach surely didn't need the acid. "Do you think Evan will write me another letter?"

"No," Michael said. "Tweaking you was fun. And it was a release in a sense. He could sublimate his need for recognition by savoring his access to a famous prosecutor. But now he is known. He doesn't need that release."

"Do you have any new ideas about what his next target might be?" I asked.

"I'd say keep looking at the big venues—but ones he'd be very familiar with," Jenny said. "At this point he knows that his next target will likely be his last. So what he wants now is a sure thing. A place where he feels most in control."

"And I think that means somewhere in the San Fernando Valley," Michael said. "He can't risk traveling, and he was here for the Cinemark shooting. So I'd guess he's still local."

Jenny sighed. "I know that's still a huge amount of territory to cover—"

"It is," Bailey said. "But we're trying."

We wrapped up our meeting, and as we walked to the parking lot, it started to pour. Naturally, I'd left my umbrella at the station, so by the time I got to the car, I was soaking wet. Bailey handed me some paper towels she kept in the middle console.

I wiped my face and neck, then rubbed my hair dry. "The thing is, he could've been preparing for his next target for the last six months—or even a year. I've been thinking he'd need to score another AK or AR. But he doesn't necessarily have to use guns—"

"No. Matter of fact, I'd be surprised if he hadn't set himself up with Molotovs, pipe bombs, the kind of thing he can build himself. And you're right, he's had plenty of time."

"He'd need a place to store it all."

"Yeah. But a car would do." Bailey pulled out of the parking lot.

I stared out the window. "Jenny's right. He's not far."

"I agree."

Which only made the question of Evan's whereabouts more aggravating. Worse still was the possibility that we wouldn't have the answer until it was too late.

76

When we got back to the station, we checked in with Graden to find out if there'd been any tips worth hearing about.

"Evan's been sighted everywhere from Eureka to Tijuana, and they're not even a quarter of the way through them all. We're running down every one that's even marginally close, but none of them look good so far."

I looked at the television in Graden's office that was perpetually tuned to the local news. "I have to believe he'll try to disguise himself."

Bailey nodded. "Yeah, a wig—or even just a hat and a pair of shades would probably be enough to do the trick."

"But at least now people will be looking," I said. "And we're going to show Jax our photo of Evan and see if he can make some kind of ID."

Graden looked hopeful. "He saw Evan close-up?"

"Yeah, but I'm not all that confident. He said the guy was wearing a baseball cap and shades. All he could give us was a general height and weight—"

Bailey moved toward the door. "Which fits Evan and about ten million other guys."

"It doesn't matter," Graden said. "We know we've got the right guy. Evidence will pile up fast when we catch him. And you've got a nice start with those letters he had Amanda send you."

"Is she . . . ?" I asked.

"Just fine," Graden said. "And she hasn't heard a thing from our Bachelor of the Year."

We headed to Bailey's desk. "Mind if I use your computer?" I was desperate for ideas about where Evan might strike, and I thought it could help to check out the stories of the other mass killers—juveniles in particular. I'd just finished looking at the entries for the two middle school shooters when Bailey got an urgent message on her cell.

"Yeah?" Bailey listened for a few moments, then quickly pulled out her notepad. "Give that to me one more time." She made some notes, then said, "I'm leaving now," and ended the call. She stood up and handed me my purse. "Let's go."

I ran to keep up as we headed for her car. She peeled out of the parking lot so fast I had to hold on to the dashboard to keep from being thrown against the door. I waited until she'd steered us through the Harbor Freeway and onto the 101 northbound. "Okay, Mario Andretti, want to tell me why we're setting a land-speed record?"

"They spotted the car—"

It took me a moment to catch on. "You mean Logan's car?"

"Yep. It was parked in front of a Chipotle on Topanga Canyon Boulevard."

I waited for her to give me the rest of the story, but she fell silent. "And? Was Evan in it?"

"No one's in it right now. They've staked it out and they're waiting."

"You still have an extra vest in your trunk?"

"Of course."

I tried to tamp down the hope that was rising in my chest. I'd had too many letdowns in this case. Still, this looked good. The fact that no one had spotted Logan's car all this time was some indication that it had been hidden. And who else besides Evan would've had access to it? He was probably living in that car. After all, he didn't have much money, and this wasn't a killer with any long-term plans for survival.

In less than half an hour we pulled onto the side street where the stakeout was being coordinated. A patrol officer started to wave us along, but when Bailey held up her badge, he pointed her to a parking spot nearby. A legal parking spot. She looked peeved as she pulled into the space. "You could ask him if there's a fire hydrant around here," I suggested.

"Shut up."

We found the officer in charge, which turned out to be a lieutenant. A lot of firepower for a stakeout. Then again, this was no ordinary stakeout. Lieutenant Scott Braverman, whose buzz-cut blonde hair and muscled torso looked like a poster for a fitness video, was sitting in the driver's seat of a patrol car with the door open.

Bailey held out her badge again and identified us. He scanned the two of us. "So now you Robbery-Homicide dicks carry around your own personal DAs?"

His tone was just the wrong side of snotty. This was not an uncommon attitude in the local divisions—they really didn't dig the fact that RHD stepped in to take over all the hottest cases.

Bailey gave him a cold smile. "Not all of them. Just me. When was the car first spotted?"

Braverman's lip curled. I could see he was dying to get into it with Bailey. But this was no time to indulge his baser instincts. He reined himself in with an effort and looked at his watch. "Just about forty minutes ago. The car's parked in front of the Chipotle, but he could be anywhere on that corner."

We'd passed the corner on our way here. It was the size of about four city blocks. Chipotle, a small Mexican fast-food diner, was on the outer edge of a complex that included two large grocery stores, a Petco, a FedEx store, three restaurants, and several specialty boutiques.

Bailey stood with her hands on her hips and looked toward Ventura Boulevard. "You have any officers inside the Chipotle?"

The lieutenant's jaw muscle bounced. "No. I didn't have any plainclothes available and I didn't want to send any unis in there."

Bailey looked at him steadily for a long beat, then nodded. "We'll take it then—"

"You and...her?" He looked me up and down. "You're kidding, right?"

Bailey turned to me. "You're locked and loaded?"

I nodded. I knew she'd asked the question only to show I was a tough guy too, and I appreciated it. The problem was, Evan had seen both of us on television. He'd recognize us in a heartbeat. But I didn't want to say that to Bailey in front of this jerk. So I followed her as she turned and headed down the block. I trotted to get alongside her so I could talk without being overheard.

"Uh, Bailey, that guy's an asshat, but this might not be the best idea you've ever had."

Bailey stared straight ahead and spoke out of the corner of her mouth. "Yeah. I thought of that about two seconds after the words fell out of my damn mouth."

I started to chuckle and she shot me a look. I cleared my throat to stifle the rest of my laugh. "Too soon?"

"A sane person might think so."

True, it wasn't funny. We were about to walk into a tiny fast-food joint to confront a murderer who might well have more—and bigger—firearms than all of us put together. I opened my purse and kept my hand on my gun as we walked. We'd just turned onto Topanga Canyon Boulevard when a young man in jeans and a hoodie stepped out of the diner and headed toward Logan's car.

Bailey whipped her gun out of the shoulder holster and shouted, "Police! Drop your weapon!"

At that moment, the rest of the officers, who'd been hiding behind the bushes that separated the parking lot from the sidewalk, sprang out with guns drawn and pointed as they shouted at him. "Put your hands on your head! Get down on the ground! Now!"

He put his hands in the air and slowly backed away from the car.

"Stop!" Bailey and the officers shouted. "Get down! Now!"

But he kept backing up until he bumped into the front door of the Chipotle. Then he reached behind, pulled it open, and slid inside.

77

We ran toward the diner, just steps behind the officers. Lieutenant Braverman came pounding up, bullhorn in hand, as the unis took cover behind cars and around the sides of the building. At least seven squad cars screeched into the parking lot and surrounded the restaurant. Four officers balanced assault rifles on the hoods of their cars and trained them on the front door.

Braverman raised the bullhorn to his lips, but before he could speak, the door opened, and a burly Hispanic man in a white apron and paper hat emerged holding the young man by the back of his jacket. His arms dangled helplessly, like a puppy held by the scruff of its neck.

The Hispanic man hauled him outside. "This the guy you want?" Braverman confirmed that it was. Before the lieutenant could issue a further order, the Hispanic man tossed him out as though he were a heap of garbage. He fell face-first onto the asphalt.

So much for Hotshot Braverman's moment of glory. The officers swarmed the young male, and when they stood him up, we finally got a chance to move in and get a closer look. He was tall, skinny, and had long, dirty white-guy dreadlocks that looked like they might house a family of small rodents.

One thing was immediately clear: it wasn't Evan. I hadn't realized how much I was banking on this being the end of the road until just that moment. My spirits crashed and burned as I watched the officers load the now-docile suspect into the back of a patrol car. We followed them back to the local station.

I stared out the passenger window, feeling bitter and frustrated. "Maybe this fool has some connection to Evan or Logan."

Bailey was in no better mood. "If he does it's probably useless."

When we got to the station, the guy—who looked like he was in his early twenties—was already set up in the interview room, one hand cuffed to a ring in the table. Two burly unis stood on either side of him, their hands on their weapons. Neither of them looked particularly concerned, and I could see why. The guy was a string bean, not a muscle in sight, and he was cowering in his seat, looking pale and sweaty. A paper cup of water was in front of him, and when he reached for it, his hand trembled so badly he spilled half of it on the table.

A detective came in and handed Bailey the booking form with his information. I offered my hand to the detective and introduced myself and Bailey.

He took my hand and shook it warmly. "Dwight Rosenberg, nice to meet you."

"Where's Lieutenant Braverman?" I asked.

"He'll be here."

"Good, I miss him."

Dwight's lips twitched. We weren't the only ones who thought the lieutenant was a jerkweed. We sat down across from the suspect, and Bailey led off.

"Charlie Herzog. It says here you're twenty-two, that you live with your parents and you're unemployed. That right?" He nodded. "So how do you know Evan Cutter?"

Charlie licked his lips, which were cracked and dry. "I d-don't." He picked up the cup and gulped some water. "I d-didn't have any idea who he was back when I s-saw him."

Bailey waited for him to continue. When he didn't, she prompted him. "But you know who he is now."

Charlie nodded. "They just told me."

"They?" Bailey said. "Do you mean the officers who arrested you today?"

Charlie nodded. It was bad procedure to tell a suspect anything before questioning. Annoyed, I looked up to catch Dwight shaking his head.

"Okay, let's make sure we're on the same page," Bailey said. She pulled out the photograph of Evan we'd used in the public release. "Do you recognize this guy?"

Charlie stared at it. "I'm, uh, not sure. Dude was wearing sunglasses and a baseball cap. That might be him, though. Looks pretty similar."

"Tell us how you met him."

"I saw an ad on Craigslist. A guy was looking for a straight trade, said he might throw in some cash if it made sense."

A straight trade? The light began to dawn. I stepped in. "Of cars?"

Charlie nodded. "Yeah. I had this old junker Chevy my folks gave me when I graduated high school. I figured, what the hell? It couldn't hurt to see if he'd go for it."

Pretty friggin' clever. "And he did."

Charlie gave a short chuckle, remembering the sweet deal he'd scored. "Yeah, I couldn't believe it. Dude was crazy to do a swap like that. I mean, his car had a little body damage. But hell, it was about a thousand times better than my old piece of sh—" Charlie stopped. "Uh, junk."

I hadn't had the chance to look at the car yet, but I remembered Jeremy had said Logan sideswiped his car as he and Evan fled from the school. "When did you make the trade?"

Charlie looked up at the ceiling. "I'm not great on dates. Five, maybe six days ago?"

"Do you have any paperwork?"

"At home, yeah."

That might nail it down. Though given what I'd seen of Charlie, it might not. He had *stoner* written all over him. But if his estimation was right, then Evan had made the trade right after the Cinemark shooting. Which was well before we'd identified him. No way Charlie could've known who he was dealing with. He might be in violation of some DMV registration laws, but not much more. I'd leave it to the local cops to decide what to do with that.

Bailey put the photo back in her notepad. "Where did you meet with him when you made the swap?"

"Just down the block from my folks' place."

"You didn't want them to know about the trade?"

"Nah, I didn't care about that. If it was righteous, I was getting a sweet deal. But I didn't know this dude. I didn't want to be too close to my parents' house in case he was, you know... a problem."

I was kind of touched that Charlie was protective of his parents. Then again, he might've just been protecting his meal ticket. And I thought I couldn't get more cynical.

Bailey nodded at me. "You got anything else?"

"No, thanks. We should get the car to Dorian for processing." I knew Evan would've done his best to clean out any evidence, but his best was no match for the superhuman abilities of Struck.

Bailey thanked Charlie for his time and nodded to Dwight and the unis. They'd just taken Charlie away when our buddy Lieutenant Braverman walked in. I could see that Bailey enjoyed telling him we'd already finished. "I'm not recommending any charges," she said. "But if it's important to you, there might be some vehicle code registration violations." Translation: "There's some chicken shit over there in the corner for ya."

Braverman's face locked up and his eyes narrowed. "We can process the car out here." Translation: "If there's some glory to be salvaged from this wreck, I'm taking it."

Bailey gave him a cold smile. "Thanks, but it doesn't make sense to bring anyone else in. Dorian's handled all the other crime scenes, so she'll know what to look for." Translation: "Go fuck yourself."

We left the station with a spring in our step. It wasn't as big a victory as we'd hoped. We didn't net Evan Cutter. But we did have a line on the car he might be driving now. That was something. We who live on crumbs demand very little for a feast. Bailey called in the description and plate of Charlie's car to get out an alert, and we spent the rest of the ride back downtown laughing at Bullet Brain Braverman. By the time Bailey took the off-ramp at Sixth Street, it was after six o'clock.

My stomach grumbled, reminding me that I hadn't eaten since breakfast. "You hungry?"

"Apparently you are." Bailey glanced at my stomach. "We were just at Chipotle. We could've picked something up."

I laughed. "Yeah. I'm sure the manager would've been thrilled to serve us. Biltmore bar?"

"Sold." It'd be nice to sink into the plush quiet with a glass of Pinot Noir. Or a martini. And I knew Bailey hadn't seen Drew in days. For that matter, neither had I.

Bailey made up for her obnoxiously legal parking job in the Valley by selecting a space in the red zone right in front of the hotel. We slid into the booth closest to the bar. "What're you having?" I asked.

"A tiny Martin."

"Sounds good. And an appetizer?"

"How about a grilled artichoke?" I gave her the thumbs-up, and Bailey went to the bar to order. And make kissy-face with Drew. She came back with him bearing two icy martinis.

He set them down as Bailey sat. "I heard you two had a wild ride today."

We gave him the highlights. Drew laughed out loud when Bailey told him about the manager dragging Charlie out by the scruff of the neck. "I wish I'd seen that."

"You still might," Bailey said. "I wouldn't be surprised if someone caught it all on a cell phone."

"I'll keep the TV tuned to the news." Drew headed back to the bar.

I raised my glass and we clinked. "To a wild ride."

We sipped our drinks, and I thought about what we'd gained from it. "We might not find anything in Logan's car, but if Evan didn't dump the one he got from Charlie, we now have a license plate and description of what he's driving. Are the unis still pulling all stolen license reports?"

"Yeah. I'm not sure that'll pan out fast enough, though. If Evan's been planning all this for as long as we think, he could've ripped off a plate a year ago."

"Yeah. Well, at least we know what the car looks like. That's something." I sighed. "It feels like I've been saying that a lot lately."

Bailey gave me a little smile, then looked over my shoulder. Her smile disappeared. "Oh, no you didn't. You little turd." She pointed to the television above the bar.

And there, in all his pixilated glory, was Charlie Herzog. The crawl said that the footage was being broadcast courtesy of TMZ—a tabloid television show. It figured. I shook my head. "They flashed the cash, so of course he went for it."

Bailey went to the bar and asked Drew to turn up the volume. Charlie's voice drifted over the clink of glasses and soft chatter. "Yeah, when I swapped cars with the dude a few days ago I had no [*bleep*] idea who he was." Charlie leaned in and cocked his ear at the reporter. "What?" The reporter said something we couldn't hear, and then Charlie said, "My car? Oh, my car was a beige 1999 Chevy. Back bumper's a little dented, and the driver's side door's got a ding in it. Oh, and the front passenger door's kind of messed up too." Then he gave the license plate. The reporter asked another question, and Charlie smiled. "Nothing unusual about the dude at all. He was just a regular guy, about so high." Charlie gestured six inches below his head. "Had short hair... uh, that's about it."

Bailey and I exchanged a look. I shrugged. "We should probably thank the fool. The whole world's going to be looking for that car now."

"That ought to tighten the screws on psycho boy."

78

FRIDAY, OCTOBER 18
7:08 A.M.

I was having a nightmare about being chased by a man in a ski mask—it doesn't take Freud to figure out the symbolism in my dreams—when my hotel phone rang. I sat up before I grabbed it, hoping that would make me sound more awake. "'Lo?"

"I woke you up." Bailey sounded triumphant.

"No, you didn't. I was just lying here thinking about what to wear."

"Sure you were." I can never get away with anything. "I just wanted to warn you to wear boots and a heavy coat since we're going to be sitting outside for a few hours."

Outside? Then I remembered. Today was the memorial for the victims of the Fairmont High shooting.

They'd chosen the San Juan Theater, a lovely outdoor amphitheater on the north side of the Santa Monica Mountains. The stage was set into a steep hill planted with beautiful multicolored shrubs and scrub oak trees. Above the entrance to the theater was an open rooftop that afforded a north-facing view of the mountains. That space was used for private parties, and I'd had the chance to attend one a few years ago. A flamenco troupe was performing that night, and standing there under the stars, seeing the dancers move against the dramatic backdrop of the mountains, was an incredible experience.

"Nine o'clock?"

"I'll pick you up at eight."

79

FRIDAY, OCTOBER 18
7:14 A.M.

"He's here! He's at the school! I saw it! I saw his car!"

The 911 operator spoke with deliberate calm. "You need to give me a name. Who's there? And where are you?"

"The shooter! That guy from the school! He's here!"

The dispatcher stared at the blinking dot on her monitor, then put out the call.

7:15 A.M.

"Zero hour"—when band members and athletic teams had practice—was at seven thirty at Taft High School. The janitor opened the doors to the main entrance and found two tenor sax players and a wide receiver already waiting. They straggled in, still half asleep. "Good morning to you," he said with an amused smile.

The principal and three teachers pulled into the faculty parking lot. An older Honda Civic stopped in front of the main entrance and three students carrying instrument cases got out. Then it headed for the student parking lot, which faced Ventura Boulevard.

No one noticed the beat-up beige Chevrolet parked in the middle of the lot.

But a few minutes later, a squad car slowly cruised down Ventura Boulevard, past the school. The officer in the passenger seat tapped the driver on the arm. "Hey, there it is."

The driving officer pulled to the curb. "Call in the plate."

The passenger officer called it in. "I can't tell whether anyone's in the car," he told the dispatcher.

Within seconds the dispatcher confirmed it was the car Evan Cutter got from Charlie Herzog, and reported the sighting to the Valley Division. When she came back on the line, she relayed the captain's orders. "Stay in the area, but do not approach. Repeat, do not approach. Stand by for backup."

As the squad car slowly circled the block, five male students in workout sweats poured out of a van and entered the school.

Principal Dingboom sat down at his desk, a steaming mug of coffee in his hand. The hour before regular classes began was always a welcome quiet time. He'd just raised his mug to take a sip when the phone on his desk rang. Startled, his hand jerked, and coffee spilled on his desk and dribbled onto his lap. He grabbed a Kleenex and wiped his trousers as he picked up the phone. "Principal Dingboom," he said.

"This is Captain Vroman of the West Valley station of LAPD. I need you to listen carefully and do exactly as I say." The captain told him that Evan Cutter's car had been sighted in the school parking lot. "I need you to lock the front doors, then round up everyone in the school and evacuate them through the back doors. Immediately. SWAT officers are on their way. Do you understand me?"

The principal's throat tightened. He barely managed to choke out "yes." He dropped the phone into its cradle with a shaking hand. Outside, he saw five more students and two teachers walking up the front steps of the school. The principal yanked open the bottom drawer of his desk, pulled out his set of keys, and ran.

Seconds later, four SWAT officers pulled up behind the school and hurried to the gate in the chain-link fence that surrounded the football field. The team had just begun to warm up. The officers called out to the coach. He stared for a moment, then hurried over and let them in. The coach's weathered face blanched as he listened to what they said.

When they'd finished, he blew his whistle to gather the players. They huddled around him and a SWAT officer stepped forward. "Don't ask questions, just do as we say. You're going to exit through the back gate, fast and quiet. Follow your coach. Do it now."

The players, too stunned to question the orders, rapidly filed out. The coach handed his keys to the officer, who gave his final order. "Take those kids as far away from the school as you can. Then call the station. They'll have someone pick you up."

The coach joined his players outside the gate, raised an arm, and gestured for them to follow as he ran down the street. The SWAT team headed into the school.

Outside, officers had begun evacuating all homes and businesses within half a mile of the school and were cordoning off the entire area.

West Valley Detective Dwight Rosenberg and his partner, Meg Wittig, drove up in an unmarked car and badged their way through the line of officers guarding the perimeter. They stopped at the west edge of the school parking lot, five hundred feet behind the beige Chevrolet. Seconds later, three other unmarked cars lined up behind them.

Meanwhile, the SWAT officers shepherded the principal, the teachers, and all the remaining students out through the back door of the school, where squad cars waited to take them out of the neighborhood. The SWAT officers then went back inside and continued to clear the building.

Within minutes, more backup arrived. A dozen uniformed officers and four canine units swarmed in through the back door of the school and fanned out through the hallways. They combed every inch of the school for bodies, bombs, spring-loaded guns, and IEDs. Lockers were swept, trash bins turned upside down, bathrooms, classrooms, and offices searched top to bottom.

Finally, the SWAT officer in charge reported that the building had been cleared. All officers left through the back door.

At the front of the school, all was quiet. Unnaturally so. Traffic had been diverted for a six-block radius, and more than three dozen officers encircled the outer perimeter of the school grounds. All had their guns drawn and ready.

Detective Rosenberg remained at the edge of the student parking lot, behind the Chevrolet. Without taking his eyes off the car, he asked Meg, "Did someone put in the call to Detective Keller?"

"Captain said he'd take care of it."

Dwight got out and peered into the driver's side window of the Chevrolet. He spoke quietly. "You see someone in the driver's seat?"

Meg nodded. "But it looks like his head is covered—"

"A ski mask."

Meg swallowed, her heart pounding. "Yeah."

"Where's our sniper?"

"On his way."

Dwight shook his head. He didn't like any of this. Precious minutes were being wasted. If that was Evan Cutter, he could come out blasting at any moment. Dwight pulled out his bullhorn. "This is Detective Dwight Rosenberg with LAPD. I'm ordering the occupant of the beige Chevy to exit the vehicle immediately with your hands up."

There was no response.

Dwight signaled to the detectives in the unmarked cars to get ready to move. He again raised the bullhorn and ordered the occupant of the car to exit the vehicle.

There was no response.

Sharpshooter Officer Butch Cannaday pulled into the parking lot behind the detectives and came running. Dwight nodded and pointed to the car. The sharpshooter pulled up his high-powered rifle. Sighting through his scope, he focused on the driver's seat of the beige Chevrolet. He lowered the gun but kept his eyes trained on the car as he spoke to Dwight. "Someone's definitely in the driver's seat. Wearing a black balaclava."

"That's our boy's MO," Dwight said. "All right, kill the car."

Butch raised his rifle and took aim. Four out of four shots hit the tires.

Dwight again used the bullhorn to order the occupant out of the car.

There was no response.

Dwight's cell phone buzzed at his hip. It was the West Valley captain, who'd been monitoring the events on his radio. "Dwight, fall back and wait for the bomb squad."

Dwight grunted. Another delay—the last thing they needed.

"Dwight? Don't fuck with me. That's an order."

Dwight ended the call, relayed the order to Meg, and muttered under his breath. "We're just giving this shitbird more time to do his worst."

Meg nodded, but she agreed with the captain. If it was Evan Cutter in the car—and she was fairly sure it was—she wanted all the backup they could get. Meg liked the idea of being a hero, just not a dead one.

Dwight signaled for the detectives parked behind him to fall back. They retreated and crouched behind the open doors of their cars.

Police helicopters arrived, and the air above the school parking lot filled with the *whop-whop* of their propellers. Off in the distance, media helicopters hovered, waiting for the chance to move in.

Dwight's cell phone buzzed again. "Yeah?" he answered, irritated.

It was the head of the bomb squad. "We're trying to get there, we've got sirens and lights going, but the traffic's a bitch—"

"How long?"

"Hard to tell right now. Maybe fifteen, twenty minutes."

"Shit." Dwight huffed. He gave Meg the news.

"Figures," she said. "It's morning rush hour. Nothing they can do about that."

Dwight shook his head. He didn't care whose fault it was. Cutter obviously couldn't escape, but Dwight didn't think that was the plan. He was staging his finale. Dwight fully expected him to come out shooting at any second. That'd be just his style. And what if he had grenades? Dwight looked at all the officers and detectives holding the perimeter. How many would die? They couldn't afford to wait for the bomb squad. Dwight spoke to Meg in a low whisper. "Stay back and don't let the others move until I tell you."

She opened her mouth to argue, but before she could say a word, Dwight had turned and begun to move toward the beige Chevrolet.

Hunkered down to make a smaller target, his gun held out in front of his body, arms shaking with tension, Dwight slowly edged toward the car. Meg couldn't let him do it alone. Against her better judgment, she followed. But she held up a hand to signal that the detectives behind them should stay back.

The detectives, seeing her signal, exchanged looks and reached a silent agreement. All six of them quietly fell in behind her. Slowly, the phalanx inched forward, guns held at the ready.

When he got to within ten feet of the car, Dwight thought he saw movement in the driver's seat. He stopped and tried to peer in through the rear window. Behind him, Meg and the other officers stopped and watched. Meg could feel a pulse throb at the base of her throat, imagined a bullet—or a piece of shrapnel—lodging there. She swallowed and tried to slow her breathing.

Dwight stared at the driver's seat. Another movement? It looked like it. He raised his gun and took a step forward. But in that moment, he heard a low rumble, like the sound of a gas flame igniting. Dwight yelled, "Get down!"

Everyone dropped to the ground just as a thunderous explosion split the air. Fire shot out through the cracks in the doors, and flames engulfed the car. Seconds later, two smaller explosions, muffled and weak, followed. Smoke billowed out and spread through the parking lot.

For a brief moment, Dwight, facedown on the asphalt, heard nothing. Was he dead? But a few seconds later, he noticed that his ears were ringing. Not dead. But he couldn't feel his arms, his legs. His heart began to race as panic set in. He'd had nightmares about being paralyzed ever since his former partner took a bullet to the spine. Squeezing his eyes shut, he begged his body to move. With an effort, he managed to roll onto his side. He could at least move his body. He opened his eyes. The smoke stung and made him tear up, but he could dimly make out shapes through the haze. He could see. He inhaled but pulled in smoke, and his body convulsed in a hacking cough. But as he struggled to catch his breath, his knees reflexively drew up. His legs felt okay. He straightened his arms, then curled his hands into fists. A smile spread across his face, and he almost laughed with relief.

Slowly, head still swimming, he stood up. He leaned forward, hands on his knees, and took a few shallow breaths. He looked down at his body. Unbelievably, there were only minor cuts and scrapes. Behind him, he heard coughs and sputters. Dwight turned to see that all the other detectives had advanced with him, Meg in the lead. Jesus, what had he done?

Dwight helped Meg up. Her forehead was badly scraped, but she was able to stand and dust herself off. She was wobbly, but okay. "Why didn't you stay back?" he asked.

Meg shrugged. "Didn't want to miss the fun."

His heart was heavy with guilt. Dwight should've known she wouldn't let him move without backup. He looked back at the rest of the detectives, who were wiping blood off of palms, cheeks, foreheads. "You guys okay?" The detectives nodded.

Dwight looked at the Chevrolet. He tried to see Cutter's body, but flames and smoke obscured his view. When they'd cordoned off the parking lot, Cutter must've realized it was over and decided to make his grand exit. It struck him again just how reckless his move had been. If they'd gotten just a little closer, or Evan had a little more firepower... Dwight didn't want to think about it.

The bomb squad arrived just as he was pulling out his phone. He restrained the impulse to say that "better late than never" really wasn't their best motto. The truth was, he was glad to see them. He doubted the car was rigged with any more "surprises," but after what they'd just been through, he was happy to let the experts make sure of it.

The head of the bomb squad, a big beefy type, jumped out of the truck and stomped over to Dwight. His voice was hot. "Ya just couldn't wait, could ya? Ya had to be a friggin' hero. You're just damn lucky you didn't get your whole team killed." Dwight heaved a sigh, but said nothing. He'd known this was coming. And he knew he deserved it.

Dwight turned back to look at the Chevrolet. Now the only sound coming from the car was the crackle and whoosh of flames eating whatever would burn. They stood and watched, and waited.

The bomb squad took statements from Dwight and his team, examined the debris that had blown from the car, and studied the car itself through binoculars. After they'd huddled, the head of the squad marched up to Dwight, his jaw clenched. "Rosenberg, I know I said you got lucky. But now we have a better idea of just how lucky. You need to hear this: he had three bombs rigged up. Only the smallest one detonated. The other two were duds. If things had gone as this asswipe had planned, you, your team, and a whole lot of others would've been blown to smithereens." He gave Dwight a hard look. "Get it?"

Dwight swallowed. He hadn't thought he could feel any worse. "Got it."

"Good. You can let the fire dudes in now." He headed back to his truck.

The fire department moved in and put out the fire. Now even more smoke poured out through the shattered windows. Dwight grabbed a rag, doused it with water, and covered his eyes. He wanted to move closer, but the heat coming from the car was still so intense it was hard to breathe.

When the air had cleared somewhat, Dwight moved in and peered into the driver's seat through streaming eyes. The body was charred, burned, and now soaking wet—with odd bits of the black balaclava still clinging to the head—but it was Cutter.

Dwight ran back to his car and pulled out his cell phone. He called the captain and gave him the update. Then he called Bailey. It went to her voice mail, so he left a message. "Detective Keller, it's Detective Dwight Rosenberg. If you're on your way here, you can stand down. We got him. Cutter's dead. It's over. I'm heading over to the memorial right now. I should get there in about twenty minutes."

80

Bailey and I moved into the amphitheater behind a group of students. Their arms were draped over each other's shoulders, heads tilted together. It had been sunny when Bailey picked me up at the Biltmore, but now clouds had gathered and the air smelled like rain. As we walked down the aisle on the right side of the amphitheater toward the front section, I noticed the governor and his wife, the chief of LAPD, and several councilmen. And, of course, Vanderputz, who was cozying up to the governor's entourage, hoping to worm his way up to the man himself. There were no cameras, at the families' request. But I'd seen reporters, both print and television, packed into the back seats, near the entrance. The police presence out front had been impressive.

The families of the victims were all around us, and grief hung damp and heavy over the theater. Some cried, others stared vacantly, unable to absorb the cataclysmic loss. Ushers moved through the theater with baskets of tissues. Surviving students walked with heads hung low and shoulders hunched. They embraced their dead friends' parents awkwardly, eyes cast downward.

The floral arrangements were so massive they took up the entire back half of the stage and the lower part of the hill behind it. At either side of the stage there were open wings, and I could see Principal Campbell standing with the clergymen at stage left. From the crowd behind him, it looked like all denominations were represented.

As we took our seats, my cell phone buzzed. It was a voice mail from Graden, asking if we'd heard the news. He didn't want to say what it was on the phone. I told Bailey. "Have you had any calls?"

"No." She pulled out her cell. "Shit! The battery's dead. Jesus H. Christ. I can't believe it."

I popped the battery out of my phone and gave it to her. Bailey took it and moved to an alcove across the aisle on our right. I watched volunteers dressed in black pants and long-sleeved shirts guide elderly family members to their seats. Other volunteers carried in armloads of still more flowers, some wobbling under the weight of the larger arrangements.

As the last of them placed a huge wreath on the stage, I noticed another volunteer on the hill behind the stage, wheeling out what looked like a small trash can. Bailey came back and spoke into my ear in an urgent whisper. "They got him! Evan's dead! He parked in the student lot at Taft High School. Rigged it up with a bomb—"

I pulled back and looked at her with alarm. "Was anyone...?"

"No. No one was hurt."

I exhaled, relieved. "And they've got Evan's body?"

"Yeah. It's in the car."

It was over. I couldn't believe it. I was glad. I was. Especially because no one else had been hurt. But I was angry too. He'd gotten his wish. I'd never get the satisfaction of seeing him cuffed and caged like the animal he was. "Should we get out there?" I asked.

"To do what? Dwight—he left me the message—said he's on his way here. There's nothing left for us to do. Except celebrate." Bailey gave me a grim smile, but she didn't look all that elated either.

"You wanted to bring him in too, didn't you?" I asked.

Bailey nodded. "I didn't think it mattered till now. But yeah, I guess I wanted to see him locked up. This way..."

"He kind of gets what he wanted."

"Exactly."

My eyes drifted back toward the hill. The volunteer had left the trash can in the middle of the hill and was now moving toward the wings at stage right. Were they planning some display up there? I started to ask Bailey, but Principal Campbell walked onto the stage, leading the procession of clergymen. When he got to the microphone set up in the center, he tapped it and cleared his throat.

"On this saddest of all days, I welcome our Fairmont High families."

At that moment, a booming explosion shook the theater. On the hill behind the stage, a fireball burst into the sky. Hot orange flames leaped into the trees. Jagged metal pieces of the trash can shot out through the air, sharp and deadly. Principal Campbell dropped, face-first, onto the stage, and a flower of red spread across the back of his head. Deadly metallic shrapnel rained onto the stage and the front rows of the audience. The clergymen fell to the floor. Fire crackled on the hill, and sparks flew into the floral arrangements at the back of the stage.

Screams of terror filled the amphitheater. The audience jumped to their feet and tried to head for the exit, climbing over one another in a blind panic.

Damn, I knew it! "Bailey, that was Evan! That volunteer on the hill was Evan!" And I knew exactly where he was headed. The wings led into the building that wrapped around the back of the theater and out to the open terrace that overlooked the only point of exit or entry into the theater. He'd be able to fire straight down into the fleeing crowd. Like shooting fish in a barrel.

With the audience clogging the entrance, the police would be stuck outside for precious seconds. We were the only ones who could get to him in time. I grabbed Bailey's arm and pointed to the wings at stage left. "Go that way! He's got to be heading for the terrace over the exit!" Bailey took off running. I snatched my gun out of my purse, put it into my coat pocket, and ran toward the wings at stage right.

The fire roared all around me; trees crackled and splintered as they burned. The heat from the flames was so intense I could feel it blistering my face and hands. But it hadn't spread onto the stage yet. The earth was slippery with mud from the recent rains, and I kept sliding back down the hill. I managed to grab the low branches of a scrub oak and pull myself up the muddy incline. As I pushed my way up the hill, the branches of the shorter trees stabbed at my eyes and scraped my face and neck. Finally, covered in mud, eyes stinging with sweat and the blood that had trickled down from my scalp and forehead, I reached the ledge. I put my hands on it, jumped, and levered myself up onto the stage. Ahead was the enclosed hallway that would lead me to the open terrace.

Where I was sure Evan was now headed.

The hallway was dark. As I stepped inside, the abrupt shift from daylight to darkness blinded me. I forced myself to move slowly at first to let my eyes adjust, and tried not to imagine that Evan was drawing a bead on my forehead. After a few seconds, I was able to see well enough to run. I took out my gun and stayed close to the wall.

Knowing that Evan might be just steps in front of me, my heart thudded hard against my rib cage, but I kept running. I found the door to the stairway that would lead me to the rooftop. He might be waiting for me behind that door. But there was no other way. I had to risk it.

I crouched down and twisted the knob as slowly and quietly as I could. Then, using all my strength, I threw the door open and held my gun out in front of me. The door banged into the wall and bounced back so fast it almost knocked me down. I pushed it open and flew up the stairs to the roof. Like the one on the floor below, this was an enclosed hallway and it was pitch-black, but I pounded down the corridor, heart beating like a trip-hammer, lungs on fire.

I stopped at the curve just before it opened onto the terrace. And there he was, the monster we'd been chasing since this nightmare began. Evan Cutter stood just a hundred feet away. He'd shaved his head and was wearing dark-tinted aviator glasses. He was slamming a magazine into a forty-caliber Smith and Wesson as he watched the fleeing audience. His lips were twisted in a sick, gleeful smile. I knew that gun held eleven rounds, and I saw another seven clips on the wall in front of him. Even if that was the only gun he had, he'd be able to take out dozens.

He took aim and began to fire at the crowd below. The shots echoed loudly in the hallway, mingling with shrieks of terror. Without thinking, I ran straight at him, gun in hand. Desperate to stop him, and afraid I might miss at this distance, I screamed as loud as I could, "Evan! Stop!"

His head jerked around. He turned and fired. But at the same moment I dropped down to a crouch. The shot zinged over my head and ricocheted off the wall to my right. I raised my gun and aimed for his torso—the biggest mass, as my father had taught me—and pulled the trigger. Once, twice, three times. The first two shots missed, but the third hit him square in the gut. He staggered backward and looked down at his stomach, where a neat, black hole began to fill with blood.

I straightened up and prepared to shoot again. But in that moment, Cutter suddenly raised his gun and lunged toward me. I dived again, catching a brief glimpse of muzzle fire as gunshots exploded above me. Just before I hit the ground, I felt a searing heat slice through my body. I landed hard on my back and my head slammed onto the concrete floor.

When I opened my eyes, he was standing over me. "Perfect," he said. I stared into the muzzle of his gun. Dizzy and disoriented, I raised a hand to push the gun away and tried to roll out of range.

Another shot split the air. And then, all was quiet. My head hurt. Badly. I put my hand to my forehead, where Cutter's gun had been aimed. No blood. How could that be? I managed to raise up just enough to see Evan Cutter lying at my feet. He was on his side, facing me, eyes vacant. Dead. My head began to swim, and bile rose in my throat. I sank back onto the floor and swallowed to keep from throwing up.

"Knight? You okay?" I looked up and saw Bailey running toward me, her gun at her side.

I realized that the last shots I'd heard were Bailey's. She took my pulse and leaned over me. I smiled up at her worried face.

"I don't need CPR, Keller," I croaked through a dry throat. "So don't be using this as an excuse to pound on me."

"Shut up." Bailey opened my coat and lifted the hem of my sweater.

I knew I'd been shot. "Is it…?"

"I don't think it hit anything major." She pulled off her scarf and wrapped it tightly around my body.

I remembered the image of Evan Cutter firing down into the crowd. My heart thumped, and I struggled to sit up. "Was anyone…?" I asked.

Bailey put a restraining hand on my shoulder. "I don't know yet. Now stop talking and lie down or I'll knock you out, I swear."

I wanted to argue, but my eyes wouldn't focus, and the queasy feeling in my stomach told me that if I tried to sit up again, I'd regret it. I heard the sound of sirens wailing in the distance. I closed my eyes and listened as they got louder and louder.

81

The next time I opened my eyes, we were surrounded by police. An officer with sergeant's stripes gestured toward Evan's body. "That him?"

Bailey nodded. Only then did I notice the smell of smoke. "The fire—"

"It's out," the sergeant said. "Fire country up here. They keep plenty of fire extinguishers on hand. They got it before it could reach the audience. Scorched the back of the stage pretty bad, though."

Bailey gestured to me. "Paramedics coming? She got hit."

He nodded. "Should be here in a few seconds."

One more second, actually. The paramedics arrived carrying two gurneys. I pointed to Evan Cutter's body. "You only need one. I'll be okay. Just give me a few minutes."

The younger paramedic shook his head. My theory—that God made paramedics good-looking so you got to see something beautiful before you died—was once again proven true. He was a dead ringer for Brad Pitt. Blue eyes and all. He knelt down, checked my right side, then swapped out Bailey's scarf for a big gauze pad and an Ace bandage, which he began to wrap around my torso.

"See, just the fact that you said something that ridiculous shows you've got a nasty concussion," he said. He shined a light into my eyes, checked my pulse, and with the help of another paramedic, lifted me up onto a gurney. He was about to wheel me away when the sergeant who'd spoken to Bailey walked over. "How're you feeling?"

"I'm okay." I gestured to the paramedic. "Pay no attention to Brad Pitt."

The officer smiled and shook his head. "We'll take your statement at the hospital. After another 'know-nothing' like Brad says you're able. But

I want to be the first to say that you and your partner over there are heroes. You saved a lot of lives today."

I tried to raise myself up again, but Brad Pitt gently pushed me back down. "Did he get anyone?" I asked.

The sergeant looked at me sadly. "I heard five got hit."

I closed my eyes. "God, no."

"Yeah," he said. "But so far it looks like two, maybe three are going to make it." He leaned down and spoke with intensity. "Listen, it's bad. But it would've been a helluva lot worse if it hadn't been for you and that detective."

I guess I should've been consoled, but I wasn't. At least two more had died at the hands of this monster. As Brad Pitt rolled me away, a hot ball of anger burned in my gut. I'd been determined to see Evan Cutter brought to court in chains and made to live out a life of miserable anonymity behind prison walls. But he'd managed to go out in a hail of bullets—in a bloody shoot-out with a cop and a prosecutor, no less. It may not have been exactly the ending he'd fantasized about, but it was close.

Bailey insisted on accompanying me to the hospital. It turned out she was right: the wound was through-and-through, no vital organs involved. I'd heal cleanly. But I did have a concussion, which meant I'd have to spend the night there. I hate hospitals. Too many sick people. "You can let me go home," I said. "Bailey will stay with me." I looked at her. "Won't you?"

She started to answer, but the doctor—a young Asian man with a ponytail—held up a hand to stop her. "I don't care if Mother Teresa wants to stay with you. You're not going anywhere. We need to monitor you for twenty-four hours."

"Twenty-four hours?" I rolled my eyes.

"They tell me that's only one day. One day to make sure you don't die of a brain bleed. Is that so much to ask?" I started to say yes, but he glared at me, then turned to Bailey. "She always like this?"

Bailey shrugged. "Pretty much."

He muttered something under his breath that sounded a lot like "wing nut," then turned on his heel and walked out.

After the doctor left, I remembered the sight of Principal Campbell as he fell face-first onto the stage. I asked Bailey if she knew how he was.

"I'll call around, see what I can find out."

I must have fallen asleep, because when I opened my eyes, Bailey was across the room, curled up in an armchair, covered with a blanket. Graden was standing at the foot of my bed, whispering to my warden, the Asian doctor.

Graden smiled when he saw I was awake. "How many of me do you see?"

"Just two. But one of you has a ponytail."

The doctor chuckled. "Not bad for a few hours after a concussion." He gave me a stern look. "But you're still not going home."

I started to fold my arms across my chest, but it hurt, so I let them drop. "You're a real buzz kill, you know that?"

"Yes." He patted my foot and walked out.

Graden came over and kissed me on the forehead. "You'll have to start giving your statement pretty soon." He nodded toward Bailey. "She's already given hers a few times."

I knew we'd both be giving statements for days to come. No matter how obvious it was that shooting Evan Cutter was justified, there would be a full investigation. And that meant endless questioning.

But I had some questions of my own. "Have you been able to find out what kind of bomb he used at the amphitheater?" I asked. I told him about seeing Evan on the hill with the trash can.

"They're pretty sure it was a propane bomb." Graden saw my expression and nodded. "Same as Klebold and Harris."

Klebold and Harris had put propane tanks with alarm-clock timers in the school cafeteria. The timers had been set to go off when the cafeteria was at its most crowded, but something went wrong. The bombs malfunctioned and never detonated.

"How'd he make it work?" I asked.

"I didn't get all the details. But from what I heard, it can be done if the valve on the tank is jammed and unable to release pressure—for example, by putting the tank upside down in a trash can. Then, all he had to do was start a fire in the can. The pressure builds and..."

So Cutter had managed to "outdo" Klebold and Harris once again.

Graden's phone buzzed. He looked at it and frowned, then looked away.

"What?" I asked.

He sighed and took my hand. "I don't want to give you this news right now, but I don't want you to get blindsided. There were two more casualties."

A lead weight dropped into the pit of my stomach. "Who?"

"Officers. They were patrolling the hillside behind the stage. I don't know if you know them. Craig Silvers and Dwight Rosenberg. Silvers is critical, but Rosenberg didn't make it."

Dwight. I couldn't believe it. Hot tears pricked my eyelids. My voice was thick. "How?"

"We had security patrols set up around the entire amphitheater. But we only had a few on the sides of the hill because it was the least likely point of entry. Dwight came here straight from the Taft High scene and saw we were a little shorthanded there..." Graden paused and took a deep breath. "Silvers wasn't able to say much, but it seems Evan was dressed like a volunteer. He rolled up with the trash can, and when Silvers asked to see some ID, Cutter shot him. Dwight came running when he heard the shot. Silvers passed out at that point, but based on what we saw, our guess is Evan Cutter got the drop on Dwight."

I was so miserable I could barely move my lips to speak. I stared out the window. "And so that despicable piece of shit gets his damn blaze of glory, doesn't he? They'll write about how he got the jump on the police and managed to set off a bomb and got killed in a shoot-out with a prosecutor and a cop."

"They were going to write about him no matter how it ended, Rachel. He bought himself a place in history with the very first shots he fired at Fairmont High."

Fame is amoral. It was such a bitter, bitter pill to swallow. "And right now, there's another monster out there, salivating over his chance to show the world how he can do it better."

"There probably always will be. We can take them out when we find them, but we can't stop them from being born."

EPILOGUE

Graden worked through the night, but Toni and Bailey stayed in my hospital room with me. The next day, before I was released, Graden came by to tell us the rest of the story. We figured Evan had been living in his car all along, and we were right. A car had been found parked at the side of the hill near the amphitheater. It had been stolen early on the morning of the memorial from a location near Taft High. Clothing, food, three handguns, and a notebook that had the plans for all the shootings, plus a detailed diagram of the San Juan amphitheater, were found in it. The writings in that notebook revealed that Evan and Logan had planned to do the Cinemark shooting together, but that Logan had lost his stomach for the killings after Fairmont. He'd committed suicide. Evan had waxed eloquent in his disgust for Logan's "pathetically inferior weakness," saying that he didn't need that "fucked-up loser." He would win this "competition" on his own.

Evan used Charlie's car as the decoy at Taft. And there had indeed been a body in that car. A canvass of the neighborhood near the school turned up a good lead as to whose it was. The cashier at a 7-Eleven on Ventura Boulevard saw a white male matching Evan's description talking to a Hispanic man who regularly hung out at the store, looking for work. The Hispanic man was last seen getting into a car with that white male. The car matched the description of Charlie's beige Chevrolet. The charred remains in the car hadn't left much to work with. They were still trying to get a positive ID.

Bailey and I were both taking time off. We hadn't slept much in the past two weeks, and that plus the endless rounds of interrogations had left us thoroughly depleted. My gunshot wound was healing, but it was no picnic.

We probably could've slept for the next two weeks straight if we'd had the chance. But we didn't. From the moment we left the hospital, Bailey and I had been besieged by requests for interviews and appearances by every news program in the country.

Neither of us had much love for the spotlight, and after so many had died, we didn't feel like there was anything to celebrate. We kept our appearances to the bare minimum. The City of Los Angeles had voted to award us a sort of medal of valor—or, as the mayor put it, a "warm, heartfelt thanks for your courage and bravery." It was a big honor. Beyond that, it had the unexpected charm of annoying the hell out of Vanderhorn. That camera-loving, face-time-sucking publicity whore, who would've had a hard time choosing between seeing me and suffering a bout of food poisoning, was forced to stand on the stage and clap for us. His smile was so strained he looked constipated. I asked one of the friendlier reporters to see if he could get me some still photos that'd be suitable for framing.

The following week, with police interviews and most media appearances done, we finally had the chance to wind down. Bailey was going to spend the time with Drew, which meant she'd be hanging around the Biltmore a lot. That worked for me.

But Graden was swamped. The fact that both suspects were dead didn't end the investigation. How they'd acquired their weapons, where they'd stored them, and, most important, how to prevent this atrocity from happening again were among the many questions that still needed answering.

Toni, on the other hand, had finished her trial and was available to play. We spent our first day off getting mani-pedis and taking in a movie at the iPic in Pasadena. It's a theater that features recliner loungers for seats and serves food and liquor. We ordered martinis and watched a goofy rom-com starring a hottie whose name I forgot five minutes after it ended. It was decadent fun.

I spent the next day going through my closet. Toni had proposed a shopping trip, and I wanted to see what I needed. Midway through the afternoon, I decided I couldn't try on another skirt. I'd just decided to call to see if Graden was up for lunch, when my hotel phone rang.

"Hey, Rache," Graden said. "Want some company?"

"I was just about to call *you.* It's about lunchtime. Want me to order something here? Or you want to go out?"

"Let's eat at your place. Order whatever you think sounds good."

I ordered a cheeseburger and fries for Graden—actually, the fries were for me—and a Caesar salad with salmon for myself. Then I put on some makeup, fluffed my hair, and spritzed on some cologne. If I played my cards right, I might get lucky.

But Graden's expression when he walked in the door told me "lucky" was not on the menu. He gave me a warm kiss and a hug, but his expression was serious. "How are you feeling?"

"I'm good," I said. "Really good."

Room service had already delivered our lunch. We sat down to eat. I asked him about the investigation, but Graden gave me short, terse answers. When we'd finished lunch, he put down his napkin and leaned forward.

"I have news. It's about the bug in your office. Are you ready?"

I sat up. My heart began to pound. "No, but okay."

Graden gave a tight little smile. "First, we figured out who put it there. It was a woman on the cleaning crew."

I sat back and thought about that for a moment. "Someone hired her, didn't they?" Graden nodded. I started to speak, but my throat constricted. I did—and didn't—want to hear the answer to my next question. "Who?" Somehow, I knew an instant before he said the name. "Who was it?" I asked again.

"Lilah Bayer."

A knot twisted in my stomach. "How?" As far as we knew, Lilah wasn't even in the country.

"The cleaning woman has family in Croatia. She met Lilah there last spring. The woman wanted to bring her children to the States. Lilah promised her money and visas."

I nodded slowly. "And she didn't know why Lilah wanted my office bugged."

"Or care," Graden said. "But we know why. Lilah wanted to keep tabs on us, on you. To find out whether we were closing in on her. And whether Chase Erling has recovered and started talking."

"Croatia? We'll never get our hands on her."

Graden smiled. "Actually, we have a source who says she's in the States now. I don't want to say any more at the moment. But I can promise you this: we will get her. And soon."

I didn't know whether to laugh or cry. Graden came around the table, pulled me to my feet, and put his arms around me. "It's over, Rachel. You're safe."

That night, Graden and I celebrated the good news in a quiet but spectacular way in my suite. The next day, I went shopping with Toni—a less quiet but only slightly less spectacular celebration.

I was a little apprehensive about the expense, but Toni scoffed. "You've been through a lot, right?"

"Yeah."

"Therapy's a good idea, then, isn't it?"

"So they say."

"Retail's the best kind I know."

We drove to the Premium Outlets at Camarillo—I'd spotted them during our travels on the case—and spent the day finding lots of things we didn't need and a few things we did. We'd made plans for all of us to have dinner later at the Pacific Dining Car.

After an insanely fun day of spending—shoes, jeans, tops, and *no* suits—Toni and I returned to my room and changed for dinner. When we went down to the bar, we found J.D. there, talking to Bailey and Drew. J.D. stood up and gave me a hug. "You've sure been through the wringer. How are you feeling?"

"Like I haven't seen you in forever," I said.

J.D. shrugged. "It's been about three weeks..."

"Seriously? It feels like three years." I shook my head.

"You know how time flies when you're having fun?" Bailey said. "It goes slower than shit when you're not."

"I'll drink to that," Toni said. "Anyone else?"

It was unanimous. We all piled into J.D.'s car, with Bailey on Drew's lap, and headed to the Pacific Dining Car. Toni and Bailey and I ordered our usual. Ketel One martinis, very dry, very cold, straight up, with olives on the side. Drew and J.D. opted for a bottle of Ancien Pinot Noir. Graden ordered a shot of Glenlivet.

"Did you see the letter Evan's parents wrote to the families of the victims?" Graden said.

"No," J.D. said. "It was a public thing?"

"Yeah," Bailey said. "They posted it on the Fairmont High Facebook page—"

Evan's parents—like Logan's—had been bombarded with death threats and hate mail, so they'd moved away. But shortly after relocating, they'd written an open letter to all the victims' families, including the family of the as yet unidentified man Evan had used as a decoy at Taft.

"What did they say?" J.D. asked.

"The only thing they could say," Toni said. "How sorry they were, how they'd have done anything to stop it if they could—"

"'If they could,'" Bailey said. "It just gets to me the way they had no clue—"

I nodded. "The way they *still* have no clue."

"And the victims' families?" J.D. said. "Did they respond?"

"They're going to. They sent me a draft to look at. It's incredible. They said they know the parents aren't to blame and that they'd lost their children too. Just asked that they help Jenny and Michael with their project—"

"Your shrinks?" Drew asked.

"Yeah," I said. "They're heading up a study on these mass shooters. The plan is to come up with a handbook to help parents and teachers spot the warning signs."

"Damn," Toni said. "That *is* incredible. So they've already found a way to make something good come of this."

J.D. shook his head. "Those people... those families. Amazing."

"They really are," Bailey said. "I'm not sure I could do that."

We all fell silent for a few moments. Then Graden asked what Toni was up to.

"Just finished a kidnap/attempted murder. The wife wanted a divorce. The husband didn't. So of course he had to kidnap and kill her. What else could he do?"

"He didn't say that," Bailey said.

"Yeah, he did. Well, close. It was a version of 'the bitch had it coming.'"

"Kind of weird a case like that wound up in Special Trials," I said. Sadly, a husband killing his disenchanted wife was not unusual.

"Not so weird. He was a cop down in Riverside. They moved up here because he got a job with LAPD."

"Oh, man," Drew said. "That's crazy."

Bailey looked aghast. "We hired him? He couldn't have been around long."

"Try twelve years," Toni said.

Bailey groaned. "Embarrassing. Just friggin' embarrassing."

Graden shook his head.

"Hey," I said. "We've got Vanderhorn."

Graden laughed. "Right. You win."

"Lucky, lucky us," Toni said.

We all laughed and drank to that.

It had been a while since I'd laughed like that. Living through so much darkness, I'd forgotten about the light—about the goodness that would always ultimately outweigh the evil. I thought about the strength of the Fairmont High parents, the selfless forgiveness and determination to do all they could to prevent others from suffering the same tragedy. But most of all, I thought about the bonding love that would somehow get them through. Then I looked around the table.

I raised my glass. "To families."

ACKNOWLEDGMENTS

My profound thanks go to Dr. Bethany Marshall, who gave generously of her time to explain what is known of the psychological makeup of psychopaths in general and this type of killer in particular. I could not have written this book without her brilliant insights and expertise. I also thank her for recommending the published works of Dr. Robert Hare and Dr. J. Reid Meloy on the subject.

For research regarding the actual killings at Columbine High School, I relied upon *Columbine,* the definitive nonfiction book written by Dave Cullen.

Once again, I am forever indebted to Catherine LePard. I would never have taken the leap into novels had it not been for her. To Marillyn Holmes, I again thank you for your keen eye and knowledge. To beloved friends Lynn Reed Baragona and Hynndie Wali. I love you all!

My profound thanks, as always, to Dan Conaway, the best agent, bar none.

My deepest thanks to wonderful editor in chief Judy Clain and to Mulholland executive editor Josh Kendall. I am so fortunate to be working with you. And thank you to Amanda Brower for your excellent assistance. And my thanks once again to senior production editor Karen Landry for yet another terrific job.

My endless gratitude to the fabulous publicity team, Nicole Dewey, Fiona Brown, and Pam Brown. And to all the wonderful people at Mulholland Books, a million thanks to you for all your hard work, creativity, and brilliance.

ABOUT THE AUTHOR

Marcia Clark is the author of *Guilt by Association, Guilt by Degrees,* and *Killer Ambition.* A former prosecutor for the state of California, she is now a frequent media commentator on legal issues. She lives in Los Angeles.

Prospect Free Library
0001500098783